Beyond Grey

Beyond Grey

Ella Cook

Stories that inspire emotions!
www.rubyfiction.com

Published 2022 by Ruby Fiction
Penrose House, Crawley Drive, Camberley, Surrey GU15 2AB, UK
www.rubyfiction.com

A CIP catalogue record for this book is available from the British Library

ISBN: 978-1-91255-042-5

Printed and bound in Great Britain by Clays Ltd, Elcograf S.p.A.

For Geraldine, Joan, Alfred and Nona – gone from our world, but never our hearts.

And for anyone who has ever faced the pain of bereavement – know that you're not alone.

Acknowledgements

No book ever makes it into the world without a lot of love, support and encouragement from a lot of people – so there's always a lot of thanks to make.

A huge thank you to everyone at Choc Lit and Ruby Fiction – without you, this story wouldn't have made it into the world. So, special thanks for the Tasting Panel Readers (Deborah Warren, Janice Butler, Gillian Cox, Jenny Mitchell, Fran Stevens, Jo Osborne, Alan Roberton, Hilary Brown and Gill Leivers), the Choc Lit team for taking a chance on me. And my editor – for the edits and patience!

Thank you to my amazing beta readers, Steph, the fabulous Friday Night Therapy Group (you know who you are, ladies!). Thanks to Ann and her wonderful Monday Night Wordsmiths – who helped me rediscover my love of writing fiction.

And thanks to Alex, Dad and my friends – for putting up with me being distracted and late because I'm writing, and for not minding when I start talking about my characters as if you know them.

I can't thank you all enough.

Chapter One

The Worst End to a Year

JENNIFER

You know that old saying some people have about "today being the first day of the rest of your life?" Well it's not true. At least not for me, and not for today. Because today's the day I died.

It didn't really hurt. In a way I think it should have. Something so monumental as being ripped out of the world should have been marked by something. It takes so much pain to enter the world that I feel like there should be just as much when you leave.

But there wasn't.

Then again, it's someone else's pain at birth, and there are definitely plenty of other people suffering now.

I'm not sure I even woke up before I died. I suppose I should consider myself lucky to have gone so quickly and quietly, but I don't. In truth, I feel a bit cheated. If I'd been given the chance to plan my death, it would have been safe and warm and peaceful, surrounded by the people I love the most. And a lot of years from now. I wasn't ready for this. It isn't fair. I don't want to be here.

But I didn't get a choice. There was a sudden jerk and shock that slammed into me, which melted away into empty coolness. Then I was here, watching myself fall. No pain or fear. Just the peculiar feeling that I was dropping away from the living world and falling into this one.

Watching my husband though, that hurt. More than any other pain I've ever felt. Including breaking my leg at fifteen and giving birth to our children. More than the lorry crashing into me.

I watched as David blinked and came back to life after the accident, pushing the airbag out of his eyes. His face was smeared with blood and I wanted to reach out and comfort him, to ease his pain and soothe him the way I'd done for years. But I can't do that any more.

I watched as he fought against his seatbelt, struggling against the straps until he could turn and reach me. Panic filled his eyes and he screamed my name over and over again. But my ears were already deaf to him.

Other hands appeared, reaching through the tortured, twisted metal to pull us free. They half-supported and half-lifted David to safety. Then they reached for me. They hesitated, fingers fluttering at my throat, trying to find the signs of life that should have been there. They paused in their hopeless search before pulling me out anyway.

Soon flashing blue lights arrived, and other hands took hold of me. They manoeuvred me to the side of the road, and pummelled and punched at me, jabbing me with needles as they tried to drag me back into their world and hold me there with them. Then we were racing towards the hospital.

I did try to hold on like the voices begged me to. I tried to push my way back into my body, but I was too far gone from it. The coldness had already sunk in and wrapped around me, dragging me away.

I didn't live an extraordinary life. It certainly wasn't the one I'd planned in a fit of teenage optimism all those years ago. But there's another saying about that, isn't there? Best laid plans and all. Something like that. But I did love my life. I loved the kids I taught, I loved the home and family that David and I had created in Hillingdon. If you don't know it, it's a borough at the edge of London, pretty much at the end of the tube lines. Halfway between city and country, it was just another suburb, but I loved it. Unextraordinary, unassuming, and utterly perfect to me.

I wasn't particularly religious when I was alive. My sister, Sarah, had always been the good girl who paid attention in Sunday School and kept up with church as she'd gotten older, but me? I'd been too busy living my life to really think about it all. But if I had found the time, this wouldn't be what I would have pictured as the afterlife. I suppose if I had thought about it, I would have expected warm lights and fluffy clouds. A welcoming hug from my dead mum or gran, maybe. I don't know. But it wasn't this.

I didn't expect to be stuck in this odd place where nothing seems to have any meaning, and everything is nothing. Time, distance and feelings. It's all here, but nothing is quite right. It all echoes too much, with everything amplified and softened at the same time. It's all just … nothing. And everything. All at once. All of time and all of space. Right here, in this strange, grey world.

I didn't want this, but there's no going back. No matter how much I want to.

DAVID

It all seems so unreal. They let me out of the hospital this morning. Once they'd stopped the nosebleed and stitched up my forehead, there wasn't really much else they could do. I think the overnight observation was really only out of pity.

My keys got left in the car, so I had to use Jenn's to get back into the house. I must have used them before, but I couldn't remember which key was which, and it took me three attempts to get the door open.

I flicked on the lights and turned the answerphone off while still on autopilot, then wandered into the living room. It could have been any other day when I got home before

Jenn, and part of me waited for her to walk in the door a few minutes from now.

Everything looked the same. It was just our living room, a bit messier than usual, but it was always a bit messy at this time of year. The Christmas tree was starting to wilt, and the last few presents that still needed delivering were piled up underneath. It's strange, this time of year. Things seem to change so quickly. A week ago all the sparkle and tinsel was exciting and full of promise. Now it's just tired looking, and another job waiting for me. The house always looked tired at this time too. The couch appearing slightly more faded, the wallpaper that was starting to peel, just a tiny bit, in the corner above the door, all the more noticeable.

The mirror mocked me, flinging my haggard reflection back at me. Jenn had always claimed to like my dull blond hair and brown eyes, but to me they just looked ordinary – though now my eyes were swollen with tears and bruising, and my hair was matted and darkened against my head. I looked closer to seventy than fifty. The face that stared back at me didn't seem to be mine, but that made sense because the life I had been living in recent hours doesn't feel like mine either.

Jenn's scarf was still there. She'd changed her mind at the last minute and flung it across the back of the chair. Her cup rested on the table next to it, half an inch of tea still in the bottom. I rolled my eyes. Why couldn't she ever remember to use a coaster? Then I remembered.

I picked up the cup and cradled it between my hands. It was ice cold, but the print of her lips still kissed the rim where she'd taken a sip after applying her make-up. She always did that just before we walked out the door. I loved watching her put on her make-up. Some women take forever, primping and fluffing and doing God only knows what. But not my Jenn. She patted on that cream stuff quickly, swept colours over her eyes, then flicked the mascara over the top. A quick swish of the pink brush, a kiss of lipstick and she'd be done. She'd smile at me in the mirror and give her hair a final brush, and then she'd be ready. She always laughed and teased me about how long I take to get ready. But it's easier for her. She looked gorgeous from the second she rolled out of bed. Even when she was tired and creased from sleep, she was still the most beautiful thing I've ever seen. I wish I'd told her more.

How can she be gone?

It feels like she should walk through the door any second, kick off her shoes in the hall and chuck her coat over the banister. She always promises to put it away later, but usually forgets, distracted by something far more interesting and exciting. Invariably I'll take it upstairs for her and hang it carefully in the wardrobe. I always complain about it, but really I don't mind. I like looking after Jenn.

Liked. The word is liked now. With a very final, solid extra *d*. One single, innocent looking letter that takes my wife from "is" to "was". From living to ... not.

I don't understand any of this.

Her slippers still sat on the floor, slightly trodden down at the back, and the book she'd been reading still balanced on the arm of her favourite chair. The cushions were still piled up oddly, all leaning to one side, and I could clearly see the dent from where she always rested her elbow as she tilted the book to catch the morning light.

How could she possibly be gone?

I sat on the sofa, and stared at her chair. I could still remember when we bought that. It was a few years ago. Jenn saw it in one of those antique stores by the market and had to have it. I hated it on sight and swore it wouldn't fit in with the colour scheme. That it was the wrong shade. That it was too big. That it was plain ugly. We'd argued about it, and she'd won. She usually did. She'd been right of course. It fits into the alcove perfectly and makes the room seem a bit warmer and cosier. Especially when she was curled up in it. She'd tuck her feet into one corner and balance a cup of tea on the arm while she read, or worked on lesson plans and marked homework, a soft smile usually playing at the corners of her mouth.

It didn't make sense.

I couldn't understand the idea of Jenn not coming back and never sitting in her chair again. It can't be real. It has to be a mistake, or a bad dream that I'm going to wake up from. I stared at the cold cup caught between my fingers and concentrated on that instead. I'm not ready to think about a world without Jenn. I don't think I could survive in a world like that.

I didn't hear the key click in the lock, or register the thumps as bags hit the hall floor, but a few seconds later one of the few voices left in the world that could reach me echoed through my thoughts and dragged me back to reality.

'Dad?' I looked up to see Charlotte standing in the doorway, her eyes red and blotchy against her too pale skin.

People say she looks like me, but I don't see it. When I look at her, it's Jenn's dreamy hazel eyes that I see, Jenn's stubborn chin, and Jenn's soft mouth that's always quicker to smile than frown. But now those lips were pressed together tightly, and they trembled as Charlotte tried not to cry. Two decades melted away in a moment, and the pink streaked hair, battered jeans and shredded top disappeared. In my mind Charlotte was four years old again, warm in her princess pyjamas and upset because she couldn't find her favourite teddy.

Only it's not that easy any more. I couldn't fix these tears with a hug and game of aeroplane. It's not as easy as finding Ted behind the sofa, or in the greenhouse dressed as a pirate.

'Dad?' She gave her heavy bag a kick with one of her clunky boots. 'I brought stuff to stay for a while. I can go home whenever, but I thought you wouldn't …' Her voice broke and she swallowed hard. 'I couldn't bear to think of you being alone right now.'

I stared at my baby girl, once again amazed at the beautiful, thoughtful person Jenn and I had created. 'Thanks, sweetheart, that sounds good.'

'I talked to Aunt Sarah. She's flying in via Edinburgh and driving down with Matty. She didn't want him driving down alone. Oh, Daddy …' Her face crumpled and her voice broke as tears streamed down her cheeks.

I held my arms out to her, not knowing what to say or how to take the pain away. I didn't know how to make it better for myself, let alone her.

Chapter Two

JENNIFER

Maybe this is hell. Being trapped in nothingness, where all you can do is watch the people you love suffering.

It feels like hell.

It's horrible being here, seeing the people I love hurting because of me, but not being able to ease their suffering. I hate myself for what I'm doing to them, and the pain that they are feeling because of me. I'd take their pain a thousand times over if it would stop them hurting and make them happy, even for a few minutes.

Matty arrived home with my sister, Sarah. It's sweet of her to have detoured her flight to Edinburgh so he didn't have to drive the hundreds of miles back home by himself. She's always been like that, my big sister. Thoughtful and caring. I missed her when she moved to Germany with her husband, even though we talked every week. But I guess I'm going to miss her even more now. I'm going to miss them all.

Matty looks worse than the others, if that's even possible. His dark eyes, the same colour as his dad's, are red and swollen, bloodshot from the salt of too many tears. His hair, which is as dark as mine, is sticking up all over the place and getting greasy from where he's been worrying at it too much, and his suit's crumpled. It's so far away from the smart, slick solicitor he's become that I find myself welling up.

It's so unfair.

This whole thing is so bloody unfair. What did I do to deserve this? I'm a good person. Or at least I was, wasn't I? I treated people well and did my bit for charity when I could. I was always the one organising the charity events at school and encouraging the children to think of someone else instead of just themselves. And with teenagers that wasn't always easy, but my students still liked me! I was a good mother, and wife, and a good sister and daughter.

Oh God, why did you do this to me? I'm a good person. Didn't I always try to do right by other people? And try to make the world a little bit better? All right I wasn't perfect, but who is nowadays? There are plenty of bastard people worse than me. Plenty of terrorists killing innocent people. Plenty of murderers, and rapists and paedophiles. Plenty of people who beat and abuse their children. I've had enough of the victims crying in my office to know. So why not one of them? Why do this to me God? Why put my family through this? What did any of us do to deserve this?

What did I do?

Why not just kill me and have done with it? Why bring me here to this place where all I can do is watch helplessly? And don't give me any of that mysterious ways rubbish. What did I do to make you hate me and want to hurt me and my family so badly? It can't just be because I didn't go to church.

This isn't what I believed in. This isn't what I wanted. This isn't fair!

Send me back. Please God, send me back. Please let this be a nightmare. Let me open my eyes in my own room and see the sunlight streaming through the crack in the curtains. Let me hear David snoring next to me. I'll be a better person. I'll quit my job and work for charities. I'll go to church every weekend. I'll go every day. Just please send me back.

DAVID

I haven't been sleeping. In truth I don't really want to. I know if I go to sleep, that I'll eventually have to wake up and face reality. And once I wake up, everything will stop being a bad dream, and I'll have to accept that Jenn's really gone. I'm not ready to do that. I don't think I ever will be.

So tonight instead of trying to sleep, I wandered around the house and made coffee that went cold before I could drink it. I'd needed something to do with my hands, but then I was left in the ridiculous position of having cold coffee. I've always hated cold coffee. I've never been one of those people who would order an iced chocha, mocha thingy and drink it with a straw. Proper coffee should be scalding hot and black.

So like an idiot, I sat there staring at the cold coffee while I tried to work out what to do with it. I didn't want to drink it cold, but pouring it away seemed so wasteful and wrong that I just couldn't do it. I should have gulped it down while it was hot rather than putting myself in the awful position of having cold coffee.

Oh God, why did I have to drive that day? Jenn had offered to. She'd known I was tired and that I had had a couple of drinks with lunch. Was I drunk six hours later? They'd breathalysed me at the scene, and I was well under the limit – but I've heard it said that even one glass could make a difference. Were my reactions slower than they should have been? Was I so tired that I had drifted into another lane? Was it my fault?

The thoughts filled me with ice.

It's my fault she's gone. I killed Jenn. I should have been in the passenger seat. I wish I had been. I wish we hadn't been on that bloody road. I wish that truck hadn't been there. I wish we'd stayed for that second cup of tea. I wish it had been me instead.

Jenn was such a wonderful, beautiful, special person. She could make other people smile just by being near them, and she made the world a better place just by being in it. What good do I bring it? It should have been me instead.

I wish it had been me.

Maybe if I just curled up here and died, Jenn would be allowed to come back. Maybe if I just gave up moving and breathing, she could somehow come back to life.

Maybe if I never moved again, none of this will have ever happened. Or maybe I could stay in this strange, cold, suspended reality forever. Not moving, not living, but not hurting either.

JENN

Oh no you don't, David Hughes. Don't you dare! I'm still here and I'm trying to reach you. Can't you feel me?

I can't watch you curl up and disappear. It's bad enough that one of us is gone, don't you dare try to follow me here into this nothingness.

It's all right to be sad – I'd be hurt if you weren't. But not this David, please not this. And not in my name either.

The man I married isn't a quitter, so pull yourself together and get on with it. I know it hurts, God knows I know it hurts, but there are the children to think about. They might be adults with their own lives, but they are still my babies. And they need their dad, just as much as you need them.

Please love, don't give up now. You're an amazing, strong person. Please don't lose who you are just because you've lost me.

I love you David, but giving up is not an option. So what are you going to do next?

DAVID

For some reason I found myself wanting to smile. It seemed so wrong, wanting to smile just days after my wife died, but it suddenly occurred to me what Jenn would have said if she could have seen me.

She'd have booted me up the behind. She'd tell me it's all right to be sad, and to miss her. And then she'd ask "So what now?" as she demanded to know what I was going to do next. And sitting around moping would not have been an acceptable answer.

She would remind me about the children too. She would tell me how much they need me, and that they're still our children, even though they're off living their own lives. She'd be right too. She always is. Was? That sounds wrong. I'm still not ready to think of Jenn as a was. I don't think I ever will be.

I remember when we first met, back in college. We were friends then, almost from the moment that we were introduced. There was always an attraction between us, but the timing was never quite right. She had a boyfriend, or I was dating someone, or we were taking exams that seemed so important back then that they eclipsed everything else. And then one warm day in that long, heady summer before we headed off to university, everything fell into place. We've been together ever since. I've literally spent my whole adult life with Jenn. How am I ever going to function without her?

'Dad, are you all right?'

The light flicked on, half-blinding me, and for the few blinks that it took for my eyes to adjust, I was convinced that Jenn was sitting next to me, but she disappeared as my vision cleared and Matty sat down.

'You can't just sit here in the dark, Dad. It's not healthy.'

'I know.' I scrubbed my hands across my face. 'I was just thinking.'

'About Mum?'

'What else?'

'Want to tell me?'

'I was just thinking about how she'd react if she could see me sitting here.'

My son snorted with dark humour. 'She'd kick you up the arse.'

'I know.' I laughed with him, the tears barely held back. 'Seems a bit wrong, laughing.' Guilt still assaulted me, digging under my skin and tearing into me.

'I dunno.' Lottie stood at the door, her mum's purple dressing gown wrapped tightly around her, swamping her small frame. 'I think she'd be all right with it. She never had much patience for pity parties.'

'True enough.' Matty shrugged and sighed. 'There's so much to do. I don't know how we're supposed to start planning everything. It seems so wrong. I still feel like she's going to walk in the door any minute.'

Lottie nodded in agreement. 'I know what you mean. I feel like I'm walking around in a bubble, or watching a bad film. It all seems so unreal.'

I sighed, already feeling the tears well up again. 'I wish it were. I don't know how to sleep without her. I never realised how big that bed is.'

'Oh, Dad.' Lottie's eyes filled with tears and she wrapped her arms around me. 'You can have my bed if you want. I'll curl up down here on the couch.'

I couldn't help myself. The tears just ran down my face unchecked. A few seconds later, Matty's hand patted my shoulder awkwardly, before he wrapped us both in a big hug.

Chapter Three

JENN

Ugh. I am so glad that's over with. Watching your own autopsy must be the most disgusting thing ever. It was like a bad horror film. Gory, bloody, and utterly depersonalising, but I couldn't look away. They pulled me out of the drawer, manhandled me onto one of their cold, shiny tables, and left me lying there under stark, bright lights.

I know I'm not part of that body any more, but it was still mine. I looked after it for the best part of five decades. OK, it wasn't a perfect body, and there were definitely a few more pounds and inches on it than I would have liked, but not everyone has hours to spend down the gym, or the money for personal trainers.

All that aside, I was in pretty good shape. I loved the stretch marks over my belly and hips that my children left me, and I liked the funny little scar on my forearm from the day David and I moved into our home. I'm still fond of the bent little finger that never healed quite right after I broke it at school. I even liked my wrinkles, because they're reminders of so many nights of laughter with the people I cared about, usually with a little bit too much wine.

OK, I didn't always think that way when I was alive, but now I can see the imperfections for what they really are. Reminders. A lifetime mapped out in scars, stretch marks and wrinkles. I loved that body.

Watching someone cut it up was horrible and degrading. An invasion of privacy. The final insult. And despite me having left that body, it still hurt.

But at least it was over quickly. Once they'd cut me open, even I could see what killed me. There was blood everywhere, pooling around my heart and lungs. A traumatic dissection of the thoracic aorta. That's what the coroner called it. I'd literally died of a broken heart.

He'd been right about the other thing too. It was so quick I hadn't even felt it. But he was wrong about that being a blessing. I'd rather have been in pain and had the time to tell David how much I loved him once more.

But then again, if I'd had the choice, I'd still be alive.

DAVID

The coroner called this morning. They're going to release Jenn. The inquest and final verdict won't be for a few months yet, but we're going to get Jenn back to bury. I haven't been able to decide whether it's a good thing or not. In a way it's both. I'm relieved she's not going to be in that horrible place any more, and will be going with the undertakers. They seemed really nice and promised to take excellent care of her.

But the whole thing scares me too. Because it means I have to start thinking and making decisions. I have to start planning the funeral, and getting ready to say goodbye to Jenn.

The local newspaper found out about her death. Apparently it makes a good story. I didn't know anything about it until I wandered downstairs one morning and found it sitting on the doormat.

'Beloved teacher dies in crash.' The headline screamed at me from the front page, an obnoxious reminder of the worst day of my life. Another twist of the knife that's been digging in my chest since those last, precious minutes on a cold roadside. They mention me of course, but as usual get my job wrong – I'm a draftsman not an architect. I turn other people's ideas into the technical drawings and maps that make sure buildings end up the right way up. But most people think it's all the same thing.

But it wasn't all bad, because below the black, tormenting letters was a full-colour picture of Jenn, smiling out at me. The photo wasn't one I knew. She was sitting cross-legged on the floor, her bare toes just peeping out from under one of those gypsy skirts that she loved. Her hair was blowing gently in the breeze, and she was surrounded by daffodils. Her smile was filled with such love and warmth that she had to know the photographer. She looked incredibly beautiful.

'It's one of mine,' Lottie admitted as she peered over my shoulder. 'They were going to print a photo anyway, so I figured it should be a good one. You know she'd have been furious if they used some stupid passport photo, or her school ID. You don't mind, do you?' Worry sounded in her voice.

'No. I think it's lovely. When did you take this?'

'When she stayed with me a couple of Easters ago. Just before I graduated. You were working, me and Mum were both on Easter holidays. It's around the back of an old church in some little village a few miles from the uni. The daffodils seemed to go on for miles. She lit up when she saw them.'

'She always did.' I smiled, remembering. 'They were her favourites. She always said she knew spring was really here, and the world was coming back to life, when she saw the daffs.'

Lottie laughed, and for a brief moment sunshine filled the kitchen. 'She once told me fairies pushed up daffodils to make the sun want to come back. I think I was about four.'

The visits started that afternoon. People who were "just dropping by", with twee cards covered in crosses and lilies and rainbows. And sunsets. As if I needed the reminder that things were ending. We're in everyone's prayers and God is apparently with us in our time of need.

Just what I didn't want to hear. What about out on that cold roadside when Jenn was dying? I could have done with some divine intervention then. But after Jenn was gone and my life was falling apart? Too little, too late. It was all I could do not to rip up the twee cards and throw them back in the faces of the nosey busybodies masquerading as sympathetic well-wishers.

And as if the cards weren't bad enough, there were all the flowers and food. I had half expected the flowers, but the food was a complete surprise. Plates of cakes and cookies, endless casseroles and dishes of cheesy, tuna pasta. Did people actually think endless plates of food would help fill the hole that Jenn's left in our lives? She didn't even like tuna when she was alive, and they had managed to make her whole house stink of it.

Lottie and Matty were great. They smiled graciously and accepted the condolences and food with heartfelt thanks. It's better than I would have managed. Lottie even made some sort of list to make sure everyone gets the right dish back.

But me? I did my best to stay away from them all, but struggled to avoid everyone. I couldn't bear all the false sympathy. They were as bad as those bastards who slowed down to stare at the accident. What is it about some people that makes them so interested in the pain and suffering of others? Maybe that was the real reason for all the food. Come see the grieving family, it's a bargain price! Admission is just one plate of horrible food that you'd never eat.

And then when they'd seen enough, they give another sympathetic smile, and maybe touch my arm. 'We're so sorry about Jenn, such an awful thing, a horrible tragedy, a terrible loss. If there's anything we can do?'

I gave myself a headache trying to control the urge to

smile back and respond sarcastically, 'Really? You mean that? How about building a time machine so I can undo that day? That would be just great!' But instead I forced myself to smile and thank them for their kindness, all the while counting the seconds until I could politely escape.

Then, job done and gossip gathered, they skip off happily and smugly, heading back to their own, perfect, whole, unbroken families.

It's been days since the article was published, and people are still turning up with dishes and plates. I wish they'd stop with all their sympathy. I wish they'd stop filling the house with nasty tuna casseroles and mangy lilies. Jenn's always hated lilies. They made her sneeze and depressed her. Now I can't move for the blasted things.

I wish they'd all just leave us alone. I wish none of this was real.

JENN

Oh love, you don't mean that. I know you think you do, but you really don't. These are our friends, and they are only coming round to offer their support. And to get some back. I know I'm your wife, and I've been incredibly proud and lucky to call you my husband, but these people are my friends and colleagues. They were part of my life, and I was part of theirs. They lost me too.

Besides, I'm a little flattered by all the attention. It's a shame you have to drop dead before people remember how much you mean to them. Then it's too late, and everyone's filled with regret for every phone call they forgot to return and every evening they postponed. I wish I'd realised when I was alive. Then I could have made more of an effort, and not wasted my time watching so much rubbish on television. Or at least I could have watched rubbish with my friends, instead of without them.

There aren't many things I regret. But that's one of them. I should have made more time for the people who really mattered. I wonder how many nights I wasted worrying about things I couldn't change, and that didn't really matter. I used to think that so much mattered, and now it all seems so pointless. The only thing that really matters is people, and the people who matter to me are hurting so badly right now. It's agony. Their pain wraps around me, dragging at me and exhausting me. I keep trying to reach them, especially David, but the pain and anger just buffets me away.

DAVID

I don't know what's going on with me lately. It's like I'm not really myself. I'm so angry all of the time. And confused. I can't work out what I'm supposed to be doing, but I know it's not yelling at my children.

It's like being really, really drunk. There's a tiny part of me inside that's watching everything I'm doing, and screaming to be heard, and begging me to stop. But it's drowned out by the all-consuming anger that leaves me numb and aching.

Oh, Jenn, why did you have to leave me? I need you more than ever right now. I'm taking my anger out on the children, especially Matty. I hate myself for it, and I know it's wrong, but I can't seem to stop. Everything Matty does annoys me. Even when he's trying to be helpful, he manages to irritate me. Doesn't he know you're supposed to rinse the soap off dishes before drying them?

Then I hate myself for not being the father that Matty and Lottie need right now. They need me to be strong, and to support them both. They deserve that. And I am trying, but I don't know how to deal with Matty. He's not a little boy any more. He's not even the cocky teenager I waved off to university years ago. I don't know how to be a dad to this adult. I don't even know how to talk to him.

So I snap and I snarl instead, and I hate myself for it.

But I hate you too, Jenn. I hate you for leaving me and letting me turn into this monster. I hate you for breaking your promise to me. We were supposed to grow old together. Now you've left me and I can't work out how to live without you. I'm scared and confused and … Damn it, Jenn, I'm furious. Forever was supposed to be a lot longer than this. It was just a stupid accident. I walked away from it, and I don't understand why you didn't. Sometimes I think you should have tried harder to stay with me.

I hate you for not being here right now.

JENN

I'm sorry, David, I really am. But I didn't exactly choose this. I'd give anything to be back with you all. I hate to see you hurting because of me, but there's nothing I can do to change it.

I want to be with you and I want to help you, but your anger is pushing me away. I still love you, but I can't fix this for you. You have to do it for yourself. And you have to work out how to fix it and start talking to your son again. The only way you're going to get through this is together.

Chapter Four

MATTY

Something inside me just snapped. I couldn't bear the tension and sadness in the house any more. It was getting so bad that the air was starting to vibrate with pain and anger, and bring out the worst in us all. Lately Dad and I don't seem to be able to talk to each other without arguing. About anything. Even working out what to have for dinner and who should wash up sparked another row. You would have thought a company solicitor would be able to manage his temper a bit better, but I swear when I'm around Dad at the moment I feel like I'm reverting to my teenage self. It wasn't pretty the first time around, and with all the stress of what's happened to Mum, I seem to be permanently on the edge of another argument.

It was getting to the point that even Lottie couldn't keep the peace between us, and that's not fair. I'm her big brother. I'm four years older than her, and I'm supposed to look after her. The last thing she needed was to see her dad and brother at each others' throats.

Lottie's always got upset when people argued around her, ever since she was little. Dad and I had been arguing over something so stupid I forgot what it was, almost immediately, and then I'd caught the look on Lottie's face, and I realised I couldn't bear to hurt her any more. So I just upped and left. I didn't even remember to throw on a coat or change my shoes, which turned out to be a mistake. But I really didn't care. I just had to be moving.

It was freezing cold and icy underfoot, and my breath steamed in the air around me, but I ignored it. The weather was much colder back home, and a bit of English frost was nowhere near as bad as what I was used to in Edinburgh. I shouldn't have been so arrogant.

I started to run almost as soon as I turned the corner. I hadn't ran in ages, and jeans weren't exactly the comfiest clothes for running, but it felt so good. Every time my foot slammed into the pavement I squashed another angry thought and forced back another wave of tears.

I had been heading for the shops, thinking that I could be cheeky and cut across the park the way I always did when I was younger. I only made it as far as the park gate before I hit a patch of black ice, and my feet skidded out from underneath me. There was a strange moment of weightless freefall, and then I was flat on my back with my muscles screaming in protest. I was completely disorientated and for a few moments, all I saw were stars. They twinkled down, laughing at my expense. I glared up at them angrily, furious that they were so cheerful when my world was falling apart all around me. Didn't they know Mum had died and that nothing in my life was ever going to be the same again?

The cold seeped through to my skin, and I tried to stand, but my feet skidded again. I ended up sitting on my arse in a puddle of icy slush. For a moment, dark humour filled me, and I realised Mum would be laughing herself sick at me right now. I started to laugh, and laughed harder as the stars seemed to join in.

My phone vibrated in my pocket and made me jump. I wriggled it out of my pocket. Lucy flashed on the screen. My sweet, wonderful Lucy.

'Hi honey.' Her voice filled me with warmth, even over the phone when she was hundreds of miles away. 'How are you doing?'

'So-so I guess.'

'You sound strange, are you all right?'

'Yeah, no. Yeah. I'm fine.'

'You sound really strange, are you sure you're all right?' Lucy's voice was filled with concern. 'Where are you?'

'Sitting in a puddle, since you asked.'

'What? Are you sure you're all right?'

'It's all right, I'm fine. Really. Lucy, I'm fine.' I tried to reassure her.

'I'm sorry I'm not there with you …'

'It's all right, I understand. You can't just drop everything.'

'I wish I could be there, though.'

'I know. And I love you for that. Hang on a minute.' I struggled back to my feet. 'Sorry, just crawling out of the puddle.'

'What?' Lucy laughed, and for a moment the world didn't seem quite so dark.

'Nothing, it's all right. I'm all right. I promise.'

'Good, that's all I needed to know. So, why were you sitting in a puddle?' I could hear her trying not to laugh.

'Well it seemed like the sensible thing to do. I needed to cool off.'

'Matthew …' There was a warning tone in her voice. I sighed. Lucy's always been really good at refusing to let me get away with some things, especially talking about stuff.

'Dad and I had another argument. I can't even remember what it was about this time. Something stupid and silly and pointless. Oh Lucy.' I scrubbed my eyes with my free hand. 'I just don't know how to talk to him. Not about this.'

'You talk to me. How is it any different?'

'I don't know. It just is. It's my dad. He doesn't really talk to me. He never has. When I needed to talk to someone when I was growing up, I always went to Mum.'

'But your mum isn't here any more, sweetheart. You have to talk to your dad. You, he and Lottie need each other so much right now.'

'I know. But he's so angry all the time.' I started to walk

again, taking care to avoid any more ice. 'It's like he blames her for leaving, and is angry at me for being here.'

'But that's sort of natural isn't it? Don't people often get angry when someone dies suddenly?'

'I guess. But angry at me? It's so bloody stupid.'

'I said it was natural, not that it made sense.'

'I don't know how to get past his anger, Lucy.'

'I know you don't.' Lucy sighed quietly. 'But you have to find a way to reach him. I know you can do it.'

'What makes you so certain?'

'Because I know you, Matthew Hughes. You're not going to give up. You'll work out how to talk to him. And if you don't, when I get down there, I'll knock both of your heads together.'

I laughed. 'Thanks Luce. I'll call you later.'

'OK. Speak to you later. Love you.'

'Love you too.' I paused outside a shop to slide my phone back into my pocket. I glanced at my reflection in the shop window, and twisted to see how badly my unplanned skating session had messed up my clothes. Something in the store caught my eye, and I found myself grinning idiotically at my own reflection. Maybe I did know how to get through to Dad after all.

CHARLOTTE

My brother's lost it. He's totally and utterly insane. He was having yet another stupid argument with Dad, and then he turned and looked at me. He froze for a few seconds, and then stormed out. He just disappeared. He didn't take his coat or keys with him, and it's freezing. I tried his phone half a dozen times, but it just rang out. Clearly he didn't want to talk to me.

Then finally, after I'd worried myself sick, he strolled back in. He had sludge and ice all down his back, and a bottle of whisky in his hand, but he just grinned and shrugged as if having a huge row over who had eaten the last biscuit and then disappearing for an hour in the freezing cold was a completely normal and sane thing to do.

But I have to admit, it did work.

Once Dad stopped complaining and started drinking, all the anger and hatred seemed to fall away, and he finally started to talk to us. It was awful and painful, but in a weird way, nice as well.

I hadn't realised why Dad had been so angry, but once he started to talk, it all began to make sense. Mum's death had really hit me. Parents are supposed to be indestructible and untouchable. They're not supposed to die when you're still young and still building your life, so losing Mum really messed me up, but I'd had no idea how badly it affected Dad. I'd selfishly been thinking about myself and worrying about what I was going to do, but I'd not totally realised that in losing Mum, Dad had lost the centre of his universe. He and Mum had been together since they were teenagers, which is just about forever. Even trying to imagine how he was feeling made me want to cry.

But it was nice to talk about everything properly. And I was so relieved to see Dad and Matty finally get past their anger and start talking again. I'd really been starting to worry about them both. But it finally looked like the rift was starting to heal.

When I crept back from the bathroom, I paused by the door and listened, but all I could hear was silence. I took a deep breath and opened the door, worried that I'd find the spell broken, and that they'd be glaring at each other from opposite sides of the room again. But instead, Dad was on his hands and knees in front of the TV, and Matty was digging around the sofa cushions.

'What's going on?'

'We're putting on a film. Except Dad's lost the remote again.' Matty rolled his eyes.

'I didn't lose it,' Dad complained.

'Well who did then? It didn't exactly grow legs and walk away.'

'Umm ... you're putting on a film? Now?' I still wasn't sure what was going on.

'Sure, why not? It's Friday night and we're all here. That means movie night.'

'Or it will be if I can find the bloody remote,' Dad added grumpily.

'I guess I'll make some popcorn then.' I shrugged and headed to the kitchen. 'By the way, the remote's on the windowsill behind Mum's chair.'

Chapter Five

DAVID

I'm glad Matty and I were able to sort things out between us, because we've all had to pull together over the last few days. There has been so much to organise, and so many decisions to make. It's amazing how complicated death can be.

I had to go to the registry office to let the officials know about Jenn. Then there were the insurance companies to call, the banks had to see the death certificate so our joint accounts stopped being joint, and the solicitors needed to be contacted about the will – not that there's much of one. We only bothered with the basics, but at least it will make everything else easier to deal with. I had to deface and return her credit cards, transfer her car into my name and cancel her insurance. And all that was before I could even start thinking about the funeral arrangements.

I'd handled similar situations in the past when Jenn's parents had died, but I'd forgotten how much there was to do when someone died. In a way I suppose it's good. As painful as it was to tell people I needed to change policies, account details and information because Jenn had died, it's better than actually having to stop and realise what that means. I've found I'm OK, or as OK as I can possibly be, so long as I stay busy. It's when I run out of things to do, and I'm forced to stop, that's when it hits me again.

Sarah, my sister-in-law, and Lottie have been so good. They've helped me make all the decisions I just couldn't handle. I had no idea how to answer the questions the funeral directors asked. My brain just froze. I'd never even thought about half of the things they needed to know. I didn't know if Jenn would rather be buried or cremated. She was a free spirit, and she loved life, but whether that meant she'd rather be scattered or buried I just couldn't decide. We never really talked about things like that. We were both too young and healthy to worry about it.

'Buried.' Sarah had nodded firmly. 'Somewhere sunny and with trees. She'd have liked to be somewhere we could visit her. She was always scared of fire, so better to bury her and cover her grave with flowers that bloom every year.'

I nodded in numb agreement, wondering how I could have forgotten how careful Jenn had always been about checking the smoke alarms, and making sure there was nothing left on the stairs that could trip us up if ever we needed to get out fast. What other things was I going to forget?

Then there was the coffin to discuss. Did we want traditional wood, wicker, bamboo or even biodegradable cardboard? What type of wood, what handles, what lining? Question after question was thrown at me, forcing me to drag myself out of the numbness and think. What was the best answer? What should I do? What would Jenn have wanted? I struggled with the answers to their questions.

Where to hold the funeral was probably the easiest one to deal with. I would have preferred a quiet, small ceremony where I could have said goodbye to Jenn privately. But over the last few days I'd come to realise that's not what she would have wanted. She loved people, my Jenn, and they loved her. That's part of what made her such a good teacher – the fact that she really did care. She would have wanted to make sure everyone who was part of her life would have a chance to say their farewells, and to support each other. So when the question of where we should hold her funeral came up, I knew the answer as clearly as if Jenn had been sitting beside me and answering for herself. It had to be the church around the corner from her school. It was big and friendly and welcoming, and near enough to the school that the students could come if they wanted to.

The rest of the plans flew by in a blur. Yes the minister at the church would be fine as Jenn knew him through the school, yes we'd get back to them with hymns and readings, yes members of the family and close friends would probably want to say something, yes we'd like to have photos of her on display – Lottie would sort that, and yes Matty and I both wanted to help carry her in. I'd carried her over the threshold of every home we'd shared. It seemed appropriate, that when it came to her final resting place, it should be my arms that carried her.

'No, we'll organise the flowers, thank you.' Lottie shook her head. 'I don't know about the rest. Dad?' She turned to me, her face pale. 'What do you think?'

'About what?'

'We were speaking about the personal items you'd like Jennifer to have with her, such as favourite clothes, photos or trinkets.' The undertaker explained gently. 'I'd asked if you wanted to see her again, when you dropped them off.'

'See Jenn?' My heart juddered against my ribs. Of course I wanted to see Jenn – I always wanted to see Jenn. Every time I turned a corner or walked into another room, part of me still expected to see her, hoping against hope that she'd be there.

'Mr Hughes? David?' The man leant across the desk. 'You don't need to answer now, but it's something you should think about.'

'How ...' Lottie paused and took a deep breath before she could continue. 'How does she look? Have you seen her?'

'Yes.' The man nodded. 'She looks peaceful, as though she's asleep.' He squeezed my daughter's fingers. 'You can't see any signs of the accident.'

'Good.' Lottie studied her fingers. 'That's good. I'm not

sure I want to see her, though. Is that wrong?' She looked around helplessly. 'Is it weird that I don't want to see her like that?' She bit back tears as her aunt wrapped a comforting arm around her.

The man shrugged slightly. 'Some people find it helpful and reassuring. They find it easier to accept the finality of the situation once they know their loved one is resting and at peace. Others prefer to remember them as they were. There is no normal in grief. One way is not better than another. All you can do is what's right for you, and your family.'

I nodded as relief flooded through me. That was the first thing that had made sense in this whole crazy situation. 'Thank you. I'll think about it.' I shook his hand gratefully.

'It's what we're here for,' the man reassured me. 'If there's anything else we can do, any questions you may have, please don't hesitate to call us.'

I nodded numbly, suddenly feeling drained and tired as Sarah led us all out into the fresh air. She peered at me with concern. 'I'm worried about you David, you look exhausted.'

I shrugged. Sleep hadn't been coming easily. I'm not sure I've slept properly since. There's been drug-induced unconsciousness from the painkillers the hospital gave me, but it's not the same. In all honesty I still don't want to sleep. The thought of being alone in our bed still terrifies me.

'Look, I can put my phone calls off until later, and come to the florists with you,' Sarah offered as she unlocked the car and slid into the driver's seat.

'It's all right.' I shook my head. 'Just drop us off on your way back, and we'll walk home afterwards.'

'Are you sure you're all right?' Sarah persisted.

'Yes.' I forced myself to smile, trying to reassure her. 'I'm all right. Thanks for all your help. You've been brilliant.'

'No need.' Sarah shook her head. 'Jenn's my little sister.' She paused, concentrating on the road. 'She was my little sister.' The correction hurt her, tearing at her throat and strangling her voice. 'I'm used to looking after her.'

I nodded and stared out the window, not knowing what to say. I felt like my brain had turned to mush, and I couldn't think straight any more. My eyes burned every time I closed them, and my nose and sinuses were bunged up and raw from crying. I stared out of the window and watched the world slip past us, barely registering what I was seeing as people went about their lives, unthinking, unknowing and unhurting. What I wouldn't have given to be one of them again.

'Daffodils aren't really in season yet,' the florist explained. 'And they're not really suitable for a funeral. What about something more classy and elegant, like lilies? A little more upmarket? After all, you want to give her the best possible, don't you?'

I found myself nodding numbly, watching as the woman bustled around her shop, gathering up roses and lilies. I thought daffodils would have been nice, that Jenn would have liked them, but the florist was right. She deserved the best, and what did I know about flowers anyway?

'No.' My head shot up at the sound of Lottie's voice. 'I'm sorry, but no.' She shook her head firmly. 'No lilies. Mum didn't like them. She found them depressing and they made her sneeze. She wouldn't have them in her house. She didn't like them in life, so why should we give them to her in death?'

'Well they are traditional.'

'I don't care.' Lottie shook her head. 'And while you're at it, the only roses she liked were the old-fashioned scented ones. And the ones in your hand don't look like they're going to meet either criteria very well. Her favourite flowers were daffodils. And she loved tulips and irises too. Especially the white irises.'

'They're not really in season.'

'But roses and lilies are?'

'No. We import them.'

'Well can't you import the daffodils and tulips?' Lottie was insistent.

'I don't know.' The florist shrugged. 'I suppose we could, but as we're buying so early in the season, it's likely to be difficult. Which means expensive.'

'I don't care.' I shrugged. 'My daughter's right. Daffodils were my wife's favourite, so that's what she should have. She lived the life she wanted, and did things the way she wanted, and if tradition didn't like it, tough. Can you help us?'

The florist nodded. 'I'll do my best.' She flashed a quick, sympathetic smile at us both. 'I'm sorry for your loss. She sounds like she was very special.'

'One in a million.' Lottie grinned. 'Mum's one in a freaking million.'

The tiredness that had been creeping up on me and seeping into my bones for days finally hit me, full force, as we walked home from the florist. My knees wobbled and I could feel the world spinning around me.

'Dad? DAD?' Lottie's voice echoed towards me from far away. She was somewhere beyond the spinning, roaring world that was closing in on me. I could feel my heart thumping in my ears, and dizziness swamped me. Maybe this was it. Maybe I was finally getting my wish and I was dying. I was caught in a spinning grey whirlpool that dragged me down and, as the colours around me blurred and light faded out of my world, I realised I didn't even care.

Then everything changed. Right at the moment when I was about to lose consciousness, the blurring colours briefly twisted into a shape so familiar I could recognise it even in that state.

Floaty skirts and hair swirled around the figure as she turned to face me. Her eyes widened with shock and confusion, then her face lit up with a warm smile, and she stretched out a hand towards me. But as I reached mine out in return, a sharp pain across my cheek jerked me back into cold reality.

I blinked a few times, trying to focus as I stared up at Lottie. 'Dad! Are you all right?'

'Did you hit me?' I rubbed my stinging cheek.

'Yeah.' My daughter grimaced. 'Sorry about that. You zoned out. I thought you were going to collapse or something. What happened? When did you last eat or sleep properly?' Concern and worry etched her face as she pulled a bottle of water out of her bag.

'I saw her. I saw Jenn.'

'Oh, Dad.' Pity and sadness filled Lottie's eyes as she slid her arm through mine. 'We're just round the corner. Do you think you can make it?' She waited for my nod. 'When we get home, you really need to eat something and go to bed.'

She chattered away as she helped me home, talking about everything and nothing with the forced cheer that everyone seems to be using around us at the moment. What she was going to make for dinner, how nice the weather was for the time of year, how good it was to see the green tips of snowdrops and crocuses peering through the dirt, coaxed out by the early sun. Spring would be here soon, along with Jenn's favourite daffodils.

I let her talk, and mumbled encouraging sounds when it seemed like she was about to stop, but I couldn't concentrate on what she was saying. I'd seen Jenn. And she was real. The look of shock and confusion on her face convinced me of that. If it were just my imagination, I would have pictured her happy and at peace, not confused and surprised to see me. This was real. Somehow, Jenn wasn't really gone. She was still with me.

I know a lot of people think they see their loved ones after they've died. That they mistake people in the street for someone who's gone, or that they think they see them at the edge of their vision, disappearing around a corner. But this wasn't like that. This was actually, honest to God, my Jenn.

JENN

I can't believe he saw me. I've been trying to reach him for days, trying to let him know I'm still here, just so I could ease his pain a little. I was starting to think this was all in my head, and that I was going mad in this horrible, grey, empty place. But I'm not. He finally saw me.

I've been so worried about him. He's exhausted. I don't think he's slept properly since the accident, and I know that every time he tries to eat, his stomach just ties itself into knots. He's so tired that he doesn't know what to do with himself. Maybe that's it though. Up until now his pain and anger have just pushed me away. But maybe now he's just too tired to hurt any more. Maybe his anger is finally wearing away and that's why I've finally been able to reach him.

And I know he saw me. He saw me, and reached out to me.

I thought he'd seen me that first night at home, in the second when the light snapped on, but it was so fast I convinced myself it was just wishful thinking. I mean, I don't even believe in ghosts. But I'm starting to think what you believe in doesn't really matter all that much. After all, I'm here, wherever here is, and whatever I am.

But it doesn't matter because he saw me. He actually saw me! I'm so excited I feel like I'm buzzing. I managed to make David see me. I've no idea what this means, but it has to be good. The fact that I could reach him has to be good, doesn't it?

No, it's definitely a good thing. Because if I can do it once, then I can do it again. And maybe there's more that I can do. What if I can actually communicate with David? And I don't mean any of that mumbo jumbo stuff. I don't see myself rattling chains, wobbling photos or moving around upended glasses. I mean real, true communication. Actually talking to him. Maybe I could reach him again, and let him see that I'm OK. Maybe I can still be there for him, for all of them, and help them through this.

Maybe I don't have to leave them at all.

It would make sense. I mean there has to be a reason I'm still here. I know I'm dead, but in a strange way, I think I'm coming to terms with it. But spending eternity here, in this pointless place where all I can do is watch my family hurting? That would be unbearable and far too cruel for contemplation. So I must be here to help them. It's the only thing that makes any sense.

It's horrible knowing that I'm dead and my life is over, but apparently that doesn't have to mean that I'm gone. At least that's something. I'll take anything right now.

There were so many things I thought I had wanted to see and do, but I know I've already done the most important things. I never made it to the Taj Mahal, but I met David, and married him, and had Matty and Lottie and helped them grow into the wonderful people they are now. Next to that, no amount of marble or gold can ever measure up.

Life is scarily short. I've had plenty of time here to work it out. If you're lucky you get maybe 85 years. Less than three quarters of a million hours. And most people sleep for a third of them, so that's a quarter of a million gone just in sleep. Plus there's work to consider. Probably most people spend 80-100,000 hours commuting or at work, in their lifetimes. And that's without thinking about school and exams and studying when you're younger. Half your life spent unconscious or at work. It's quite scary really. I wonder how many hours I wasted watching TV, or arguing over things that seemed so important at the time, but really didn't matter in the long-run. Not a nice thought. Especially when your life's already been cut short like mine.

I was never the type to give up in life. I'd always be fighting and swimming against the tide. But sometimes you just have to know when you're beaten. And trust me, there's nothing like being dead for forcing you to accept that you're beaten. It's an odd sort of peace that descends when you finally accept that you just can't change a situation. So I've stopped fighting, and now I'm going to embrace this afterlife and see what I can really do.

I'm not gone yet, and I've had plenty of time to think about what that means. I've decided there are too many stories of hauntings and ghosts across the world for them all to be imagination or fiction. Some of them have to be real. And if they are real, they had to start somewhere, and maybe that somewhere was here. If others can make their presence known, then so can I, and I will do it. Once I set my mind to something I never fail.

I'm going to get through to David again, and this time as more than just a glimmer in the corner of his eye or an exhaustion-induced hallucination. Once I've done that, I'm going to do everything I can to make sure he, and my darling Lottie and Matty, know I'm still here. And I'm going to look after them.

I know they'll grieve for a while, but if I give them the support and encouragement they need to get over my death, then they can go back to living the happy, fulfilled lives they deserve all the sooner.

I'm going to make sure they have wonderful lives, and that they don't waste a single moment of them.

Chapter Six

DAVID

I couldn't be bothered to move when I woke up. It was so comfortable there, curled up under the duvet where it was warm. The sun filtered through the pale curtains, making the room far too light. I knew there was something I was supposed to be getting up for, but I didn't want to move, and I could hear Jenn pottering around in the kitchen. With any luck, she was whipping up her scrambled egg and muffin breakfast. With sausages. Then maybe I'd pull her back into bed with me, and we'd laze a few more hours away.

That was when it hit me. The curtains were letting in too much light because they weren't mine. I was in Charlotte's old room. Without Jenn.

I really do hate mornings. They're the hardest part of the day. Every time I wake up I have to remind myself that Jenn's gone. It's sheer agony. I wish I could wake up without the few minutes of peace and warmth every day when I think that she's still with me, and avoid the half an hour of pain that follows when I have to remember what my new reality is.

I want to stay asleep forever, because in my dreaming world Jenn still exists. She's far more than lingering perfume and unfinished books that fill the house and mock me. In my dreams, Jenn is as bright and beautiful, and as warm and real, as she's ever been.

But Jenn would never forgive me for lying around in bed, especially when there was so much to do.

Yesterday I packed all the things I thought she would want. One of her favourite long, floaty skirts, and the top she always hand-washed so carefully. Lottie picked out beaded sandals, and Sarah found a necklace that apparently matched. I'm glad the girls were there to help me, because I've always been a bit useless with things like that. I don't think I really paid enough attention. There are so many things I wished I'd paid more attention to.

We filled up a bag with all the things we thought Jenn would want. Letters and photos from the children, and her favourite book of poems, which I wrote my own message in. Sarah slid in a few photos of her own – one of them recent, and one of them from years ago, when they were both giggling little girls. And I put in the book that had been sitting on the arm of her chair. I don't even know if Jenn was enjoying it, but she hated to leave things unfinished. I don't think she ever started a book that she didn't finish. I remember when she lost one on holiday somewhere. When we got back, we had to drive to three different libraries before we found a copy of it – because she couldn't bear to not find out how it ended. At least this way she'll know the ending.

At the last second I grabbed her mobile and dropped it into the bag. I know it's silly, and it's not like it'll even work, but I hate the thought of her being all alone in the dark. She always had a phone near her, whether it was on the bedside table or in the bottom of a bag. Admittedly half the time her bags were so big that she wouldn't be able to find it before it stopped ringing, but she always had it with her. I wasn't going to take it away from her.

Making sure she has all the things she would want is very nearly the last thing I can do for Jenn. I'm determined to get it right.

It took me nearly an hour to get to the funeral home. I hadn't realised that I'd be driving through rush hour, or that there were roadworks clogging up the high street. I've lost track of everything at the moment. There aren't really days or times, just a never-ending list of different tasks. Lottie offered to come with me, but I knew she didn't want to see Jenn, not really. She wants to remember her the way she should – full of life and happiness, and that magical sparkle that made her Jenn. And I can understand that. I want to remember her like that too, and I'm really scared to see her now, without that sparkle. But at the same time, I don't feel that I have any other choice. I have to see her one last time. I have to make sure that everything is the way she would have wanted it to be. And I have to make sure that she's all right, even though I know she really isn't. It doesn't make sense, but in a way it feels right. It was me and Jenn for years before the kids came along, so it seems fitting it should be just me and Jenn now.

Lottie fussed about me driving by myself, worrying that it was too soon and that I wasn't ready – like I haven't been driving for her entire life and longer. Besides, I didn't have much choice. I couldn't afford to take cabs everywhere, and the thought of sitting alone on a bus surrounded by noise and chaos made my skin crawl. And there was something comforting about climbing into Jenn's car, smelling her fragrance on the headrest and hearing her music streaming from the speakers.

The traffic was horrendous, and in a way it really pissed me off. Didn't they know Jenn had died? How could they just carry on with their lives as if nothing had happened? I didn't even know how the world kept turning. I felt like mine had stopped moving, back on that roadside.

Maybe that's why I feel so disoriented and sick all the time, because I'm standing still when I should be spinning through life. It's like the whole world is moving on around me, blurring with speed, while I'm frozen in time. I'm living in the past, in flashbacks of Jenn. Moments when she's smiling, when she's crying, when her hand tightens around mine. I see her full of life, crying and laughing at the births of our children, vibrant and beautiful, moving beneath me in our bed, yelling at me in anger so intense it burned. I wondered how many times she'd kissed me, how many times her hand slipped into mine. A few thousand? A hundred thousand? I could probably have worked it out, but it would be pointless. Whatever the answer, it just wasn't enough.

When I got to the funeral home, I found myself standing behind a cold, quiet door, a sombre man next to me, waiting for my decision. Did I want to see Jenn again? Or just leave her stuff with him?

In the end there wasn't any choice. I don't know why, but I had to see her. I guess I had to be sure. I had to be certain she was really gone.

Even though I'd been with her at the hospital, and watched them working on her, then finally shake their heads and tell me how sorry they were, it hadn't been real. It had been too bright, busy and noisy to be real.

Besides, hospitals were places that people went to to get better, and where good things happened. The last time Jenn was in a hospital, she came out with Lottie wrapped in her arms, a cooing, wriggling bundle of new life and hope. How can you die in a place like that? It was too silly and contrived, too like a scene from a TV drama to be real.

But the quiet, cool room on the other side of the door was real. The professional, comforting voice at my side was real. Jenn, peaceful and silent on the table, her eyes closed and arms by her side, that was real.

I wanted her to look like she was asleep, like she'd flutter her eyes open any second, and roll over towards me with a smile. But she didn't. She looked cold, and small, and alone. And far too still.

The waxy fingers I stroked weren't hers, nor were the cool cheeks or lips. But I kissed them anyway. I sat there for a while, holding her hand and stroking the soft hair I knew so well. It was Jenn lying there. I knew that. I knew every single inch of that body, every freckle and mole, every wrinkle and tiny imperfection. But at the same time, I didn't know that strange, empty shell at all. The woman I fell in love with, who had been the centre of my world for decades, wasn't there any more. There was no light or joy or laughter. But it was all I had left of her.

I sat there numbly, not knowing what to do. I wanted to shake her, to yell at her to wake up and make everything OK again, but it couldn't happen. The harsh, cold reality finally hit me. It seeped beneath my skin and made me shiver.

Jenn was really gone. She wasn't going to walk into the room and laugh about this big, silly mistake. And no matter how many corners I walked round, she was never going to be waiting there to greet me.

I wanted to run from the room, screaming at the unfairness of it all. I wanted to tear the world apart to find her again. But I couldn't move, and couldn't release my fingers from her grasp. Even if I could have torn myself away, there was nothing to find because she was right beside me. And this would be the last time I'd ever see her again.

I held her hand to my cheek, trying to recapture the feeling of her skin against mine, unable to say that final farewell and let go of her enough to leave. The numbness flooded my body and weighed me down.

I was struggling to breathe through the tears, gulping and gasping at the air that couldn't get past the lump in my throat. Sweat poured off me, and my stomach twisted with pain so intense that it blotted out everything else. It raced up to form a huge, choking lump in my throat. I couldn't breathe from the pain, and tears blinded me, rushing down my face in burning floods. White hot loss seared through my brain, leaving me unable to even think. Useless. Pointless. Empty. That was my life from now on.

I buried my face in her hair, trying to breathe in its

scent and capture the last precious essence, while my tears drenched her.

That was when it happened again.

It was stupid and clichéd, the type of thing you see in straight-to-TV movies, but I felt a presence in the room. Then coldness shot down my arms, and wrapped around my back. There was a whiff of that scent I'd been trying to find – honeysuckle perfume and apple shampoo – and then peace. It cut through the pain that had frozen me to the spot and pushed it away, soothing the burning horror that filled me. I saw her out of the corner of my eye. A flash of brown hair and the swirl of a long skirt as she turned. Jenn.

Icy warmth filled me. Goose pimples raced up and down my arms, but I was filled with warmth and strength that flooded through me. The room around me, and cold hand folded into mine, faded from my mind as the sensation consumed me.

I could feel Jenn's ghostly presence as vividly and as real as if she'd walked up behind me and slipped her arms around my waist. I could almost feel her breath against my neck and the kiss that she'd planted there a thousand times.

I knew it wasn't real, but I welcomed the insanity and fantasy. It gave me the strength to face reality and pull myself into something resembling togetherness. Jenn deserved better than this. I scrubbed my face dry on my shirt, and placed a single, final kiss on her cold cheek, whispering, 'Thank you for making my life so much brighter. Thank you for our beautiful children, and the wonderful life you gave me. I love you, Jenn. Always and ever yours. I love you.'

I don't know how I made it out of that room, or back home, but I found myself sitting on the edge of the bed. The edge of our bed. I had been avoiding our room as much as possible, but with Jenn's scent still in my nose, it felt right to be there.

I was so tired. It had been so long since I'd slept. I didn't want to sleep there without her, but I lacked the energy to move. So I rested there for a few minutes, and let the odd calmness soak into me. At least it had stopped hurting long enough for me to close my eyes.

JENN

It shouldn't be possible to be exhausted when you're dead, but I'm so drained and tired that it actually hurts. I ache all over in a body I don't have any more. I don't know if it's true pain and tiredness, or just the memory of it, but it feels real.

It's been worth it though.

I don't know whether it's because David's been feeling calmer and starting to accept everything more, or because he's been near my body, but I was able to reach him more strongly than before. This time I actually made him feel me. I saw the hairs stand up on his arm when I touched him, and his nostrils flare as he caught the scent of my perfume. I know that he saw me again, but this time he wasn't on the verge of passing out. This time he was completely conscious and knew exactly what was happening.

I could see him struggling, and I reacted without thinking. I reached out to him the same way I would have a few weeks ago, when I was still alive. I willed my strength into him, wanting to take away his pain, and it worked. I felt his resolve strengthen, and his panic subside as I poured love and support into him. And when I kissed the back of his neck, he reached up to brush the spot where my lips had been.

He thinks he's going mad, and I feel bad for that because I'd never want to hurt him. But I don't know any other way to do this, and I know he's glad of my presence. He desperately wants to believe this is real, that I'm really here, even though everything he's ever known tells him it can't be true. I guess it's up to me to prove logic and science wrong, and to let him know I'm still here, that I still love him, and that I'm going to help him.

It's working. Today's the first day he's come back into our bedroom for anything more than a few minutes. It's not surprising he hasn't been sleeping well in the spare room. He never sleeps well in strange beds, and that one's much smaller than ours, and the mattress is older and a bit lumpy. I'd been meaning to replace it.

I understand why he's been refusing to sleep in our bed, though. When he was away for just a night or two, I used to struggle to sleep properly. The bed just felt too big and empty without him; when I rolled over, half-asleep, and realised he wasn't there, it usually woke me up. Only when I woke up, I knew he'd be home the next day. Poor David doesn't get that.

The room's full of memories. Good and bad, but far more good. It's where Lottie was conceived. I remember the nights when the children were little and still scared of thunder, and they'd crawl into our bed and all four of us would sleep there together. Birthdays and Mother's Days when the children and the dog would jump into the bed together. Hundreds of happy memories. It really is a very big bed for one person.

David always used to sleep so soundly. He'd barely move in the night, except when he half-woke up, and then usually his hand would wander around under the covers until it found mine. But now he tosses and turns. Even in his sleep he's getting no rest.

I'll stay here with him, and see if I can ease his loneliness and fears. Maybe I can even slip into his dreams and make them sweeter and more peaceful.

DAVID

When I finally woke up, it was nearly midday. I stared at the clock and found myself smiling. For the first time since that awful day, I had woken up gently, and without the agonising stab of memory and realisation.

Nothing had really changed. Jenn was still gone, and that could never be changed, but the knowledge came with sad resignation rather than pain. Jenn was gone and I would have to get on with that. It's what she would have wanted me to do.

Besides, as stupid as it sounds, there have been moments when I've felt like she was near me. It's hard to describe, but you know that feeling when you know you're being watched? When the hairs on the back of your neck stand up, and you can feel someone else near to you? In your personal space? It's a bit like that, but stronger. I know it's Jenn.

I don't know if I'm imagining it. I mean everything I know, every logical thought is telling me it's in my mind, but ... I really want to believe it's real. I don't want to accept that every part of Jenn could be wiped from the world so totally and quickly.

I wandered downstairs blindly, following the lure of fresh coffee into the kitchen. The children were sitting at the table, with Lottie's laptop in front of them. Jenn smiled out at them both from the screen, still watching over her children even after death. I wonder how many times I had come in and found all three of them sitting there in the past, planning a party, or, when the children were younger, covering the table with paint, glitter and glue.

I peered at the photo more closely, and found myself smiling a little. It was a beautiful picture of Jenn, a moment of her happiness and joy caught on film and captured forever, pinned down and protected from ever changing. A perfect memory preserved behind the glass of the screen. She's so talented, our Lottie. She thinks she gets it from me, but in truth all I do is draw different shaped boxes with rulers and protractors. Like with most things, all the best bits I see in both of my children come from their mother.

'This is beautiful, Lottie. No one could have captured her better.'

'Thanks.' She tried to shrug nonchalantly. 'It's what I do.'

'And you do it brilliantly,' her brother reassured her. 'You're going to be huge one day.'

'I hope so.' Lottie shrugged. 'I'm getting bored of shooting weddings and babies smashing birthday cakes. Don't get me wrong, I'm lucky to make any money out of photography, I know that. Half my course mates are still in the same shop and bar jobs they had at uni. I just want to do so much more than candid snaps.'

'You will.' I rested my hand on her shoulder, and watched the screen as she flicked through more photos, each one another moment of Jenn's life preserved forever.

'We're putting together a reel for the funeral. I thought it would be a good way for people to remember her.' Matty looked up. 'Do you like it?'

'I love it. It's beautiful.' I couldn't tear my eyes away from the screen. I didn't notice Lottie was crying until her shoulders started shaking beneath my hand. 'Lottie?'

'I just can't believe she's gone. I only took some of these last month. It feels so weird being here without her. I keep wondering when she's going to come home, then remembering she never can again.'

I pulled her out of Matty's hug and wrapped her in one of my own. 'I'm sorry, Lottie, I'm so, so sorry.'

'What are you apologising for?' Matty asked, concern and grief etching new lines in his face as he stared at me over his sister's head.

'I don't know.' I rubbed my forehead tiredly. 'I keep wondering and thinking maybe I could have done something different ...'

'Dad this isn't your fault!'

'It was my friends we were visiting. If I hadn't insisted we go, and ...'

'And nothing. It was a horrible accident. There's nothing you, or anyone else, could have done to change it. You can't blame yourself for something you couldn't ever have changed.'

'But I was the one driving!' I snapped, yelling at them both, and regretting it instantly as Lottie's face crumpled further and she pulled away. She looked at me strangely, like she barely recognised her own dad.

'Do you really think you caused her death? Please tell me you're not actually blaming yourself for Mum's death.' Her voice was an incredulous whisper.

I couldn't find the strength to meet her eyes, and I didn't have the words to answer her.

'Dad, you didn't do this. You've nothing to feel guilty for,' Matty whispered forcefully.

'But I do. Every day. I'm here and she's not. It's not fair.' I hung my head. 'She should have survived. She should still be here.' I bit my tongue, not wanting to finish saying the thought aloud.

But Lottie knew me too well. 'What? You think it should have been you instead? You think we should be going to your funeral tomorrow instead of Mum's?'

'Yes. I do.' I shrugged, unable to take the words back once they'd escaped.

Lottie sighed hugely. 'Dad, I love you. We both do. But you're being an idiot. It was an accident. Horrible, and terrible and awful, but still just an accident. They aren't anyone's fault, that's why they're called accidents.'

'You weren't there, you don't know for sure.' I tried to argue.

'No, we weren't,' Lottie shot back. 'But we know you.

You'd never do anything to hurt any of us. We've all heard what the police said. Accident.'

'And you know Mum would hate it if she knew what you were putting yourself through,' Matty added. 'You can't torture yourself like this. It isn't fair.'

'Nothing about this is fair,' Lottie agreed. 'But this isn't making it any better. We need to pull together to get through this, especially over the next few days. It's the only way any of us are going to make it out the other side.'

'Agreed.' Matty nodded and stood, stretching. 'You've got to stop beating yourself up. This whole thing is hard enough without you making it harder.'

'All right. I'll try.'

'Promise?'

'Promise.' I nodded.

'Good.' He peered at his watch. 'I've got to get to the airport. Lucy's getting in at three.'

'She's coming?' Lottie pursed her lips.

'Yeah. She is my girlfriend, Charlotte. Mum liked her, even if you don't.'

'I don't dislike her,' Lottie complained. 'I just don't get her. Or what you see in her.'

'Yeah, well I don't get what you see in half of your boyfriends either,' Matty challenged, glaring at her. 'Who was that last guy you dated? No one should have that much metal in their face. I don't know how he blew his nose.'

'You mean Dom? Well at least he wasn't afraid of expressing himself. Better that than looking like corporate Barbie.'

'Lucy does not look like corporate Barbie!'

'*Puuhleeese.*' Lottie rolled her eyes. 'She must get up at the crack of dawn to put on all that make-up and squeeze herself into those miniskirts. And I don't know how she even walks in those shoes. Her feet must be ninety percent bunions.'

'Her feet are just fine,' Matty snapped back, before turning to look at me in surprise, and I realised I was laughing out loud.

'Something amusing you, Dad?'

'I'm sorry,' I gasped out between guffaws. 'It's just ... hearing you two squabble like this takes me back about ten years.'

Lottie stared at me, an odd look in her eyes as she tried to fight her own laughter. She glanced over to Matty, and lost all self-control, collapsing into fits of helpless giggles. 'Go on.' She waved at her confused brother. 'Go pick up your Barbie doll. Make sure her little plastic shoes don't fall off.' She collapsed against me, laughing hysterically.

JENN

It's good to see my family laughing, even if it is because of squabbling. Lottie's far too hard on Lucy. She's really a lovely girl, even if she is a tiny bit tarty, in the nicest possible way. She's blonde, slim, big-boobed and likes make-up and short skirts. But beneath all the primping, fluffed hair and preening, she's got a heart as big as a house. And it's solid gold. There's nothing she wouldn't do to help someone out, especially someone she cares about. Besides, I guess maybe that look works in her PR job.

And she loves my son so much. She's good for him, and she makes him happy. I'm glad she's going to be there for him tomorrow. It's going to be a long hard day for them all, so I'm glad he'll have someone there to support him. Someone who would do anything to ease his pain and make his life better. She'll cry tomorrow, just like the others, but it won't really be for me, which makes me smile.

Don't get me wrong, we got on well when we saw each other, but I know half the reason she'll be crying is for Matty's pain, not her own, and that makes her incredibly special in my mind. I don't think he knows it yet, but I'm pretty sure Matty's going to spend his life with Lucy. They're going to be so, so happy together. I just wish I'd been around long enough to see him realise that Lucy is his "one".

I hope Lottie manages to see beneath the push-up bras and hair spray, and realise how sweet and kind Lucy really is. She'll make a good big sister for Lottie. She's as organised and business-like as Lottie is creative and scatty, and I think they'll bring out good things in each other. Eventually. When they stop judging each other and realise how alike they really are.

Still, it's good to see my children squabbling and laughing. It fills me with hope for their futures.

I slipped into our bedroom as David opened the door that evening, and felt a rush of pleasure as he paused, recognising my presence. I wandered over to the wardrobes, and fingered the suit already hanging on the door. The collar on the shirt was crooked, so I tugged at it, trying to smooth it flat and chase away creases with my fingers.

I don't know what's going to happen tomorrow. It's the day I'm going to be buried and laid to rest. I don't know what that means for me as I am now, but I'm scared. I desperately want to be close to David tonight.

I've come to the frightening conclusion that maybe there's no one in the odd grey world I'm inhabiting because they've all moved on to ... I don't know where. Anything I used to believe about the afterlife, I'm now questioning. But I can't help thinking and feeling that after I'm buried, and the people I love have said their farewells, things might change. That scares me because I don't think I'm ready to leave yet.

For now I'm just going to stay here and rest my head beside my husband, and make sure his sleep is peaceful and healing. He'll need a good night's sleep before he can face tomorrow.

Chapter Seven

DAVID

Pain hit me almost as soon as I woke up. It was the day I'd been dreading. The day I had to say goodbye to Jenn.

I don't know how I slept, but I'm glad I did, because I dreamt Jenn was with me, warm, comforting and loving. When I first opened my eyes I could have sworn I saw her disappearing in the bright morning light, leaving nothing behind except the vaguest hint of honeysuckle and apple. Somehow that helped to push some of the dread away.

The sun shone through the curtains I had forgotten to close, and the sky was clear. Such a beautiful day. I couldn't help thinking that I would have preferred it if it was raining. Somehow it would have seemed more respectful if the day were grey, sombre and overcast, instead of bright, fresh and vivid.

Though I'm sure Jenn would have disagreed. Even when it was freezing, she'd have been out in the garden, drinking her morning tea and breathing clouds of steam into the winter air.

It all seemed so bizarrely unreal. My dark suit and crisp white shirt hung on the door, and when I put the shirt on, I got a whiff of sweet chocolate from the cocoa butter hand lotion Jenn always wore. It must have been one of the ones she'd ironed and put away that morning, before we left the house together for the last time. I almost didn't want to wear it, because then it would stop smelling of Jenn and just become another dirty, meaningless shirt. And it would be one more part of Jenn that would be gone from me forever. But then again, she ironed it for me. I should wear it.

Flowers arrived all through the morning. The first florist, our florist, turned up at about eight, while I was still in my slippers and dressing gown. She did a wonderful job, and managed to get the daffodils and irises we'd asked for. Huge, beautiful explosions of yellow and white that filled the house with their fresh, cold smell while they waited to be collected.

There was nothing for me to do. Lucy, Matty's girlfriend, had arrived yesterday evening and flipped straight into organisation mode. There wasn't much we hadn't already done, but it seemed to make her feel better. She zipped between the church and the house, dropping off orders of service, tied with ribbon in Jenn's favourite shade of yellow, and checking that every last detail was in place. She even produced dozens of those little packets of tissues from somewhere.

What it all meant was that I had nothing to do but sit around awkwardly and wander between the kitchen and the living room trying not to crease my suit and nursing tea so hot that it scalded my fingers through the mug. It hurt, but I couldn't move. If anything I was grateful for the pain, because it kept me grounded in reality.

I slipped one of Jenn's hair clips into my pocket. I knew it was silly, but I desperately needed something of hers to hang on to throughout the day. It was almost like a talisman to keep her with me. Because that way, even after we were finished, I'd still be able to take a bit of her home with me, and the thought of not doing that was unbearable.

As I slid my fingers into my pocket and wrapped them around the clip, the door swung open to reveal Lottie, far too pale and dull in her smart black dress and the scarf covering her pink streaked hair.

'Dad?' She offered me a weak smile. 'She's here. Mum's home. It's time to go.'

I am so proud of my beautiful, sweet, brave family. I love them all so much, and I am so lucky to have known them. How did I get lucky enough to be surrounded by such wonderful people?

Every single decision they've made has been perfect. I love the flowers. I don't think I've ever seen so many daffodils and tulips together. And not a single, hated, lily in sight. They found white irises too. They must have bought out half of Holland. Everywhere I look there are more flowers, and huge baskets of pure white tulips at the door.

The location was perfect as well. They picked the church just down the road from the school I'd taught at for so many years. I knew the vicar well, and it meant some of my children could come. I'm stunned by how many of them did. Not just my current students either. Plenty of my former pupils who long ago left school to start their own lives came too. The fact that so many took time out of their lives to come and wish me farewell is incredibly flattering. I didn't realise I'd touched so many lives so deeply. I mean, you spend your life trying to help people and make a difference, but to see so many faces at your funeral, and to know you've actually succeeded, is incredible.

The church was so packed with people that the children ended up sitting on the backs of the pews, dangling their feet over the shoulders of their friends, while the girls sat on their friends' and boyfriends' laps. Even like that, and with the extra chairs, there were still young people standing at the back, spreading halfway down the aisle, and leaning against the walls and pillars. Some even ended up shoving candles out of the way so they could perch on the windowsills. I know it's just a local church, but it was still humbling to see it so packed with people.

I loved the way that, after a few seconds of shocked silence, everyone burst out laughing at the first song, and then joined in singing. Spirit in the Sky. It wasn't a song I had especially liked in life – I didn't dislike it – it just wasn't anything special to me. Not until I saw all my students, and my friends and family, singing along and snapping their fingers in time to the beat. Some people even started swaying and dancing. Then I got it. Whoever's choice that was, it was perfect. If I'd anything left to bet with, my money would be on my sister, if for no other reason than the slight smile on her face.

And I'm blaming Lottie for the projector and slideshow of photos. I didn't even know that the church had a projector, but there I was, up on the wall and smiling down at everyone. Lottie's done a wonderful job. She's so talented.

Then all the music and dancing stopped, and it became much more serious. Tissues were passed back and forth and I could feel all the hurt and pain in that room, and all the sadness that was hidden behind brave smiles washed over me.

I could see people squeezing one another's fingers, or leaning up against others for support. They fiddled with jewellery, or bits of tissue, or just their fingers, and looked around awkwardly as the vicar began to speak. For some reason most funerals seem to start like that, with everyone watching everyone else, nervous and worried that they're going to react wrongly and be judged. Within seconds I could already see a few shoulders twitching with nervous laughter, but I didn't mind. People handle things like grief differently.

There was no laughter in the front rows though, not even the nervous kind. David did well to start with. He was pale and kept clearing his throat, but his tears didn't really start until the vicar caught his eye and described me as a loving wife. Lottie had already buried her face in his shoulder and was sobbing quietly, in that horrible, shoulder-heaving way that lasts for hours.

Matty was pale, his mouth tight and eyes too bright as he stared ahead, not really focusing on anything as he squeezed Lucy's fingers more tightly, the knuckles of his hand turning pure white. Lucy's slim fingers must have been creaking under the pressure of Matty's grief, but she didn't wriggle or complain, just leaned against him a little more, offering her silent support.

Sarah sat on the other side of the aisle. She looked tiny wrapped in her husband Gary's arm, with my nephews on either side of them.

The service sped on, and lots of lovely things were said about me. Matty gave a beautiful eulogy, but to be honest most of the funeral, most of my funeral, passed in a blur. The sadness and grief of my friends and family was so overwhelming that pain seemed to ricochet around the church. Every soft sob and sniffle echoed in the air and struck a blow against me. Just when I thought the pain had peaked, David stood up and walked to the front. He paused at my coffin, and for a second seemed frozen to the floor. I tried to reach out to him and lend him my strength, but his grief was thick and heavy and I couldn't push through it. He rested a hand briefly on the warm wood surrounding what was left of the physical "me", then visibly straightened his shoulders and walked to the lectern.

He cleared his throat nervously, and looked out across the crowd. He seemed to draw strength from them, but I suppose that's the point of funerals. To come together and share your memories, stories and strength as you say goodbye to someone you care about. When he spoke his voice was rough with tears, but clear and strong.

'I've been trying for days to find the right words for this

moment. Those magical perfect words that would sum up Jenn's life in a few short sentences and describe how much we'll all miss her. And I've been failing miserably.' He took a deep breath. 'But it's not until I stood here in front of you all that I realise why. What made Jenn really special, was how she was with other people. She was bright and beautiful and clever and kind, and everyone loved her. She inspired people and made them want to be better than they were. She saw the best in people, even when others didn't, and she brought it out.

'Jenn could light up a room just by walking into it. But you already all know that. That's why you're here today, and Jenn would have been incredibly touched and grateful to see this church overflowing with the people who cared about her.' He paused briefly as murmurs echoed round the congregation.

'If she were here, she'd thank you all for coming, and remind you to take care of each other. So in her stead, I'll tell you what I know she'd have said: "Look after each other, take the time to remember the things most important to you, and make the time to tell those people who they are".

'I've been dreading this moment, and, as I said, I haven't been able to find the right words, so I decided to leave it to an expert. This poem was one of Jenn's favourites, and one some of you might be familiar with. Especially if you've been in one of her English classes.'

David smiled at the young people lining the back of the church, amusement briefly filling his eyes as some of them nudged their friends, whispering. He was right, almost every English class I'd ever taught poetry to knew these words.

He took a deep breath, and his hands trembled slightly as he started to recite the poem that we both knew so well. We'd discovered it in an old book decades back, when we'd been split apart by different universities and study courses.

For years, the last line had been how we'd signed every card, letter and even note that we'd given to each other. A silly, private little way of reminding the other of how we felt in our private relationship.

'I wanted you in the darkness, when I didn't know you yet,
And I fell for you in the grey dawn
light, when our souls first met.
In the noon sky brightness, when we saw each other's flaws
I knew that you still loved me, and I loved you all the more.
I've loved you through to sunset,
through pink pains of eventide
And even as the light dims, I'll stay here by your side.

Because I'll love you in the morrow,
and in every one to come,
And I know I'll still love you, when time itself is done.
There's no doubt in my mind, and of this I am beyond sure,
For I know I'll love you for always and forever,
And that I'll be always and ever yours.'

His voice finally gave out on the last line, choked by tears. The final words were barely more than a whisper, but it didn't matter because the whole church was silent enough to hear his ragged breath. When the music started again, a few people jumped, and then nervous, relieved laughter followed. They'd survived the horror of the funeral and most people would walk out of the church relatively unscathed. Papers rustled as orders of service were shoved into bags and pockets, or smoothed carefully to be kept as mementoes.

The doors at the back swung open, bathing the church with cold, bright light. There were a few moments of confusion as the undertakers had to usher children out of the aisle to make way for my final journey.

The pallbearers walked solemnly towards my coffin, and I could feel David's tension growing as they faced me, bowed, and lifted me to their shoulders in a single smooth movement. They paused for a moment as David and Matty took up position between them on either side, taking me onto their shoulders as well.

The whole church stood, their eyes on me, or at least my coffin, as I was walked back up the aisle. The flowers bounced jauntily in time to "Angels" by Robbie Williams. It did seem a little inappropriate but that's what daffodils tend to do.

It's only a relatively short aisle, no more than seventy-five feet or so, but every step was agony for David. I could see his fingers tightening against the hard wood of the coffin as he carried it, trying to press into the wood to be closer to me. As his knuckles turned white, I knew what he was thinking. He desperately wanted to reach inside and pull me back to him, to wrap his hand around mine and never, ever let go.

There were only scant inches between our fingers, and yet we'd never been further apart. And we'd never be as close ever again. It's enough to break what's left of my heart into dust.

I knew David's other thoughts clearly as well. I could read it in his eyes as he thought about the last time he walked me up an aisle. Then it had been in a blur of hope, promises and love wrapped in silk, lace and dreams for the future. He'd slipped a gold ring onto my finger, promising we'd love each other for our whole lives, until death do us part.

Neither of us had expected it to be so soon. And I don't think either of us had really considered an ending like this. I know all I'd thought about was how lucky I was that this sweet, wonderful, handsome, clever man had chosen me, of all people, to spend his life with.

Pain and grief have aged him so much that I hardly

recognise him as the man I married all those years ago. He's as worn as the gold band that's wrapped around his finger, digging into his skin slightly where he's gained a little weight over the years. I wish I could wrap myself around him so tightly. I wish I could let him know I'm still here, but his pain buffets me away. I'm helpless to do anything except watch.

DAVID

We buried Jenn at the cemetery just half a mile from the church. It seemed a little silly, loading her into the car for such a short journey. In life she'd have laughed and taken the mickey of anyone jumping in a car for a five minute walk, but what choice did we really have?

I sat in the hearse with Sarah, her husband, and Lottie, Matty and Lucy. Lottie wove her fingers through mine tightly, but didn't say anything. None of us seemed to know what to say. I knew I should have been talking, that I should have thanked Sarah and Lucy for all their help organising everything, but I just couldn't. I couldn't tear my eyes away from the hearse in front of us. I couldn't take my eyes off Jenn's coffin. It was all so terrifying, knowing that I was never going to see her ever again. I wanted to remember every last detail. Even if it was just the polished grain of a mahogany coffin.

It was all over so quickly. Within minutes they had Jenn carefully balanced at the top of the open grave, waiting for the last few words from the vicar. Then they slowly lowered her down. It was so easy for them. I found myself wondering how many thousands of times they'd done it, and whether they felt anything behind their solemn, professional masks.

If they had somehow found a way to numb themselves to the pain, then I wished I was one of them, because every inch they lowered Jenn was another stab of agony through me. Another flash of memory, another realisation of all the things we'd never do together again.

My hopes and dreams shattered as they lowered Jenn into that cold hole, and my future unravelled in front of my eyes. I'd never see her eyes fill with proud tears as I walked Lottie down the aisle. If she ever does get married, Lottie's going to be like that girl in the awful charity commercial – standing alone in her wedding dress and wishing her mother was there. I'm never going to see Jenn laughing and playing with her grandchildren, and we're never going to walk barefoot along a beach on one of those holidays for pensioners that we'd teased each other about. She's not going to grow old with me, and we're not going to retire and buy a little cottage in the country. There's so much Jenn's never going to get to do. I don't know how I'm going to live without her – I don't think I can even breathe. They should throw me in the ground and bury me with her. I'm already dead inside.

In a way, I'm glad there were so many people there. Otherwise I might have actually climbed in after her. God knows I wanted to.

The students from Jenn's school filed past the grave, holding the pure white tulips from Lucy's basket. Most of them were sniffling, and a few cried outright, holding on tightly to each other for support as they dropped the tulips into the grave. Some paused to whisper a few words. 'We'll miss you, Miss. Won't be the same without you.' A couple of the older students even paused to shake my hand and murmur a few words of comfort. To tell me how much they'd miss Jenn, and that school wasn't going to be the same without her. As if I didn't know already.

Then it was over.

People streamed from the cemetery, a few pausing to look back, but most just walking away. I wish I could walk away and go back to my life so easily, but it's lying in the ground with Jenn. After a few moments, Matty and Lottie left my side, whispering their own farewells to their mum as they left. Sarah squeezed my fingers tightly, and peered down sadly. 'Goodbye little sis, sweet dreams.' She dropped another flower into the grave and brushed away her tears.

Then I was finally alone with Jenn.

I peered down into the grave and almost burst into tears again at the huge pile of flowers covering her coffin. Every person who'd come to say farewell had dropped a single, pure white tulip in for her. The wood of the coffin and carved brass plaque were almost completely hidden beneath the tulips. There were hundreds of them, lying haphazardly over Jenn in a chaotic display of love and grief. The summary of my kind, clever, beautiful, loving wife's life. Hundreds of tulips piled up, one for each person who would be missing her. I think she'd have been quite touched to see them all. I wished she had been there with me so I could have shared it all with her, and let her know how many people love her.

I wish I'd told her that I loved her more. But I think she knew.

There were people waiting for me, and I had to go, but I didn't know how to move. I didn't know how to leave Jenn there in that cold, empty, lonely hole. I didn't know how I was supposed to say goodbye and just walk away from my wife forever.

That's when the cold warmth flooded over me again, and warm breeze ruffled my hair and pulled at my jacket. I wiped away the tears I hadn't even realised were streaming down my cheeks, and caught a whiff of cocoa butter hand lotion. There was a flutter of movement in the corner of my eye and honeysuckle tickled at my nostrils, but I couldn't bear to turn my head and look properly. If it was Jenn, then I didn't want her to disappear, and if it wasn't her, then I didn't want to know. I think something brushed against my cheek, but the touch was so delicate it could have been my desperate mind imagining it.

Either way it gave me strength. I stared at the tulip I'd been holding so gently and stroked its soft petals. I could see why she loved the flowers so much. They were delicate and beautiful – just like her. I kissed the petals gently, and let it drop in with all the others.

'Thank you for the wonderful life you've given me, and our beautiful children.' My voice broke and I had to whisper the final words. 'Ever yours, Jenn. I'm always and ever yours.'

We'd organised the wake to take place back at the church hall. I couldn't get into the car with the others. I needed to be by myself for a few minutes and I needed to be moving. I couldn't sit still and think about what I'd lost. I waved the driver on as I walked past the cars. It sounds silly now, but then I felt like if I kept moving, I might just make it through the awfulness of the day.

I didn't know what I was going to do the next morning. Funerals are funny things. Everyone views them as the end. The goodbyes have been said, and most people can go back to their normal lives, with their grieving pretty much over and done. Even the rest of the family will move on. Matty will go home with Lucy, Lottie will go back to her flat in Farringdon, and Sarah will fly home with her husband and children, and everyone will go back to their normal lives. Of course they'll still be grieving for Jenn too, but they won't have to wake up to an empty bed and silent house where she should be.

For me the funeral's just the beginning. The day after there's less to do. Less to organise. There aren't flowers or readings or songs to think about. There aren't any distractions. There's just me. Without Jenn.

In a way I didn't want that awful day to end, because the funeral was still a link to Jenn. Albeit a painful one. Once the funeral was over, I knew I would have to start getting my life back together, which meant working out how to live without Jenn.

I walked back to the church hall slowly, using the time to pull myself together. I paused at the doors, not entirely ready to face everyone waiting inside for the wake. If I'd had my choice, I would have headed home to collapse on the sofa with a bottle of whisky to keep me company. It's not something I'd usually do, but right then I just wanted to be alone with my memories. And to maybe drink enough to pretend that none of this had even happened. Though that might be something I should knock on the head soon. I've been going through the alcohol cupboard far too quickly lately, and Jenn would never have approved. But it seems to help a bit, and I just can't seem to find the will to care all that much. Anything that helps is good. I'll think about it another day. If I can be bothered.

But as much as I'd like to crawl into a corner and just drink until I forget everything, Jenn wouldn't have wanted me to do that. She would have wanted me to go in and socialise, and spend time with other people, remembering her. So I took a deep breath and swung the doors open, and stepped into a room full of memories of Jenn.

Lottie spotted me as soon as I walked in, handed her drink to a neighbour and rushed to my side. 'Are you all right? We were worried.'

'I think I'll be all right,' I answered honestly. 'Is that the same thing?'

She slipped her arm through mine and led me towards the back of the room. 'I think maybe it is. Shall we get a drink? I think there's a bottle of whisky back there somewhere.'

'Thanks. I could do with it.'

A few minutes later I was nursing a glass of amber fluid that burnt as I swallowed it, and filled me with warmth.

'Mr Hughes?' The polite voice didn't match the heavy leather coat, black jeans and long hair. And it really clashed with the gothic rings and piercings.

'Yes.' I shook the offered hand gingerly.

'My name's Stu. Stuart. I'm sorry to disturb you. I just wanted to say how sorry I am about Mrs Hughes.'

'Thank you. How did you know Jenn?'

'I was one of her students nearly ten years ago. I don't think she ever stopped nagging me.'

'Oh, I'm sorry about that.' I didn't know what to say.

'I'm not.' He grinned. 'She kicked my arse up and down the corridors for five years. And it was exactly what I needed. I was way too smart for my own good back then, and nothing but trouble. Everyone else lost patience with me, but not Mrs Hughes. She wouldn't ever stop pushing and nagging at me. She never left me alone. And I couldn't be more grateful. I got through college, and now I'm doing a part-time course in social care and working with other troubled kids. All because of her.' He took a deep breath. 'I don't think I ever really thanked her. I should have. So I wanted to say it to you instead, and make sure that you knew. We all loved Mrs Hughes. She really was one of a kind.'

I'd known Jenn was popular at work, how could she not be? But I hadn't realised she'd made such an impact on the children she'd worked with. She literally changed people's lives. 'Thank you.'

'No worries. Like I said, I just wanted to make sure you knew. If there's anything I can do for you, let me know, all right?'

I nodded, not fully trusting myself to speak.

I was right to be worried. Once the wake was over, and David and the children had gone home, I found myself being pulled back into the grey place. It seems to happen more when I'm tired. After today, and so many people's emotions pulling me back and forth, I'm exhausted.

Anyway, that's when it happened. A bright red, slightly battered rubber ball appeared from nowhere, and rolled to a stop at my feet. I stared at it in surprise, thinking that I knew it from somewhere. It was the first thing I'd seen here since arriving, and the colour was so bright it seemed to glow. I picked it up to study it more closely, and bounced it between my palms, trying to decide where I knew it from.

When it finally clicked I nearly dropped the ball in surprise. Of course I knew this ball. How could I forget? It belonged to Daisy, our border collie. I sat on the floor batting it back and forth between my hands. I couldn't believe I'd almost forgotten Daisy. Sweet, faithful, loving, clever little Daisy. David brought her home when Lottie was about three years old. He'd thought all children should have a pet, and that a dog was the perfect addition to our family. She was a scrappy little bundle of scruffy, yappy fluff and we all fell in love with her at first sight. She was part of our family from the moment she'd clumsily scampered into our lives and we all loved her dearly.

She'd treasured her bouncy balls, and for some reason the red ones were always her favourite, even though she was supposedly colour blind. When she finally had to leave us at nearly seventeen, we buried her with a collection of her favourite toys, with her beloved red ball by her nose. I think I cried for the best part of a week. I know that Lottie did, even though she was far beyond being a kid at the time.

I had no idea what the red ball meant, but it had to be important so I kept it with me.

A while later a cold, snuffly nose thumped against my hand and made me jump. As soon as Daisy saw she had my attention, she sat, begging for her favourite toy.

'Hello girl. I've missed you.' I wrapped my arms around her and buried my face in her riotous black and white fur. She felt warm and solid, and I could feel her tail thumping excitedly on the floor. She looked almost the same as I remembered her, only younger and healthier. She wriggled against me and tried to sniff me all over, whimpering and snuffling until finally deciding she was happy, and headbutting me so hard I fell over. She nuzzled at my hand, licking at my fingers, trying to free her toy.

'All right, all right.' I gave in and tossed the ball, and laughed as she shot off after it, grinning from ear to ear. Within a few seconds the ball was back at my feet, Daisy beside it with her tongue lolling out happily. She barked hopefully and nudged the ball with her nose.

I scooped it up and threw it for her again, this time harder. She bounded after it, grabbed it, and streaked back towards me. I laughed out loud, glad to have found a friend in this dull, lonely place.

Then the game changed. Instead of bringing the ball back, Daisy dropped it a few feet from me. I shrugged and stepped forward to pick it up, but she dived in and snatched it away from me, then raced away. She dropped the ball and looked back to me, tongue lolling out and tail wagging, wanting me to follow.

That was when I realised how much my world had changed. While I'd been playing with Daisy, the grey melted away to bright green grass and the sky had taken on golden and pink hues. For the first time since I'd died, I felt warm, and the air was filled with the scent of daffodils and freshly baked pie. Apple, cinnamon and walnut pie. The way my mum used to make it. I'd tried the recipe myself a dozen times, but it just wasn't the same – I didn't have my mum's magical way with pastry and spices.

Fear froze me to the floor as realisation dawned. Daisy barked impatiently, wanting me to follow her. I shook my head. I wasn't ready for this. If I followed Daisy, and I desperately wanted to, it would mean leaving David, Matty and Lottie. It might mean giving up and accepting that I was dead, and leaving them all. I might not be able to be part of their lives any more, and I wouldn't be able to support them and help them move on.

Daisy dropped the ball and ran back to me, darting around my legs and trying to nudge me forward.

'No Daisy, no. I don't want to.' I tried to explain as she sat down and stared up at me in confusion, worry in her brown eyes. I knelt down to comfort her, and she leaned against me. Peace, warmth and love flooded through me, and in that moment, everything I'd experienced in my life made sense. Every moment of pain and sadness faded away to be replaced by knowledge and understanding. Even my death made sense.

These were the things I'd chosen to experience long before I'd been born. Things that I had to experience before I could move on again. I'd been here before, many times, and this time I'd chosen to go back and help other people. That's why I had become a teacher, to guide others and help them experience the things they needed to. I'd done everything I was supposed to, and lived the life I wanted.

Now that was over, I was being offered something far bigger and more wonderful than any words could describe. All I had to do to get it was follow Daisy. There would be joy and happiness, and peace so tangible that it was like being wrapped in a blanket, protected from harm, and sadness, and worry forever. As if you could wrap yourself up in love and light. It was a place where I'd never feel anger, fear or hurt ever again. I'd never be lonely, and I'd never suffer. If I let it, I knew the warmth would take me over and fill me up, moving me to where I was supposed to be.

And then David's face flashed across my mind.

I didn't want to move on. Not yet. I didn't understand it well enough. How could I think of my family without feeling sadness or grief? It's important because you can only feel grief when you've loved someone or something dearly. And grief is supposed to hurt. If this wonderful place was somewhere without grief and pain, then surely it meant it was somewhere I was supposed to forget my family. I didn't know how I could ever do that. I couldn't see how I could move on to eternal peace and contentment when they were still hurting so badly. Especially after I promised myself that I'd stay and help them.

I knew I'd still be able to watch over my family and see them live their own lives. And I knew that when their physical lives were through they'd join me in the light, but the idea of seeing them and not hurting for them was too alien and scary for me to accept. Even for a few decades that would pass as quickly for me as mere hours and days would for them.

Daisy whined sadly and pawed at my knee, and I realised this wasn't really the Daisy I knew. This creature was brighter and more beautiful, and shimmering with golden light. A guide who'd come to show me the way home, but taking a form that would make me feel relaxed and happy.

'No Daisy, I can't come yet. It isn't the right time for me.' I went to ruffle her silken ears but she ducked out of my way and streaked out of sight. Pain hit me like a tidal wave, slamming over me and leaving me gasping. The colour and warmth drained back out of the world, and I was left alone in the cold empty grey. Panic gnawed at me and I fought the urge to yell for her to come back and take me with her. Had I done the right thing?

Just as I thought I couldn't bear the pain and emptiness for a moment longer, Daisy reappeared, ball held proudly in her mouth and tail aloft.

She paused, her tail wagging as she invited me to play. I shook my head firmly, half-smiling at her persistence. It sure seemed like Daisy. She gave a snort and half-shrug before dropping the ball on the floor and nudging it to my feet.

Instantly I understood. It was for when I was ready. The light would wait for me.

I picked the gift up and tossed it back and forth between my palms. My family still needed me. One day, when they were healed, then I would be ready. But not today. And now, thanks to Daisy, it's my choice when that day will be.

Chapter Eight

DAVID

I was supposed to go back to work a few days ago. Now I have to go and see the Human Resources department as my compassionate leave has run out. Apparently they've been very understanding and already given me more than the contracted three weeks, in consideration of the fact that I was in the accident too. Offices and houses are still being built, and people are still wanting extensions on their homes. It doesn't matter that my family, and life, has shrunk by one very important person – other families are still growing and their houses need to keep up, so someone, like me, needs to draft the plans.

Three weeks. Twenty-one days to get over a car accident, a few minor injuries and the loss of your wife. That's not even a day for every year I spent with Jenn as the centre of my world. Not that it would make any difference. Jenn is still everything to me, even though she isn't here any more. She's still the first thing I think of every morning, and the last thing on my mind at night. She's embedded into my heart and my skin. A habit that I never want to break. I still feel her hair brush against my skin and smell her perfume in the air. Sometimes I still think I see her out of the corner of my eye, before I'm fully awake in the morning.

Matty and Lucy have already had to head back up north. He took off as much time as he could, but he was needed back at work. It seems contracts don't wait any longer than building blueprints. As I've found out recently, losing one of the most important people in your life apparently doesn't warrant more than a few weeks off. I mean Jenn only carried him for nine months, went through hours of agony to bring him into the world and spent two and a half decades dedicating her life to him. Why should he need more than two weeks to get over losing the woman who did all that and a million other things besides?

At least Lottie has been able to stay longer. She's still trying to set up her career, so most of her work is freelance or short contract. I keep trying to tell her to go home, that I don't need her here looking after me, but we both know it's a lie. Really, I'm glad of her company. I'm not ready to be alone in Jenn's and my house yet. I still feel like I'm trying to work out how to breathe without her, let alone how to live and function.

The meeting with HR and my boss was a complete blur. Somehow I got through it and found myself sitting in the car in a daze, trying to remember what had been said. It was pretty clear to everyone in the meeting, myself included, that there's no way I'm ready to go back to work. I struggled to concentrate on anything, and even when I did try really hard, it seems that my memory's shot to pieces.

They want me to go see a doctor and be signed off work formally, and the occupational health nurse mentioned that she thinks I could be experiencing depression. I think they're overreacting myself. Who wouldn't be in pain after something like this? There are times when the grief is so overwhelming that it becomes physical agony. I mean, yes, I am struggling to sleep, having nightmares about that bloody awful day, and I have lost my appetite, but surely that's to be expected when going through a major trauma. Can there really be anything more traumatic than losing your wife?

That's when it happened again. The cold warmth wrapped around my left hand and seeped up my arm. I breathed in honeysuckle and apple, and closed my eyes. A moment later hair brushed against my shoulder, as delicately as a butterfly.

If I hadn't been sitting silently, waiting for it, I'd probably have missed it. I found myself smiling. Jenn was here. I didn't want to open my eyes in case she disappeared, but I didn't need to. I knew she was there as strongly as if I'd just rolled over in the darkness in bed and found her lying beside me.

There was no questioning it, and no fear for my sanity either. It had happened so many times before, so clearly, that questioning Jenn's presence and refusing to accept it would be the true measure of insanity. Besides, the more time I have spent thinking about it, the more I have come to realise that it would be insane to have believed Jenn would really have left us completely. If there was ever any way she could have stayed with us, I know Jenn would have found it. She was always a fighter in life, pushing hard to achieve whatever it was she wanted and needed.

It seems that Jenn's set her mind to staying with us, or at least with me. I have never been so glad of anything. Before this year, I hadn't really thought about death or what happens after it. I'd always assumed that it would either be nothing at all, or the full-blown pearly-gated heaven. I'd never really thought about ghosts or hauntings as anything more than the basis for stories around a campfire or Halloween films. But now that I have started to think about it, it makes so much sense. Jenn wasn't expecting to die. She definitely wasn't ready to leave us, any more than I'm ready to face life without her. I like the idea that she's still here, in some form. I'm not ready to be alone yet.

JENN

Oh David, sweetheart, I'm not going anywhere until you're ready. I'm not ready to leave you either. Especially not when you're still hurting. I've got all the time in the world. I'll be here for your whole life, and I'll wait at the end of it to greet you if that's what you need.

But I'd rather you worked out how to live again, and found other things that make you happy. You're not just my husband, David, or the father of my children. You were a wonderful person before we met – I would never have fallen in love with you otherwise. You had a life before you met me and it's time you remembered that. You're going to have to rediscover who you are, and I know it's scary, but it's exciting too. How many dreams did you give up to be with me? You always talked about travelling when you were younger, before Matty and Lottie came along. You could do that now. Or learn to fly, like you always threatened, or even just go back to your painting. You were always brilliant at capturing a feeling and pinning it down to paper. It's not me Lottie gets her creativity from: it's you.

You've spent your whole adult life being "Jenn's husband" and "Matthew and Charlotte's daddy", and you've been incredible in both of those roles, but now it's time for you to be David. It's up to you who that's going to be.

But whoever you decide to be, and whatever you decide to do, you're going to be wonderful. You always are.

I have a confession to make. I'm feeling a bit guilty. I knew Lottie was planning to go back to her shared flat, and I knew David wasn't ready for it. So I decided she should stay. I'm blaming David for my actions though. He should be able to talk to his own daughter. He should have been able to tell her that he wanted her to stay a little longer. She was never going to say no. If anything, she was waiting for the invitation. But those two are as bad as each other. He's too proud and scared to ask for help, and she's too self-sufficient and stubborn to offer it freely.

So I took matters into my own hands.

Yesterday evening, when Lottie was getting ready to leave, I stole her keys. She was packed and ready to go, but she kept pausing at the bedroom door and chewing the side of her thumbnail, like she always does when she's worried. I could see David wandering back and forth downstairs, stopping every so often to stare up at the ceiling helplessly.

I love them both dearly, but sometimes they can be so stupid. I'm worried about what's going to happen to them now, because they're just useless at talking to each other. It was obvious to me that neither of them were going to make the first move, so I decided to make it for them.

It was so easy. One moment Lottie's keys were sitting on the dressing table in front of the mirror, and the next they were in my hand. Lottie hoisted her bag onto her shoulder and looked around the room vaguely, checking to make sure she'd got everything. She stared at the spot where her keys rested a few seconds before, then shrugged.

She clomped down the stairs and dropped the bag on the hall floor with a thump, then peered into the dish on top of the bookcase, looking for her keys. She lifted it up, then tutted in annoyance and yelled for David.

'Dad, have you seen my keys?'

'I thought you took them upstairs.'

'I thought I did too.' Lottie dropped to her knees and tore open the zip on her bag. She yanked the clothes out, shaking them and chucking them haphazardly to one side. 'They're not in my bag.'

'Have you tried the bookcase?'

'Already looked there.' Lottie pursed her lips thoughtfully. 'I could have sworn I left them on the dressing table. If I don't leave soon I'm going to catch all the traffic.'

'I'll help you look,' David offered, ever the good father. Forty-five minutes later they'd pulled the house half-apart, yanking out drawers, scouring Lottie's bedroom, searching through the hall and living room, even pulling books off the shelves. I laughed when Lottie opened the fridge and peered inside. Nice try kiddo, but not good enough. She slammed the door shut, making the bottles rattle.

'I've got no idea where they are. This is freaking ridiculous. Keys don't just grow legs and walk away!'

David sighed and ran his hand through his hair, clearly getting frustrated with his scatty daughter. 'You must have put them somewhere.'

'I didn't! I last saw them on the dressing table.'

'All right, all right.' David held up his hands in surrender. 'I'll check your room again. You look down here.'

'What's the point? We've already looked everywhere.'

'They have to be somewhere.' David climbed the stairs tiredly.

Lottie groaned and grabbed the cushions off the sofa, throwing them to the floor in frustration. She pulled the sofa apart, yanking out the seats and running her hands down the sides and underneath. After a few minutes she gave up and stared at the ceiling, hands on her hips as she huffed and puffed. 'That's it, they're not here. It looks like I'm staying whether I like it or not!'

'What was that?' David's voice echoed down the stairs.

'Nothing.' Lottie shook her head.

'Oh.' David sounded disappointed.

I gave Lottie a gentle nudge. She sighed and folded her arms. 'It's just, well ...' She wandered out to the hall. 'If I didn't know better, I'd think I was being told to stay here.'

Upstairs, I felt David freeze. 'I suppose you could.' He tried not to sound too eager. 'If that's what you want.'

I stared at Lottie, wanting to scream at her to say yes.

'All right. I don't need to rush back. I suppose I can stay for a bit longer. I don't have to be back for a few more days. I'll stay at least until the weekend.' Lottie stuffed her hands in her pockets and sauntered back to the living room.

I smiled to myself. That was exactly what I'd wanted to hear. Mission accomplished.

Lottie grabbed the cushions from the floor and stuffed them back into place, thumping them a few times for good measure. She collapsed on the sofa with a sigh, and froze at the soft jangle. Surprised, she bounced up and down, listening carefully. 'I don't believe it.' She jumped to her feet and lifted the cushion again. The keys sat underneath it innocently, spread out in a perfect star that stretched from their ring. 'What the ...?' Lottie stared at the keys, astonished. Surely she'd checked there a few seconds ago? No one else had been in the room. 'Um, Dad? I've found them.'

So you can see why I'm feeling slightly guilty, although I'm struggling to feel that bad about it, because Lottie's staying a bit longer and I think it's what they both need right now.

I watched as David crept down the stairs, leaned over the banister, and carefully shut the hall door. I wondered what he was doing, so followed him back up the stairs. He sat on the edge of our bed and grinned. 'I know you're here.'

I stared at him in surprise.

'I can feel you all around me, Jenn. When you're here the air changes slightly. Do you remember when Lottie was little and kept using all your bath salts? How she said they made the water feel softer? Well that's what this is like. I know you're here because the air feels ... softer.' He paused and rubbed his eyes tiredly. 'I miss you so much.'

I miss you too. I wish I could tell you how much, but I don't have any way to let you know. I still love you. I'm here.

'Oh my God.' David shook his head. 'I can't believe I'm talking to a ... ghost. A month ago I didn't even believe in them. I half think I'm going insane.'

I wanted to reach out to him and reassure him, to let him know I was still there and that he wasn't going mad.

On the bed David smiled. He leaned back and tucked his hands behind his head. 'I can feel it when you do that. At least I think I can.' He shook his head. 'You know, that was a pretty rotten thing to do to Lottie.' His eyes creased with amusement. 'But, thanks.'

I rested next to him, pouring love, happiness and reassurance into him.

Chapter Nine

DAVID

It's quite incredible how strange a thing it's possible to accept as normal when there's no other choice, or when the alternative is too big and scary to contemplate. Six weeks ago I would never have imagined that I'd be regularly talking to a ghost. I never even used to believe it was real. I used to think it was just something bored teenagers and slightly crazy middle-aged hippies did. I definitely am not a teenager, or hippy.

Still, it doesn't matter. Because it is real. Spirits, ghosts, ghouls, souls, whatever people choose to call them, do exist. I have the proof of that. I have Jenn.

Jenn's with me all of the time, and I probably talk to her more than when she was alive, because then we didn't always need words. We could finish each other's thoughts without even needing to speak, but now she's gone I have to do the talking for both of us. So I chatter on, telling her about everything and nothing, just to keep talking and keep her with me a bit longer. It's been a lot easier to talk to her since Lottie went back to her flat-share. Recently, she'd started to give me some strange looks, and as much as I tried not to worry her, I know she's heard me talking to Jenn.

She wanted to stay longer, but I convinced her to go home. She pays enough for that tiny Farringdon flat – even sharing the bills, it still costs her a fortune. She should be able to have the freedom of living there. And, although I know she means well, sometimes I just really want to be alone with my wonderful Jenn.

There are times when I don't feel her around me and then I wonder what she's doing and where she is. But even if Jenn wanted to give me the answers, she's not able to. Now she communicates in feelings that rush over me, tiny changes in the air, feather-light touches and moving things around. She leaves gifts of tiny white feathers as reminders that she's still in our lives.

And her scent. It wasn't something I really noticed before, but now it's the thing I notice the most. I could happily spend the rest of my life just sitting in her presence and breathing in her scent.

But Jenn knows that, and I don't think she's too happy about it. She keeps leaving me little hints and trying to entice me out of the house. Sometimes it's the smell of freshly baked bread, or the maddening smell of pastry, eggs and nutmeg. It insinuates itself into my mind, and I find it difficult to think about anything other than biting into cool, creamy custard wrapped in buttery pastry. And then I realise that, as usual, Jenn's right. It is about time I ate something other than cheese and ham sandwiches. Food has lost a lot of appeal lately, so I'm not always bothering to eat. Partly it's that Jenn did a lot of the cooking for both of us, and partly it's that I just find it so much effort when it's just for me. All the planning, shopping, and all the effort of cooking and cleaning up. It just doesn't seem worth it, so I sometimes don't bother. But the thought of a custard tart right now? Delicious.

Supermarkets have to be just about the most depressing place in the world. I'd never noticed how hard it is to be a single person in a supermarket. Almost everything comes in packs of two, or three or four. Who needs a dozen pork chops? Surely I should be able to buy some sausages without ending up with so many that I'm eating them for four days straight. If something is £1.50, but two for £2, I think I'd rather just have the first item for £1. I just don't have the need to buy things for two any more.

I soon found myself standing by the fridges in front of the fresh cakes. All I wanted was a single custard tart, but that wasn't an option. I could have a pack of four, or even six, but not just one.

When did the world become so anti-single? I felt like a leper or some sort of criminal. Like I'd done something wrong and was being punished for it. I stared at the cakes helplessly and wondered how on earth my life had brought me to this point.

A polite cough sounded at my ear and a hand rested on my arm. 'Sir?' The girl was dressed in the brightly coloured uniform of the shop, and her face was a mess of concern and acne. She looked about twelve. When did shop assistants get so young?

'Sir? Are you all right?'

'What?' I stared at her in confusion.

'Only you've been standing here staring at the cakes for nearly twenty minutes,' she explained awkwardly. 'Can I help at all?'

Twenty minutes? How could I have been stood there for twenty minutes? I swallowed hard and forced a smile onto my face. 'I'm fine thank you. Just a million miles away.' My laugh sounded forced, and the girl nodded nervously. I grabbed the packet of tarts and chucked them into my basket to reassure her, then forced my feet to move. Where was Jenn when I needed her? The whole blasted outing was her idea.

I kept my head down, refusing to meet anyone's gaze as I headed for the checkouts. It felt as if everyone was staring at me with pity in their eyes, and at the same time, they shied away, not wanting to be caught in my lonely hopelessness. I'd never realised it before but the whole world seems to be designed for couples and families. There's no room in it for a sad, lonely, single old widower like me.

JENN

I really don't know what it is with the white feathers. They just keep turning up around me. I don't know where they come from or why they appear, but they feel nice so I left a few around David. He seems to like them, and they reassure him that I'm not just a figment of his imagination. They give him proof and offer him something physical to hold on to. I suppose that probably is the point of them.

It's strange being part of this world still, but at the same time being part of another one. I feel as though I'm walking along the top of the fence separating the dead and living worlds, and I can see into both. I never realised how many things I didn't see clearly when I was alive. It's like I've drawn aside a lace curtain, and everything's much brighter and clearer. I can see and understand things I'd never even considered before. I can see the flow of energy across a world that's alive with colour and feeling, and it all has meaning.

Most of it's beautiful, but when I look at David I see clouds of darkness surrounding him. It's all his grief, anger and hurt, and it's pressing down and choking him, cutting away all his hope and joy. It's easy to see why he's struggling. And although I try to keep them at bay, his nightmares have started sneaking back in. At first it was only the odd one that I could easily soothe away, but recently there have been ones so bad, and so vivid, that he wakes up in a panic, having relived the accident again in all its technicolour misery.

Oh, my darling David, I wish I could make you hear me properly. You've been doing so well lately. Please don't let a silly incident in a supermarket set you back. You're so much better and stronger than that. I know you think your life is over, but I promise you it isn't. You have so many wonderful things still left to experience. I just need to help you see that.

Maybe we should concentrate on something else for a

while. You've seemed happy lately, but I can't help worrying that it's a fragile happiness. I worry you're focussing too much on me, and doing things for me instead of yourself. Don't get me wrong, I love being with you and feeling your emotions wash through me, but you need to remember the other things that make you happy. I need you to find your inspiration and passion for life again, and I'm going to help.

DAVID

Over the last few days my fingers have been tingling, an irritating itch under the skin that I just can't get rid of. I've been trying to ignore it, but it's getting worse.

But on the other equally itchy hand, Jenn's presence has been getting stronger. I can feel her all around me from the moment I wake up until the moment I fall asleep again.

She's so vivid and real that the rest of the world fades away around her. I spend my days wandering around in a world that glows and shimmers with her presence. Even the rain clouds seem beautiful as they take on new hues of purple and blue that I've just never seen before. I'm so grateful to Jenn for showing me all this, and I'm even more glad that she's back with me.

The intensity of her presence makes my mind spin, and I'm glad of it. All around me people are talking about Valentine's Day, even though it's over a week away. The world has exploded with paper hearts and tacky gifts. As if there were roses beautiful enough, or a card honest enough, to express the monumental truth of love. Even the biggest, most overstuffed fluffy teddy in the world is just a sad attempt at expressing something beyond words. There's nothing that captures the intense joy and pain of love. Nothing that really explains the feeling when two hands, or bodies, fit together so perfectly that the sweetness is unbearable and makes you shiver. Or the sheer joy of just being with the person who understands, accepts and celebrates every part of you. Realistically, what chance does a shiny, mass produced card have against that?

And nothing that describes the agony of having it ripped away.

Matty called to check up on me. We spoke for maybe an hour, but I can't remember much about the conversation. He said his work is going well, and Lucy is fine, but that's about all that managed to stick between my ears.

But I may have been distracted, because something really important did happen during that hazy phone call, although I didn't realise it until I looked down at the phone pad. It was full of doodles and tiny little sketches that I hadn't realised I was drawing. In one corner a daffodil flowered. Its leaves twisted and wandered across the page to morph into a speeding car whose skid marks skipped into a black and white dog. In the centre of the page, eyes stared out at me from under brows that arched in a quizzical expression so like Jenn's that my breath caught in my throat.

I could feel her beside me and tension filled the air, like she was waiting for something. I stared at the doodles, knowing they were important to Jenn, but not fully understanding why. That's about when I realised that my fingers had stopped itching.

How long had it been since I'd spent any real time painting or drawing? Everything I did now was on a computer at work. By the time I'd finished for the day, all I wanted to do was go home and spend time with Jenn and our children. I'd spent the last couple of decades too busy creating a family and a home for them, to worry about works of art. But now I found myself staring at those absent-minded doodles and my fingers itched to pick up a brush again.

I eventually found my stuff packed away in a box at the

back of a cupboard. The brushes were fine, but the paints crackled in their tubes. I could have split them open, remixed them and found pots for them, but I couldn't be bothered. I needed paper and canvases anyway. The only sketch book I could find was already filled with my drawings. They were actually pretty good. I wondered if I could ever be that good again.

It should have worried me, the thought of trying something without Jenn, but if I'm honest, it excited me. Painting and drawing was one of the few things in my life that I truly loved before meeting Jenn. The idea of picking up a brush and smoothing colour across a blank canvas to create something was enticing. I could feel my fingers tingling with anticipation at the thought of having something that belonged just to me again. The only problem was the supplies I still had were woeful, and the only way to get new ones was to order them and wait for days until they turned up, or risk going out to the shops again.

I actually enjoyed visiting the art shop. I tried to avoid it at first, thinking I could order everything online, but it just wasn't the same. As soon as I'd found an art supplies website I realised I didn't want to look at photos of what I was buying. I wanted to feel the paper between my fingers and smell the paints. I wanted the inspiration and experience of the store, and to see all the possibilities and promises of success lined up in rows of tiny tabs and tubes of brightly coloured paints.

I paused when I first reached the shop, overcome by nerves. I didn't want it to be another moment like the supermarket. But then I spotted the brushes and palettes in the window and they lured me in.

It was actually nice. The shop assistant gave me a friendly smile as I edged in, and then the smell of the store hit me.

The woody, pulpy dryness of blank paper mixed with the metallic, oily weight of paint and the heady acrid scent of chalk to create an air of exciting promise. How many masterpieces were sitting on these shelves and racks, just waiting to be put together?

I breathed in the old familiar scents and felt my shoulders relax. This was a part of my life that didn't revolve around Jenn, so maybe it was somewhere I could find a little happiness, instead of just more things that reminded me that I'd lost her.

I felt instantly guilty for trying to find some joy so soon after Jenn's death, but she washed love and reassurance over me. She wanted me to have this, and was pushing me towards it.

JENN

I never thought I'd find anything good about being dead, but I love being with David like this. The painting is making him happier, which is helping to push away the darkness and clouds surrounding him, which makes it easier for me to reach him.

As sad as it is that we're not together in the usual sense, this new relationship is exciting in its own way. We're getting to know each other again, but in a completely different way. It's like falling in love all over again, but on an incredibly intimate level. I thought I'd known David as deeply as you can know anyone, but I had no idea.

Our life together now is so vivid that it almost replaces the memories of our last life. My physical life with David was full of touch and sensation, but this new existence replaces touch with colour, and passion is shared through emotion so intense that it might as well be tangible.

It's so intensely intimate that I struggle to put it into words. I feel his emotions wash through me, and I can feel the beat of his heart and the rush of warmth through his veins. It's exciting to feel his body react to me. I remember the nights we shared in our life together. Moments of intense desire and desperation where I just couldn't pull him close enough to me, where the passion was so overwhelming that we wanted to be part of each other. Now we can.

I can make him shiver and moan with a single thought, and he opens his mind to me further, drawing me in even more. The closeness is delicious. I can feel his every sensation, and give him mine in return while tasting his pleasure and joy with every part of me. I feel like I'm starting to blur around the edges and blend into David's consciousness. I can't see where I end or he begins, and I've never been more content.

I stay with him afterwards, while his body still shivers. I stroke goose pimples up his arms and over his chest which still heaves with a mixture of laughter and tears. He begs me to stay with him and I nuzzle against him, soothing him and teasing with a wash of emotions.

In moments like this I don't feel dead and gone any more, in fact I've never felt more alive or connected.

David's making great progress. I had started to worry a little about whether I was doing the right thing by spending so much time with him. When I tried to pull away, even just for a little while to visit Lottie, Matty or my sister – who I still want to check on, even if I can't communicate with her – I could feel David withdrawing and collapsing back into himself. He needs me with him. We've been a team for so many years, that he's almost having to re-learn how to be and who he is as David who isn't part of the David and Jenn couple. In a lot of ways, we were quite traditional in our roles. Yes, I knew which end of a drill was which, and he could work the oven, but he enjoyed DIY and caring for our home, just like I enjoyed cooking. And now he's struggling and suffering. When I am with him, he does so much better. Which makes leaving him so much harder.

He's painting and drawing more, and I've been using that to coax him back out into the world. I make sure that he looks out of the window and sees all the beautiful things that are out there.

I managed to get him to go back to the supermarket, although it wasn't easy. It took me days of convincing and support. In the end I had to slip into his dreams. I played on his weaknesses and filled his waking thoughts with the tantalising smell of fresh garlic bread and spicy tomato pasta. After a couple of days he gave in and ventured back into that nightmare place, me by his side and reassuring him all of the way. When he finally sat down to that garlic and tomato mess he had created, he looked so proud of himself. It was the same look he'd get when he'd finally finished wrestling together a swing for the children, bikes on Christmas Eve, or flat-pack furniture. It was such a small victory, but an important one nonetheless.

A few days later he went back to work. It's only for a few hours a week, but he's back, which is the important thing. He needs to be working to get back to something resembling normality. The truth is, as much as he makes jokes about his job just being drawing boxes, he enjoys his work. Or at least he used to.

The first couple of days were really hard for him. Friends and colleagues offered their sympathies again and asked him how he was holding up. At first they treated him too softly, like they thought he might break, but the people who didn't know him that well were worse. They talked about him in the corridors, hushing their voices as they pointed him out and shared the gossip. But it didn't matter. They all quickly came to see that David could do his job as well as ever, and everyone relaxed back into their routines.

I've come to the conclusion this is the key to helping David rebuild himself. If I can help him get into a routine, then he can sink back into the ebb and flow of normal life and let it wash away his pain and grief. It's not very exciting, going to work, cooking and eating, but it's a normal routine, and that's important. While he's carrying on with routine, he can start to heal and realise there is still a point to his life.

Once he's settled into that healing routine, I can encourage him to try more things, until he discovers other things that fill him with joy, like painting does. Then maybe I can stop the nagging feeling that he's relying on me a little too much.

Chapter Ten

DAVID

It felt so good to be out of the house. I hated to admit it, but giving in to Lottie's gentle nagging and Jenn's non-too-subtle temptations to go for a walk was the best thing I could have done. For days she's been sending me visions, easing doors open and blowing fresh air through the house, teasing me with early spring warmth on my skin that makes me crave the outdoors.

As usual, Jenn was right to push me. What with it being Valentine's Day tomorrow, I really needed the push to get up and do something. My usual refuge of the TV has betrayed me, with every other programme or advert being another loved-up, nauseating Valentine's special that serves to remind me of how alone I've become.

It was brisk and cold outside, but the sun was warm on my back and my mini sketchbook and camera were comforting, bouncing weights in my coat pocket. A good day to be alive. Almost as soon as I'd finished the thought I felt the usual twinge of guilt, but the warm sun and Jenn's soothing presence soon eased it. She wouldn't want me wasting my life feeling bad. Especially on such a beautiful, sunny day. Had Jenn still been alive, she would have been the first one to bundle herself up in a scarf and gloves, and then drag me out to enjoy the day. It's easier to remember her like that: happy and full of life.

If she were here now, I know exactly where she would have wanted to go. It would be the park to see if the daffodils had started to peep through. It had long ago become a Valentine's tradition for us. And then Jenn would have come back every week to check on their progress and make sure she'd catch them in full bloom.

I didn't have anything else important to do, or anywhere I needed to be, and it seemed a nice idea to go and check for the daffodil shoots. Another little way to remember Jenn. I think she would have approved of this one, because at least it meant I was out in the fresh air and getting some exercise.

It didn't take me more than a few minutes to reach the cul-de-sac that the park and daffodil field backed onto. As I sauntered through the gates I could feel my muscles starting to relax. I hadn't realised how tense I'd been until the warm winter sun began to melt the stress away.

I started to whistle as I sauntered through the gate, across the park and through the treeline. When I caught sight of the fields, I felt like I'd been sucker-punched in the stomach. My throat closed up and I struggled to breathe. The beautiful green grass had disappeared and been replaced by heavy, grey mud churned up by workmen and their machines. The daffodils I'd come looking for were far too easy to find. Instead of being tucked safely beneath the soil, they had been ripped out and chucked carelessly aside into loose piles, along with all the other rubbish dragged out of the earth. I leant down and picked one up. The damp, papery skin was soft against my palm, and I could see the white shoots where it was starting to grow again.

'Excuse me, what's going on?' I shouted to one of the workmen, my fingers still wrapped tightly around the bulb.

'Clearing out all the rubbish to make way for the foundations to be laid in a few days.'

'What?'

'The council's new housing estate. Where have you been, mate? It's been in all of the papers.'

'Distracted.' I forced down the tears that were threatening to choke me. 'I've been distracted.' I stared at the bulb in my hand, thinking of all the memories of Jenn that were wrapped up in its brown skin. This was yet another thing I associated with Jenn that was disappearing forever. There'd been so many things disappearing lately, so many memories fading away. Jenn always smiled so brightly when she saw the tiny green daffodil shoots appear. She's never going to be able to smile again, and these bulbs were never going to burst into life and welcome spring back to the world again. I couldn't bear to see all those thousands of bulbs lying in muddy, unloved piles. Something inside me snapped.

'How much do you want for these?'

'What?' The workman spun around.

'The daffodil bulbs. How much do you want for them?' The man stared at me blankly. 'I'll buy them off you.'

'You're mad, mate.' He shook his head and started to walk away.

'I'll give you a hundred. One hundred pounds. And I'll pick them up, every single one of them I can find.

'I'm from the council, mate. I don't want your money.' He turned away.

'Please. Just, please ... don't throw them away.' I forced back tears as I tried to explain. 'My wife ... she loved them. Seeing them flower was one of her favourite times of the year. She's gone and I couldn't save her, but maybe I can save these. Please?'

Confusion and then sympathy filled his eyes. 'You know they're probably all dead, right? We dug them up.'

'It doesn't matter, I've got to try.'

'All right.' He nodded, clearly still confused. 'If it means that much to you. But they've got to be gone today.'

'Thank you. Thank you so much. I'll be right back.' I shook his hand hard and clapped him across the shoulder before running home. I was panting so hard by the time I got back that I struggled to get the keys in the door. I raced around the house, grabbing bins, boxes, buckets and bags. Even the washing basket got thrown into the car. The thought of all those bulbs lying in a dirty pile and never being able to flower again was heart breaking. I had to rescue them.

Two hours later, Jenn's little car was completely filled with muddy, papery daffodil bulbs. I'd packed them into every bucket, box and bag I had, and they were stuffed into the boot, balanced on the seats and crammed into the footwells. I was covered in mud and sweating despite the cold, but grinning happily as I brought the last load to the car. I'd managed to gather up nearly a third of the bulbs already. My back gave a painful twinge as I heaved the last bucket up and wriggled it into the only gap left.

I drove home carefully, making sure not to smack against the speed bumps or bump up the kerb too hard. I didn't want to risk spilling the precious bulbs or damaging them any more. Within an hour I'd unloaded them all gently onto tarpaulins on the garage floor, and headed back to gather up more of their friends.

I was on my hands and knees sifting through the dirt to find more bulbs when a cold, wet nose snuffled its way between my fingers. I looked up into big brown eyes and a toothy, cheerful grin attached to a bullet shaped head and raggedy ears. There was a lot of staffie in him, and his brown coat was brindled with golden stripes, making him look almost copper coloured.

'Jasper, c'mere. Stop bothering the man. Not everyone wants you to slobber all over them.'

'It's all right.' I rubbed the battered ears gently.

'Mr Hughes?' Dark eyes peered at me over darker glasses. 'Are you all right?'

'Umm … yeah.' I shook my head. 'Sorry, I know I know you from somewhere, but I can't quite remember.'

'It's all right. We met at the wake. Didn't expect you to

remember.' He held out a hand covered in heavy silver rings shaped like skulls and claws. 'Stuart Tomkins.'

'Right.' I nodded. 'Jenn's old student. Aren't you a social worker now?'

'Not yet.' He grinned. 'But I will be soon. Now I work up at the school where I try to make sure even the disadvantaged kids get the same chances as everyone else.' He looked around again. 'What are you doing?'

I took a deep breath and nervously tried to explain.

When I was done, Stuart just shrugged. 'Makes sense to me.' He flicked his long leather coat out behind him and knelt down. So what are we doing with ones like this?' He held up a damaged bulb.

'Umm ... I thought I'd take them anyway. They might grow, but if not they'll probably just compost and help the others grow better. What are you doing?'

'Helping.' Stuart dragged a bucket towards him and started dropping bulbs in carefully. 'You'll be here all day if I don't.'

'I really don't need help.'

'Yeah you do.' He grinned and reached for another bulb. 'And I don't have anything else I need to be doing. But if you want some privacy, I understand. This is kinda personal.'

I shrugged. 'It's all right. I could do with a hand.'

'Then you've got it. Besides, Jasper seems to be enjoying himself.' He glanced over to his dog who was already up to his front knees in mud.

'Thanks.'

'Don't mention it. We going to get on with this?'

An hour later I dragged another bag of bulbs back to the car and carefully lifted them into the boot. I leant against the car roof to catch my breath and spotted a lump of paper shoved under my windscreen wiper. I tore it out hastily and skimmed it. It was a badly written note:

IT IS EELEGEL TO PARK HERE.
THE POLISE AND COUNSIL HAVE BEEN TOLD.
DO NOT PARK HERE! I WILL
MAKE YOU REGRECT IT

I looked around in confusion, trying to work out what I had done to prompt such an angry response. In places the pen had actually torn through the paper. All right my parking wasn't great, and I was a little across one drive, but I certainly wasn't blocking it. I shrugged and shoved the note into my pocket, slammed the boot shut, and started back towards the daffodils.

'Hey!' A voice sounded behind me and I was surprised at how much venom a single word could contain. 'Hey, I'm talking to you. What the hell do you think you're doing?'

I spun around to stare at the woman in disbelief. 'I'm sorry, are you talking to me?'

'Is that your car?'

'Well, sort of.' Her badly dyed hair distracted me. It's funny the things you notice sometimes. Did she actually think she looked good with beetroot hair screwed up on top of her head? I know my daughter dyes her hair too, but I don't really agree with that either, even if it does sort of work with her odd dress sense. Plus she's young, and experimenting is what she's supposed to do. But the harridan screaming at me was much older. Older than me. Certainly old enough to know that beetroot isn't a good colour for hair, especially as her face was starting to match it.

'Are you even listening?'

'I'm sorry, I don't really see what the problem is,' I responded politely.

'You don't really see what the problem is?' The woman repeated in disbelief. 'I'm fucking fed up of people like you thinking you can park wherever you want. It's illegal to park on a kerb. You're blocking me in. Who the hell do you think you are?'

'Umm ...'

'What if I want to get out to go shopping?'

'Do you want to?'

'Not right now – but I might. You're making it impossible for me to get out.' Her spit landed on my cheek. I wiped my face and stared at my fingers in disgust. I felt my grasp on my temper start to slip. Then the stupid woman prodded me with a dirty finger. She actually prodded me.

I felt the anger bubble up as a growl in my throat. 'Madam I am not blocking you in. I'm three foot away from your precious driveway, and actually it's not illegal to park on a pavement so long as you're not causing an obstruction. Your driveway was empty when I got here, and now it's not, so clearly you did manage to park.'

'Well I had to struggle. And I had to walk on the road. What if a car sped along and knocked me over?'

'In a cul-de-sac? Don't be ridiculous. And frankly, if you can't get your car out of that huge gap, you shouldn't be on the roads! How dare you come out here and start shouting at a complete stranger. What on earth is wrong with you? For your information, the men from the council working just over there,' I pointed a shaking finger back towards the daffodil field, 'told me I could park here.'

'Well I said you can't.'

'Whatever.' I started to walk away, realising I sounded like Lottie, but not really caring. 'I'll be gone soon enough.'

'Well I've called the police, 'cause you're parked illegally and it ain't right. Selfish git.'

'What did you say?' I span on my heel to glare at her, but she refused to repeat herself. For some reason, her spinelessness angered me even more. 'I don't think the police care, because they're not here, are they? And by the way, illegal doesn't have four Es in it. And it's not illegal in any case, and even if it were, can't you make an exception for a few hours when I'm causing no one any harm at all?'

'It still ain't right of you to park across my drive.'

Tears started to choke my anger. 'If you want to talk about what "ain't right" then I'll tell you what really, really "ain't right". Losing the only woman you've ever loved in a stupid, senseless accident is about as far from right as anything can be. For all you know I'm doing something really important. For all you know my wife just got ripped out of my life and that the daffodil field the council are digging up was one of her favourite places in the world. For all you know I'm trying to rescue every single last bulb because I've already lost so much in my life that I can't bear the thought of a single, solitary daffodil bulb being left lying around to rot and shrivel up. For all you know this is the first time I've left the house for anything other than work or shopping in ... I don't know how long. For all you know, this is the first time I've actually been driven to DO anything in weeks. But you don't know any of that, because you're too busy yelling at me and stomping around to bother to ask.'

Her face was pale by the time I'd finished my rant, and her mouth opened wordlessly.

I stumbled backwards, horrified at the strength of the anger I'd thrown at her. 'I'm sorry, I'll move the car.'

'No. You won't.' Stuart stood a few steps away, his arms folded and Jasper sitting calmly at his feet. 'Because his car being parked here isn't really that much of a problem, is it? After everything he's been through in the last few weeks, his car being parked slightly over your driveway for a few hours, really isn't that big a deal. Right?'

'So all what he just said was true?' She eyed Stuart warily.

He nodded. 'I was at thc funeral.'

'Oh.' The woman bit her lip and looked slightly awkward. 'You'll really be gone in a few hours?'

'The second I put the last bulb in the car.' I nodded.

'Fine. But you know them bulbs are probably dead?'

'So I've been told.' I nodded tiredly. 'But I have to try.'

In the end it took us three more runs to collect up all the daffodils, but even with Stuart and his dog taking up space that I could have filled with bulbs, we still finished earlier than I could have hoped. Stuart's a really good guy. He insisted on staying to help unload the last of the bulbs and make sure they were tucked away safely in the garage. His dog lolled around happily in the garden, sunbathing and rolling cheerfully on the patio. When we were finally finished, I dusted off my hands.

'So, can I get you a beer or anything?'

'Usually I would.' He grinned easily. 'But I have to get moving.' He glanced at his phone. 'I promised my mum I'd meet her for dinner. If I turn up in this state I'll never hear the end of it.'

'Oh.' I felt disappointed. 'Well, you'll have to let me buy you a drink one day soon. I really don't know how to thank you for all this.'

He shrugged the thanks off. 'It's no biggy. Mrs Hughes did a lot more for me. C'mon Jasper. Let's go see the biscuit lady.'

'Biscuit lady?' I felt my eyebrows rise.

'Yeah. This dog's disgusting. Couple of times my mum gave him a biscuit when we visited, now he runs straight into the kitchen and sits beneath the cupboard begging. He won't move till he gets his biscuit.'

'Smart boy.' I fondled his ears.

'Yeah, he is.' Stuart agreed with a disgusted snort. 'Too

smart for his own good most of the time. Anyway …' He held out a hand. 'See you round.'

'Oh my God, Dad. What have you done?' Lottie's voice echoed through the house. 'What the hell is all this in the garage?' She held a loose bulb in her hand. 'I nearly broke my neck tripping over these. You could have warned me. What on earth is all this?'

'Daffodil bulbs.' I flicked the kettle on and reached into the cupboard for mugs. I didn't want to meet Lottie's eyes. The events of the day suddenly seemed a lot less sane than they had earlier.

'But there are thousands of them.' I could feel Lottie's gaze on my back. 'Dad, look at me. Please. Tell me what's going on.' She sighed irritably when I didn't answer her. 'Where did they come from?'

'The fields over the back of the park. They were digging them up.'

'That's a real shame, but what are they doing here? You know these are probably all dead? They've been dug up.' She thumped the bulb down on the worktop.

'They might not be,' I argued. 'I saw Jenn dig them up and move them about in the garden.'

'Not in February you didn't. Not at the start of their growing season.'

'I don't care. I couldn't just leave them there to die.'

'I think I get that.' Lottie handed me the milk.

'I'm going to plant them. They'll grow. They have to.' I concentrated on stirring the tea.

'Where? Are you going to carpet the garden with them? And then the house?'

'I haven't really decided yet.' I handed Lottie her tea and felt panic descend. She was right. I had no idea what to do with all the bulbs. I'd rescued them, and now they were probably going to die anyway. I couldn't plant them all, and just planting a few in our garden seemed ridiculously pointless. Maybe I really was going mad with grief.

JENN

Matty came to see me today and he brought the most beautiful flowers. At first I wondered why he was here, and what had brought him so far away from his job, home, and Lucy, but I could see he was troubled from the moment he arrived. He fidgeted with the wrapper on the flowers, and kept stuffing his hands in and out of his pockets awkwardly. I tried to comfort him by washing warmth and reassurance over him, and eventually he relaxed.

'Bloody hell, Mum, I miss you so much. I always miss you, but I really wish you were here right now. I've got a huge problem. I don't know who to talk to about it. I keep picking up the phone and finding that I've dialled half your number before I remember that you're here now.'

He ran his hands tiredly through his hair as he stared at the headstones around me. 'I don't know what to do, Mum. I wish you were here to help me figure it all out.'

He leant against the tree that shades my grave, and sighed sadly. I settled next to him and rested my head on his shoulder. It's all right, Matty, I'm still here. I tried to soothe his worries and smooth out the wrinkles from his brow. I wished I could take away his pain. He's been through so much lately that he doesn't need any more stress.

He stared across the gravestones as he spoke. 'It's Lucy. She's been offered a job. Her dream job. It's exactly what she's been working towards for years. It's a good company and they're offering her a great deal, but it's hundreds of miles away. Back in England. There's no way she can do it without moving.'

Oh no. Not Lucy. Horror shot through me at his words.

She and Matty were so good together, and she's helped him so much in the last weeks. I couldn't bear to see him lose her now. Besides, they're supposed to be together forever. I'm not just saying that as his mother, I'm saying that as someone who can actually see parts of the future. I look at Lucy and Matty together, and I see a bright, loving future filled with happiness. When I try to think of them splitting up, all I see is darkness and emptiness for each of them.

'She wants to take the job, Mum. I know she does, and she should. It's a fantastic opportunity for her. But she's asked me what to do. She wants to know where our relationship is going before she makes the decision. She's willing to stay for me, Mum. All I have to do is ask her to.'

If I'd still been breathing, I would have held my breath.

'But I don't know if I can.' Matty's jaw was clenched and I could see the muscles in his throat working as he struggled with the next words. 'I don't know if I want to give that much of myself to someone. I don't want to be like Dad. We all saw him the day we buried you. It was like we'd buried part of himself too. He's a mess, Mum. He barely seems to know how to function any more. I don't ever want to be like that. I don't want to love someone so much that I fall apart without them. Lucy wants everything. She wants me to tell her whether we have a future together or not. She does want a future with me, she's made that much clear. But I don't know if I want to give her that much of myself. I don't ever want to feel the way Dad is feeling now.' He dashed angry tears away from his eyes.

I felt like crying myself. Was this what I'd done to my son by dying? Had I taught him to fear love instead of embracing it? Horror and sadness filled me. I'd left my family's lives too soon, and it seemed that I'd stolen something incredibly important in the process.

I understood now why Matty had come to see me. For his

entire life he'd been a mummy's boy. We had an incredibly close relationship, and whenever anything had been bothering him, it was me he talked to. When he was worried about exams, it was my phone that rang. When he broke up with his first girlfriend, it was me he wanted to tell about it, and when he was first considering moving so far north for work, it was me he turned to. He swore blind it was me he'd miss the most. He was too like his dad and too unlike his sister for them to really get on. He doesn't have anyone else he can talk to about this.

I've no idea how I can make this right, but somehow I have to. I refuse to let my death ruin my son's life.

It suddenly occurred to me to wonder again why Matty's really here. I know he's struggling with a big decision, but he's far too practical and grounded to drive hundreds of miles to stand and talk to a grave. The flowers are beautiful and thoughtful, but I can't believe he came all this way just to leave me flowers. Even if he needed some space and time to think, he's got closer places to run and nearer boltholes than this. I know this is his childhood home, but in truth my house hasn't been Matty's home for a lot of years. It's barely Lottie's any more. Both of them are always welcome here, it'll still be their home even when they've got children of their own, but they're off building their own homes now. I do wonder if talking to me is the only reason he's here.

Chapter Eleven

Spring

DAVID

Life has been good lately. I went back to work properly, and while it was a little odd at first, it is good to be back. It's nice to have normal conversations again where the biggest worry is getting a project completed by the relevant deadline. I've been sketching and painting more too, which is making me happy.

But almost all of my happiness is down to Jenn. Her presence has been so strong that I can sometimes hear her words and thoughts. She's wrapped all around me and twined through me, in my every thought and movement. She's my whole world again. She's with me at night soothing me into sleep, and she eases me into waking every morning. She gives me the reason to get up and fills me with a lust for life. For the first time since the accident I've been able to see the world as a bright and beautiful place filled with hope and joy. It's like I've woken up and put on glasses, and the whole world has snapped back into focus. I owe it all to Jenn.

I still miss her and would give anything to have her back in my arms, but she's been showing me a whole new world through her eyes. I wonder if this bright, colourful, passionate world that tingles and buzzes with energy is the world Jenn always saw. It would make sense if this different view of the world was what she'd spent her life seeing. She always managed to look past the obvious and see the good in people, no matter how deeply it was buried.

I could happily spend the rest of my life just living through Jenn. Most of the time. But lately, just on occasion, I find myself feeling weird. A bit fed up, and ... numb. That's the best word for it. Numb. Even when Jenn's beside me I've found myself distracted and a bit separated from reality. But I don't think anyone else has noticed, so it's probably nothing.

Lottie was in the living room, talking animatedly. I smiled when I saw her guest. 'Hey Matty, this is a nice surprise. Is Lucy here too? Are you staying for long?'

'No, she's not, and I'm not really sure yet.' Matty's smile didn't quite reach his eyes, and I found myself feeling worried.

Lottie licked her lips nervously. 'Dad, we umm ...' She took a deep breath before she could continue. 'We wanted to talk to you.'

'We're worried about you,' Matty added in a rush.

'Why? I'm fine.'

'You don't look fine, Dad. Lottie showed me the bulbs.'

'And? They were being dug up. I couldn't just leave them to die.'

'But, don't you think it's a little odd? I mean what are you going to do with them all?'

'I don't know yet.' I rolled my eyes. 'So, I've got a few hundred daffodil bulbs, it's not that big a deal.'

'It's more than a few hundred,' Matty argued.

'I've heard you talking to yourself,' Lottie added quietly.

'Is that all? I'm not talking to myself, that would be insane. I've been talking to Jenn.'

'Dad.' Matty exhaled sharply. 'Don't you realise that sounds insane? I miss Mum too. I visited her grave this morning, and yeah I chatted a bit, but I know she's not really there. I don't expect her to answer me back. We buried her weeks ago.'

'I know that.'

'So you know you can't be talking to Mum?'

'But I am. I'm talking to her every day,' I argued.

'I know you think you are, Dad, but she's gone. We miss her too, but Mum's gone.'

I buried my head in my hands, and tried to find the words to explain to my children. I knew they were just worried about me, but I was getting annoyed. Who were they to write off Jenn so quickly and easily? They didn't know what was happening, or what I've been experiencing and feeling. Jenn and I share an incredible love that is, quite simply, stronger than death. If my own children couldn't understand that, then they were being idiots.

I felt Jenn wrap around me, soothing and warm. It was so intense that for a moment I couldn't catch my breath. The children weren't being idiots at all, they were just missing their mum and worried about their dad, I saw that the second Jenn's hand slipped into mine, and suddenly I had the words to explain.

'I'm not going insane, really I'm not. I'm not sitting up all night calling psychic chat TV.'

At least that much was true. I'd seen it before and suggested it to Jenn, but the air around me turned ice-cold as she made her displeasure known. It made sense. She'd hated people coming between us in life, and she wasn't going to accept it in death. I forced my mind back to the conversation.

'I'm not buying tarot cards or messing around with ouija boards.'

'But you still think you can talk to Mum?'

'Not like I'm talking to you, no.' I took a deep breath and let Jenn's feelings flow into me and add strength to my words. 'Love's the most powerful force in the universe. It can bring people together against all odds, overcome barriers beyond belief and last for an entire lifetime and beyond. Your mum loved us all desperately. We were the most important things in her life, and she'd have done anything for any of us. Our love was so powerful it couldn't be contained by just two people, so it made you both. Do you really think feelings that strong can be snuffed out, or disappear in the blink of an eye?'

Neither of my children could meet my eyes.

'Do you really think, that in a world so full of beautiful miracles as this one is, that it's completely impossible for a spirit to come back? And do you think for a moment, that if there were a way, your mum wouldn't find it?'

'You really believe in this, don't you?' Lottie asked softly.

'Yes, I really do. But at the same time I don't.'

'I don't understand.' Lottie shook her head.

'I don't believe or disbelieve in this. Your mum's here, just the same as the room's full of air that we're breathing. You don't need to believe in something that you know.'

'You said here. Is she here now?' Lottie gulped, her face caught somewhere between fear and hope.

I nodded.

'How do you know?'

'I can feel her.' I tried to keep my tone easy and nonchalant. I already knew how I probably sounded to them. 'See the goose pimples on my arms? I'm completely warm. But I get goose pimples whenever she's nearby.'

'Has she ever done anything else, like moved things?' Lottie asked very quietly.

'Don't tell me you're buying all this,' Matty snapped.

'No, of course not, but ...'

'But what?'

'Nothing.' Lottie shook her head sadly.

Matty leant forward. 'We're worried about you, Dad. Look at this place, it's a complete mess. You never go out, and you look like you haven't slept properly in weeks. This isn't healthy.'

'I go to work.'

'But you don't go out with friends, or spend any time with people.'

'Why would I want to spend time with other people? It's just time away from Jenn.'

‘This is exactly what I’m talking about.’ Matty rubbed his forehead in exasperation. ‘We want you to see a doctor and get some help.’

‘Help for what?’ I shook my head. ‘There’s nothing wrong with me.’

‘Then there’s nothing to worry about.’

‘It’s a waste of time,’ I argued.

‘Dad.’ Lottie leant forward and squeezed my arm. ‘Please? Will you do this for me. I’ve already lost my mum, and I’m scared I’m losing you. I can’t lose you too. Please, Dad? Will you do this for me?’

I looked at the tears filling her eyes, and gave into the guilt stabbing me in the gut. ‘OK, I’ll see the doctor, but just for you.’

She nodded. ‘Thanks Dad.’

I saw the doctor today. It was so embarrassing going in there and trying to explain I was there because my children were worried about me. Lottie had offered to come with me, but the thought that I’d become so doddery and loopy that my twenty-four-year-old daughter needed to hold my hand was so insulting that I instantly refused. I know they’re only worrying out of love, but I hope I’m a lot of years away from needing to be ferried to medical appointments.

The appointment wasn’t that bad. The doctor nodded and made sympathetic noises, then talked me through a questionnaire on the computer. Was I sleeping well? What were my dreams like? Was I tired in the day? How much was I drinking? Was I finding myself more easily irritated? Was my appetite different? Did I carry feelings of guilt for anything? Was I finding it difficult to concentrate on things properly? Had I lost interest in things I used to enjoy? Had I thought about hurting myself?

I tried to bite back my sarcasm and answer honestly. It wasn’t like it would change anything. I was really only there to reassure the kids. So what if I struggled to concentrate sometimes, or to sleep. It wasn't a big deal. And I could do with losing a few pounds anyway, so skipping meals was hardly a concern. And everyone at work knows what's happened, so they're not really that worried about a few little mistakes.

After a few more minutes of questions, the doctor patted my hand kindly, and told me she understood. Then she sent me out with a prescription and the number for a local bereavement group. Like I really want to spend more time around depressed, grieving people. I get enough of that looking in mirrors. Besides, it would mean more time away from Jenn, and that really is a depressing thought. Although the doctor is worried I might be heading that way already, and wants to see me in a few weeks to check up on me. She says I've been traumatised by Jenn's death – like I needed a medical professional to tell me that – and while my feelings of sadness and lethargy are normal, and even healthy, she's worried about how long the symptoms are lasting.

Maybe the prescription wasn't such a bad idea though. I was tired. It wouldn't hurt to take something to help me sleep. It would keep the kids happy too I supposed. And Sarah who had called from Germany to check in on me.

The doctor did say the antidepressants would help me, and she should know best. It could only make things better, right?

So I took the slippery bit of paper to the chemist and swapped it for a paper bag that rustled. It felt so light that I peered inside to check the pills were actually in there. Once I took them out of the box I was surprised by how small they were. The tablets I took for headaches or when I'd strained my back were bigger, and they did a lot less.

I left the bag sitting on the table all day. At one point I pulled the packet out and studied the shiny sheet of pills that were cheerfully labelled with the day and little arrows to make sure they were taken right. Did everyone think I was so out of touch with reality that I couldn't be trusted to take a tablet without step-by-step instructions? I still managed to get to work every day, and do a decent job, yet the manufacturers of these tiny little tablets had taken extra pains to label them.

So what if I sometimes had to stop and think about what day it was. Or if I occasionally missed an appointment or skipped the odd meal. Does that really make me depressed? Isn't it normal to not want to go to sleep when sometimes you still wake up drenched in icy sweat because you're reliving the worst moment of your life in a nightmare so vivid your ears sometimes still ring from the sirens?

I'm sure my occasional moments of absent-mindedness have nothing to do with depression – they're just happening because I'm enjoying myself so much with Jenn. Of course I get a little distracted when surrounded by so much love and joy.

I did my best to ignore the pills all day, but when it came to the evening I found my attention being pulled back to them more and more. I'd made a cup of tea and headed up to bed. I'd meant to leave them on the table, I really had, but at the last second I found myself grabbing the bag.

I popped one of the pills out and sat on the edge of the bed. If everyone thought it was a good idea then maybe it was for the best. I rolled the pill around in the palm of my hand as I studied it. It would be so, so easy to tilt my hand and let it slip into the bin – it was so small it probably wouldn't even make a noise as it buried itself amongst the tissues and random crap that half-filled it. But I didn't know how much longer I could keep up the pretence of "normality" around my kids, though I don't think I was really fooling them. And to be honest, I was starting to get fed up of trying to fool myself.

After long moments of contemplation, I popped it in my mouth, swallowed dry, and crawled into bed.

Chapter Twelve

JENN

I'm not sure I like this. I'm glad David is getting help and starting to talk about his feelings, but antidepressants? I know the kids are worried about him, and can't believe that he's really talking to me, but he'd been doing so much better lately.

I blame those silly daffodils, at least partly. It was an incredibly sweet, romantic, thoughtful thing for David to do, but utterly insane. I wish he hadn't seen them, but he did, and seeing something I loved ripped up and dying like that was the unexpected blow that's knocked him back into a phase of not looking after himself properly again. He's not eating or sleeping properly, and I've lost count of the amount of times he's opened the garage only to peer at the bulbs, sadly.

I know medication does help some people, but I'm not so sure this is such a good idea for David. He's miserable and down because I'm dead, not because he's depressed or suffering from a chemical or hormonal imbalance. Surely things like grief are supposed to be felt. How can you recover from something without going through the healing process? I just worry this isn't going to help him in the long-term. That it will remove an essential part of the process.

It's become so hard to push through the darkness and reach him recently. I suppose it makes some sort of sense. When I first died it was so surreal for him – so utterly unbelievable – that there was part of him that truly expected me to walk back into the house any second. Maybe it was that part that made it so easy to reach him. But lately, it's been harder for me to reach him, and he's been having moments when he's almost disconnected ... from me and from his life. Seeing all those daffodils dead and dying seems to have cemented things for David, even more so than my funeral. I'm gone from him, and can't ever get back. This ... whatever it is ... is the best it's ever going to be again in his lifetime. It's heart-breaking enough for me, and I'm the one who has left.

I can see why the daffodil situation has worried the children. What on earth is he going to do with all the bulbs? It would be really sad to see them all shrivel up and die, but I can't really see another option. David's not going to take it well. I would hope that he's just going to forget about them, but there's so many that there's no way that's going to happen.

On the other hand, the daffodil incident did achieve one good thing. It brought Stuart into my family's lives. It was really sweet of him to insist on helping David dig out all the bulbs, although I can't say I'm that surprised. He always was a sweetheart, despite the attitude, tattoos and love of everything leather. A lot of people would judge him just on the way he looks, and miss the heart of gold that's beating beneath the heavy metal T-shirts. He was troubled as a youngster, but I always knew he had a good heart, and that he'd grow into a good man. That's why I was so pleased when he sauntered up the driveway and Lottie, on another of her overnight visits, opened the door.

'Umm, hi.' Lottie ran her fingers through her currently purple hair and smiled at him. I knew from the glint in her eye that she liked him instantly.

'Hey. I'm Stuart.' He gave her a warm smile. 'Is Mr Hughes in?'

'Dad? No, but he'll be back in a bit.' Lottie leant against the door frame casually.

'Do you know when? I can come back. I wanted to talk to him about an idea I've had.'

'He only went for a walk. Should be back in a few minutes. You could wait inside.'

'You probably shouldn't invite me in. You don't even know me.' Stuart's eyes crinkled with laughter.

'Sure I do.' My daughter shrugged. 'You were at the wake.'

'I'm sure I would have remembered you.' Stuart was trying not to smile and I realised that he was flirting with her.

'I didn't quite look myself.' Lottie tugged a strand of her hair. 'This was all covered, and I wasn't dressed quite so ...'

Stuart looked down at her tight jeans, shredded top and bright bangles. 'Hotly?' He offered the word and I found myself blushing on Lottie's behalf. He really liked her. This was interesting. They would make quite a cute couple, and Stuart was genuinely nice. After all the rubbish Lottie's been through lately, she could do with a nice guy in her life. And I had a good feeling about this.

'So are you coming in to wait?' She ignored his compliment, although I knew she was pleased.

'What about him?' Stuart's eyes dropped to the dog sitting patiently at his feet.

Lottie looked down in surprise. 'Oh, he can come in too.' She stepped away from the door.

Stuart paused as he passed by her. 'I'm sorry about your mum. She really was someone special. She changed my life.' He pulled a face. 'Sorry, I probably shouldn't have said that. I hope I've not upset you – I shouldn't have brought it up.'

'No.' Lottie shut the door quietly. 'You're right. Mum was amazing. It's sort of nice, you wanting to talk about her. Everyone's being so delicate and treating me so gently. They all walk around on eggshells all the time. It's nice to actually have someone talk about Mum normally. Even if you did spoil it by apologising within three seconds.'

'In that case I apologise for my apology.'

Lottie treated him to a grin before spinning on her heel.

'In that case I might just let it slide. Do you want tea or coffee?'

DAVID

I hung my coat by the door and wandered into the kitchen, where I came face to face with a toothy grin and rapidly wagging tail. Strong, heavy paws slammed against my legs as the dog leaped up with a slobbery, cheerful greeting.

'*Ugh*, get off.' I tried to remember his name. 'Jake ... Jim ... Jet ... Jules ... *Jasper!*' Wild brown eyes looked up at me. 'There's a good boy. Get down!' The slobbering continued unheeded until a sharp whistle sounded from the living room. He looked up at me with reluctance in his eyes. A second whistle caught his attention and he gave a half-amused snort before shooting into the living room. I followed him, wondering what on earth Stuart's dog was doing here.

The answer was sitting on the sofa, holding a mug. His black leather coat, metal studs and muscular dog clashed with the quiet comfortable feeling Jenn had created in this room, but he seemed relaxed and at home as he grinned at me. 'Hey, Mr Hughes. I hope this big lump didn't scare you.' He nudged the staffie cross with his foot.

'Awww, he's a lovely boy, aren't you Jasper? Not at all scary.' Lottie fussed the dog who fawned shamelessly. 'Besides, we used to have a dog of our own, didn't we Dad?' She shot me a look.

'Yeah.' I grinned. 'He was probably just in the kitchen scrounging for food.'

'More than likely.' Stuart laughed. 'So how are you doing, Mr Hughes?'

'I'm all right thanks. But don't you think it should be David? You did fight a gorgon-woman with me and dig through a mountain of dirt to rescue thousands of daffodil bulbs. Besides, your Jasper seems to have made himself right at home.' I glanced over to the dog who was wriggling happily on the floor as Lottie scratched his belly.

Stuart pulled a face. 'Sorry about him. He's got no manners at all. It's actually the daffodils that have brought me round here.' Stuart stood and looked around awkwardly for somewhere to put his mug. Lottie took it from him in an easy move. He flashed her a smile before turning back to me. 'I hope you don't mind me just dropping round, but … Do you still have all the bulbs?'

'Yes. I'm not sure what to do with them.'

'I've got an idea about that. If I get the school to bring over the mini bus, could you load them up?'

'Why? I'm not dumping them.'

'He's not asking you to, Dad. He's got a brilliant idea. That's why he came round. I think you're really going to like it.'

'So are you going to tell me what it is?'

'Nope.' Lottie shook her head. 'We're keeping it a surprise.'

I followed Lottie and Stuart up the path towards the school. 'Are you sure this is all right?' I didn't like the thought of being on school grounds at the weekend. I'd been there lots of times with Jenn, usually roped into helping with one of her fundraising activities, but this felt very different.

'It's fine.' Stuart held up a bunch of keys. 'I told you I work here part-time. The staff liked my idea, so gave me the keys to the gate.' He shrugged easily. 'Besides, if anything happens, the head and caretaker both know where I live.' He jiggled a couple of keys into the padlock on the gate before finding the right one. 'Come on. It's just up the top of the hill.'

I hung back slightly to let Lottie and Stuart talk. I couldn't quite put my finger on it, but Lottie seemed different around him. I trudged up the slope behind them, wondering what this was all about. It had taken Lottie a lot of nagging to convince me to join in with their game, and I was starting to regret it.

Stuart turned to face me when he reached the top of the hill that was the back of the sports field and the edge of the school grounds. The rest of the hill disappeared beyond the heavy steel fences that marked the boundaries.

'Well? What do you think?' Lottie asked excitedly.

'I'm not sure what I'm supposed to think.' I looked around and spotted odd designs that had been spray painted over the grass. There were long, sweeping curves that cut through the slope of the hill and ended in a big circle. Huge squares broke up the sweeping patterns, and long, skinny rectangles sat along the edge of the fences.

Stuart took a deep breath. 'These squares are picnic tables. The circle would be benches and curved seating, and the long thin ones are normal benches. The curves are pathways and everything else, well, that's where the daffodils could go. If you like the idea.'

I stared across the slope and paint as I tried to take in the patterns and understand what they meant. I didn't realise how long I'd been silent until a small hand slipped into mine. I looked down at the bright blue nails as they squeezed my fingers.

'Well, what do you think, Dad?'

I shook my head. I didn't want to hope this could really happen. 'It would take forever to plant all the bulbs.'

'Not as long as you'd think.' Stuart folded his arms. 'We asked for volunteers. Half the school's already signed up. Everyone here loved Mrs Hughes and wants to be part of remembering her. If you like the idea, it could be a nice memorial.'

I nodded slowly, not trusting myself to speak past the

lump in my throat. When I looked out across the fields again, I could almost see the green grass disappear in a haze of yellow heads that waved cheerfully in a non-existent breeze. 'It sounds perfect. Jenn would have loved it. Thank you.'

The next Saturday I was stood in the school playing field by eight a.m. I stuffed my hands deeper into my pockets and blew a cloud of frozen air across the empty grounds. 'You still think this is a good idea?' I glanced over to Lottie and Stuart who were pulling on gloves and flinging open the doors of the school mini bus.

'Yup.' Lottie gave me a cheerful grin as she grabbed the first bucket of bulbs.

'But no one's here.'

'It's still early.' Stuart reassured us both as he lifted out another bucket of bulbs. 'They'll come.'

He was right. Within an hour people had started turning up carrying all manner of trowels, forks, and other gardening implements I didn't even recognise. The car park quickly filled with people who happily double-parked and blocked each other in, and still more people streamed through the gates. Tables were carried out of the school, and steaming urns and huge boxes of cakes and biscuits appeared. Someone somewhere must have found more power outlets, because music started blaring out across the field.

Other teachers and parents I knew from fundraising events, meetings, and school shows Jenn had brought me along to, gathered around Stuart and Lottie. A few minutes later everyone was spreading out and starting to dig and twist holes out of the solid ground to make new homes for the thousands of daffodil bulbs.

I looked at the hundreds of people who had dragged themselves out of their nice warm beds and were giving up their weekend. They were braving the freezing weather just to do something nice for my Jenn. Then I was reminded again that she wasn't just my Jenn. She belonged to them too. Here were her colleagues, students and the parents she came into contact with every day, and each one of them had a different story and experience of Jenn to share. Each one of them had cared about her enough to be here this morning. Suddenly the cold seemed to lose some of its bite.

I flipped the small shovel in my hand, grabbed a bulb from one of the buckets, and joined Jenn's friends digging into the hard ground to make way for the sunny memorial we were all working to create.

Thirty-something bulbs later, a steaming cup of coffee was shoved in front of me.

'Thought it was about time you had a break.' Lottie's nose had turned pink from the cold.

'Thanks.' I cradled the coffee between dirty gloves, enjoying the painful heat it brought. My back creaked as I stretched. 'This is incredible. I can't believe how many people turned up.'

Lottie nodded. 'It's pretty cool. But so was Mum.' She gave me a bright smile. 'There's more people here than you think.'

'What do you mean?'

'The guy in the posh coat by the tea table? He's a journalist. Matty called a couple of Lucy's media contacts to tell them about what we're doing. I guess they wanted to do something even if they couldn't be here. He wants to talk to you, Dad.'

'Why me?' Panic flooded through me. 'Why not you or Stuart? You two organised this.'

'He's already talked to us both. And a lot of other people. This is more your story to tell than ours. There was supposed to be a photographer too, but apparently he's snowed in somewhere up north. But I've been taking plenty of photos, so maybe they'll use them. He's right over there waiting for you.'

'All right.' I nodded slowly. 'I'll talk to him.'

'Great. Thanks Dad!' Lottie planted a quick kiss on my cheek and raced over to the man, grabbing her camera off the table on the way.

The man followed her back, and held his hand out in greeting. I stripped off a dirty glove to shake his hand while shooting a questioning glance to Lottie. She gave me the tiniest of nods, trying to reassure me.

'Morning. I'm Gareth Brady. Impressive ... event you've got organised here. Sorry for your loss, by the way.'

'Thanks.' I silently wondered when strangers were going to stop apologising for the death of someone they'd never met. 'It is pretty amazing how many people have turned up.'

'Especially on such a horrible day.' He held up a tiny recorder. 'This OK?'

'Sure.' I nodded. 'So, which paper do you work for?'

'None at the moment. Used to work for one of the dailies, but now I'm freelance. Have had things in the Telegraph, Times, Star, Observer, Herald and Gazette. There's others, but they're the main ones. Oh, and the Post.'

'Quite an impressive list. Do you really think this,' I gestured to the now muddy field, 'is interesting? Do you really think you'll get a story out of a school field being planted?'

'I wouldn't be here if I didn't. Listen, David ... Can I call you David? I'll level with you. Your wife's death was tragic and awful, and the way it happened was shocking. All that makes for a potentially good story. I'm sorry, but that's just the truth of things.'

'Oh.' I felt sick to my stomach thinking of Jenn's death as a good story.

'But what really makes this interesting, and something

that people will want to read, is how you've reacted. Your son told me about how you collected all these plants from the council.'

I nodded. 'They were digging them up to lay the foundations for a new housing estate. They were going to throw them away.'

'But you saved them because your wife liked them. And now hundreds of people have turned out to help you replant them. That's interesting. People like things like this. I've already got bites from two editors, and that's just from a couple of quick phone calls.'

'It's human interest, Dad.' Lottie squeezed my hand. 'People like to be reminded that there's still good in the world, and that people still care about each other enough to come together in difficult times.'

'Exactly right.' Gareth nodded. 'Tragedy and then hope. People like it, which means they buy it. So, shall we start with you telling me about what the daffodils meant to you and your wife?'

The story came out a week later. It was in two of the papers, maybe three. I can't remember. It was nice though. They used Lottie's photos. She was so excited and I wanted to be excited for her too. I wanted to share her joy and energy, but I just couldn't. I'm so tired that I just couldn't really care about anything. I should care about that. I should have been worried that I wasn't being a good dad, but I just didn't have the energy.

And worse, Jenn has disappeared. I didn't know where she had gone, or why, but I couldn't feel her any more. I couldn't feel anything. It was like someone shoved a hoover into me and sucked out everything. There's nothing left. Just tiredness. I feel like my head has been stuffed with cotton wool. Not like me at all any more.

I was right to be worried about David taking the antidepressants. He's not been himself lately. I feel like he's slipping away. To everyone else he looks all right. He's still going to work, and forcing himself to smile and laugh with his colleagues, but it's all an act. If you look closely you'll see that his smile never reaches his eyes.

He's not eating properly. I know he was skipping meals before, but it's far worse now. He's always tired and lacking energy, but he doesn't seem to be able to sleep. He just lies on the sofa watching late-night television. He flicks through the channels as the evening wears on. The programmes get worse as the hour gets later until, eventually, he passes out watching shopping channels. But it isn't really sleep, and it isn't helping him heal or feel rested.

I can see the tiredness around his eyes, and in deepening lines on his face. It scares me. This tiredness eating away at my darling husband won't be cured by a good night's sleep. It's sinking into his bones and dragging him down. Why can't anyone else see how much pain he's in? The last few mornings getting out of bed has physically hurt him, but he still gets up and goes to work because that seems like it will take less effort than having to call in sick and make up an excuse.

He's not painting any more either. He seems to have stopped feeling almost everything. There doesn't appear to be anger or pain, no joy or hope. No love. He doesn't respond to me. I'm not sure he even knows I'm here. He's being sucked down into a pit of darkness, and that same darkness is pressing down on top of him and pushing me away. I don't know how to help him. The antidepressants have created a wall of fog and confusion in his mind. It's stopping him from hurting, but it's pushing me away too. It's suffocating him. He knows there's something wrong, but his mind is too muddled to work out what, or how to fix it. And I don't know how to reach him to help. Nothing seems to be reaching him right now. Not even me.

I don't know what to do. I don't know how to help him.

Except … if it is the medication, even this particular brand of antidepressants or dose that might not be a good match for him, then the solution is simple. He needs to stop taking them. I need to stop him taking them, but I don't know how. Since he's stopped responding to me I've felt weaker. It's crept up on me so slowly that I didn't notice at first. But now it's getting harder and harder to leave my strange, grey world, and the grey nothingness seems heavier.

I feel like I'm underwater. My senses are duller and weight drags at my every movement. Even my thoughts are clouded and just thinking leaves me feeling tired. There's other things I need to be doing. I need to watch over Lottie, and help Matty answer his questions about Lucy, but David's emotions are dragging me down.

I'll have to come up with something. I just don't know what.

DAVID

I'd forgotten just how forceful Jenn can be when it came to making her feelings known. It was one of the things I'd always loved most about her. I got a very sharp reminder last night. I hadn't seen or felt her clearly for days, and I was starting to think maybe she'd passed on, or crossed over, or whatever it is that happens when you die. And the idea of that happening had been so terrifying to me that I'd barely been able to function for the last few days.

But then, when I'd just finished brushing my teeth and looked up into the mirror. Even though the bathroom was cold, the mirror was foggy and distorted my reflection. I swiped my hand across the cold glass a couple of times, and looked up into Jenn's warm eyes. My breath caught in my throat. I didn't even want to risk blinking in case she vanished again. It had been so long since I'd seen her, and she was silent. The air around me felt oddly cold and empty.

'Why can't I feel you?'

Jenn shrugged at me apologetically and shook her head sadly.

'Why are you only in the mirror? Don't you want to be with me any more? Have I upset you somehow?' I didn't care how desperate or pathetic I sounded.

Jenn shook her head, waving her hands frantically, her mouth forming silent words, but I knew her expressions well enough to understand her. No, absolutely not. I wasn't the problem.

'So what is it, love?'

She mouthed something to me, but I couldn't understand. She tried again and again, her frustration clearly growing as I let her down further, still failing to understand her meaning. She covered her face with her hands, clearly upset.

'I'm sorry. I don't know what's happening, or how to make this right.'

She shook her head sadly. She didn't know either.

I rested my head against the cold mirror, desperate to be close to her again. My breath steamed the mirror, and as I went to wipe the obstruction away, I hesitated. Jenn had held up a finger. She had an idea.

Slowly, an image appeared in the fogged glass, drawn by her finger. A rectangle filled with small, evenly spaced dots in four neat rows. What on earth?

Jenn looked at me expectantly, waiting for me to understand her drawing and meaning.

'I'm sorry, I don't know what you mean.' I stared at the image, trying to figure out what it meant. 'Connect 4? Do you want to play a game?'

Jenn shook her head.

'A box of chocolates?' Another no. 'Some sort of jigsaw? A big Lego block?'

Jenn smacked her hand against her forehead in frustration. As I watched, her eyes closed and her lips pursed in concentration. The mistiness surrounding her swirled and thickened, obscuring her beautiful face and leaving just the finger-drawn image. It seemed to glow and twist, taking on a greater depth and shine. As Jenn disappeared completely, the image became more defined and finally I could see that she'd drawn a packet of pills. The anti-depressants the doctor had prescribed to me, which I'd been so carefully taking, hoping they would help.

As loathe as I was to leave the first contact I'd had with Jenn in weeks, I raced to the bedroom and came back with the pills so tightly grasped in my hand that the edges of the packet bit into my palm. The image of them on the mirror was already fading, to be replaced by my lovely Jenn. But she wasn't her usual, vibrant self. Instead she looked drawn and as tired as I could ever remember seeing her. Was talking to me really so painful and draining to her? I felt horrible that I'd caused her so much more pain.

'This is what you wanted?' I held up the packet. 'I've been taking them, I promise.'

Even though she was faded, I could see Jenn nod tiredly. She knew I'd been taking them. Of course she did. She flicked her hand towards me, a gesture of irritation I'd usually only seen when she was incredibly frustrated about something – or with someone.

'I don't understand.' As glad as I was to see Jenn, the tiredness that never left me was making it hard to think. 'What are you trying to tell me?'

She pointed at the pills in my hand and gestured to the corner of the room.

'I still don't know what you want.'

Jenn's lips pursed and I could almost feel the muscles tensing along her jawline. She was getting annoyed with me, but I couldn't work out how to make her happy. I popped out one of the tiny pills and reached for the water beaker.

Jenn rapped on the inside of the mirror glass and scowled at me. When she knew she had my attention she shook her head firmly and wagged a finger at me.

'You don't want me to take this?'

Her face lit up in a relieved smile.

'But I thought they were supposed to help me.'

Jenn held her hands up and shrugged. She was right, of course. I'd tried taking them – which was the sensible thing to do. They'd been prescribed to me for a reason. While they might help other people – most don't have ghostly communication to think about. They just weren't working for me.

'I suppose I haven't really been feeling like myself.'

Jenn pulled a face.

'Is this why you haven't been around?' I held the pack up to her.

She nodded, and that was enough reason for me to dump what was left of the pack in the bin.

My hand shook as I now pressed my fingers against my side of the mirror. 'I miss you, Jenn.'

Her smile was so full of love and happiness that I could almost feel warmth through the cold glass as she tucked a loose strand of hair behind her ear before pressing her hand up against mine. She'd got her message across, and I hoped she'd be back with me as soon as the drugs worked their way out of my system. For the first time in weeks I went to bed smiling, and woke up feeling rested and happy.

I saw Lottie briefly today. She has gone back to her own

place, but she still drops round every couple of days. Keeping an eye on me and making sure I behave. I don't think she was too happy to learn I had stopped antidepressants.

She didn't say anything, but I could see it in her eyes. I tried telling her not to worry, but I was pretty sure she would be calling her brother, and quite possibly her aunt, the second she was out of the garden gate.

I don't like to worry the children, but I'm not taking those things again. Jenn's started to fade back into my consciousness, and the stronger her presence becomes, the lighter my world feels. When she's near me I can actually feel the tension start to wash out of my muscles. Colour seems to be pouring back into my world, and my fingers are itching to draw and paint again. I'm seeing things more clearly and it's because of Jenn. I'm not giving her up again.

JENN

It's good to see David smiling again, but I feel bad that his happiness is causing the children so much concern. Lottie's really worried about her dad, and I'm worried about her. She's wearing herself out trying to live between two homes, and keep her own life going while looking after her dad. Finding out he's stopped taking medication is really worrying her, but she's wrong. He tried it, and it just didn't work for him.

Matty seems to be handling it a bit better, but I think it's easier for him because he doesn't see it up close every day. Plus he's distracted trying to work out what to do about Lucy. I've been keeping an eye on him, but I don't want to guide him in the wrong direction. He needs to make his own decisions. I just hope he hurries up and makes the right one before his lack of action forces Lucy out. But I don't think it's likely to happen. He's never been great at making decisions about his life, which is odd given he makes such big ones at work all the time. I'll just have to keep a close eye on him.

I need to keep a closer watch on both of them.

It's good timing really. There's not much I can do for David right now. It's horrible to be leaving him again, but he knows I'm still here, and that I'll be back by his side as soon as I can. Until the drugs leave his system, it's really hard to appear as anything more than a blur to him. I'm glad I worked out how to make myself visible to him in reflections, but I'm getting fed up of shimmering in and out of mirrors. Even just letting him know I'm nearby takes an incredible amount of effort to fight through the dark clouds and leaves me drained and exhausted. But David knows it was only the drugs making him feel so rough, and now he's stopped taking them he's filled with new hope.

Besides, Lottie could really use a bit of extra support now, even if it is from a ghost she's not sure she fully believes in. She's still carrying so much anger and fear with her, which is bubbling below the surface. If she doesn't stop burying her feelings, and face up to them, I'm worried they're going to pull her apart. I hate seeing her like this. It's like she's thirteen again, only this time I can't make her hot chocolate and wrap my arms around her until it's all better.

I think I need to try and reach her more, and let her know she's not alone. Maybe it'll help her to know I'm still here. She already wants to believe that her dad's right, but she's scared and upset. She lost me and her dad fell apart in front of her eyes, so she did what any little sister would do. She went to her big brother for help.

Unfortunately Matty lives in a world full of science, reason and evidence, and nothing about this grey, ghostly world is reasonable or proven. Matty responded the only way he knew how and turned to science for help. But science is nowhere near understanding this, and it's not even close to understanding me. So I'll have to find a more creative way of making sure Lottie knows I'm here.

Chapter Thirteen

CHARLOTTE

I should've been excited. Stu was going to pick me up and take me out. Out, out. He's sweet and funny and kind, and really hot. We've been texting each other since that day he came round about the daffodils, and we've met up a couple of times, just as friends. But the last time we talked he was a bit weird, and I teased him about it. That's when he told me he kinda likes me as more than a friend. And, to be honest, I fancy the pants off him.

So I should have been really excited, but I was too worried about Dad to relax. I had only just found out that he'd stopped taking his medication. It scared me. He said that he's happier without the drugs, and that he can see Mum more clearly, but that worries me even more. I don't think he's lying exactly, but he still talks about Mum like she's really here. I want to believe it's true, but it's pretty far out there, even for me.

I brushed on another flick of mascara and checked the mirror. It wasn't perfect, but it was pretty good and it would have to do. It was nearly time for Stu to pick me up. I ran down the stairs and yanked on a jacket. I dug my lace gloves out of my pockets, and something clattered to the floor and rolled across the hallway. I stared at it in surprise and found myself hesitating. I had to force myself to pick up the shiny, silver bangle. It was icy cold and the bright turquoise stones stared up at me innocently. I knew this bracelet. I'd given it to Mum one birthday. What I couldn't work out was how it ended up in my pocket.

I got halfway upstairs, intending to shove it to the back of a drawer, but something stopped me. Without knowing why, I wriggled the bracelet onto my wrist.

'So …' Stu studied me over the table. 'Are you going to tell me what's on your mind?'

'Sorry?' I fiddled with my wine glass.

'Well call me vain, but I kinda thought you liked me.' Stu shrugged. 'You've been quiet all night. I figure either I've misread this totally, or you've got something bothering you. I'm hoping for the latter myself.'

'I'm sorry.' Guilt flooded me. He'd been trying so hard, and here I was letting worry eat away at me and ruin our first date. I took a deep breath. 'I'm worried about my dad.'

'So you do like me?' His eyes sparkled.

'I didn't say that.' I tried to smile back.

'You didn't not say it.'

That did make me smile. 'I'm sorry I've wrecked tonight. I did really want to be here. It's just … Dad.'

Stu shrugged. 'It's just one night. Seeing as it's you, I might let you have a do-over.' He sipped his drink. 'So, as this just officially became a non-date, and there's nothing you can worry about wrecking, what's up with your dad? He seemed all right the other day.'

'He's stopped taking his antidepressants. He says they mess with his head, and when he takes them he can't …' I looked around, realising how busy the restaurant was. 'Fancy a walk?'

'Sure.' If Stu thought the sudden change of topic was weird, he didn't say anything. Instead he quietly paid the bill and held my coat out to me.

We walked down the road in silence, not holding hands or anything, but so close together that his arm brushed mine every few steps. After a while, Stu turned to me. 'Well, it's pretty quiet here.' He gestured to the nearly empty street. 'You going to tell me?'

'I don't think I want to.' I stared up at the sky, trying to see the stars through the clouds.

'You have to. It's part of the do-over deal. Full disclosure and explanation or no second chance.' He flashed me a grin. When I still didn't speak he sighed. 'Look, Lottie, whether you want to tell me what's going on or not is up to you. But you have to promise to let me know if there's anything I can do to help, OK?'

'Is this another do-over rule?'

'No.' Stu shook his head and looked down. He caught my hand in his and threaded his fingers through mine. The heat of his bare skin through my gloves made me shiver, and I struggled to meet his eyes. 'I like you Lottie and I want to help you.'

'You are helping.' I squeezed his fingers through my gloves. 'This helps.' Warmth flooded through me, and I suddenly felt safer and more relaxed than I had in weeks.

'Then let me help more.' His whisper filled the air between us with his frozen breath. 'Whatever's going on with your dad is clearly upsetting you, and I've got a shoulder spare if you want it.'

'You'll think I'm crazy.' I desperately wanted to tell him everything. I wanted Stu to make it all better, but I really did like him, and didn't want to scare him off.

'Would it help if I told you I already did? Just a little bit?'

'You think I'm crazy?'

'Well you like me, so you must be.'

'I didn't say I liked you.' I felt his fingers tighten around mine.

'You didn't say you didn't.' He grinned down at me. 'Spit it out, Hughes.'

I took a deep breath and let the words tumble out in a rush. 'Do you believe in ghosts and stuff like that?'

'Umm.' He looked confused. 'I dunno.' He studied my face closely, trying to work out the right answer. 'If you're asking me about scary bed sheets, clanking chains and glow-in-the-dark eyes with Hollywood special effects, then no. But if you're talking about spirits and guardian angels and things ... then maybe yes. I know too many people who've had too many weird experiences to say I don't believe in anything like that. Myself included.' He shrugged easily. 'I'd say I'm pretty open-minded about it all.'

'Weird like what?' I was intrigued, and hopeful. Maybe Dad wasn't losing his mind after all.

'A few things,' he admitted. 'Odd feelings and dreams that have turned out to mean something. But the biggest one was when a mate and me were in an accident a few years back. It should have been really bad, probably fatal. The bike was totalled, but we both walked away without a scratch. The paramedics couldn't believe it. We couldn't believe it. I believe someone was watching over us that day. But the other stuff? Most of it's just silly. Things going missing, or moving around. Things you'd thought you'd lost turning up in strange places. Just lots of things that could be odd coincidences, except there were too many of them. Do you know what I mean? Lottie?' He sighed. 'Now you think I'm crazy.'

'No.' I shook my head and rubbed my fingers over the bracelet. I showed it to Stu and explained about it and the keys. Then everything started pouring out of me. I hadn't meant to say so much, but I couldn't stop once I'd started. I told him about how Dad thought he could still talk to Mum, and how my big brother and me convinced him to see a doctor who prescribed antidepressants. The weight that had been crushing my shoulders started to feel lighter, so I told Stu everything Dad said about the antidepressants stopping him from seeing Mum, and how much it scared me that he wasn't taking them any more.

Stu didn't interrupt. He just let me talk, nodding and

making encouraging noises whenever I faltered. I forced myself to look up when I was done. 'So, what do you think?'

Stu took a deep breath and replied slowly and thoughtfully. 'I think there's a lot of things in this world that we don't understand. Especially when it comes to death. Maybe your mum really is watching over you all and trying to help your dad feel better. If it helps your dad to believe she's still around, then does it matter what the reality is?'

'It matters if he thinks he's talking to a ghost.'

'Can you say for sure that he isn't? Are you completely and totally one hundred percent sure? Truly?'

My keys weighed heavily in my pocket and the bracelet seemed to burn around my wrist. I didn't know what I believed.

'Besides,' Stu carried on. 'Even if it's not true, you said it makes him feel better to believe it. All I know is you guys are going through one of the hardest, shittiest things that can ever happen. Anything that helps you get through that has to be good. Even if it is unconventional.'

'I hadn't thought about it like that,' I admitted. Warmth and peace wrapped around me, and my skin tingled beneath Mum's bracelet. What Stu said did make sense. I desperately wanted to believe Dad, and know that Mum was still around somehow, looking after us. I wanted to believe that when my keys vanished in her house, it was because she wanted me to stay with Dad for a bit longer. I wanted to believe she'd somehow slipped her bracelet into my pocket as a reminder and promise she was still with me. It felt right to believe it, even though everything I've ever been taught told me it couldn't be real.

'It's not like you have to decide your entire belief system right now.'

'True.' I watched as Stu blew on his hands and rubbed them together. 'You're cold.'

'Not really.' He shrugged.

'Well I'm cold, so you must be. Why aren't you wearing gloves?'

'It's supposed to be spring. Honestly, I don't feel cold at all.' Stuart smiled at me, and I felt my insides melt. Suddenly I didn't feel quite as cold either. It was as if the sun had come out. I didn't want this to end.

'Do you want to come back to mine? It's only a quick hop on the tube from here, and I'm pretty sure my flatmate is out tonight. I'll make coffee and you can defrost a bit.'

'Are you asking me back for coffee or are you *asking me back for coffee*?' He winked suggestively.

Oh God, I didn't know the answer to that. I tried to keep my voice steady. 'If you don't like coffee, I can make tea.'

Stu gave me an odd grin, like he was trying to work me out, and then burst out laughing. 'All right. Tea it is.'

We talked for hours. About everything and anything. I have to admit I can't even remember everything he talked about, because at times I got distracted just watching him speak. That probably sounds really weird, but it's the truth. I never really thought about a guy having gorgeous lips until I met him.

I don't remember when his arm slipped around my shoulders, but it was probably after I swapped the empty mugs for a couple of glasses of wine, and started flicking through the TV channels. I do remember it felt easy and comfortable, and even my flatmate's giggly appearance at 2 a.m. didn't spoil it. I hadn't felt so relaxed in a very long time.

Neither of us realised how late it was until grey light started to seep in through the living room window. Nothing else happened. We just sat on the couch and talked the whole night away. I swear it's the truth, despite the knowing looks and giggles of a certain flatmate when she came back in to look for coffee.

Well. Almost nothing. Stu couldn't get the front door open. He didn't have the hard-earned knack of jiggling the latch in the right way to make it release. I gave up trying to explain the twist, shove to left and jiggle motion he needed, and leant across him to open the door. He looked down at me and smiled in a way that made me really aware of how narrow the hall was.

'So, am I going to get this do-over?' I tried to keep my voice casual and not let him know how desperately I wanted him to say yes.

'I don't know, Lottie.' He shook his head slowly. 'I think I kinda like how our non-date turned out after all.' His fingers brushed against my cheek and his breath was warm as he bowed his head. After what felt like an eternity his lips met mine softly. His hand slipped around the back of my neck and my fingers tangled in his hair as he drew me more firmly against him. I could feel the heat radiating from his body as I kissed him back firmly. When I teased his lips with the tip of my tongue, stroking them ever so gently, he groaned and shifted slightly, wrapping his arm tightly around my waist.

I couldn't tell you whether it lasted a few seconds or an hour, I was so focussed on him. For those moments, Stu filled my world and consciousness completely, like a warm, blindingly white light. I couldn't have thought about anything else if I'd wanted to, and I didn't want to. The whole thing felt natural and easy. And good. Really, really, really good.

When we finally broke apart for air, I leaned back against the wall, loving the feeling of being trapped and protected by him at the same time. My breathing was too fast, and I could feel the heat rising in my cheeks. Wow, that boy can kiss. If I hadn't had the wall and Stu to support me, I think my knees would have given way and I would've ended up on the floor.

'No.' He grinned down at me, his thumb still stroking my cheek gently. 'Definitely no do-overs.'

JENN

Lottie and Stuart have been spending a lot of time together. They're definitely "an item" as she'd say. I'm so pleased. He's a good man, and he's making her happy. She's less angry and seems to be getting over my death a little more every day. She's excited about things again and glowing with new energy and hope. I'm not sure, because things like this take time to set and fix themselves into the universe, but I'm starting to think that maybe Stuart and Lottie might be soulmates, and maybe they're meant to be together.

Of course, it doesn't hurt that Stuart's one of the nicest, most level-headed pragmatists I've ever known. He's a lot more mature than his years, and has more sense in his head than most adults I know. He doesn't discount ideas as quickly as most people, and has a very open-minded way of looking at life. I think that's what makes him so good at helping special needs children.

It's what's made him so supportive of David not taking the antidepressants any more. His simple response to Lottie, when she pushed him for an opinion, was that David seemed happier, calmer and more together without the medication, and if he was sane enough to make the choice for himself, then he probably didn't need it.

He's very open-minded about the idea of a spirit world too. He's also clearly besotted with my daughter. What more could a mother ask for?

Stuart turned up at Lottie's door this morning. I don't know how he managed it, but his dog was sat on the doormat, grinning up at Lottie through a mouthful of daffodils when she opened the door. She grinned and bent down to rub his ears and tell him what a lovely dog he was.

A second later, Stuart peered round the wall and held up a brown bag. 'We thought we'd bring you breakfast and see what you were up to today. It was all Jasper's idea.'

Aww, he really is a sweet guy. I crossed my fingers and hoped Lottie had been up long enough to get past her usual morning grumps.

'Well that was very sweet of Jasper.' Lottie laughed. 'I've not really got much planned. Thought I'd just be lazy and chill out.'

'Sounds like a good plan to me. Want some company?'

'Sure.' Lottie opened the door fully. 'Come on in Jasper. You can bring Stu too, if he promises to be good.'

'Doubtful.' Stuart shot her a wicked grin.

Jasper zoomed through the house, straight past me and into the kitchen. Stuart followed and I saw him roll his eyes. 'Stop begging you muppet, Lottie will think I never feed you. Besides, she hasn't got anything for you.'

'Says you.' Lottie broke a biscuit in half.

'He's going to get fat,' Stuart complained.

'No he won't,' Lottie argued. 'If he puts on a single ounce I'll take him running. All right?'

Happy once he'd gulped down his treat, the dog streaked into the living room. I hadn't expected him to move quite so fast, and didn't have time to move out of his way, and he barrelled through me. He screeched in fear and shot backwards, quivering against the wall. I felt awful. I would never want to scare a dog.

Lottie dropped to her knees on the living room floor next to the shaking dog, who snapped and snarled at her fingers. She pulled her hand back easily and stroked his flattened ears gently while murmuring soft, soothing noises. 'What's the matter with him? He looks terrified.'

‘I’ve no idea.’ Stuart knelt down beside her. ‘Last time I saw Jasper like this, he’d just been attacked by a cat.’

‘A cat? Really?’

‘Yeah. Bloody mean thing. I’m sorry, he usually doesn’t act like this. He didn’t mean to snap or growl.’

‘It’s all right.’ Lottie reassured them both.

After a few minutes, Jasper calmed down and started to show an interest in me. I pulled out the red bouncy ball that Daisy had left with me, and started tossing it between my hands. Jasper watched with fascination. I bounced the ball on the floor and watched the dog’s brown eyes follow the movement.

‘Well he seems all right now.’ Lottie shuffled up onto the couch. ‘So what happened to that breakfast you promised?’

While Stuart went into the kitchen, Jasper edged over to me. He wriggled across the floor on his belly until he could sniff my outstretched fingers. After nearly a minute of suspicious sniffing, his ears pricked up and his tail started to wag. He nudged the ball hopefully with his nose. I sent it spinning across the floor and he chased after it gleefully. He snatched it up and skidded to a halt at my feet, tail beating on the floor. I wrestled the ball off him and threw it again.

Lottie laughed. ‘Your dog’s mad. What on earth does he think he’s doing?’

‘I’ve got no idea,’ Stuart admitted. ‘But he looks like he’s having fun. He gets that look when he’s playing. It’s kinda nice. I’m usually busy looking for another ball or trying to wrestle it off him to throw it again, so I don’t get to see it from this angle.’

‘I can fix that.’ Lottie leaned over Stuart to grab her camera. With a few quick beeps she changed the settings so the lens clicked and whirred crazily, capturing I don’t know how many images per second. She followed Jasper’s antics across the room as he ran back to me, and I found myself wishing desperately that she could see me. I wondered how many thousands of photos she'd taken of me before. I'd give almost anything to be able to offer her a few more photos.

'Here, what do you think of these?'

'This one's great.' Stuart peered at the camera screen over her shoulder. 'I love the look on his face. It's just like he's grinning. Shame his front paw is blurred though.'

'Don't worry.' Lottie grinned. 'I had it on rapid fire.' She started clicking through the pictures more quickly.

'What's that? At the corner of the frame? It almost looks like smoke ...'

'I don't know. Dust on the lens maybe?' Lottie flipped the camera over to check. 'Looks clean enough.' Her eyes widened as she flicked through more of the photos.

'What is that?' Stuart stared at the tiny screen. 'It almost looks like there are hands reaching out of it.'

'I know.' I couldn't see the screen, but Lottie's jaw clenched as she clicked through the photos more quickly.

'Jeez ... that looks almost like a face.' Stuart's voice was hushed.

The camera clattered to the floor as colour drained from Lottie's face. I edged forward to look at the screen. Right in the corner of the room, half obscured by Jasper's excitedly wagging tail, was a hazy figure outlined in shimmering light. If I squinted I could make out a floaty skirt and cloud of dark hair surrounding oddly familiar features.

'Shit ... that looked just like ...'

'Mum.' Lottie's voice was choked. 'It's my mum.' She looked straight at me for a few seconds, and for a moment I thought she could see me. Then her eyes dropped back to the camera on the floor. She watched it like she thought it might suddenly jump up and bite her.

Stuart wrapped his arm tightly around her shoulders. 'Want another look?'

Lottie nodded silently and reached slowly for the camera. She cradled it between her hands and stared at the screen. 'Oh God, it's my mum.' She shook her head in disbelief and stroked the screen. When she looked up again her eyes were overly bright with tears, and I had to fight the urge to reach out and comfort her. 'Mum?' Her voice was breathless. 'Are you still here?'

I tried to answer her, to fill the room with scent or to move something, anything to let her know I was there. But the greyness and exhaustion were already gnawing at me.

Lottie laughed nervously, but there was sadness in her eyes. 'I guess not. I'm not imagining this, am I?' She offered the camera to Stuart. 'Please tell me I'm not seeing things.'

'If you are, then I am too,' he reassured her. 'And I don't think Jasper's got that good an imagination anyway.'

'You think Jasper knew she was here?'

Stuart gave her a warm smile. 'Like I said, he only gets that look when he's playing with someone. Most animals are a lot more sensitive than we are. I don't see why he couldn't see her.'

'Then you really believe my mum was here?'

'Yeah. And I think you do too.' He tapped the camera. 'And I think anyone seeing these pictures would believe it as well.'

'Yeah.' Lottie looked down at the screen again. 'You know, I've kept thinking that I could feel her around me. I don't know. A weird warmth and a hint of perfume every so often. Things that kept moving about. But I was scared it was just wishful thinking. But this ... this is pretty undeniable.'

Stuart squeezed her more tightly and kissed her forehead. 'It's kinda cool.'

'Yeah.' Lottie nodded, before looking up at Stu again. 'Thanks for believing in me and not thinking I was crazy.'

'Never a problem, babe.' Stuart grinned and leaned

back, spreading himself out on the sofa as he got more comfortable.

'I can't wait to show these to Matty and Dad. And Aunt Sarah.' Lottie paused and gnawed on her thumbnail. 'Actually maybe not Aunt Sarah. I don't know how she'd react to it.'

'Why not?'

Lottie sighed. 'She's Catholic. I'd be worried about upsetting her.'

'How'd you mean?'

'Well, she believes Mum's in heaven. If she's really here, playing with your dog, then clearly she's not. Wouldn't you be upset to be told your beliefs are wrong?'

'I guess. Except I don't think the photos prove that. Why can't both things be true? Why can't she be in heaven, but still visit you?'

'I guess.' Lottie hesitated. 'But that doesn't feel right. I don't know why, but it doesn't.'

Chapter Fourteen

Summer

JENN

The antidepressants seem to be taking forever to leave David's system. I'm finding it so difficult to keep my patience. I just want to reach out to him again, but the medication seems to affect me too. It makes everything blurry and drains me of energy, then throws me back towards the grey place more quickly. I can still wave to him through mirrors and other reflective surfaces, but I can't push past their shiny surfaces and reach out when it comes to being around David. I don't fully understand it, but there are so many things I don't fully understand about this whole situation.

I'd been spending more time around Lottie recently, but now she and Stuart are getting closer, and their friendship is becoming something more. So, Lottie wouldn't want her mum hanging around, and from my point of view, there's such a thing as too much information, especially when it comes to your daughter and the guy she's dating.

Besides, Matty needs me at the moment. I was really hoping he could sort out the whole Lucy problem by himself, but he's doing exactly what I worried he would. He's let himself get caught up worrying about what-ifs and maybes, and he's trying to build and cross every possible bridge the future might bring.

He's got his thinking so twisted with worries that he's forgotten the whole point of what he should be thinking about. Whether he loves Lucy enough to ask her to give up the opportunity of her career to stay with him, or to give up his own career to follow her. There aren't that many firms willing to take a risk and give a young solicitor a chance like Matty's company did, and he's loved being there. But as rare as a dream job can be, the chance at love can be ever rarer. He does love her, he really does. More than anything. But he's so busy worrying about what might happen one day fifty years from now, that he's forgotten that.

He's been like this since he was a little boy. Always such a little worrier. I remember his sixth birthday. We were going to buy him a "proper big boy bike", but he saw a safety video about what happened to children who didn't wear helmets. He got it into his head that somehow his helmet would come off and then he'd get hurt, which would make me sad. It took us two weeks to convince him to stop worrying and to just enjoy the bike.

He knows he does it, that he lets himself get distracted by worries, and that they can derail his life. That was the point when my phone would ring. We could talk for hours when he had something on his mind, but I'd always try never to tell him what to do. I'd just let him talk and bounce ideas off me until he'd worked it all out in his head.

But that's not an option this time. I know he's in pain and needs my help. His agony of indecision and worry is dragging at me and pulling me towards him. He wants me, or someone, to tell him what to do and make the decision for him, but I really don't think I should. I've always tried so hard not to influence his decisions in the past.

But he needs help, and I'm still his mum, even if I can't pick up the phone or hug him any more. He's not going to ask his dad. He won't want to "bother him when he's dealing with his own stuff". He won't talk to Lottie either. He thinks big brothers should fix problems, not burden their little sisters with them.

*

Matty is so down. He really doesn't know what to do about Lucy. She's pushing him for an answer, and I don't blame her, but it's the worst thing possible she could do to Matty. As soon as you start pressurising him, he stops being able to think straight and starts to panic.

I know what I need to do. I need to give him some sort of sign to reassure him that what he keeps thinking about, and what he really wants to do, is the right thing. Maybe then he'll stop second-guessing himself so much.

I think I've worked out how best to do it. I've discovered metal is really easy to work with. Whether it was Lottie's keys I moved to get her to stay with David a bit longer, or my bracelet which I dropped in her pocket to let her know I was still with her, metal seems to respond well to me. I think it's because it absorbs the energy of the people carrying it around, so keys and jewellery are the easiest by a long stretch. I was a bit nervous about whether something new and unhandled would have enough energy in it for me to work with, but it had to work because Matty's hurting.

I spotted him trudging down the high street. His smart work coat was buttoned up tightly and he'd shoved his hands deep into his pockets. He looked cold, tired and miserable. I could almost feel the worry pouring off him.

Look up, Matty. I'm right here. I was listening when you came to talk to me. I know you're worried and scared, but I'm still here for you. I just need you to look up and pay attention to me for a few seconds. Please Matty, look up.

I concentrated everything I had on trying to get his attention. If he didn't look up soon, it would be too late.

Come on Matty, just look up! I screamed in frustration. His step faltered and he glanced towards me. For a moment he froze and stared at the window behind me.

This was the moment I'd been waiting for. Rows of rings, necklaces and bracelets nestled in velvet trays in the window, glowing under the carefully placed spotlights. The ring I'd chosen sat close to the window, proud on its glass stand. I needn't have wasted my time and energy worrying about it responding to me. It didn't have the energy of something carried around with someone for years, but had its own energy. It was full of hope and excitement. Making it sparkle and flash with light was easy.

Matty stared at the ring and the rainbows that flashed out of the diamond at my gentle nudge. 'Mum?' His voice was barely audible.

Oh my God, can he see me?

A blast of wind shot through the high street. Matty shivered and shook his head sadly. He pulled his coat tighter and turned away, head down as he trudged sadly towards home.

Damn, damn and buggerations. I really thought that was going to work. For a moment I could have sworn Matty looked right at me, and that he'd understood what I was trying to tell him. But he never was any good at taking hints.

I could feel the despair and loneliness drifting off him in waves. If anything he seemed worse than before. I'll just have to come up with something more drastic. Something that even Matty can't manage to ignore.

MATTHEW

I can't believe the photos Lottie showed me when I visited her in London this weekend. They're just incredible. At first I thought it was some big joke she was playing on me, but she swears it's the honest, simple truth. Mum's really here. I feel awful. Dad's been telling us she's been here all along, but instead of believing and supporting him, I bullied him into seeing a doctor and taking antidepressants. I really want it to be true, especially now.

For a moment yesterday, I thought Mum was with me. On the high street, by the jewellery store, I thought ... Oh I don't know what I thought. It was probably nothing more than wishful thinking. I'm so confused right now. I don't know what to do. I can barely trust my own mind.

Lucy's been offered a brilliant new job. It's a huge step up in her career, and a massive pay rise. She should take it. It's a fantastic opportunity. Except, she doesn't seem to want to. She keeps asking me what she should do, and if there's any reason for her to stay.

She wants me to give her that reason. I want to, I really do. We've been together for years and I love her like mad, but I don't know what to do. I always thought I'd marry her, that we'd settle down and have a family. But after watching the pain Dad's been through, I'm scared to care for anyone that much. I don't ever want to feel the way he's been feeling. The way he's still feeling.

Except, the thought of not having Lucy in my life makes my stomach tie in knots and physically hurts. So what am I supposed to do?

I wish Mum were here with me. She'd be able to tell me what to do. *Please Mum, I really need your help to figure this all out. I'm sorry I didn't believe Dad, and that we left you in the ground. I'm so sorry. But I really need your help. I don't know what to do. I don't know how to deal with this. Mum, I need you.*

I don't know when I started crying. I think I've cried more in the last few months than I have in the last decade. That's when the strange warmth started. I know it could have just been imagination, but I really don't think it was. It started in my right hand, a strange, tingling warmth that quickly spread up my arm and slipped around my shoulders and back. It was a little scary at first. I had goose pimples all over, but was warm. And then I swear I could smell Mum's perfume. That comforting mix of flowers and fruit that's been there in my life for as long as I could remember.

I know every logical thought and almost every accepted belief means there's no way this could be anything but desperation and imagination. But, it doesn't feel like that, and after seeing Lottie's photos, I couldn't help but think it's more.

Except, if Mum really is here, and really can communicate, then I can't believe she'd leave me hanging like this. I can't believe she wouldn't help me work out what to do about Lucy.

It had been really late when I got back home to Edinburgh, but I decided to go for a walk anyway. After hours of driving, my legs were stiff and I needed to be moving. Plus I didn't want to go home while Lucy prowled around, snatching things off shelves and adding them to the growing piles of "her" stuff all over the house. Every time she looked at me I could see sadness and disappointment in her eyes. All I needed to do was ask her to stay, and tell her that I wanted her in my life. It sounded like such a simple thing. It should have been, because I do love Lucy.

The thought of not having her in my life is enough to make me feel physically sick, but people break up all the time. People get over break-ups. I don't know if Dad's ever going to get over losing Mum. I can survive another break-up, I've done that before. But I don't think I could ever get over losing someone I loved that much. If ever I had to watch Lucy die, I think it would kill me too. So maybe it's better just to avoid ever being in that situation. If I never get married, I can never be that badly hurt.

Except that the thought of my life being Lucy-less is like a stab in the gut. I really don't know what to do.

I pulled my coat tighter and shoved my hands deep into my pockets. My fingers brushed against something small, cold and round. My thumb traced around a narrow edge. It was smooth, except for one bit that was larger and rough with lumps and bumps. My finger tip slipped into a small circle, and I carefully pulled the alien object out.

Surprise made my fingers clumsy, and I had to fumble to keep hold of the tiny treasure. I moved under a street lamp to look at it more closely. It was a small, gold ring, and the roughness I'd felt was a row of stones that glittered and flashed with blue and white light. Warmth seemed to gather around me as I studied it more closely. It wasn't new. There were tiny scratches around the band, and the gold was thinner at the back. It looked like it had been worn and loved lots. I don't think I was even breathing when I reached for my phone and hit Lottie's speed dial.

'Ugh ... what?' My sister sounded less than thrilled to hear from me.

'Lottie? Are you all right?'

'Matty? Is that you? Have you any idea what time it is?'

'Umm.' I checked my watch. *Oops*. 'Sorry, sis. I just wanted to ask you something.' I heard muffled voices, as though she'd covered the phone with her hand. I couldn't help but notice one sounded a lot deeper than hers, and my big brother response was impossible to hold back. 'Lottie? Have you got someone there?' My suspicions worsened when I heard what sounded like a dog whimpering and Lottie apologising. 'Are you even at home?'

'Actually, not that it's any of your business, I'm at a friend's. But if you rang me at ugly o'clock in the morning and woke me up to ask about my love life ...'

'I didn't, I didn't.'

She sighed with frustration. 'So what did you want?'

'What did Mum's engagement ring look like?'

'What? Hang on.' I heard rustling and a few seconds later a door clicked shut. 'What?' Her voice was clearer.

'What did Mum's engagement ring look like?' Even as I asked the question, I already knew the answer. It was staring up at me from the palm of my hand.

'Why? Matty are you all right?' Lottie sounded confused and worried. 'Where are you?'

'Back in Edinburgh. I drove home. I'm fine. Charlotte, what did it look like? Please.' I almost never used her full name.

'Umm. Sapphire and diamond, part eternity set into gold. Why?'

'Sapphires? They're the dark blue ones, right?'

'Right.'

'And eternity means they're all in a row?'

'Uh huh. What's going on?'

'What happened to it?'

'I'm not answering any more questions until you tell me what's going on,' Lottie snapped.

'I'm fine Lottie, just tell me what happened to it. Please.'

'I don't know,' she replied quietly. 'We did talk about burying it with her, but I don't know what Dad decided in the end. Why?'

'Thanks Lottie. I'll call you later.'

'What? You can't just ...' I snapped my phone shut halfway through her indignant squawk and turned it off.

I cleared my throat awkwardly. It's a good thing it was late, because I'd have felt like a right idiot if I thought anyone could have heard me. 'Mum?' Warmth flooded through me and the air filled with fragrance. 'Is this your answer? Is this what you think I should do?' I held the ring out. Happiness joined the warmth. If she'd shouted yes in my ear, the message couldn't have been any clearer. I shook my head. 'It's not that simple, Mum. If it were, I'd have asked her already.'

A question hung in the air around me. 'I love her. I really

do, but I don't know if I can do this. I'm scared. I've never been so scared in my life. I'm scared of losing her, and scared of having to live without her. If she leaves now, then she's just left. But if I ask her to stay with me, she will. Then I could lose her forever. She wants children one day, Mum, but women still die in childbirth. She could get hurt, or sick, or die in a car crash like you. And then I'd have to watch her die. I couldn't survive that.'

Softness brushed against my wet cheeks and left a trail of goose pimples as calm patience and understanding flooded through me. It was all right to be scared. That's what Mum always told us growing up. That almost everything worth doing was hard, and usually a little bit scary.

I twisted the ring and looked at it again, thinking about what it could mean. The light hit it at an odd angle and flashed back into my eyes, almost blinding me with colour and brightness.

An image formed out of the spots in my vision. I was little again, and Mum's fingers were wrapped tightly round mine. We were at the top of a roller-coaster, and I was terrified. I'd always been scared of them, but my friends were going to a theme park, and I desperately wanted to go with them. So Mum had brought me here and held my hand through the whole ride, even though she hated roller-coasters too.

I knew what she wanted to tell me as clearly as if she'd said the words. This is what love's usually like. It isn't easy and smooth, it's full of ups and downs and terrifying moments when all you want to do is scream and run away. But it's also exciting and wonderful, and nothing else in the world is like it. And you almost never regret it.

There was another flash of colour and emotion, and I saw her marrying Dad. She'd never told me she'd been shaking with nerves on the day, or that Dad had been crying.

Next, I saw myself as a baby, wrapped up in a blanket in

her arms, and I felt the rush of terror and joy that she'd felt the first time she'd held me. All the hope, all the fear, and all the happiness.

Then the image changed, and the baby was in Lucy's arms. She smiled at me. 'Look what we did.' Her voice was filled with pride and astonishment.

I can't even begin to explain what that felt like, but as the image faded away and the real world came back into focus, desperation filled me. I thought I knew what it felt like to really want something in my life. There were toys that I thought "I'd literally die" if I didn't get when I was younger, the exam results that got me into the university I wanted, and my dream job. I had thought these things were important, but they were nothing compared to that blink-long image of Lucy smiling at me, exhausted, happy and proud.

Until that moment I'd only ever thought about having children in the abstract. That yeah, maybe one day it'd be nice to have a family. But that one image that lasted less than a second, took it from a dreamy possibility and shoved it into reality.

I wanted that. I wanted a family in my future, and I wanted Lucy as the main part of it. I needed her. Who did I think I was kidding? The thought of not having that future together was so painful that it made it hard to breathe.

Bloody hell. Was this how Lucy felt? No wonder she'd been trying to get me to decide. If she felt even a fraction of this, then having me bumble around not telling her whether or not we had a future together must have been sheer agony. She really is incredible. If she'd hurt me like this, I don't think I could have even looked at her without feeling pain and anger every time. I had spent so much time worrying about myself, I'd barely stopped to think that the situation might be hurting her too. I think I'd rather have my heart ripped out through my throat than hurt her any more. I had to get home and apologise. I'd been a complete arse.

The air around me had filled with amusement, and I knew Mum was laughing along with me. I'd finally got the point and realised what I should have known all along.

The rest was easy. I guess that means it was the right thing to do. By the time I got home my heart was pounding, though I think it was more because of what I was about to do than because I had just ran all the way back.

I crept up the stairs and to the room I usually shared with Lucy. The door creaked as it opened, and I froze as she turned over in bed. A shaft of light hit her face and I swear my heart skipped a beat. She's so beautiful, sweet and kind. She could have anyone in the world, but she chose me. I can't believe she chose me.

I crept into the room and sat on the edge of the bed. 'Luce?' I shook her gently. 'Luce, wake up. I need to talk to you.'

She moaned and opened her eyes, squinting against the light. 'Matty? What on earth? I thought you were still at your dad's.'

'I got back a few hours ago. I'm sorry. I didn't want to wake you, but I need to talk to you.'

'Can't it wait?' She squinted at the alarm clock.

'No. It can't. I'm an idiot, an arsehole and an inconsiderate bastard. I don't deserve you.'

'I'm not going to argue with you, if that's what you're waiting for.'

'I know I've hurt you Luce, and I am so, so sorry. I want to spend the rest of my life making it up to you. There are a hundred reasons why you should say no, and I can only think of one why you should say yes, but … I love you, Lucy. I want you as part of my life. For ever and ever. You are my life. I'm an utter moron for taking this long to realise it, but Lucy, please don't leave me.'

'You are an idiot, and a moron, and a lot more besides.'

'Agreed.'

'But I love you too.' She buried her face in my shoulder, and I could feel her shaking. 'But what about the job?'

'You should take it. You've worked hard for it, and you deserve it. I'll come with you. If you'll let me.'

Lucy chewed her bottom lip. 'But what about your job? You've worked hard to get where you are.'

'I don't care.' I laughed. 'I'll get a transfer, or another job. It's just a job, Lucy. I can find another. I can't find another you, there's only you for me. You said you love me. Do you love me enough to forgive me? Enough to stay? Or let me follow you wherever you go?' She nodded against my shoulder. 'I need to hear you say it.' I brushed her hair away from her face and smoothed it down her back.

'Yes. I love you enough.' Lucy smiled softly, and my heart warmed.

'Enough to marry me?'

'What?'

'Marry me. I'm asking you to marry me, Lucy.'

Her eyes narrowed and her lips pursed. 'Not good enough.'

'What?' That wasn't the answer I'd been expecting. Panic grabbed at me.

'I'm not going to give you an answer unless you ask me properly.' She kicked back the duvet and swung her long legs round until she was sitting on the edge of the bed. She pointed to the floor with a wicked grin. 'On your knees.'

'All right.' I shrugged and got down on one knee. I owed her this and a hell of a lot more. 'Lucy Anne Kingsley, I have loved you since the month I first met you.' I caught her fingers in mine. 'You make me feel like the luckiest man who's ever lived just by smiling at me. You light up my entire life. These last few years have been a complete roller-coaster ride, but I've never been happier than when I'm with you. I'd like to spend every day from here until eternity making you feel as special and as loved as you deserve. If you'll let me. Lucy, will you marry me?'

'Of course I will.' She flung her arms around me and kissed me thoroughly, her body warm and welcoming against mine. When her hands started pulling at my shirt, I pushed her away with a groan. It took every ounce of my strength, but I wasn't finished yet.

'Wait. Wait. There's something else.' I flicked the lamp on.

'What?'

'This.' I fumbled with my coat and pulled out the ring.

'Wasn't that your mum's?' Lucy's breath caught in her throat as she stared at the ring in my fingers.

'Yeah. She'd have wanted you to have it.' My eyes widened as a horrible thought occurred to me. 'Unless you don't like it. I can get something else if you don't.'

'No.' Lucy smiled and held out her hand. 'I think it's perfect.' She gasped when I slid the gold band around her finger. 'Look, it even fits.' She pulled me back against her and kissed me again, before pulling me into bed for the most fantastic make up sex of my life. I could have drowned in her and been happy. The last thing I remember thinking as I fell asleep, my arms wrapped tightly around her, was bloody hell, this woman's going to be my wife.

Lucy moaned and wriggled against me, her long legs twisting round mine. She shifted uncomfortably and wriggled a hand out of bed. A blast of cold air shot between us.

'Checking it's still there?'

'More like checking it was ever there, and that it really happened.' Lucy smiled at me. 'Are you sure about this?'

'About you wearing Mum's ring, or the whole thing?'

'Both, I guess.' Worry crossed her face.

'I'm still sure. Are you?'

She groaned as she rolled over. 'I've been sure about this for a year.'

'A year?'

'Yeah. That long weekend we spent down in the Lake District? I think I knew then and there that I wanted to spend the rest of my life with you.'

'So you've just been hanging around for a year ...'

'Waiting for you to catch up with me.' She nodded and wriggled closer. 'Don't worry. You're worth the wait.' She kissed me gently. 'So, what was it that changed your mind?'

'Well ... you might think I'm a bit crazy, but ... Mum did.' I pulled her closer and told her everything.

CHARLOTTE

Oh. My. God. I swear when I get hold of Matty that I'm going to kill him. What type of person rings up their little sister in the middle of the night, worries her sick asking weird questions, then hangs up and turns off his phone? And what happened when I'd finally found the number to the landline? It just rang and rang and rang. The bastard must have unplugged it. I'm gonna rip him a new hole. I'm gonna freaking well skin him alive. I've left him about a dozen angry messages, including two on Lucy's phone. If he doesn't get back to me soon I'm gonna jump in my car and drive all the way up there, just so I can have the pleasure of beating the crap out of him.

Stu's been trying to calm me down, but I just couldn't settle enough to go back to bed. Every time I closed my eyes, horrible images of Matty jumping off a bridge or something crashed into my mind. I'll tell you what, he bloody better have. It'll save me the murder charge when I do get my hands on him.

Stuart pushed a steaming cup of tea into my hands. 'I thought you finished the milk in one of the dozens of cuppas you made last night?'

'I did.' He shrugged. 'But you didn't drink half of them, so I found the least scummy looking one and nuked it in the microwave.'

'Umm, thanks.' I stared at the cup suspiciously. Somehow the death skull staring back at me didn't fill me with confidence. 'What are you drinking?' I glanced at his steaming mug.

'Black coffee.' He grinned back.

When my mobile finally did ring, I jumped so far I spilt the tea all over myself. 'Answer it, just answer it!' I yelled while trying to mop up the scalding hot tea out of my lap. 'Oh get away, Jasper.' I shoved the dog's head away while apologising to Stu for drenching his cushions.

'Don't worry,' he whispered as he handed me my phone. 'It's easily cleaned.'

'Charlotte?' Lucy's voice was tinny and far away, and I rolled my eyes. Barbie. Not the person I really wanted to talk to just now. 'I just turned my phone back on and picked up some really peculiar messages. What's wrong?'

'Nothing, I was just trying to find Matty.'

'He's in the shower.' For some reason Barbie sounded almost pleased with herself.

Bloody great. I've been worrying myself sick for hours, and he's in the freaking shower. This had better be really, really good.

'Do you want me to go get him?' Barbie asked, all helpful.

'No, just get him to call me back when he's done. He's all right though?'

'He's brilliant,' Barbie trilled happily.

'Thanks.' I sighed tiredly. Whatever happened last night, Matty was all right. At least he would be until I get my hands on him.

'Well?' Stu raised his eyebrows in question.

'He's fine.' I gave Stu a tired smile. 'Apparently he's in the shower.'

'Fair enough.' Stu held his arms out to me, and I sank into them tiredly. 'But do I still get to be pissed off with him for upsetting you?'

'Yeah.' I rested against his shoulder. 'I think that's OK.'

Eventually my phone started to jingle and buzz, and flash with Matty's image. 'You've got five seconds to explain last night before I get to start yelling at you.'

'Yeah, sorry about that. Guess I was pretty thoughtless.'

'Two seconds.' I took a deep breath.

'I asked Lucy to marry me.'

I fumbled and had to scoop him back up off the floor. 'Sorry, dropped the phone. And?'

'And I said yes!' Barbie's voice squealed, deafening even from hundreds of miles away.

'Oh, wow. That's … not what I was expecting. I guess maybe I don't get to yell at you.' I remembered myself. 'Congratulations.'

'Thanks.' I could hear the smile in his voice. 'But listen, don't tell anyone else yet. I … we want to do it ourselves.'

'Of course.' I settled back more comfortably and took a gulp of the microwaved tea and grimaced. 'So what on earth was last night all about? Was it this?'

'Sort of. You know how you showed me those pictures of Mum, and said that you thought she'd been moving your things?'

'And you laughed and ripped the mick outta me?' I snapped back.

'Yeah. I'm sorry about that, sis. But … I believe you now.'

'Really?' I was starting to wonder if my brother had been brainwashed. Or discovered drugs. First the weird phone call, then proposing to Barbie, and now apologising to me and admitting I was right about something.

'Yeah. I think ... no scratch that ... I know she's been with me.'

'And?' I was so excited I started pacing. Jasper yapped excitedly and started following me up and down.

'And she helped me work a few things out. Everything really. Oh my God, it was amazing, Lottie. Her presence was so strong. It was like she was hugging me and telling me everything was going to be all right. She helped me work out what to do about Lucy and—'

'Hold up. What do you mean, what to do about Lucy?'

'Oh, we'd been having some problems. She's been offered a really good job down south, and I was trying to figure out what to do about it. Anyway, Mum ...'

Barbie and Matty were in danger of splitting up? I know I don't really love her, but she made Matty happy, so that was good enough for me. 'Why is this the first I'm hearing of this?'

Matty sighed down the phone and I grimaced, expecting a "Big Brother Lecture". 'Charlotte, you're my little sister. I'm here to look out for you, not to whinge about my own problems.'

'Matthew David Hughes, you are ten kinds of stupid! You really are the most arrogant, pig-headed, stupid, dim-witted idiot I've ever known.'

'Hey, I thought you weren't going to yell at me.'

'Well I didn't know how stupid you'd been! I'm not a little kid, Matty. And I'm clearly smarter than you. You should freaking well talk to me about things like this. No wonder you've been so weird lately.'

'Do you want me to tell you about Mum's visit or not?' Smart git knew that was about the only way to shut me up.

'All right. But I'm nowhere near done on this topic.'

'Whatever.' He brushed my anger aside. 'Anyway, Mum left me a little present too.'

'Her engagement ring.' Everything suddenly added up.

'Yeah.'

'Bloody hell.'

'Yeah I know.'

'So Lucy's going to be my sister-in-law? I guess I'd better stop calling her Barbie.'

'Yeah. You can knock that right off.'

'Fairy snuff.'

'What?'

'Fairy snuff. As in fair e-nough. Try to keep up. Anyway, tell me more about Mum.' I sat back down and took another sip of the nuked tea. It really wasn't all that bad.

Chapter Fifteen

DAVID

The coroner's report and inquest findings were finally released today. The policeman who'd been involved in the aftermath of Jenn's death brought it round himself.

I hadn't bothered to go to the inquest. The police said it wasn't necessary. They'd already got my statement, and it was a pretty straightforward case. I could have gone along to question the other witnesses, but it seemed so pointless. I was the main witness and I didn't really want to relive that day again. It's already branded into my memory as it is. Besides, I don't think there's actually anything that useful I could tell anyone.

All I really remember was the world-shattering noise, and pain slamming into me. Then I remember Jenn, slipping away from me. And the cold. I don't think I'll ever forget the cold. It seeped into me and lasted for days. Even wrapped up in blankets at the hospital and drugged out of my mind, I was still shaking with cold.

The policeman sat awkwardly on the sofa, and waved away my offer of tea. He was just dropping the report in on his way home to make sure I found out about it properly, and that he could answer any questions I had. That was nice of him. He'd handed over a thin envelope, and watched as I read it. It seemed such a ridiculously short document to sum up the worst day of my life.

The inquest status was "officially concluded". Jenn had died of "exsanguination by cause of catastrophic internal haemorrhage" caused by "traumatic dissection of thoracic aorta".

It was nothing new. The doctors at the hospital explained all that to me. The next bit was mildly interesting, as it confirmed what I'd thought all along. The cause of death was given as a "motor vehicle accident" where the "secondary vehicle spun on ice and impacted to the passenger side".

Accidental death. The words screamed at me from the box marked "final verdict".

Jenn died in an accident. I honestly didn't know if that made things better or worse. There was no one at fault, and no one to be angry with. But equally there was no one to blame. Jenn's death had just been a pointless accident. A conspiracy of fate. We'd just been in the wrong place at the wrong time. It's a very depressing thought.

Then again, maybe it isn't. Maybe it doesn't have to change anything. Maybe it just is what it is. That's certainly how Jenn would have viewed it.

JENN

I'm glad David took the inquest results so well. I was worried they'd upset him, and that I still wouldn't be able to reach past the antidepressants and help him deal with it. But he did just fine. Better than me, actually.

I don't know why, but I think I might have felt better if there had been a better reason. Someone to blame and be angry at. Not just a load of bad luck and worse weather. I wanted my death to have been more than just a random mess of coincidences and bad timing. If we had stayed for that last cup of tea, we wouldn't have even been on that fatal stretch of road at that turning point in time. Or maybe if I'd driven we'd have been further back. I always drove a little slower than David. A few seconds would have made all the difference. A moment would have saved my life.

Then again, maybe it was just my time. Maybe we'd have missed that accident only to have another worse one where David was taken with me. I guess when your time is up, it's up.

But I still think I might have liked to have someone to be angry at. Someone to blame, who could take responsibility for my death. Maybe their hurting would have taken away some of my pain. Then again, maybe not. I never really bothered with holding grudges in life, and I've got things to do that are much more interesting and important than starting to hold them now.

I want to share Matty and Lucy's happiness and excitement. I want to help Lottie get back to the path she should really be on, and help her make herself a happy future.

I want to visit with my sister instead of just checking in on her quietly without trying to interact with her or revealing my presence at all – Lottie's right, it would upset her to think I'm not in heaven.

But most of all, I want to get back to David. Properly.

The antidepressants are finally wearing off. They're not trapping him in an impenetrable cloud any more. It's not completely over yet, but it's getting better. I keep reaching for him, but his consciousness slips away into a fog. It's so frustrating. Like trying to catch a bubble. But every time I reach for him, the slip away is a little slower, and I know it's only a matter of time before I can wrap around him again, and slip into his mind.

He knows I'm here. I see him smiling at windows, and I know he's caught a glimpse of me as we've walked by. Well, as he's walked by. He still talks to me as if I'm with him, even though we both know I can't respond yet. Still, soon his system and mind will be clear again, and we can get back to being together. I can't wait.

I think it's going to be even better than before. The more time I spend around my family, absorbing their happiness, the stronger I seem to become. The grey place that had trapped me seems further away, and things in the real, living world respond to me better. I'm not just moving around rings and keys any more. Now I can do other things too, like turn on the television or radio, and move around other small objects. Like David's paintbrushes. Maybe I'll even be able to write him a message one day. Wouldn't that be something?

It's not a normal relationship, but who cares? So long as we're both happy it doesn't matter what shape that happiness takes. And we are happy. Everyone is. The whole of my world seems to be glowing with energy and the light of my family's happiness.

It's utterly blissful.

DAVID

Life just seems to be getting better and better lately. The antidepressants must have finally worn off, because Jenn's back. She slammed into me without any warning and wrapped around me. It felt fantastic. Like stepping into a warm shower.

She feels stronger than ever. Things seem to move around more often, and the house is filled with her perfume. I keep finding myself humming her favourite songs absent-mindedly, and the tiny white feathers that often mark her visits have been appearing in the strangest places. Yesterday I found one balanced on the tip of a paintbrush. I've even found them in the fridge when she thought I wasn't eating properly.

But it's so much more than that. The house just feels ... different. It feels like Jenn's here, laughing and filling the place with light and warmth, just like she did when she was alive. She's nagging me again. When I started to feel a little down the other day, the radio flicked on to one of my favourite songs, and my paintbrushes started to jump up and down in their pot. She's right of course. Painting always makes me feel better.

I don't know if it's my perception improving, or Jenn's

presence growing stronger, but she has definitely been more noticeable. It would make sense. Our children are both happy. Matty and Lucy are engaged, and Lottie seems to be half-living with Stuart and never stops smiling. Jenn would want to be close by to share in this happiness. Maybe I'm sharing it too, and all the good news has pushed away the last of my anger to make way for more happiness.

It's such a relief to have Jenn back. I actually feel like I can face the world again. Getting out of bed every morning doesn't hurt any more. I'm eager to see what each day will bring. Life is inspiring and exciting. I'm starting to see the beauty in the world again, and the old familiar itching to pick up a paintbrush has returned. I want to try to capture the beauty around me before it fades away forever.

The only thing is, it seems like the images and colours are fading away more quickly than they used to. Or maybe I'm just not capturing them as fast as I once had. Everything seems a little more sluggish. I don't know, I must be tired, or getting old. Or maybe the antidepressants haven't totally worn off yet. Actually, now I think of it, it must be that. It couldn't be anything else.

JENN

David's almost as glad to have me back as I am to be back. He spent half the night sitting up, drinking wine, and just talking to me. Telling me about all the things he'd worried I'd missed, and everything that was on his mind.

I miss this.

I miss the way we used to sit up for hours, just talking and catching up on each others' lives. I miss curling up on the sofa and just being together. I miss the way he'd absent-mindedly play with my hair and twist it into curls around his fingers. I desperately want to feel his breath against my skin again, and to wrap my fingers around his.

But there's no point dwelling on sadness and what can never be, especially now. Now's a time for joy and celebration, for hopes and dreams for the future. Because Matty and Lucy are getting married! I'm still not tired of thinking about it. I'm so pleased for them both. It really is the most wonderful news. Finding someone you love enough to spend the rest of your life with, and realising that they love you too, is truly something special and wonderful, and worth celebrating.

It's something worth fighting for. Maybe the only thing in the world that really is worth it. Even if you are scared of getting hurt, it's worth the risk. Even when it seems impossible and the barriers between you seem insurmountable, it's still worth it. Love deserves every chance and every ounce of strength, faith and hope you can give it.

I need to remember that. I need to remember why it's so important.

I need to focus on the positive, and what David and I still do have together, instead of regretting and mourning what we've lost.

Besides, there are other positive things to focus on, because Matty isn't the only one with good news ... only Lottie doesn't know about hers yet. I can't wait to see her face when she finds out. I only wish I could tell her myself. But it wouldn't be the same if I did. Even if I could work out how to do it.

It's all so exciting when things just fall into place perfectly. I'm so pleased for my daughter and the news she doesn't know is coming yet. I just buzz with energy whenever I start to think about it. It's yet another good thing that's happened because of my death. I'm glad, because it makes being dead a little bit easier to bear.

This time I didn't have all that much to do with it. It's mostly thanks to Stuart and David, my wonderful colleagues, and all the children at school. And my beautiful daughter's unsquashable ability to see the beauty in every situation.

Maybe there was some good old-fashioned luck too. And a little spiritual guidance, if you get what I mean.

All right, maybe more than a little.

It must have been a really slow week for news, because my coroner's report was published, along with Lottie's photos from the great daffodil planting at school. They really are quite lovely, but I've always thought that about her work. I almost believe there's something magical about her camera. She always manages to capture things, and people, at their very best. People come alive in front of her lens and her rapidly clicking fingers, and she captures them that way. Alive, powerful, and brimming with feelings and energy. She sees beauty that other people miss, and she captures it and pins it to paper in a way that suddenly everyone else can understand. Then they can see it too.

She gets that from her dad. I never understood how either of them could look at something boring and ordinary, like the multi-story car park, and see beauty in it. That was a place I could never follow them to. But somehow, when I saw the pictures afterwards, it was always so obvious. Even now, in this strange place from where I can see the whole world differently, I still struggle to see what they see.

But anyway, back to Lottie's soon-to-come brilliant news. A certain photographer, employed by a certain paper that had previously published Lottie's photos, might just have failed to turn up to a certain photo shoot he should have been at. I happen to know it's because he was in a slightly dodgy-looking hotel in Scarborough with a model he picked up at a recent photo shoot, but that's not really important.

What is important, is that a dozen models were being paid to sit around in bathrobes with nothing to do but munch on celery and gossip, at the expense of the editor who was fast losing his temper. It turned out that his staff photographer was covering a festival somewhere up north, and his two main backups were at a mutual friend's wedding.

From there, it was almost too easy. The most recent editions of the paper were piled up in a corner of the room. It didn't take much effort to knock the editor's coffee over his laptop, and send him racing for the papers to soak up the liquid before it destroyed the delicate electronics.

It took even less effort to make sure that the page at the top was the one with Lottie's photos from the daffodil planting. Even now, months later, the image still glowed with the energy and feelings of the day. Love, hope, peace and laughter. Fond memories still spilled from that one image in a rush of energy. Like I said, my daughter has an almost magical ability with a camera.

The editor stared at the image as the coffee slowly soaked into it, staining it brown. He grunted to himself and reached for the phone. He didn't notice the single, pure white feather that drifted off the edge of the table and twisted in a lazy circle before hitting the floor.

Chapter Sixteen

CHARLOTTE

I rolled over in bed and stretched luxuriously, but refused to open my eyes. I was way too comfy to want to give in to morning yet.

'I know you're awake. Stop faking.' A finger ran its way along my ribs and I shivered with the deliciousness of it.

'So what if I am?' I rolled over.

'So come here.' Stuart slid his arm beneath me so I could snuggle against his shoulder. He was so warm and comfortable that any complaint I might have been thinking about making melted out of my brain. He often seems to have this effect on me. Damn it, the man even managed to smell good. It's not fair. From the feel of it, my hair's a knotted mess that's going to hurt like a bitch to brush out, and I'll just bet that my mascara's turned me into a panda.

He just lolled back into my pillows looking hot. So. Not. Fair. Still, I guess there are worse things to worry about than having a hot guy between your sheets. Especially when he looks at you the way Stu looks at me. I swear he can turn me into a puddle with just a look. I snuggled closer to hide my blushes.

'What you thinking?'

Oh my God! A guy who cares what you're thinking about when you're naked. If it weren't for all the evidence to the contrary, I'd swear he was gay. 'Nothing really. Just ... wondering.'

'About what?' I could hear the smile in his voice.

'About when you stopped thinking of me as a friend.'

He shifted beneath me and rolled over to catch my face

between his hands. His dark eyes were so intense it felt like he was trying to read my mind. I lost all track of time until he suddenly grinned and kissed me on the nose. 'You're still my friend, Lottie. The fact that you make me crazy horny is just an added bonus.'

'Just an added bonus?' My heart dropped. Was that all he thought of me? 'Do you have added bonuses with other friends?'

'Would it bother you if I did?' I couldn't read his expression or tone of voice, no matter how hard I tried.

'Yes.' I wanted to bite the word back as soon as it escaped. I didn't want to be so needy and demanding.

'Good.' Stu grinned. 'Coz I'm not having ... added bonuses with anyone else, and I don't want to be. Are you?' He struggled to keep the smile from his face. Arrogant sod.

'You know I'm not.'

'Just checking. I like you, Lottie. I've liked you since the moment you opened your dad's front door to me, and you bent down and petted my brute of a dog. That's what you wanted to know, wasn't it?'

I shrugged, not wanting to admit it. 'What was I wearing for you to respond like that?'

Stu sighed. 'I wasn't staring at your tits or arse, Lottie, though for the record both are just ... wow. There was just something about you. I liked you then and there.'

Huh? I hadn't realised he had feelings back then. I thought he'd just been a nice guy. 'So why did you wait so long before ... you know?'

'Putting the moves on ya?'

'Yeah.' Except that it sounded so icky when he put it like that.

His arms tightened around my waist and I instantly forgave him. 'You were hurting when I met you. You'd just lost your mum.' Even now, in my safe, cosy bed months later it still hurt. Even curled in Stu's warm arms, it still hurt.

'You're still hurting, Lottie.' He tilted my chin up so I had to look at him. 'I didn't want to rush you. I didn't want to be some weird rebound thing that just made you feel better for a couple of weeks.'

'You really think I would have done that?' I wasn't sure how I felt about that.

'I think people do some strange things when they're grieving. I wanted to give this ... us ... a fair chance.'

'So you just waited?'

'Yup.'

'How long would you have waited for?'

'As long as you needed.'

'And if you were still waiting?'

'Well ...' He drew the word out. 'About now I'd probably ask you to make sure that, if I died of frustration while waiting, you'd have me cryogenically frozen until you were ready, and then defrost me.'

I started to laugh, but Stu pulled me tightly against him and smothered my giggles with slow kisses. His fingers traced goose pimples up and down my spine, and I completely forgot what I had been laughing about. I squirmed happily and arched my body against him. His lips followed his fingers across my bare skin, chasing down the shivers and goose pimples with trails of fire. I gasped when his warm breath hit my belly button.

I groaned with frustration when the phone rang.

'Leave it.' His eyes begged as they met mine.

'Definitely. They can leave a message.' I barely heard his reply as he murmured it into my stomach. I twisted my fingers through his hair and pulled him back up to me so I could kiss him properly and slide my tongue between his lips. He groaned and moved against me, and slid his hand around the back of my neck.

We both froze when the phone rang again. 'Leave it. Lottie, please leave it.'

'*Argh*. I can't. It's the second time. Who'd be ringing this time on a Sunday morning? It might be important.'

'Aren't I important?'

'Urgent. It might be urgent.' I rolled away and grabbed for the phone. 'I'm sorry. Hello?' I tried not to giggle and give away the fact that Stu had followed me and was slowly kissing his way up my back.

'I'm looking for C Hughes.' The voice was gruff and didn't introduce himself. Oh please don't be a sales call. Do not tell me I just pushed away a crazy hot guy who wanted nothing more than to kiss me until I screamed, for a freaking sales call.

'Speaking.' I kept my voice curt. If this was a sales call, they were gonna get it!

'This is James Barrow. From the Gazette. Are you the same C Hughes who took the photos of all the tulips being planted?'

'Daffodils.' I wriggled and gave Stu a gentle shove. Stop it, I warned him with a glare.

'Tulips, daffodils, they're all the same to me. Was it you?'

'Yeah. They're my photos. Is there some sort of problem?' I sat bolt upright, and could feel Stu's eyes on me as I held my breath.

'For me, yeah. For you, nope. You near Middlesex?'

'Yeah.' Ish, I fibbed.

'How fast can you, your camera and all your gear get to the marina? 'Cause if you can make it to the shoot there in the next hour, you've got a job. To be honest, you'd be doing me a favour.' He rattled off the details quickly while I scrabbled for a pen. Shit. Could I make it all the way over there in an hour? It'd take at least fifteen minutes for me to get everything together and into the car. Forty-five minutes to get out of the city was pushing it, and to find the right place? I shoved the address at Stu and mouthed 'in an hour?' to him.

He nodded firmly. No problem.

'Umm .... Can I ask what the fee is?' I gawped at the answer. 'Yeah. I'll be there.'

He laughed. 'Good. I thought you might. Bring a laptop. I need to see the first proofs before lunch. The shoot manager will fill in the rest when you get there.'

'Umm ...' A thought hit me.

'Yes?'

'What type of shoot is this, exactly?'

'Fashion. What else do you think you'd be shooting on a Sunday in the marina? Anything else?' The phone clicked off before I could even respond, and I stared at it.

'Oh my God, Stu, I've got a job. A *real job*. I've got to get moving.' I rolled out of bed.

Stu groaned reluctantly. 'I'll give you a hand. Just tell me what you need me to do.'

'Thanks.' I shot him a grateful smile and rushed into the bathroom. Thank goodness no one else was about.

'Hey, Hughes?' Stu tapped softly at the door. 'You're going to make this up to me, right?'

It was really scary at first. I was nearly late getting there. We'd both forgotten about the Sunday markets and got caught up in traffic, and then struggled to park. When we finally found the right address the lift wasn't working, so we had to lug my camera, my back up, all my tripods, lighting gear and laptop up four flights of stairs. By the time we actually got into the shoot I was sweaty, out of breath and getting more stressed by the second.

The harassed looking shoot manager with a clipboard met me at the door. 'You the replacement photographer?' I looked pointedly at the camera bag resting on my hip. 'Thank goodness. We've been set up for ages, and we're losing time. And time is money. You ready to go?'

'Just need to set up.'

'And how long will that take?' He tapped the clipboard impatiently.

'Depends on what you want.'

'They haven't even briefed you yet? *Ai me* ...' He started rattling off unpleasant sounding phrases in Italian. Within five minutes, Stu had calmed him down and got my laptop set up and connected to the internet, ready for my photos to whizz their way to the editor. He helped as much as he could with the rest of my gear, but most of it he'd never even seen before, so he just stuck to lifting the heavier things and holding them in place while I bossed him about. It was kinda cool. And just knowing he was there seemed to make it easier. Like I was drawing strength from him or something.

A couple of times I think I felt Mum too, but there was so much going on, it was hard to know for sure.

I did the shoot they asked for, focussing on showing the clothes in the best possible light. The sets were already in place, and the models were clearly well-briefed and knew what they were doing. All I really had to do was adjust some lighting, tweak a few poses and keep adjusting my shooting settings to capture the movement of the scene. But it was exhilarating.

I shot set after set of photos, pausing just long enough in between to move a few limbs around and flick out a skirt or ask the make-up team to touch up a sweaty forehead. Halfway through the shoot, Stu waved at me and tapped his watch. Damn, he was right. I needed to get proofs over to the editor.

'All right everyone, take a break. Back in ten, please.' I felt stupid saying it, like why should these people listen to me? The models were beautiful and elegant, and the shoot manager was brisk and efficient. They were all seasoned professionals, and I couldn't see why any of them would listen to me, but within seconds the set had cleared and the room filled with chatter.

It took me less time to upload the photos than it did to actually hit send and share the link with the editor. But I couldn't stop remembering that all my hopes and dreams were resting on that single press of a button. Stu watched over my shoulder as the images flickered across the screen.

'Just hit the button, Lottie.'

'I can't,' I whispered back.

'Why?' He dragged a chair over.

'It's too big.' I shook my head. 'It's too much. What if he hates them?'

'The editor?'

I nodded miserably.

'You're scared.' Stu's voice was filled with disbelief.

'I am allowed to be,' I snapped back.

'No, no. Of course you are. It's just ... I've never seen you scared of anything.'

'Yeah, well ... this is really big.' I tried to explain. 'All of my hopes and dreams. All my plans for the future. That's what that button really is. Until now, photography's just been a nice idea. Something I played with in between jobs and at the weekend.'

'You've photographed weddings and events and stuff.'

'For friends. And friends of friends. Hardly the same.' I dragged my fingers through my hair. 'If I press that button, I'm gonna find out for sure if I have a future in all this.'

'Isn't that a good thing?'

'Only if the answer's yes. What if it's no? Then I'm

left with nothing. At least if I don't send the photos, I'll always have the idea and the dream. There'll always be the possibility that I can do it.'

'But if you do send them, you're scared you'll be told you'll never make it.' Stu laughed.

'This isn't funny!'

'It kinda is. Look around, Lottie. This is just about the worst possible time for a crisis in confidence. You're in the middle of a shoot. There are models and make-up people and dressing people all waiting for you to tell them what to do next. Across the city there's a guy sitting by his computer waiting for you to save the day. He's waiting to see what you can do.'

'Oh my God, Stu, do you actually think reminding me of all that is helping?' Cool warmth wrapped around my shoulders and Mum's bracelet seemed to burn with cold on my wrist. She was here. Of course she was here. If I didn't know better, I'd have suspected that she set the whole thing up. I covered my eyes. I didn't know if I wanted to laugh or cry.

Stu pulled my hands away from my face. 'Look around, Lottie. You're right in the middle of your dream. Of course you're a bit scared. Dreams are scary. Once you've got them, you have to do everything you can to make them real, otherwise they'll haunt you forever. They'll never let you go until you've made them come true. Of course this is scary.'

I looked up into his dark brown eyes in surprise. 'That might just be the deepest thing I've ever heard.'

'Well I'm not done yet.' Stu grinned. 'You're good, Lottie. Really good. I honestly think you can do this. And I'm not just saying that because I'm sleeping with you. That's just a nice added bonus.' He chuckled. 'Seriously. Your photos are good enough to make your dream come true. You're good enough. You've just got to make sure the rest of the world knows it. This is your chance to do that.'

'You really think I'm that good?'

'Yes. Now just hit the bloody button and get on with it.' He shoved my computer at me and warmth tingled through my fingers. I guess Mum agreed with him.

I flaked out on the couch as soon as we'd got home and unloaded all my stuff. Even that was hard work. I couldn't believe I'd just finished my first fashion photo shoot. And it had gone really well. I'd got all they'd asked for, and a few more besides. Just ideas I had during the shoot. Stuff I wanted to try. I nearly didn't send them, but Stu was having none of it. So I just emailed the editor everything that made it past my first quick edit.

I was so tired that I could hardly move. Every part of me ached from lugging around heavy equipment and twisting myself into weird positions to get the right shot. I was so shattered that Stu ended up driving home. Even though he isn't exactly insured on my car.

But oh my God, it was so worth it. The shoot was just fantastic. It was just a fashion supplement for a local newspaper, but wow, the buzz. If I had any lingering doubts about my future, they're gone now. Photography is what I want to do. More than anything. If a genie appeared from a lamp right now, that's what I'd wish for. End of.

DAVID

Everything seems to be going well for my family. Matty and Lucy are blissfully happy now they've stopped having the arguments they didn't tell anyone about. Lottie's already got three more jobs booked, none of which are weddings or baby pictures, which thrills her no end. Although she's already promised to do Matty's. Apparently the last minute photo shoot she did the other weekend was a huge success, and the editor loved her style and way of looking at things.

I've already spent twenty quid buying up copies of the paper so I can send them to people like Matty and Sarah. Maybe I'll have one framed, like Jenn would have done.

Speaking of frames ... I sold one of my paintings to someone at work. It was just a charity event, and everyone was asked to donate something they'd created. There were a lot of cakes, dried flower displays, wooden ashtrays, knitted dolls and toilet roll covers. And one of my paintings. It wasn't anything big, or worth a lot of money, but it's good to know my work is good enough that other people will pay for it. Maybe I should take part in some of the community galleries I keep reading about.

The best thing is that I know Jenn's behind all of this. The painting that sold was one of the ones I created soon after she started pushing me to paint again. Then Matty rang me up to nervously explain how he'd come to propose to Lucy, and exactly which ring he'd used. He was worried it might upset me. I told him he was being silly. I'd given that ring to Jenn decades before. It stopped being mine the second she'd said yes and I'd slipped it onto her finger. It was up to her what she did with it now.

If I'm honest, I'm glad she did it. I wouldn't have known how to deal with Matty's problem, and I love the fact that even when she couldn't be with me, she was with the children. I'm glad she's still with us all. Sticking her nose in, helping us figure out what's right, and nagging us until we do it. I'm gladder still that the children have finally realised the truth.

I'm not sure how yet, but I'd also bet good money that she was involved in Lottie's photo shoot too.

It's so good to have her in our lives still. She's always brought so much goodness into them. Tomorrow would have been Jenn's birthday. While we can't give her gifts any more, she's clearly found a way to give them to us instead. I love that woman so much.

Tomorrow everyone will be here to celebrate her birthday and remember all the good in her life. And to thank her for all the wonderful things she's given us lately. We'll celebrate Matty and Lucy's engagement, and Lottie's success, and maybe even my painting sale. We'll all remember Jenn together. It's not the typical August we'd usually have had – a break away somewhere that coincided with the school holidays and Jenn's birthday – but it's the one we're having this year.

JENN

Seeing everyone celebrating together was lovely. There were a few moments of sadness, like when they realised they'd put out mint sauce even though I was the only one who ate it, but most of the time it was just happy.

There's so much happiness in my family right now, especially for my children. Lucy is glowing with the excitement of the wedding and Matty's eyes fill with warmth and pride every time he looks at her. I don't think I've seen him this settled and happy since he was young.

Lottie's doing brilliantly too. Since the photo shoot, her career has been going from strength to strength. She's got a lot more bookings and a couple of agencies have contacted her, which is a really big deal. I'm not sure I fully approve of the way Stuart's hand keeps wandering up my daughter's thigh under the table, and the easy intimacy with which he squeezes her leg, but I do approve of the way he looks at her, and the smile in her eyes when she catches his. It's impossible not to feel happy watching my children today.

But there is a shadow over the celebrations. I don't think anyone else has noticed it yet, but David seems out of sorts. It's almost like we're slightly out of sync at the moment.

Most of the time everything seems normal and easy. He seems relaxed and happy, and smiles and joins in with the jokes and laughter of everyone else. He talks to me so easily now that the antidepressants have left his system, and smiles when I wrap around him. I could almost believe that everything's perfect.

But every so often something inside him seems to slip. It's like he snaps away from me and is distracted by some far off sound or thought as his eyes fill with a strange wistfulness I barely recognise. It only lasts for a second or two before everything clicks back to normal. At first it was so quick that I thought I'd imagined it, but now I've seen that blank-eyed, distracted stare at least half a dozen times.

It's so fast I'm sure the children haven't noticed it. They're too wrapped up in their own happiness, as they should be. I'm not even sure David is consciously aware it's happening. But I'm sure of one thing. Something isn't right with my husband.

Chapter Seventeen

DAVID

I've not been feeling quite myself lately. It's like I've got a permanent knot in my stomach. It follows me around everywhere and interferes with everything. Jenn's still with me, of course, but I can't get rid of this feeling that something isn't quite ... right.

It started the week after Jenn's birthday. Although, now I think about it, it could even have been before that, but I was so busy concentrating on her birthday that I didn't let myself think about it.

But now I've got nothing but time to think. There isn't anything I'm really looking forward to right now, or anything I can focus on. Matty and Lucy are planning their wedding, and Lottie's busy with her photography and Stuart, so I see my children less.

The friends who had been trying to jolly me along seem to have stopped bothering, and I'm hearing less and less from old friends. I think the problem is that I don't really have many friends of my own. Jenn and I had lots of friends, but they were our friends, and I'm not part of an "our" any more. I'm just me now.

Besides, I've never been that good at keeping in touch with people. Jenn was always the sociable one who made arrangements and befriended people. She sent out the Christmas cards, remembered birthdays and made the phone calls. I just tagged along.

I feel like this thing that has settled in my stomach is sapping my energy away. I don't feel like I can be bothered with things and I've lost all motivation. Colours are fading out of my world, which is an utterly ridiculous thing to say.

My eyesight is just fine, and I know the colours haven't actually changed. But something has. I feel like I'm on a slope that I'm slowly slipping and sliding down, and I just can't seem to find anything to hold on to.

It all sounds so melodramatic put like that. Completely blown out of proportion. I'm not about to do anything foolish, like jump off a building or bridge. For one thing, I don't like heights. And it's nowhere near as dramatic as it sounds. It's more that I just don't feel quite right.

It's just this nagging feeling that I can't silence any more. I feel like something is missing all the time. I'm sure it's just silliness, but the other day I found myself watching a couple who were walking down the street holding hands. Just holding hands. I felt the knot in my stomach tighten a bit more. How silly is that? To be upset by some random strangers holding hands. But then I realised it's because I don't have anyone I can hold hands with, and I'll never have that ever again.

I miss it. I miss the feeling of a warm, solid hand beneath mine that squeezes back. I miss the comfort of curling up with someone in the evenings, and feeling a warm body and a heart that beats against mine.

Damn it. I miss sex too. I miss the heat and passion of Jenn. I know I shouldn't. I know I'm an old widower and I should be past all that, but I'm not. Jenn and I had a great sex life together, and I miss it. I miss the warmth, closeness, desire and touch. But most of all, I miss the comfort of it, and the way we fitted together so well and so easily. It made me feel like I belonged somewhere. Now that Jenn's gone, I feel like I've lost my anchor in this world.

I don't want her near me right now. I don't want her knowing any of this. It's just too embarrassing. Besides, I'd worry that she'd misunderstand. I still love her and want her near me, but I want more than I can have. I need to stop being greedy and just be grateful that she's still in my life.

Plus Jenn and I are closer now than we've ever been before. I'm not sure I could even have comprehended this level of intimacy last year. She can wrap her consciousness around my mind as easily as she used to twist her fingers through mine. We can share thoughts, emotions and sensations. I love how close we've become, and how it feels to have her wrapped around me. It's the only time I really feel happy. Sometimes I think I could die happily, if only I could spend eternity wrapped in her. But it's just not the same, and, sometimes, I find myself wanting more. I want to smell the warm muskiness of a woman again, and feel silky hair brush against me. I want to feel a soft, yielding body against mine.

I know I'm being stupid and selfish. Jenn's a miracle. Somehow she beat the odds, or the system or whatever, and fought her way back to stay with me. To stay with all of us. I should be more grateful for that. It's not like I've even really given anything up.

But I still miss the physical stuff.

JENN

As if he could ever hide anything from me. Even when I was alive and David could still hide behind words and a smile, he couldn't keep things from me. Now that I can see and feel his thoughts, there are no secrets between us.

The truth is that none of this is new. I've been worried about him for weeks now. David just isn't happy, and I don't think he has been for a while. I thought, or maybe I hoped, it was nothing. Just my imagination and worries colluding to play tricks on me. But now he's realising it too.

I know what the problem is. I think he's lonely. We've shared intimacy far deeper and greater than I could ever have imagined. But it doesn't make up for, or replace, the physical. I think he needs more than half-felt touches and fleeting moments of warmth.

He deserves so much better than what I'm able to give him. He deserves all the things he's thinking about, but feeling bad for. I know he'll hold on to me and keep loving me until his last breath, but I don't know if that's right. I don't think it's fair. I'm the one who died, not him. He shouldn't have to give up living as well. And he shouldn't be feeling guilty for wanting more. He should have joy and pleasure in his life. Maybe even love too.

There's no reason he shouldn't live for another three or four decades. He's fit and healthy enough. Can I really ask the man I love to spend that long alone? Just so my feelings don't get hurt? I don't think I can. Maybe "until death do us part" are wiser words than I thought.

But I don't want to see him with another woman. I don't want to share him with someone else. He's still my husband. It's not as if we got a divorce or chose to separate. We still love each other, and I still want to be with him for every moment he has left. Until we're back together again.

But I don't want him to spend the rest of his years stumbling through life, feeling that something vital is missing. I'm not willing to be the person who holds him back. I can't help worrying that it's only a matter of time before David starts to resent me for all the things that I can't give him, and all the experiences he isn't going to have. Then all this will slip away, and love will become hate, and I'll lose my hold and anchor in this world.

So I have a choice between my husband growing to resent me, or watching him fall in love with another woman and forgetting me. I honestly don't know which is worse.

But the hardest thing is that I don't think this is about me or what I want. I'm already dead and should be gone to a place where there isn't any pain or hurt. The only reason I stayed here was to make sure that my family were all right.

So you see, this can't be about me. It has to be about them. I have to help them move on. It was so easy with Lottie and Matty because all I felt was pride for my grown up babies, and joy and excitement for their achievements and plans.

It's not going to be as easy with David, because what I'm starting to think he needs goes against my every instinct. It's going to hurt like nothing either of us has ever known.

It's a good thing I'm already dead, else I don't think I could survive this much pain.

DAVID

The horrible nagging feelings and knot in my stomach haven't gone away. If anything, they've got worse. I'm not eating properly again. It just makes the knots worse and it's too painful. I'm not painting either. It just seems pointless. All I do is go to work and then come home and sleep. Anything else takes too much effort. Maybe I'm coming down with a virus or something. I want to believe that, because I can't accept this miserableness is coming from within me.

Jenn's been after me to do something for over a week now, but I've been trying to ignore her. At first it was black bags turning up in strange places. The first was folded neatly and peeking out of her top drawer. I pulled it out and chucked it back under the sink with the others, and tried not to think about what it meant. Then they started turning up everywhere her stuff was, poking out of drawers and tumbling from shelves.

I shoved them away harder and tried to ignore them. Jenn's message was crystal clear, but there's no way I was ready to get rid of her things. I know she's probably right, that it's silly to keep everything. She's never going to need any of it ever again, but I still didn't want to get rid of anything. It felt like I would be throwing her out of my life as well, clearing her away like unwanted rubbish, when nothing could be further from the truth. I don't want to get over her. I'm scared that if I do, it will mean I never really loved her.

I kept ignoring the issue and refusing to talk about it, even though I could feel Jenn getting more and more impatient around me. I should have paid more attention. I nearly knocked myself out by walking into a cupboard door she'd opened. But even that wasn't enough to make me start clearing Jenn out of my life.

It took a visit from Lottie to make me see things differently. By the time she'd made it to the kitchen, she had a handful of those awful black bags.

'You know, Dad, maybe you should take the hint. Don't you think it might be time you thought about clearing out a few wardrobes and drawers and stuff? It's been seven months.'

'She was my wife for nearly three decades,' I complained.

'I know, Dad, but do you really think throwing out a few old jumpers and T-shirts will change that?'

'I don't want her to think I'm throwing her out,' I tried to argue.

'But it was her idea,' my daughter pointed out, irritatingly calm and logical. How could she be so unaffected by the thought of throwing her mother out of our lives?

'Dad?' She wrapped her hands around mine and I couldn't help but stare at the zebra striped nails. How did she get the stripes so perfectly even? Why didn't the colours run together and turn to a murky grey?

'This is what Mum wants. Either that or she's after you to take up litter picking. I don't really think it's that, do you? I think she's right. It's time for this.'

Warmth wrapped around us and I found myself nodding

as Jenn's perfume filled the air. 'I know it is. I just really don't want to do this.'

'I know.' Lottie gave me a crooked grin. 'I get that. I'll come over and help, OK? I'm not going to let you do this by yourself.'

I wrapped my arms around her and rested my chin on top of her head. The sad thing is, I think I've hugged her more in the last seven months than I did in the seven years before that.

'Hey, Dad.' I winced as the door slammed and Lottie's voice echoed through the house. I really didn't want to see her today. 'Dad, where are you?'

I studied the paper in front of me and tried to concentrate on the headlines, but the words kept swimming in front of my eyes.

'Dad, didn't you hear me calling?' Lottie grinned and dumped a pile of boxes and bags on the conservatory floor. How could she be so cheerful when she was about to throw away her mother's life?

'Hey. You're here early.'

'Yeah, we've got lots to do.' She stared at me for a few seconds. 'Come on, Dad. I know you're not really reading that paper.' She sighed sadly. 'I'm not looking forward to this any more than you are, but it has to be done.'

'I don't want to get rid of her.' I sounded like a whiney teenager, but I didn't care.

'As if you could.' Lottie pulled a black bag off a shelf and I wondered when Jenn had stuffed it there. I didn't remember seeing it when I got up. 'This is her idea, and she's right. You're never going to be able to move on when you're surrounded by the past.'

'I don't want to move on. I don't want to let her go.'

'Dad, we're talking about clothes and bags and shoes she's

never going to need again. She's the one telling you to clear this stuff out. I don't think she's going to leave us because you empty a few drawers.'

Warmth filled the air and I could feel Jenn in the air behind me. Clearly she agreed.

Five hours later I tied the last bag shut and added it to the pile in the hall. It actually hadn't been as bad as I feared. The first drawer was agonisingly hard. Every top I pulled out seemed to contain a whiff of Jenn's perfume and another memory that was waiting to slam me back into a world where she still existed. I don't think I would have got through it without Lottie's help. She has been brilliant.

In a strange way, it was nice. It felt good to tidy the place up, and there were a lot of happy memories that Lottie and I shared. Things I thought I had forgotten that came rushing back so easily. I just hope they don't fade away again. I don't think they will because now I know how precious they are, so I'll hold on to them more tightly.

I folded away the last thing I couldn't bear to part with – a silky black dress that Jenn had always looked fantastic in – and grabbed the final box to take downstairs.

'No, not this one.' Lottie tugged it from my hands. 'This one's mine, if that's OK.'

'What on earth, Lottie?' I stared at the pile of stuff overflowing her box. 'You're supposed to be clearing this stuff out, not just moving it to your place. You don't even have room for all this.'

'I don't care.' Lottie shrugged. 'I just need it.'

'If it's not healthy for me to keep this stuff, it really isn't for you.' I spotted a familiar bit of fabric. 'This tablecloth is ruined, what can you possibly want it for?'

'It's only a little stain.'

'Right in the middle.'

'I don't care.' My daughter snatched the bundle of checked blue and yellow fabric back and carefully smoothed the creases out of it. 'I really want this stuff, Dad. Just ... please don't ask me why, all right?'

I stared at the odd mix of things she'd picked out and shrugged. If it meant that much to her, she could take them.

JENN

It's painful watching people pick through your life and throw it away, even if it is your husband and daughter doing it at your request. But it needed to be done. David's been hanging on to things far too fiercely. It isn't healthy to live so much in the past, and I think that's why he's been feeling so down lately. So this had to be done. No matter how much it hurts me.

It was hard on them too. I could see David's fingers shaking as he reached for the first drawer. He sighed sadly and stared at our faded wedding photo sitting on top of the drawers. I wrapped warmth and reassurance around him, and nudged him gently.

I promised myself that I wasn't going to let any of my family waste their lives by living in the past and staying trapped in their grief. For David that meant doing this. As much as this was hurting him and Lottie, clearing out my clothes was the first step David needed to take in moving on. Even though he didn't believe it, I knew he was ready to make this step.

But still, it was hard watching them do it. I thought I'd reached the point where I was getting used to seeing sadness on their faces, but I don't think there is anything that could ever make me immune to the grim sorrow on Lottie's face. She tried to smile and reassure her dad, but the sentiment never reached her eyes. I thought she was going to cry when she pulled out the first top, but she straightened her shoulders and shoved it firmly into a bag.

My heart swelled with pride as I watched her help her dad through the first, hardest steps. Their faces stayed grim, and every so often one of them would pull out a skirt or scarf or jacket that triggered a memory, and tears or smiles would chase across their faces.

It's always horrible watching the people you love cry, but it got better as they finished the drawers and moved on to my wardrobes. There was less sadness in the air, and more smiles at fond memories that flashed into their minds as they sorted through my clothes.

If anything, it felt cathartic.

I was worried about Lottie, so I followed her home. As well as the box she'd taken from her dad, there were another two bags of my things. And she was acting very strangely. She waited until her flatmate had gone out for the evening before fetching the stuff in from her car. She emptied everything out all over the floor, and poured herself a huge glass of wine before settling down in the middle of the piles of fabric.

She took a much too large a gulp of wine and stared around at the bundles sadly. She fingered a soft-looking corner of green fluff. Was that my other dressing gown? She'd already claimed my purple one as her own, so why did she need the other? What on earth was she up to? I watched as she squared her shoulders and picked up an old yellow apron that was dotted with tiny purple flowers. She buried her face in it for a few seconds, then smiled.

'Mum? Are you here?'

Of course I am, Lottie. As if I wouldn't be. I wafted perfume around her to let her know I was listening.

She smiled gently. 'I'd hoped you'd be here. I guess this means Dad is OK?'

I added warmth to the air and wrapped my arms around her shoulders to answer her question. She shivered slightly and smiled as some of the fabric stirred around her feet.

'You know, I remember you taught me how to bake wearing this. I wonder how many dozens of birthday cakes this old apron has seen, and how many thousands of biscuits and scones it's baked over the years.'

More than I can count. I smiled as I remembered Lottie perched on top of the worktop as a little girl, covered in flour and happily thumping away at whatever dough I was making. Even when she'd been older she'd often joined me in the kitchen, taking her frustrations out on the dough while telling me all the things that were bothering her. So many of our deepest conversations involved being covered in flour. Problems at school, with boys. She'd first asked me about sex halfway through a batch of shortbread. That batch had come out of the oven rock-hard, but we'd been stronger for it. It was usually that way. The tougher the bread or whatever else we'd been making, the stronger our relationship had been. I'd even come to like the rock-hard scones and bread that had to be choked down with huge mugs of tea.

So what are you up to? I tried to ask her the question, but struggled to get the words out. It's easier to communicate now that I can move more things, but I still can't talk to Lottie or Matty as clearly as I can their dad. I guess maybe that's just how these things work. I tugged at the apron between my daughter's fingers.

'I guess you're wondering what I'm doing with all this stuff.'

Who needed words when they're blessed with a daughter this smart and perceptive? She folded the apron carefully and dropped it back into the box. 'Well I'm not telling you. If it works, it's going to be a lovely surprise, and if it doesn't, well no one will be disappointed if they never knew about it in the first place.' She smiled as she pulled out a red gypsy skirt, swirling with paisley patterns. 'Some of my favourite photos I took of you were when you were wearing this skirt. That Easter, when you came to stay with me at uni. Do you remember?'

Of course I did. I looked around the heaps of my old things, and realised what they represented. Here was the grey stripy cardigan I used to wear in the evenings when marking work, and there was the snuggly green dressing gown I wore for half of most Sundays, cooking breakfast and then reading the papers lazily. The bundle of blue and yellow was the tablecloth we'd used on birthdays, and Christmas, and any other time we'd got together, just to make it a bit more special and cheerful. It was the same one that had recently always had a vase of flowers on, to hide the stain in the middle from melted birthday cake candles.

She'd hoarded my embroidered denim jacket, seven or eight scarves, my favourite velvet evening jacket, and the grey suit I'd always worn when I needed to feel smart and business-like. There were other skirts and tops, the green lace dress I must have worn to half a dozen weddings and family events in the last few years, and the dip-dyed sarong I'd bought on our last family holiday together. I hadn't even realised I still owned that. I definitely didn't own the swimsuit I'd worn with it. That had long ago been thrown in the bin with a pile of other age inappropriate clothes.

Lottie hadn't picked randomly. Every item she had spread out across the floor carried its own special memories and emotions. I wondered what she had planned for them all.

The evening got even odder when her phone beeped at around eleven. I peered over her shoulder as her fingers clicked over the glowing screen, typing out her address.

Ten minutes later there was a quiet knock at the door,

and Lottie opened it to reveal a petite, pretty blonde girl. She offered a grin and her hand. 'You must be Lottie. Stu's told me a lot about you.'

'Ditto.' Lottie shook her hand easily. 'Do you want to come in for a drink?'

'Thanks, but no. Last train goes in half an hour. If I'm not on that I'll be sofa surfing tonight, and I could really use my own bed. It's been a long week.'

'They all seem to be lately.' Lottie smiled sympathetically. 'But I'd rather be busy and tired than bored and broke. I've got everything ready.' She beckoned the girl into the living room. 'Do you think you've got enough?'

The girl bent down and ran her fingers through the pile of things Lottie had folded neatly into the box. I wanted to scream at her to stop touching my stuff. 'Yeah, should be.' She shivered slightly. 'It's cold tonight.'

Lottie ignored the comment, but I saw her jaw clench slightly. Handing over my things to this stranger seemed to hurt her too.

'There are a few more bits in this bag, but the stuff in the box is the most important.' She paused. 'It's a hundred and fifty each, right?'

'Yup.' The girl squeezed Lottie's fingers briefly. 'It might take a while. Maybe even a couple of months. I really only do these in my free time at the moment, but I promise I'll make them good.'

'I know.' Lottie nodded.

'Tell Stu I'm sorry I missed him, and I'll give him a call soon.'

'Will do. Talk to you in a few weeks.' Lottie shut the door tightly behind the girl, and locked up for the night. 'Don't be annoyed with me, Mum.' She leaned her head against the wall and whispered the words to me. 'I've done this for a reason. I just hope they come out well.'

Chapter Eighteen

DAVID

It feels very odd to be in our house without Jenn's stuff. You wouldn't think that emptying a few wardrobes and giving away books and DVDs that we'll never use again would make that much difference. But it does. It's changed the feel of the house. The gaps on the bookshelves seem to resonate their emptiness throughout the room. I did think about putting a plant or something in them, but it would only highlight the gaps, and all the things that are missing in my life.

Besides, even if the plants did work, it wouldn't solve the problem of the wardrobes. Even when the doors are closed, I can still feel their emptiness. I'm trying not to think about it, because when I do the emptiness seems to grow and the knot in my stomach becomes tighter.

So instead I've been focussing on the children. I've been trying to get involved in Matty's wedding, but beyond suggesting a few guests, supplying addresses and donating some money to the day, there's not much I can do.

I've been able to help Lottie a little more, but that's not been a great success either. She's been having problems with her flat. Seems that, despite the contract they've got, her landlord wants to sell the place. Lottie and her housemate are going to have to move out quickly. I've been scouring the local papers and visiting estate agents to try and help her find a new place. It's hard work, especially in London. She really wants to stay in the city, but everything in her price range is grim and depressing, or in horrible, unsafe places that I really don't want my daughter living in.

In a way I'm grateful for Lottie's problems. Not because

I want her to be in difficulties, because I never would, but because it gives me something else to think about. It's a genuine, legitimate problem that needs my attention. Even though it's proving to be difficult to resolve, I can fix this. I can find a flat Lottie will like. It's difficult, especially in her budget, but not impossible. And it means I don't have to think about the emptiness that's echoing through the house and making it feel less like my home than it has in decades.

If I'm completely honest, I think Jenn's as relieved as I am to have something else to focus on.

CHARLOTTE

I collapsed tiredly on Stu's couch and gratefully accepted a mug full of steaming tea. 'You really do know how to look after a girl.'

'Part of my charm.' He grinned. 'Shift over, Jasper. You're not the only one who hasn't seen her all week.'

I groaned and covered my face. 'I'm sorry. Between photo shoots and editing and all the time I spend travelling back and forth, I barely have time to scratch. Any spare time I've got I've been spending at the estate agents. I'm so tired I can hardly think right now.'

'So your landlord's definitely selling the place?'

'Yeah. He's given us till the end of next month to get out.'

'How's the search going?'

'Rubbish. Everything's so expensive. I'm half tempted to move back in with Dad. At least I wouldn't have to pay rent then. I could concentrate on getting my name out there, and making sure the jobs I do get are completed perfectly.' I snuggled deeper into the sofa.

'You can't really move back in with your dad.'

'I know.' Jasper whined in sympathy and I rubbed his ears. 'I love my dad, but we're better off not living together.

Even Mum couldn't always keep the peace between us in recent years.'

'So what are you going to do?'

'I'll take one of the more expensive flats. I'll just have to get a part-time job at a bar or something.'

'I'll never see you if you're working at night,' Stu grumbled.

'Maybe a shop then.'

'Won't tie in too well with being an on-call photographer.'

'Well what am I supposed to do? I've got to do something,' I snapped. 'What are you smiling at? Are you even listening to me?'

'You're cute when you get wound up. Did I ever tell you that?' Stu grinned at me. 'Oh, and I bought you a present.'

I melted as he produced a small purple box tied with a huge silver ribbon. He was such a sweetheart. I rattled the box and bit my lip as something thumped heavily inside. Stu's arm slid around my shoulders and he nuzzled against the back of my neck.

'What's this for?'

'I thought it might cheer you up. You've been so stressed lately. Besides, do I need a reason to buy my girlfriend a present?' His breath was warm against my skin, and my stomach flipped as his lips tickled my neck. I relaxed back against him and let some of the worries pour out of me.

'Well, are you going to open it?'

'Yes.' I yanked the ribbon off, my fingers clumsy and trembling with excitement. I had no idea what it was, but if it was from Stu it was bound to be interesting. I peered beneath the lid and felt my heart sink. Nestled in a pile of tissue paper was what looked like a short, stubby, purple screwdriver handle.

'Do you like it?'

'I'm not sure. What is it? It looks like a screwdriver that's missing the screw bit.'

'Not missing.' He took the thing from me and twisted the end off. 'They're all stored in here, and each bit has two ends. It's like a dozen screwdrivers in one. And it's the right colour, isn't it?'

'Yeah. Purple's my favourite.' I fiddled with the screwdriver and tried to feel excited about it. I guess it was flattering, and thoughtful. Clearly Stu saw me as a practical, capable woman rather than some silly, fluffy thing who needed sparkly presents to hold her attention. 'Thank you.' I gave him a weak smile.

'So you like it?' His face was as eager and excited as Jasper's when someone said a certain W word.

'Umm … yeah.' I was confused. Stu seemed really pleased with himself over a tool. Overly so.

'Good. Because you're going to have to use it a lot.'

'I am?'

'Yeah.' Stu took my hands in his. 'The thing is, I've got a confession to make.'

'Really?' I watched him warily.

'Yeah. It's a bit embarrassing really. I've never really told a girl this before.'

'You can tell me anything.' Just please don't let this be some weird sex thing. I braced myself mentally.

'I'm really, really bad at putting together flat-pack furniture.'

'What?' I laughed with relief.

'Flat-pack furniture. You know, like the stuff you get from catalogues?'

I nodded, still confused.

'Well, I suck at putting it together. I mean I really, really suck at it. I just struggle to see how the pieces fit. I hoped you'd do better, being creative like you are.'

'I … guess I'm all right at it.' I shook my head.

'Brilliant.' Stu's face lit up in a grin and he grabbed my hand. I followed him to his spare room and peered around the door. The tiny room had been cleared of its usual random collection of junk and drying clothes, and instead was filled with boxes that had barcodes and heavy lifting warnings all over them.

Stu wrapped his arms around my waist from behind and rested his chin on my shoulder. 'There's a wardrobe, some more shelves, and another set of drawers. They should match the desk under the pile of CDs and books in the corner. It's not much, but you'd have your own space, and I think we could fit another chest of drawers in the bedroom.' He spun me round to face him. 'So what do you think?' His eyes filled with laughter, distracting me.

'Well, it's about time you tidied up. I always thought it was a bit wasteful to have a room filled with junk in a place this small.' Stu grinned at me again. Why did he look so pleased with himself? My mushy, overtired brain finally caught up with the conversation. My own space? 'Oh my God, Stu is this …' I took a deep breath. 'Is this for me?'

'And she finally gets it.' He rolled his eyes. 'Yes, this is for you, if you want it.' He brushed my hair back out of my eyes and tucked it behind my ear. 'Move in with me Lottie.'

'Are you serious?'

'Serious enough to trek all the way to the store, buy this lot and drag it all back here. So, what do you say?'

I desperately wanted to say yes, but it was so fast. I'd never even thought about getting this serious with a guy before, and here was one I really liked asking me to move in with him. I chewed the edge of my thumbnail, playing for time. 'It's a bit further out than I'd been looking at.'

'True, but you know the tube station is nearby, and it's

really only forty minutes or so for you to get back into the city, if you need it for work. If you get more fashion and newspaper shoots, which you will, because you're amazing. And forty minutes is much less time than you'd spend in the bar job you'd need to work in order to pay for a more expensive flat you won't even like. What do you say, Lottie – do you want to move in with me?'

'I don't know,' I whispered. 'What if it doesn't work out?'

'Well, then you'd be in the same position as you are now, and you just move in with your dad anyway. But Lottie?' His eyes glinted wickedly and I felt tingles race through me. 'What if it does work out? It might. And just imagine how much fun it's going to be finding out ...' He teased his lips down my neck and my knees went weak. 'So, what do you think?'

I struggled to concentrate while his fingers wandered over my back, tracing along the bare skin at the edge of my top. What did I think? I didn't know if I was ready to move in with a guy. I was only just starting my career, and I had no idea where it was going to take me. With any luck, it'd be halfway round the world and back. That wasn't exactly the best thing for a relationship. I hadn't really planned on getting serious with anyone until after I'd made my name. But then again, Stu's sweet and kind, and he makes my toes curl. Oh stuff it.

'Yes!' I covered his face in kisses. 'You're a genius. You're brilliant, you're wonderful, and kind and thoughtful and handsome.'

He pressed his nose tightly against mine, and the next words came out in a low, throaty growl. 'You're pretty damn brilliant yourself, Lottie Hughes.'

I wrapped my arms around him tightly as he kissed me thoroughly, and dragged me down to the floor. Oddly I didn't feel even a little bit tired any more.

It's taken me longer than I want to admit, but I've come to understand that David just isn't happy by himself. He's lonely, and the loneliness is seeping into every part of his life and making him depressed.

The only time he's really happy is when he's with the children, and that's not fair on them. They love their dad enough that they're ruining their own lives trying to look after him. They should both be happy and able to relax and enjoy the special moments in their lives. Matty's busy planning his future, and Lottie's in the first, exciting flush of a new relationship with someone who really cares about her. They shouldn't be worrying about their dad so much that it ruins everything for them.

So I have to look after David. It's appropriate really, he's still my husband and I promised to always love and protect him, in sickness and in health. That definitely has to cover this.

I've been trying to avoid thinking about this. I've been concentrating on making sure the children are all right, and now they are, I have nothing else to focus on. I'm all out of excuses. So I've had to think about David and face the truth of what's happening. It's agonising, because I've been forced to accept that David needs something to concentrate on. Something that will inspire him and motivate him to get up and enjoy life again. His painting just isn't enough to do that.

I've realised what David really needs is someone in his life, not to do these things for him, but to make him want to do them for himself. He needs someone else in his life.

Oh my God, it's so painful though. I know this is what's best for David with every part of my being. I love him desperately so I want to do what's right for him, but it hurts so much. If I could still breathe I'd choke on the pain. It's all-consuming to the point that it numbs my thoughts every time I try to consider it. I feel sick when I think about David with another woman.

There's never really been anyone else for either of us. We spent our whole adult lives together. I spent more of my life with David than I didn't. And now I'm trying to think about him being with someone who isn't me. Just thinking about it in the abstract, without any real people involved, hurts. But I have to think about this, because I have to do what's best for David. No matter how much it hurts and disgusts me.

I think I've done it. I think I've found her. It's the strangest thing to try and pick a new woman for your husband, but I know he's never going to do it for himself. He's too committed to me, even though I know I can't give him what he needs any more.

I found myself being really critical as I tried to find this perfect replacement for me. She couldn't be too bossy or controlling, because he wouldn't like that. I knew he'd never be attracted to someone who was obsessed with popular culture and which celebrity was doing what. She had to be firmly grounded in the real world. And she couldn't be someone who spends hours getting ready and messing with her hair and make-up and clothes – we used to laugh at women like that. Whoever she was, she should be someone who's just as happy in trainers as in high heels. And she had to be at least vaguely open to the idea of life after death.

The list went on for ages, but I think I've done it. I think I've found the perfect woman for David. She's clever and kind and sweet. Pretty too, but not in the vain way that would irritate my husband.

She also has a pulse, which gives her a massive advantage over me.

But I've promised myself I'm not going to think like that. I'm not going to focus on the unfairness of this whole situation, because the only thing that lies in that direction is misery and bitterness. Besides, it's hard not to like this woman. She's down to earth and easy going, and even though she's seen a lot of sadness in her life, she's still quick to smile and likes to laugh. And she's lonely too, although she's too proud to admit it except to herself at three o'clock in the morning when she's unable to sleep for the emptiness in her bed.

I think she might need someone like David as much as he needs someone like her. It really could be the perfect match. All I need to do is give them a couple of gentle nudges to make sure their paths cross. Then I can step back and see if I'm right, and whether nature and attraction will take their course. I won't interfere beyond that first introduction. As much as David needs – and deserves – to have someone in his life, I won't force anything. It has to be his choice. But I do think he'll like her almost as soon as he meets her.

It's actually going to be incredibly easy to arrange that. A water leak and overflowing drain in one road will detour her from her usual route and straight into David's path. Then all I have to do is make sure they notice each other. That's all I'm going to do. Once they've met, nature has to take over and do the rest.

Chapter Nineteen

Autumn

RUTH

Bloody roadworks. They must have hit a water pipe or something, because the route I was going to take to my next appointment looks more like a stream than a road. It was closed to traffic, so I had to detour. I thought I knew roughly where I was, but it wasn't my area, and nothing really looked all that familiar. I was at the bottom of a hill, and I couldn't really remember any hills in the area.

I was lost and running late, and I hate being late. It's one of my pet peeves – people not turning up on time – but with my patients it seems beyond rude. It's not as if they have the time to waste like other people do. If I called the office, there was a chance Mike might be able to get to Mr Blakeley's sooner than I could. He wouldn't have to get through the traffic I'd been trying to navigate.

I glanced down at the clock, trying to work out how much time I was losing, when I saw the flash in my mirror of another car approaching far too quickly. Time jerked into slow motion and my breath caught in my throat. I had nowhere to go.

The sickening crunch echoed through my car and made my bones creak as I jolted forward and was snapped back by my seatbelt. At first, all I could think was *ouch*, and a few really choice phrases about idiot drivers. My shoulder and hip ached where the seatbelt had grabbed me, trying to keep me from harm.

Then my training kicked in. Yes my shoulder throbbed,

but it didn't feel any worse than a bad jar, and I didn't think I'd damaged my collar bone past bruising from the seatbelt. All in all, I'd been pretty lucky.

I climbed out of the car with a wince and went to check on the other driver. Before I reached the window I could already make out panicked mumbles.

The other driver was a man, and he was fighting against his airbag with bloody hands, while moaning what sounded like prayers. He was begging God to not let something happen again. He was half-dazed and starting to panic.

'Are you all right?' I peered through the window. 'Can you move? Where are you hurt?'

'Umm ...' His voice was choked and his eyes were watery, and his face was smeared with blood. The airbag must have deployed with enough force to snap his hand back into his own nose.

I yanked the door open. 'Look at me. Are you all right?'

His eyes snapped into focus. 'Umm ... yes, I think so.'

'Can you move?'

'Probably.' He tried to stem the blood from his nose with his fingers. 'I'm so sorry about this. It's all my fault.'

'Worry about that later. I need to get something from my car. Are you all right to wait here?' I didn't want him slipping into panic again.

'Yeah.'

'Sure?'

'I'm fine.' He started to move.

I pushed him gently back against the seat. 'Just sit still for a minute.'

I grabbed the keys from my ignition and tried to open the boot. Come on, I wiggled the keys and yanked at the lid, but all I managed to do was break a nail. Bugger. I flung the back door open, and briefly turned back to the guy who'd hit me. 'Just a minute.' I flashed him what I hoped was a reassuring smile before clambering into the back of my car, hitting the release button for the back seat and folding it down flat. I wriggled halfway through the gap, groping blindly until my fingers closed around the handle of my work bag.

I snapped the latex gloves on with the ease that you only get after years of practice and turned back to the other driver. 'Right, let's get you sorted.'

'Do you do this often?' He eyed me nervously.

'What? Drive around with a full medical kit in case some guy runs into me and breaks his nose? More often than you'd think.' I grinned at his confusion. At least he seemed calm now. 'I'm a nurse.' I pressed a wad of gauze gently to his nose. 'Hold this here.'

'Thanks.'

'Don't thank me yet. This next bit might hurt.' I eased my fingers over the bridge of his nose gently. He grimaced, but stayed still as my fingers felt across his cheeks and checked the rest of the bones in his face. When he opened his eyes, I was shocked by how dark a brown they were against the smeared blood.

'Fingers.' I positioned them on his nose. 'Squeeze here and lean forward a bit. Once it stops bleeding we can get you out.' I picked up his other hand in mine and gently fingered the knuckles.

'Well, what do you think?'

'It doesn't look like you've broken any bones. I don't think you'll need anything more than a quick clean, some ice and painkillers.'

'Good. Thanks for this.'

'Don't worry about it.' I leant back against the open door. 'Like I said, this is what I do. But legally, I should tell you to go to the hospital and get your face and hand X-rayed by someone who can officially rule out any breaks.'

He shrugged and flexed his fingers. 'I think I'll trust your judgement on this one. But shouldn't I be leaning back? Isn't that what you do with nosebleeds?'

I shook my head. Why do people always think that? 'I thought you were trusting me? Do you want to choke on your own blood?'

'No, not really.'

'Then stay put.'

'All right.' He nodded. 'Not that I'm complaining, but shouldn't you be yelling at me and demanding insurance details by now?'

'I suppose I should, but I don't think you're in any condition to run away right now. Besides, yelling at you while you're still bleeding seems a bit unfair. It's not like you hit me on purpose, is it? It's just a stupid accident, why make it anything more than that?'

His face paled and blood started to drip over his fingers again as he lost his grip.

'Are you all right? Are you feeling dizzy?' I grabbed his wrist, but his pulse was strong and steady beneath my fingers. 'Did you hit your head?'

'No, no, I'm all right.' He waved away my concern. 'It's just ...'

'Just?'

'Bad memories.' He took a shaky breath. 'I was in a ... bad accident at New Year. I think this has freaked me out a bit.'

'Oh, well this one wasn't too bad. Come on, let's get you out. Then we can try and fix this whole mess.' Once he was out of the car and perched on the bonnet, I had a chance to properly look at my car. He'd managed to hit me on the corner and had caved in the wheel arch and part of the back. No wonder the boot hadn't opened.

His car looked worse. The bumper was half hanging off the front, at least one of the lights was broken and the bent metal looked like it was digging against the wheel. Looking at the damage, and the glass glittering on the floor, I realised how lucky we'd both been. It could easily have been much, much worse.

I flashed the guy another reassuring smile. It wasn't too bad, and he seemed shaken up. 'Not too bad. What do you think happened? Were you distracted or something?'

'No. I definitely hit the brake.' He looked confused. 'It seemed to jam. I don't know what happened. The brakes were working fine before.' He started to move, but I stopped him.

'Bad idea. You should avoid bending down too much for a few hours. Keep the pressure on your nose. I'll have a look.' I leant back into his car and twisted to reach into the footwell. After a few seconds my hand brushed against something round and papery. What on earth?

'Umm, I think I've found the problem.' I held it up. 'It's a bulb of some sort.'

He murmured something I couldn't make out, then cleared his throat and tried again. 'Daffodil. It's a daffodil bulb.' A smile crept across his face and he started to laugh, but he winced and stopped almost immediately.

'Yeah, things like that are going to hurt for a bit.' I wondered what the daffodil bulb meant to him and why, of all things, it would make him laugh now.

'I really am sorry about this.' He took the bulb from me, and I couldn't help noticing the way his thumb stroked it gently. 'I guess this is where we exchange insurance details and stuff?'

'Yeah. I guess it is.' I dug a pen and pad out of my work bag and scribbled down my details.

He peered at it before holding out a hand. 'Hello Ruth Newlyn, I'm David.'

'Hey.' I smiled back at him. 'Nice to meet you.'

Oh, I really hadn't meant to hurt David. I'd never deliberately hurt him. I just hadn't realised he would hit her so hard. I feel terrible about it.

But if I'm completely honest, I can't help smiling just a little bit. David's not really hurt badly, he's just a bit battered and bruised. Everything is working out even better than I had planned. My car, well David's now, is in a pretty bad way. Some other drivers pulled over and helped him to move it to the side of the road, but it was nowhere near drivable.

Ruth made a couple of quick calls, and stayed with him until the tow truck arrived. She'd said that it was her medical duty, and she couldn't leave David while he was still upset, but I'd like to think it was more than that.

They chatted for the hour that it took for the tow truck to turn up, and Ruth gently helped him wipe the blood from his face until he looked almost normal again, apart from the swelling. She was really kind, and sweet. If I'd met her under any other circumstances, we might have become friends. But even though this was all my idea, and she made David smile, I'm struggling to like her.

I'm still David's wife, and seeing him laughing and smiling with another woman like this hurts. Even if it is what he really needs and what's best for him. Even though I'm the one who introduced them, I struggle not to see Ruth as something of a threat. I know I shouldn't think of her that way, but I find it really hard not to.

When the car had finally been loaded up, Ruth waved David off with a smile. She's going to call him at the weekend. Allegedly it's so she can let him decide whether or not to go through the insurance companies once she's got an estimate from her garage. But looking at the damage I caused to both cars, there's no way it isn't an insurance job. There must be a couple of thousand pounds worth of damage at least. But that is what insurance is for.

If I'm right about this woman, she's more than worth the excess and any change in the premium.

I just hope David's not too upset with me.

DAVID

I slammed the door so hard the windows rattled. What the hell was Jenn playing at? What she did was stupid and dangerous and pointless.

I slammed the daffodil bulb that had nearly killed me down on the kitchen table and winced as pain shot through my hand. Was that the point? Had Jenn actually been trying to kill me?

Shock shivered through the air around me. No, she hadn't been trying to kill me. I knew that. I collapsed into a chair as sorrow filled the air. I guess even ghosts can make mistakes. She hadn't realised how much speed I was going to pick up coming down the hill, and in fairness, if I hadn't had my arm across the middle of the steering wheel, the airbag would never have hit me with enough force to do the damage it did.

With Jenn humming in the air around me, I remembered what I'd always known. She'd never deliberately hurt me. She just didn't have it in her.

'So what the hell were you trying to do? I know it was you, Jenn. I felt you in the car just before that thing ...' I glared at the bulb, 'jammed under my brake pedal.'

She stayed quiet, refusing to answer me. The feeling in the air changed, and for a moment I could have sworn it felt like regret.

'Come on, Jenn. You owe me an answer.' My patience snapped when she still stayed silent. 'Have you any idea how horrible that was for me? I felt like it was the accident all over again. I thought I'd lost you again.'

Sorrow and warmth flooded me, and I felt like an idiot. Of course she knew how I'd felt. She'd been with me the whole time. Both times. Jenn understood the pain and terror of being in a car crash better than anyone, me included. It must have been agonising for her to stay in the car beside me, surrounded by my fear and her memories, but she had stayed with me.

She moved in closer and filled me with warmth and a sense of love and peace so deep that the throbbing pain in my hand and nose disappeared. I couldn't help but smile.

'I know you didn't mean to hurt me, and I know you're sorry, but I still don't understand why you did it. What was the point, Jenn? Why did you take such a crazy risk?'

My wallet thumped to the floor and the scrap of paper with Ruth's number scribbled on it fluttered across the floor, accompanied by one of Jenn's white feathers. I stooped to pick them both up and smoothed the number flat.

'I don't understand. This is just the details of the woman I hit. She wasn't hurt, but you should already know that.'

If Jenn had an explanation, she didn't share it with me.

I stared at the words and numbers that curved across the paper and wondered what they were supposed to mean to me. I tried to find some hidden meaning in them, something that would explain Jenn's actions, but it was nothing more than a name, address and phone number. After a minute or so I came to the conclusion that it didn't represent anything other than a way to get in contact with someone. I gave up and shoved it back in my wallet.

'I don't know what this is all about, Jenn, but I'm not interested in riddles right now. I just want to relax with you, and forget this day ever happened. Is that all right?'

The air around me shimmered and blurred as Jenn wrapped around me and slid into my consciousness. Peace washed through me, and the tension in my back and shoulders melted away.

'Thank you.' I crossed my arms with a happy sigh and stared at the bookcase. 'The daffodil bulb was a nice touch.'

Her laughter echoed through the air. Why is it I can always feel what she does and hear her laughter and tears, but never her voice?

I miss hearing her voice. I miss her.

JENN

Oh good God, I think I've made a terrible mistake. I don't think I can do this. What was I thinking? Why did I start this chain of events? David's my husband. We're supposed to be together forever. That's what we promised each other. It feels so right when we're together. It's so easy and natural. Even like this. Neither of us has ever been happier than when we're wrapped up in each others' thoughts and feelings.

I don't want this to change. I don't want us to change.

Oh my God, what have I done? I've found this perfect, wonderful woman and I introduced her to my husband. What the hell was I thinking? She's going to call once she's had a chance to get a quote on her car.

It would be so easy for them to change each others' lives forever. All it would take is a tiny spark, one single moment of heated intensity, and things would never be the same again. I can already see how it could happen. The conversations to sort this mess I've made would become more than just that. Maybe a few jokes when they discover they share the same sense of humour, and then they'll talk more and discover they actually have a lot in common. They'll develop a friendship and then notice the spark between them, and then they'll be more than "just" friends.

It could all happen so easily. All because of a burst water pipe and a daffodil bulb I nudged under a brake pedal.

Oh, I don't want her to call. I don't want her and David to talk and become friends. I don't want them to notice the spark. I'm jealous just thinking about it and, if I'm honest, I'm scared as well.

What happens to me if I'm right? What happens if there is a spark between them, and they fall in love?

Without David here, loving me and grounding me in his world, what will happen to me? Will I just fade away into nothingness, or be forced to move on before I'm ready? It all sounds so silly. Why should anyone be afraid of paradise? But the truth is, we're all afraid of change. No one ever really wants to die, and this feels the same.

In a way it shouldn't really matter. I'm already dead. I'm not sure I'm even supposed to be here. As long as David is happy, that should be all that matters. I'm just not sure if it is.

I thought life was complicated, but it has nothing on death.

Chapter Twenty

DAVID

Ruth rang this morning. She was highly apologetic because she hadn't managed to get her car to a garage for an estimate yet. She'd been working longer shifts at work to cover leave and sickness, and she'd been struggling to find the time.

I told her it didn't matter. The work on my car was going to run into the thousands, so I would definitely be putting a claim in. At first the company tried to say that it wasn't worth repairing, but it was a good car with low mileage, so I'd managed to argue the case with them. I have to admit I was hugely relieved. I didn't want to get rid of Jenn's car yet.

It was nice talking to Ruth, though. The funny thing was she seemed more interested in asking how I was feeling than blaming me for the accident. She kept apologising for the inconvenience she thought she'd caused by not getting an estimate on her car yet.

'The guys at my garage are really good,' she'd told me cheerfully. 'If I drive my car up there, they'll have a look at it for me while I wait.'

'They sound better than mine. Who do you use?'

'The ones round the back of the old river industrial estate.'

'That's the middle of nowhere,' I complained on her behalf.

'Which is half the reason I've not been able to get the car there. I need my car for work, and anyone I'd usually ask for a lift is already on double shifts too.'

'I'll give you a lift.' The words slipped out before I could stop them, and I wished I could take them back. Why had I just said that? Idiot.

'Your car looked worse than mine.' She laughed and the sound was contagious even down the phone line.

'It is worse. It's going to take a week just to get the parts in, so I've got a hire car. Turned up yesterday. I wouldn't have thought this situation could get any more embarrassing, until that thing arrived.'

'Really?' Ruth sounded like she was trying not to laugh.

'Yeah. It's one of those tiny little things that looks like a normal car with its back end cut off. And as if that wasn't bad enough, it's bright orange.'

'It can't be that bad.'

'Oh it can.' I laughed. 'It practically glows in the dark and is covered in adverts. I'm driving a luminescent orange billboard.'

Ruth laughed again. 'So what are you up to today?' Her question caught us both off guard. 'I'm sorry, it's none of my business. I only called to let you know I hadn't had time to get to my garage yet.'

'It's all right.' I shrugged. 'I had contemplated going shopping to fill up the fridge, but I don't think I can handle the thought of being seen driving the glow-in-the-dark orange on wheels. Besides, now I'm waiting to see if you're going to accept my offer of a lift.'

'I really don't need a lift. I can just take my car up there and wait while they look at it.'

'How long will that take?' I already knew the answer.

'Just a few hours.'

'It doesn't seem fair you wasting half your day off waiting for your car to be checked over. Especially when it's my fault,' I argued. 'How about I meet you up there and run you back to town. It won't take that long.'

'And how will I get back?' she asked.

'I'll drop you back when it's ready.' The answer seemed obvious to me.

'If you're sure ...' Ruth still didn't sound convinced.

'I am. In fact I insist. It's the least I can do. If you can manage the embarrassment of my loan car, that is.'

'I think I can probably handle it.' She laughed.

I pulled up to the garage almost at the same time Ruth pulled up in her battered car. I winced again when I saw the state of the bumper. She waved at me through the window, and a few seconds later the door opened and a pair of green, high heeled sandals dropped to the floor, followed by feet that were bare apart from pink painted toenails, and long, lean, tanned legs. How had I missed those legs before?

She wriggled her toes into the sandals, and stood and stretched luxuriously in the sunshine, and for a second I was treated to a tantalising glimpse of tanned stomach as her T-shirt rode up a few inches. I gulped. Bloody hell she was good looking. Pain swamped me almost before I'd finished the thought. How could I be so disloyal to Jenn? I shook the thought off and climbed out of my giant orange mockery of a car as Ruth disappeared into the garage. By the time she reappeared, I'd got myself back under control.

'Hey.' Ruth sauntered over and peered at me from over the top of her sunglasses, and something stirred in my stomach. She was really pretty. 'Thanks for doing this.'

'You're welcome.' I smiled at her as I opened the car door, and peered down at the shoes she'd just put on, wondering again how women walked balanced on such precariously looking heels. 'So, do you often drive barefoot?'

'Yep.' She grinned. 'I love my heels, but I can't drive in them. And I'm too scatty to remember to leave flats in my car. I spend my working life in sensible shoes, so enjoy these when I can. Why?'

'Just wondering. So where do you want to go?'

'Well, if you drop me off in town, I thought I'd wander around the market for a bit.'

'Sounds good. I could do with picking up a few bits myself.'

'Well, then I guess we'll do that, and then I could buy you a cup of coffee to thank you for the lift. Unless you've got other plans.'

'Make it a drink in a pub garden and you've got yourself a deal. It's too nice a day to be indoors.'

We wandered around the market for a while, before settling in a pub with a nice garden. I stared at the bags on the floor and realised that I'd actually had fun. I hadn't been expecting it, but Ruth was really easy to talk to. She had a wicked sense of humour. We'd spent the morning laughing and chatting like old friends who'd just been reunited instead of strangers who'd only met that week.

Ruth reappeared. 'Two lager shandies and a couple of packets of crisps. I took a guess that you'd be a cheese and onion type of guy.'

'I don't remember crisps being part of the deal.'

'It seemed a fair reward for rescuing a damsel in distress. Even if your trusty steed is luminescent.' She grinned and stretched, and I found myself struggling not to enjoy watching her.

'Hardly. Last time we met I'm pretty sure I was the one in distress, and you were the one patching me up.' I took a mouthful of my drink. 'So what type of nurse are you? Community?'

'Not exactly.' Ruth took a sip of her own drink. '*Aaaah*, that's better. I'm palliative care.'

'Like ... dying?'

'Not always, but yes, often it is end of life care. Bit of a conversation killer, usually.'

'No, no. Not at all.' I leant forward, genuinely intrigued. 'How on earth did you get into that field?'

'I've always been a nurse, but the end of life care? I guess you could say my husband got me into that.' She followed my guilty glance to her left hand. 'I lost him five years ago. Non-Hodgkins Lymphoma.' She grimaced.

'I'm really sorry.'

'Thanks. He was a great guy. I still miss him.' Her eyes became wistful. 'Anyway, that's how I ended up in palliative care. The nurses who looked after him towards the end were so good. They helped me to bring him home and look after him there so he could be at peace and relaxed and happy.

They took us both at the worst point in our lives, and they accepted us like that. Having someone verify your feelings and let you know it's all right just to feel, is incredibly powerful. They kept us both in good humour, and even made us laugh.' She shrugged. 'They were angels. Before I met them, I didn't know how Chris, that's my husband, or I were going to cope. But they made it bearable. Better than that, they made it beautiful.'

'Beautiful?'

Ruth nodded. 'Helping someone get ready to die can be one of the most fulfilling things you can ever do. Death is always sad, but what most people never realise is that it can also be peaceful and beautiful, and even healing for the people who are left. Chris's nurses helped me see that.'

'So you decided you wanted to do that for other people?' I asked softly.

'Exactly.' Her eyes flicked up to lock on mine. 'Most people don't understand that, but I think maybe you do.'

I shrugged in reply. 'I think most people spend their lives trying to avoid thinking about death.'

'But not you?'

'I used to.'

'So what changed? If you don't mind me asking.'

'My wife was killed in a car crash at the start of this year.' The words hurt less than I'd expected them to.

'I'm so sorry.' Ruth's eyes were gentle and full of sympathy, and her fingers were warm as they squeezed mine. Just her touch was comforting. She must be really good at her job.

'Thanks.' I bit my lips together to keep them from trembling.

'So what was she like?'

'Jenn? Oh she's wonderful. Warm and full of light. People just loved her.'

'And what about you?' Ruth's hand still rested on mine. 'How are you doing?'

The question took me by surprise, probably because it seemed so genuine. 'I'm … I don't know. I'm getting there I guess. Most of the time.'

Ruth nodded. 'I remember that. As clichéd as it is, time does actually help.'

'Yeah. I guess maybe it does.' I took another gulp of my drink. 'So, this conversation's getting a little depressing. Fancy a change?'

'Sure. Kids?'

'Me? Yeah I've got two. Matthew and Charlotte. They're both grown up and long moved out. How about you?'

'A daughter, Lisa. She's off to university this year. To be honest, I'm dreading it. The house is going to be really quiet without her.' She took another sip of her drink. 'Anyway, that conversation has the potential to be very depressing as well, and I've had too nice a morning to think about miserable things.'

'So what do you want to talk about?'

'How about you? You know who I am and what I do, so what about you?' She fiddled with her drink and tucked a strand of hair behind her ear, before flicking her eyes up to meet mine.

'What about me?'

'Well, when you're not running women off the road, what do you do? What makes you tick?' She seemed genuinely interested in the answers.

That's when it hit me. Was she flirting with me? The idea seemed preposterous, but here was this beautiful, available woman laughing and chatting with me, and apparently enjoying herself. And she wanted to know more about me. The thought was exhilarating. And terrifying.

I took a long gulp of my drink before answering. 'First off, I don't make a habit of running women off the road.'

'Oh, so I'm just one of the lucky ones?'

I laughed nervously, not sure how to respond.

'Well?' Ruth prompted. 'Who are you, David?'

'I'm just me. Like I said, I've got two grown up children. My son's in Scotland and has just got engaged, and my daughter lives closer by – she's just moved in with her boyfriend. I work in the drafting department for an architect's locally. Anything else?'

'Yes. So far you've only told me about other people, and your job,' Ruth complained. 'What about you? What's your favourite food? What do you do to relax? Who are you?'

'OK. I like proper old-fashioned cooking, and I'd probably say my favourite meal is roast beef, but I'd happily eat chicken or lamb too. I hate all this nouvelle cuisine, which seems to be an excuse for charging twice the amount for half the food. Except I don't tell most people that because it makes me sound grumpy and old-fashioned.'

Ruth laughed. 'And what about the relaxing?'

'Well, this is always good.' I gestured around the pub garden. 'But I like to paint too.'

'Walls or pictures?'

'Pictures I guess, though I've painted a lot of walls in my time too.'

'So what do you paint?'

'Whatever takes my fancy. Usually landscapes and trees. Sunsets and the sky. Not very exciting or groundbreaking stuff, but I like it.'

'Not everything has to be groundbreaking. I don't think there's anything wrong with finding what you like and sticking with it.'

'So what about you?'

'Me? Oh ... hang on, I think I'm ringing.' She rummaged in her bag and pulled out a phone that was flashing and buzzing. 'You'll have to excuse me for a minute.' She answered the phone as she stood and left the table. She was back within a minute. 'My story's going to have to wait. That was the garage. They've spoken to the insurance company and finished the repairs. My car's ready.'

'Oh.' Disappointment flooded me. 'I guess we should get moving then.' I downed the last couple of inches of my drink.

'Yeah, we should.' Ruth gathered up her bags, then paused and looked up at me. 'But, we should do this again. Minus the crashing into me first.'

'Really?' I had to check, because I was convinced I'd misunderstood.

'Why not? I've had fun, haven't you?'

'Yes.' I smiled at her, surprised at myself. 'Yes I have, thank you.'

JENN

I'm still struggling to like Ruth, but it's getting easier. She and David have been out together twice more this month since he gave her a lift. Once to the market again, and once to the cinema.

They've talked on the phone at least another three times. It's quite sweet really. I've actually caught David checking the clock again and again, waiting for it to be time to call her. Last Friday when they spoke, Ruth curled up on her sofa with a glass of wine, and they talked for hours. About almost everything.

They talked for longer than either had expected to, and when Ruth started yawning, neither wanted to say goodbye to the other. So instead of saying goodnight, they kept talking. Ruth curled up in her bed, and David kept talking to her, telling her about Lottie and Matty, and his job, and his painting. He kept talking to her as her answers became quieter and less frequent, and her breathing deepened into sleep.

It's hard to dislike anyone who makes my husband smile like that. Ruth really is a nice person, but it's not just that. She makes David happy. When he's with her, he smiles and laughs. The happiness is genuine, not the mask he wears around so many other people. He talks to her openly, and I'm glad he's finally found someone who can understand what he's going through.

The funny thing is, Ruth is turning out to be even better for David than I'd first thought. I hadn't known about her husband when I found her. I'd just known that she was single, and thought that she was the type of person David would probably click with.

They do get on really well. I think that Ruth being widowed as well might be part of the attraction and friendship between them. They've found kindred spirits in each other. It doesn't upset Ruth when David talks about me, and David doesn't recoil when Ruth talks about her husband and how he died. The friendship is cathartic and healing for both of them.

However, David still hasn't told her completely about me. But I don't blame him. For all that they've quickly become firm friends, they don't really know each other all that well yet. How do you tell someone who was a stranger a month ago that you believe your dead wife is still talking to you and taking part in your life? Without ending up with a quick referral to the local mental ward, I mean. It's not exactly something you can slip easily into everyday conversation.

I do wonder about Ruth's husband though. I wonder where he is, and whether he's trapped in his own grey place like this. The more I think about it, the more I think he probably isn't. From what's been said about him, his death was expected, and maybe even wanted towards the end. He had time to prepare, and good people around him who helped him to understand and accept what was happening. He had time to say goodbye.

I didn't get any of that. I didn't even get a warning. My life was snuffed out in an instant. I think maybe it's only souls like me who end up in places like this.

RUTH

David is so nice. I really do enjoy spending time with him. He's funny and sweet and kind. When the sadness lifts from his shoulders long enough for him to smile, he's good-looking. Not that I think of him like that. He's just a friend. Besides, anyone who spends more than a few minutes with him can see he's still in love with his wife.

Poor guy. I can't imagine how badly it must hurt to lose someone like that, and I hope I never have to find out. It was painful enough losing my Chris, but in a way, I'm glad it happened as it did. At least we had time to prepare, and time enough to say goodbye to each other. As much as it hurt, we both had time to come to terms with what was happening, and to accept it. That can make all the difference.

If I have learnt anything at work in the last few years, it's that once someone accepts their impending death, it can actually become something quite beautiful. Of course death is always sad, even when it's expected and welcomed, but

I think some passings are worse than others. And from the little that David's told me, his wife's sounds like it was one of the bad ones.

But he is a really, really nice guy, and he makes me laugh, which is a big deal. I don't think I laugh as much as I should. Certainly not as much as I used to. It really is lovely spending time with David. He's easy to be around and he doesn't judge people.

He has a fantastic eye. He showed me some of his paintings, and they're just lovely. I never really thought of the old council flats by the common as anything except ugly, but David managed to capture something on canvas that I'd never even seen. All angles and shadows and light. I guess maybe he sees things differently to most people. It does make me wonder how he sees me, although I try not to think about things like that. I've been having really good fun with him. We're doing things that I haven't done in years, like going to an art exhibition. I think the last exhibition I went to was to help Lisa with her art homework, and she hasn't studied art for at least four years.

Last week we ended up in a bookshop. It doesn't sound exciting, except that it really was. It started a couple of days before, when David was a few minutes late meeting me for dinner. I'd been flicking through the pages of an old favourite when he arrived, and he instantly recognised the cover.

'It's a good book. Nice twist at the end, but I won't spoil it for you by telling you what it is.'

'It's all right. I've read it before. More than once. I've read most of his books more than once.'

'Me too.' David flashed that happy smile at me. 'The way he looks at the world and spins it is just brilliant. The wizards always make me laugh.'

'And me, but I like his witches better. They're brilliant.'

'You know he's here at the weekend? He's signing copies

of his new book in town. I didn't really want to go by myself, though.'

'We could go together,' I offered almost immediately. 'It might even be fun.'

It had been fun. The shop was packed, and people queued out of the store and around the corner to shake the hand responsible for writing such wonderful words. We stood in line for nearly two hours, but the time flew and David made me laugh so hard that my sides hurt.

When it was our turn to have our books signed, I felt as giddy as the teenager I'd been when I first read his books three decades ago. I shook the author's hand and gushed. I don't remember what I said, but no doubt I made a complete fool of myself. But David didn't seem to mind as he just grinned and took a photo.

We compared our books in a coffee shop afterwards and David laughed when he saw the kiss across the middle of the page. He told me it was because I had better legs than him, and that was the only reason I got a signed kiss and he didn't.

It's surprising how much we seem to have in common. There's the big thing, of course. We're both well acquainted with death and know the pain of having to bury our other halves years sooner than expected, so we can understand and accept each other on a level that most people are lucky enough to never have to think about. I understand why he slips into talking about his wife as if she's still here, and he's happy to ask me questions about Chris and encourage me to remember and share stories.

But it isn't just that. We have similar tastes in books and films, and I'm learning to see the beauty in the paintings and scenery that he likes.

When he called me the other night to inform me it was

going to be a beautiful sunset and to invite me to climb up the hill at the back of the school to watch it, I told him he was nuts. But he kept on at me until I agreed. Even though I complained all the way up the slope, I had to admit it was quite pretty.

I can't remember the last time I stopped for long enough to sit and watch the sun go down, but David's reminding me how important things like that are. I feel like he's helping me to find a part of me that I thought was long gone, the part of me that used to see joy and beauty all around. It was the part of me that carried a brightly coloured umbrella when it rained, because I used to think it was already dull enough without a boring black brolly as well. It was also the part of me I thought I'd buried with Chris.

But for all the laughter David and I share, every so often his face clouds over and I know he's thinking about his wife and all the pain is flooding back. I can really empathise with him. I remember that feeling, and know only too well how the pain can suddenly grab you and flood through you without warning. I can remember how crippling it can be.

I think David's getting better. I know I haven't known him all that long, but the happiness seems to be winning through in him, and I'm glad. He deserves to be happy.

Chapter Twenty-One

DAVID

Every so often Lottie does something that reminds me so much of her mother, that it's all I can do not to cry. She turned up today with a bulky parcel balanced against her hip. 'It's a present.'

'But it's not my birthday or anything. What's it for?'

'Do I really need a reason to give you something?' She perched nervously on the edge of a chair. 'Are you going to open it?'

I tugged at the string that held the brown paper closed, and a brightly coloured roll of fabric tumbled out. I shook it out and the colours blurred in front of my eyes. It was a patchwork quilt. I let my fingers wander across the different coloured patches until I found a coppery-gold silken square that triggered a memory. 'Didn't your mum used to have a scarf this colour?'

Lottie nodded slowly.

'And a blouse this colour.' I picked another square. 'I bought it for her years ago, because it brought out the colour in her eyes. I'm sure it was just like this. Didn't she have one like this?'

'She did.' Charlotte fingered another square, this time blue and yellow check. 'And a tablecloth made of this. And a skirt from this.'

'This is what you wanted all Jenn's clothes for.' It wasn't a question, but Lottie nodded anyway. I stroked another square, and the image of Jenn on a summer evening, in a garden with a glass of wine, flashed into my mind. She'd loved that skirt. I found myself smiling as I recognised more and more of the patches. Jenn's weekend dressing gown, favourite evening jacket, jeans, her apron, the dress she'd worn on our twenty-fifth wedding anniversary when all our friends and family had crowded into our garden to celebrate with us. They were all here, with hundreds of memories woven into the fabrics.

'Do you like it?' Lottie's fingers were twisting the edge of the quilt nervously.

I looked up at my daughter and my voice caught in my throat. The gesture was so thoughtful, and so like something Jenn would have done, that I didn't know whether to hug her or cry. 'It's amazing. A patchwork of memories. Thank you so much.'

Lottie sighed in relief. 'I'm so glad. I was worried it might not be the right thing to do. I didn't like the thought of her things being cut up.'

'No, you were right. It's perfect. It's the type of thing your mum would have done.' I tried to keep the emotion out of my voice as I looked at my baby girl, all grown up and so incredibly kind and thoughtful.

'Do you really think so?' Lottie smiled as I nodded. 'I had one made for myself too, and one for Matty.'

'That's incredibly thoughtful. Where did you get them done?'

'Just a friend of a friend type of thing. She makes these in her spare time. So, you really like it?'

'Yes, I do. I think it's brilliant. And you're brilliant for coming up with it.' I planted a kiss on her cheek and she shoved me away playfully.

'*Ugh* Dad, don't be gross.' She folded the quilt carefully and glanced up at me slyly. 'So, how's Ruth? Have you seen much of her lately?'

By the time Lottie left, my stomach was growling. I threw a random packet meal in the microwave and punched the buttons as the phone rang.

'So I'm at the supermarket and feeling bored and sorry for myself.' I was starting to like how Ruth rarely bothered to say hello any more, instead just launching into a conversation. 'And I thought to myself "who else would be at home and bored on a Friday night?" and came up with you.'

'I'm thrilled.' I kept my tone deadpan, not wanting her to hear the truth in the sentiment.

'Oh hush your nonsense.' I could hear the smile in her voice. 'I just wanted someone to talk to. If you're against the idea of it being you ...'

'No, no. It's fine.' I settled back against the work surface, feeling a lot brighter. 'You're right. I am at home and fairly bored. So why are you feeling sorry for yourself?'

'Because it's Friday night and I'm at the supermarket by myself. Don't think I'm too mad, but I really hate supermarkets now.'

'Because they're overpriced and seem to hate their customers? Because every time you learn where the coffee is, they go and move it again? Because all the best dates are always at the back, so you have to rummage around the fridges until your hands are freezing to make sure your packet of yogurts will last the week? And because everything is sold in packs big enough to serve a whole dinner party?'

Ruth's laughter echoed back down the phone. 'Now I think about it, yeah. Everything except the moving stuff around thing, I actually like that because it makes me concentrate instead of just blindly throwing things into the trolley.'

'So what was it before I added more to your list of reasons to hate supermarkets?' I'd given her my list of pet peeves, and was curious to find out what I'd missed.

'It doesn't matter, it's silly.'

'Sillier than rummaging around a fridge looking for the perfect pack of ham?'

'Well maybe not. It's just that I always feel really lonely here. It's like this bloody supermarket sets out to make me feel more lonely than ever. People always seem to do their shopping together. No one shops alone any more, and even when they do you can tell from what's in their basket that they're rushing home to meet someone. Half the time Lisa doesn't eat at home any more, so I'm left with a sad-looking basket that screams at the world how miserable and alone I am.' She took a deep breath. 'I told you it was stupid.'

'The first time I went shopping after Jenn died, I had some sort of mental breakdown,' I confessed.

'Really?' Ruth sounded disbelieving.

'Honestly. First time I went shopping just for myself it started in the fresh meat aisle when I couldn't find a packet of sausages or pork chops small enough to just feed me, and ended by the cream-cake chiller.' It felt good to share the experience with someone who I knew would understand. 'I stood there for nearly half an hour.'

'You're winding me up.' I could hear Ruth trying not to laugh.

'Scout's honour.' I laughed with her. Now, it did seem ridiculously funny. 'I wanted a custard tart, but I couldn't buy just one. So rather than get something else, I stood and tried to stare them all down.'

'You're a nutter. Why didn't you just go to the baker's and ask for a single?'

'I don't know.' I was laughing so hard I struggled to catch my breath. Trust Ruth to manage to make me laugh over something I'd never thought I'd get over. She was good at doing that.

'So what are you up to? I'm not disturbing you, am I?'

'Nope, just cooking dinner.'

'I'm out trying to buy some. So what are you having?'

'I don't know. Some radioactive pasta, curry, cheesy something or other.'

'Are you that bad a cook?'

'Nope. Just didn't look very closely at the packet before feeding it to the microwave.' I peered through the glass door at the slowly twirling plate. 'It's bright yellow, so I'm hoping something cheesy and pasta related.'

'*Ewww*. I think I just lost my appetite. Right in time to pass the dreaded doughnuts. Did you know they have a Krispy Kreme cabinet here?'

'Sounds lethal,' I sympathised.

'Not as lethal as your dinner. Please tell me this is just a lazy Friday dinner before you put the tele on, and not your usual cuisine.'

'Umm ...'

'Do you have any idea how much salt, fat, sugar and additives are in those things?'

'I'm guessing a lot, based on your tone of voice.' I'd never even thought about it before. 'They're easy. I can't really be bothered to cook properly when it's just me.'

'I know what you mean. I'll make a deal with you. You throw the glow-in-the-dark-possibly-pasta-thing in the bin, put a bottle of something half-decent in the freezer to chill quickly, and I'll bring round something for dinner.'

'Are you sure? I thought you were busy.' I peered in the microwave again. The maybe cheese thing was bubbling unpleasantly and the black plastic pot was starting to sag dangerously. The thought of good food and better company was appealing, but I didn't want to put Ruth out.

'Are you serious? My night just went from ice cream and old movies to actual human contact and possible laughter. See you in a bit.' The line clicked off before I could reply.

I grinned to myself. I hadn't expected to see Ruth tonight, so it was a nice surprise. It was so easy to be around her –

she's always so relaxed and chilled out. I looked around the kitchen. Damn. I really needed to wash up. I didn't think even Ruth was chilled out enough to ignore the leaning tower of dishes.

By the time the doorbell rang, the kitchen was vaguely respectable. Not as clean as I would have made it with more notice, but at least it didn't look like a bachelor pad, although I suppose that's what it is now.

I shook the thought aside and opened the door with a smile.

'Here, take this.' Ruth shoved a supermarket bag at me.

'I thought you were getting take out?' I peered into the bag.

'Oi, nosey.' Ruth tutted at me before kicking off her shoes. 'I was already in the supermarket, so thought I'd cook us something half-decent. How's ham and mushroom tagliatelle sound?'

'Better than neon-could-be-cheese-and-melted-plastic pot. Do you need a hand?'

'Just show me where everything is and open the wine.'

'All right.' She followed me through to the kitchen and rattled off a list of stuff she needed. I found everything except the garlic press, whatever that is, but she just shrugged and said she could chop it.

I sat at the breakfast bar with a still slightly warm glass of wine, and watched her bustle around my kitchen happily. The small room soon filled with steam, scented with herbs and the smell of frying bacon, and I found myself smiling. It was good to have the kitchen come back to life and be filled with energy. Lottie sometimes cooked when she was here, but usually with quite a lot of crashing pots and swearing. Watching Ruth was relaxing, and she seemed to have made herself right at home. She grabbed her glass of wine off the work surface and spun to face me.

'I brought pudding too. How do custard tarts sound?'

I laughed. She really had been listening. 'Not a traditional Italian dessert, but I think I like it.'

'Good, now grab me some plates. I'm starved.'

We ate in comfortable silence for the first few minutes, until I broke it. 'This is delicious, where did you learn to cook? I watched you, and you didn't measure a single ingredient, but this is perfect.'

Ruth smiled back at me, toying with her pasta and winding it easily into neat parcels. 'Newlyn is Chris's name. Before we got married I was a DiMarco.'

'You're Italian?'

'My father is. My grandmam taught me to cook. Can't you tell looking at me?'

'Well, no. Not really. I don't expect most blondes living round here to be half Italian.'

Ruth leaned closer. 'David sweetie, it's called dye.' She grinned. 'My natural hair colour nowadays is more grey than anything else.'

'I don't believe it.'

'You should.' She laughed. 'It's all true. If you look closely enough you can probably see it sneaking back in at the roots. It's part of the genes. Great skin and legs, but hair that lets you down. I've been grey since my twenties.'

'Well you hide it well.'

'Thanks. I've had practice.'

'Ruth, can I ask you something?'

'Sure. It's not like I actually have to answer if your question is that offensive.' Ruth shrugged. 'And I have already confessed my grey hair.'

'Do you still miss him?'

She didn't even have to ask who I was talking about. 'Do you want the honest answer to that, or the one I give the well-meaning friends?'

'Honest. Brutally.'

'Yes.' She nodded slowly and I could see her jaw clenching. 'If I am being brutally honest, I don't think there's a single day when I don't miss him, or come across something I want to share with him. Sometimes I still have bad mornings when I've dreamt about him, and then have to wake up and remember he's gone. He was my husband. We chose to get married and planned on growing old together. I'm grateful for the time we got to share, and for my daughter, but sometimes I still feel cheated for what got taken away. For one thing, I never planned on being a single mum to a teenager.' She winced and stared at what was left of her dinner, then added in a quieter voice, 'Or living alone in the house Chris and I bought together.'

I nodded and edged my fingers slowly across the breakfast bar to tentatively pat the back of her hand. 'I'm sorry. I didn't mean to upset you.'

Ruth shook her head and straightened her shoulders. 'You didn't upset me, honey. It's just … it is what it is.' Her fingers curled around mine and I was surprised by how natural and easy she made the gesture.

'It never really goes away, David, it just gets easier. And I promise you, it does get easier.' She dropped my hand and downed the rest of her wine. 'If that's enough harsh reality for one night, I'm done. Pudding while watching Friday night tele?'

'Sure, sounds good.' I cleared away the plates while she settled down in the living room. I heard the TV flick on and smiled to myself. It was nice how relaxed and at home Ruth made herself here – it made the house feel a lot less empty. Warmth gathered around me and I smiled.

'I know it isn't really empty, Jenn. I know you're always here with me. But it's nice having a friend who can actually talk to me normally. You don't mind, do you?'

The air around me hummed softly and I smiled again. Jenn wasn't annoyed or upset, she just seemed to be happy that I'd found someone to laugh with again. She really was the most amazing woman.

'I think I know what Ruth meant,' I murmured softly. 'I can't ever imagine a day that I won't still miss you. I love you, Jenn.'

The air around me shifted and I felt a slight nudge towards the living room. It seemed Jenn wanted me to spend time with Ruth. I guess she wanted me to have friends and enjoy myself again. She'd been pushing me towards this for ages. 'All right, all right, I'm going.'

I wandered into the room and settled down on the opposite end of the sofa from Ruth. 'So what are we watching?'

'Well I did find the original *Italian Job*, fancy that?'

'Sounds good to me.' I settled back into the cushions more comfortably.

In the end it hadn't really mattered what we watched, because we talked so much. I don't think we watched more than half the film between us. It was just something to look at when the conversation lapsed into comfortable silences.

'So, yet another ad break.' Ruth twirled the wine in her glass and gave me a mischievous look. 'Want to play a game?'

'I don't think I have many. I might have Cluedo or Monopoly in the loft.' I paused as she laughed. 'You didn't mean a board game. What do you mean?'

'A getting to know you game. You get to ask three questions, any three questions, and the other person has to answer honestly. You can't repeat questions.'

'Sounds simple enough. Do I get to start?' She nodded. 'All right … favourite colour?'

'Green. Boring question.'

'So what is a good question?'

'One that reveals something about you. What's your dream car?'

'Umm … 1960s Jaguar E Type. So what does that reveal?'

Ruth smiled. 'That you're not ashamed to aim high and dream, and that you like beautiful, classic, tasteful things. But that you're probably still a bit of a big kid at heart and harbour latent fantasies of yourself as some super secret James Bond type spy.'

'Probably a good thing I didn't pick an old Beetle then. By the way, Bond usually drove an Aston Martin.' I laughed.

'I'll consider myself educated then.' Ruth rolled her eyes. 'Your go.'

'Favourite book as a child?'

'Well your questions are getting better. Enid Blyton's *Faraway Tree*. So what does that say about me?'

'I don't know. It's your game. Probably that you liked to believe in magic.' I remembered reading them to Lottie, and then her reading them to me.

'Nothing wrong with that.' Ruth smiled at me and for a moment I couldn't think straight. 'My turn. If you could be anywhere right now, anywhere in the world, where would it be?'

'Here's not bad.' The words were out of my mouth before I'd even consciously thought them. 'Or maybe Hawaii,' I bluffed quickly. 'It always looks nice. Right, my last question. I want to make it a good one … What would you do with a million pounds?'

'Hmm.' Ruth studied her wine glass while she thought. 'Buy a new car, and one for my daughter so she can come home from university and visit me lots. Help her through her studies and make sure she's set up for life and can buy a house when she wants to. I'd be tempted to buy a little cottage somewhere in the country. Not too far away, but somewhere I could just disappear off to at the weekends.'

'You wouldn't give up work?'

'Probably not straight away.' She shook her head. 'I love my job, and there are people in it who need me. I'd stay for a while at least.'

'So ...' I totted her spending up on my fingers. 'Two new cars, a little cottage somewhere, university fees and a house for your daughter. By my count there's a good few hundred thousand still left. What about the rest?'

'I'd drop it in a nearby charity pot.'

'Really?' The answer surprised me. I'd known Ruth was caring, but I didn't realise it was to that extent.

'I'd like to think so. I'd hope I'm not the type of person who'd be changed by a lot of money. Apart from the suntan.'

'Suntan?'

'Yeah.' She grinned at me. 'After I've taken you to Hawaii.'

'You'd really do that?' I struggled not to picture her sunbathing on a beach. In not very much at all.

'Sure. Why not? I'm rich remember. Last question is mine.' She studied me over her glass. 'What's your favourite sexual position?'

I choked on my wine and spluttered as it burned the back of my nose. 'I'm not answering that.'

Ruth laughed. 'You think shooting wine out of your nose wasn't an answer? What's the big deal? We've done dream cars, childhood books, fantasy holidays and millionaire lifestyles.'

'Yes but they're not so ... you know ...' I trailed off, knowing my ears were burning bright red.

'It's just sex, David. You've got two children of different ages, so it's a pretty safe bet you've had sex at least that often. You know if you don't answer, you have to do a forfeit.'

'You didn't mention anything about that.'

'I know. But it's my game and my rules.' Ruth shrugged and grinned. 'Plus I really don't feel like washing up.'

'Well, if that's my forfeit, I'm delaying punishment until tomorrow. I don't feel like it either right now.' I kicked my slippers off and stretched. 'So, shall we see what's on next?'

'Sure. I can stay a bit longer. I'll call a taxi later. That wine went down a bit too easy.' Ruth kicked her feet up on the sofa, and I watched as she tucked her legs up easily, her skirt rising up and pulling tight. She caught my stare and blushed. 'Sorry. I sort of forgot I wasn't at home.' She stretched her legs out again.

'No, no. Please, make yourself at home. Seriously.'

'Thanks.' She flashed me a smile so warm that I felt it in the base of my stomach. She tucked her feet back up onto the sofa, and pulled her skirt back over her knees. 'So, have you got any plans for this weekend?'

'Not really. You?'

'Meeting up with some old friends for lunch on Sunday.'

'So you do have other friends,' I teased gently. 'I'm just the special one who gets bored supermarket shopping calls.'

'Yup.' Ruth grinned. 'You should consider yourself lucky. And yes I do have other friends. Some of them are even old ones who knew Chris too.'

'Really?'

Ruth twisted to face me. 'Why does that surprise you?'

'I've lost contact with most of my old friends.' I sighed and tried to explain. 'To be honest, I don't have many friends. Jenn and I had lots, but they were *our* friends.'

'I can understand that,' Ruth sympathised.

'Really?'

'That's becoming a catchphrase for you,' she teased gently. 'But yeah, I understand why you'd find it difficult to be around old friends, especially the ones who were Jenn's friends as well.' Ruth sighed. 'It can be hard, it really can. I'm not the same person I was five or six years ago.'

'How so?' I was fascinated at the thought of Ruth being

anything different than she was now. She seemed so together and settled all of the time.

'Well, I was married to Chris then. You can't really go through a change as fundamental, painful and intense as burying your partner without it affecting you. Do you really think you're the same person as you were this time last year?'

'Well, yeah. I don't think I've changed that much.'

'Oh really?' Ruth challenged me with a glint in her eye. 'So a year ago you were a slightly eccentric, ready-meal scoffing painter who's successfully sold work, and spends his Friday nights drinking with strange women?'

'Maybe I am a little different,' I conceded slowly, but then again maybe it was different for Ruth. After all, she didn't have her other half with her all the time. I smiled and let my eyes drift shut as I felt for Jenn's presence.

'Well?' Ruth was looking at me expectantly.

I jerked back into consciousness. 'Sorry, what did you say?'

'I asked you if you wanted to join me on Sunday.'

'I wouldn't want to intrude.'

'You wouldn't be, I've invited you. It's usually good fun.' She rolled her eyes as I shook my head again. 'Just think about it, all right? Please?'

I nodded in agreement. It was easier than arguing. It's not like she knew I had no intention of going out with a group of strangers. No, I definitely wouldn't be going.

JENN

I love my husband, but sometimes it amazes me how unobservant he can be. Despite the amount of time he's spent with her, and how much he enjoys being around her, he still hasn't realised that he's attracted to Ruth.

Although it doesn't really matter, because whether David acknowledges it or not, Ruth is good for him, and it shows. The more time he spends with her, the happier he seems to be. His confidence is growing again. He's actually looking forward to things. He's starting to care again.

It isn't just Ruth, but she's behind it all. She makes David do things, pushing, cajoling and teasing him until he gives in. He had no intention of meeting her friends, and definitely wasn't planning on having lunch with them, but Ruth kept asking and persuading until he gave in and agreed. He wasn't looking forward to it, but Ruth anticipated that and made him promise to show up. She knows exactly what David's going through because she's been there herself. And she remembers how easy it is to let yourself disappear rather than go through the effort that socialising seems to take. That's exactly why she keeps pushing him to do things, and is pulling him into her circle of friends.

It's working. Despite his concerns, David really did enjoy himself. Once he stopped feeling awkward and out of place he joined in the laughter and shared his own jokes and anecdotes. They really liked him, which was no surprise. My husband's easy to like.

For the couple of hours he was with them, I was given a glimpse of the David I'd known and loved. I knew that he'd changed after my death, but I hadn't realised quite how much until I saw him laughing and joking. It's like he's coming back to life before my eyes. He's happy and enjoying life again, and it's because of Ruth. I have to like her for that.

But then David goes and ruins everything by thinking too much. He spends too much time worrying about other things that stop him from thinking about Ruth honestly. He worries that I'll mind, but he still seems to be oblivious to my attempts to tell him that this is what should be happening. Either that or he's deliberately ignoring me. I'm honestly not sure which it is.

He needs to start listening to me, and stop feeling guilty every time he smiles at Ruth. And he does smile at her a lot, but that was why I introduced them. It's the whole point. I want him to smile and be happy again, and focus on living his life instead of worrying about me.

I can't move on while he's still holding me here in his life and his world. I'm still not even sure that I want to move on and leave my family behind, but the thought isn't as horrifying as it was a few months ago. Matty is settling down and happy. Lottie's career is moving so fast she can only just keep up, and she seems blissfully happy with Stuart, much to her surprise and my relief. In truth, my children don't need me any more.

So it's really only David that I'm staying here for. That worries me, because I've come to realise that I'm not the only one who is trapped by this situation. I can't move on while David is holding me to him so tightly, but he can't move on either. The love we shared in life always gave us freedom. It meant we could be ourselves, chase our dreams and take chances because we knew we'd always love and support each other. But now that love has twisted, and it's trapping us both. I don't really know what to do about it.

I've noticed something odd, here in my grey world. It's a tiny speck of green, not really much bigger than the head of a pin. Anywhere else I wouldn't have noticed it, but here it's the only bit of colour there is. It's bright green and glowing with life against the greyness. A tiny point of colour that's pushed its way through the nothingness to enter my world.

I've looked and looked at it, but I can't figure out what it is. I feel as though I should recognise it, that it's obvious what it is. But here, out of context, I really don't understand it. Whatever it is, it has power. It must do to have made it here when nothing else can. I'm scared to touch it. Although whether that's because I'm more scared of hurting it, or because of what it means, I really don't know.

Chapter Twenty-Two

CHARLOTTE

The door had swollen in the damp weather and was jammed again. I slammed my shoulder against it with too much force, then winced as it crashed into the wall.

'Sorry!' I closed it more quietly and kicked my boots off. 'Hey, I brought the prints from that shoot I was telling you about.' I peered into the living room. 'Where are you?'

'In the kitchen. There's fresh coffee if you want it.' The voice that echoed back wasn't my dad's.

I dropped the photos on the hall table and peered around the kitchen door. I nearly swallowed my tongue in surprise. There was a woman standing at the oven in jeans and what looked like one of my dad's sweatshirts. She looked completely at home, barefoot and poking something in a frying pan. She moved the pan off the heat and wiped her hands on a tea towel. Her honey-coloured hair was still fluffy and dishevelled from bed, and she wasn't wearing a scrap of make-up, but she was naturally pretty and had smile lines around her eyes.

She gave me a cheerful smile as she poured coffee into a cup. 'You must be Lottie.'

'Yeah, I am. And you are?'

'I'm Ruth. Newlyn.' She twisted the cup between her fingers before taking a sip.

'Oh. You're Ruth. It's very nice to meet you. I've heard a lot about you.' Everything suddenly clicked with the name. This was the Ruth, Dad had been talking about. Every time we spoke, her name somehow made it into the conversation. Ruth said this, or she said that, or thought this. Lately it's been more than that too. It hasn't just been Ruth – he's said "we". As in "*we* went to the movies", and "*we* had dinner".

I looked her over and started to smile. My dad had good taste, I had to give him that. Ruth was very pretty. If he was ready to start dating, and whatever else that I didn't want to think about for even a second, then she was a good choice.

'It's nice to meet you too.' Her smile seemed genuine enough. 'Your dad's in the shower. Do you want some eggs?'

'Right. Dad said you were going to a movie last night ...?' I let the statement hang in the air and watched Ruth closely, wondering if she'd have the decency to blush.

She stared right back, chewed on her bottom lip for a moment and then snorted in amusement. 'You can stop looking at me like that.'

'Like what?' I smiled innocently.

'Like you think you know what's going on. You don't. This,' she gestured at Dad's sweatshirt, 'isn't what you think. It was so wet and miserable last night that we decided to skip the cinema and order pizza instead. I drank a bit too much to risk driving home. I spent the night in the spare room. I'm just making your dad breakfast as thanks before I head off.'

'Oh.' Disappointment and relief flooded me in equal measure. For a couple of minutes I'd really thought Dad had found himself a girlfriend. It would do him good to stop moping around, and honestly, I think Mum would approve. 'So, you seem to know your way around the kitchen pretty well. Do you stay over often?'

'I wouldn't say often.' She gave me a quizzical look. 'Don't you ever stay with friends rather than get a late taxi home?'

'I guess,' I admitted grudgingly, not wanting to admit how many times I'd spent the night on uncomfortable couches or floors rather than pay taxi fares or risk late-night buses.

'There you go then. Now, what about those eggs?'

I shrugged. 'OK. Thanks.'

Dad sauntered in a couple of minutes later, his hair still wet from the shower. 'Something smells good out here ...' His voice trailed off when he spotted me. 'Lottie, you're early. Umm, this is my friend Ruth ... she ...'

I could have enjoyed the look of panic in his eyes, but it seemed too mean. Plus I wanted to encourage this. A girlfriend might do Dad the world of good.

'She stayed in the spare room. I know. We've already had that conversation.' I rolled my eyes. 'Are you going to stand there gawping or have some breakfast?'

'Umm ...'

'Just sit down.' I kicked the other stool out from under the breakfast bar. 'What about you, Ruth? Sure you're not joining us?'

'No, but thanks for the offer. I need to be getting home. I've got some patients to visit, and I promised I'd have breakfast with one of them. He's gone off food a bit, and it helps him to share meals.' She shrugged as if this was totally normal.

Damn. I'd been hoping she was going to stay. I wanted to talk to her more. I wasn't sure I totally bought this "drank too much" story. There was something else going on here. But I could hardly complain when she was looking after terminally-ill people. Even if I might have liked to.

'Are you sure you're all right to drive?' Dad asked.

'Yeah, I didn't drink that much last night.' Ruth laughed and leant towards my dad, her hand resting lightly on his wrist. She froze and her eyes flicked to me before she flashed a bright smile at him. 'Give me a call about Wednesday.'

'I will.' Dad went to stand up.

'Don't be silly. Stay put.' Ruth flapped a hand at him. 'I can let myself out. Nice meeting you, Lottie.'

'Yeah, you too.' I waited until the front door slammed shut before peering at Dad. 'So, what's happening Wednesday?'

'Nothing.'

'Didn't sound like nothing.'

'It is. Just said we should try to catch the film we missed last night.' Dad shrugged.

'Oh.' I fiddled with my egg. 'So, how come she stayed in the spare room?'

'She told you that. She'd drunk too much to drive safely.'

'I know why she stayed here. What I meant was why did she stay in my old room, instead of yours?'

'Charlotte! That's an awful thing to suggest.'

'Why?'

'Because Ruth and I are just friends.'

'Really?' I didn't believe him for a minute.

'Yes really. Don't be disgusting.'

'Oh come on, Dad, don't be naïve. She's pretty and you're obviously into each other. What's disgusting about that?'

'Your mum. I couldn't betray her like that.'

'Dad.' I wrapped my fingers around his. 'Mum's dead. Even though she's still here, in a way she's not. She knows that. She just wants us to be happy, especially you.'

'Even if that were true—'

'Which it is,' I interrupted firmly.

'Even if it were,' Dad continued, 'Ruth doesn't think of me like that. We're just friends.'

'Oh, Dad, sometimes I think blindness when it comes to women is a trait for the men in this family. If you and Matty are anything to go by, it's a wonder I even exist.'

'What on earth are you talking about?'

I rolled my eyes. Clearly I was going to have to spell it out for him. 'Dad, Ruth is totally into you. And you're completely into her. How can you not see it?'

'But … she's never said anything,' Dad complained.

'Of course she hasn't. Mum's only been gone since New Year. She's been a widow a lot longer. She's going to wait until you're ready. Plus she's waiting for you to make a move. It is kind of traditional you know.'

'But what about your mum?'

I rolled my eyes again. 'Mum wants you to be happy. Everything she's done so far is to look after us all, make sure that we're happy, and that we have everything we need. What makes you think Ruth is any different?'

'I don't know, Lottie. Just thinking about it feels wrong. Like I'm betraying Jenn.'

'But Da—'

'Lottie, I don't really want to talk about this.'

I shrugged. 'I think you need to talk about this, Dad. And I think Mum's with me on this one.' I paused while the air around me thickened and filled with the weight and presence that Mum always brought with her. I smiled triumphantly at Dad. 'See? She agrees with me.'

'Or she's here to disagree with you.'

'Doesn't feel to me like she's disagreeing.' I sighed irritably. 'You told me how you and Ruth met. If you don't think that's Mum giving you her blessing to start dating, what is? How much more obvious do you need her to be? What are you waiting for? A message painted in the sky?'

'Well it would be nice.' He laughed. 'Did you bring round those photos to show me?' I nodded. 'Well go get them. I want to have a look.'

'All right, but don't think this is over. I reckon Mum's going to have more to say on the matter too.'

'If you say so. Now go get those photos.'

DAVID

I don't think I can see Ruth any more. It's too confusing and embarrassing. I keep thinking about her in ways that just aren't appropriate.

I'm blaming Lottie. I love my daughter but sometimes I

could just strangle her. Ruth's been a great friend to me, but since Lottie started making her comments about us being "into each other" I can't think straight. I had never thought of Ruth like that before. Except to notice her legs, and that she was pretty. All right, maybe there was a bit of flirting, but it was harmless, and I think Ruth is just one of those really friendly people who's a bit flirty with everyone.

But now, thanks to Lottie, everything is different.

Oh, who do I think I'm fooling? I've thought Ruth was attractive since the day I gave her a lift to the garage. She's gorgeous. But I never thought about her like that, because of Jenn, of course, and also partly because I didn't honestly believe I had a chance with someone like Ruth. I mean she's gorgeous, clever, confident, and kind and I'm just me. But ever since my darling, beloved daughter made those comments I can't think straight.

Ruth and I went to see a film last night, and I honestly can't even remember what it was about because I spent the whole time focussed on her.

I struggled to keep my eyes on the screen because she was wearing this long stretchy woolly jumper thing that ended just above her knees. I don't usually notice women's clothing like that, because I'm not a pervert or something. But I really struggled not to notice that skirt as it rode up and lengthened the gap between its end and the top of the knee high boots covering the rest of her legs. I didn't know what was wrong with me. I'd seen her in shorts over summer, and she does have great legs, but they'd never affected me like that before.

The inches of caramel skin between boots and dress fascinated me, and I kept wondering what it would feel like to touch, and to brush my fingers against those long legs. Then I remembered how cold it was and realised her legs couldn't be bare. She would be freezing if they were. Which meant she had to be wearing tights. Or stockings. Oh crap, I didn't want to think about Ruth in stockings.

I tried to watch the film, I really did. I didn't want to be thinking like that. Ruth's my friend, and I'm a married man. Jenn's still with me every day. Oh God, Jenn could never find out how I've been thinking about Ruth. I concentrated on Jenn and forced myself to try and watch the film again.

But then Ruth leant down and unzipped one of the boots to scratch her ankle. It was a completely innocent movement that was over in a couple of seconds, but I couldn't tear my eyes away from the leg that flexed beneath her fingers. For the first time I noticed that her nails had been painted a rich burgundy, and for some reason that really got to me.

Or maybe it was the satisfied sigh she'd given as she'd relieved the itch. I couldn't get that stupid breathy moan out of my head, because my twisted sick mind kept wondering when else she'd make that noise.

I really did try to concentrate on the film, but those dark red nails seemed to claw their way into my mind. I couldn't stop looking at them, wondering about how they would feel running over my skin, biting into the flesh on my shoulders and back. I couldn't stop picturing them travelling lower, grasping at me, wrapping around me and squeezing. The images were so intense, and so enticingly wrong that I started to count down the current England cricket team in my head. Anything to distract myself from the growing ache and throbbing in my pants.

I think the film might have been good. I remember trying to watch some of it. I think I was starting to enjoy it, until her fingers bumped into mine when we both reached for the popcorn. How much of a cliché is that? Our fingers met over a sticky pile of popcorn. I swear an electric shock jumped right through me.

She smiled an apology at me, and went back to watching

the film, oblivious to the effect she was having on me. I couldn't watch a thing after that. I stared at the screen, but in truth I was watching her from the corner of my eye. In the flickering light from the screen I was gob-smacked by how stunning she was. Her skin looked smooth and creamy, and her lips were sticky and dusted with popcorn crumbs. She shifted in her seat and her arm brushed against mine. I held my breath as she settled, the back of her hand and wrist lightly touching mine.

I felt like a teenage boy again. My hands were clammy. I could feel sweat trickling down my back, and I couldn't concentrate on anything except this woman sitting next to me. I could feel the heat of her touch, the whole length of my forearm, and I was so tense I could feel the blood pounding in my ears.

She must have noticed something, because she turned to me and, in the half-light of the cinema, gave me a warm smile that set my pulse racing even faster. Was Lottie right? Could Ruth possibly be attracted to me? Our eyes met, and in the dark I could have sworn Ruth was reading my mind and answering the question.

Yes, I could have her. I could have all of her. In any way I wanted. In *every* way I wanted.

Then she popped another bit of popcorn between her lips and turned back to the screen.

I spent the rest of the film, which was possibly the longest one ever shown, berating myself for being an idiot. I was the worst man living. My wife's still with me every day, fighting through God only knows what to stay with me and make her presence known, to make me feel her and know I'm not alone. And there I was fantasising over a woman sitting next to me. One who trusted me and considered me a friend.

I finally managed to pull myself together enough to make vaguely sensible small talk as I drove Ruth home, but her goodnight threw me for a loop. She leant over to place a kiss on my cheek as usual, but one of us must have moved because the kiss landed on the corner of my mouth. We both froze. It was sweet agony. I wanted nothing more than to grab her and kiss her until her heart was racing as fast as mine. She moved away quickly and shot me an apologetic smile while tucking her hair back behind her ear. Then she was gone with a quick "see you soon".

I waited until her door closed before slamming my hand into my forehead. The light in her living room flicked on, and I slammed the car into gear and kicked the accelerator. When I pulled up at traffic lights, another vision of Ruth's legs crashed into my mind. I didn't realise how long I'd been staring into space until a horn sounded behind me. I jumped so far I stalled the car and growled at myself in frustration.

Ruth was attractive, hell, she's gorgeous, but she's not Jenn. I still love my wife, and she's still here with me. There's no way I can get involved with anyone else. I don't want to be with anyone else. I'd never dishonour Jenn like that. It's been her and me for as long as I can remember, and I want it to stay that way forever. That's why she came back to me, so we can stay together forever.

It's quite simple. I just won't see Ruth again.

JENN

Oh David, this is not what I meant to happen. I don't want you to stop seeing Ruth. She's your friend and you're supposed to like her. And if you like her in a way that could lead to more than friendship, then all the better. She's a good woman, David, and more than that, she's good for you. I wish you could see how much brighter and happier you are when she's around.

Damn it, David, you're supposed to be listening to me. This is what I want. And it's what you need. As much as it breaks my heart to say it, you can't keep living your life for me. You're supposed to let me go and move on. I'm supposed to move on too.

That's the problem. You don't need me any more, not like you did. You aren't falling apart. You've got yourself and your life together, and you've got reasons to live.

You're depressed because you're fighting the natural healing process. Some people can be alone and still feel happy and fulfilled. But darling, you're not one of them. You can't survive by living in the past and surrounding yourself only by memories. It isn't enough for you. You're too young and vibrant. You've only lived half your life. You've still got so much more left to see and do and experience.

I know you're scared and that you don't know what to do, or how to feel, but David, don't use me as an excuse to avoid living your life. Don't you dare do that.

You're the type of person who is so full of passion and joy that you need someone to share it with. You need someone to bring that out of you. It doesn't have to be Ruth, but why not her? She makes you laugh, and challenges you, and you're attracted to her. I'm not asking you to fall in love with her and forget about me, but there's nothing wrong with enjoying life and living it to the full.

Why do you think I introduced you two?

You shouldn't feel bad for being human, and what you're feeling is human. It's normal and healthy, so stop fighting it and stop fighting me. Stop pushing me away because you feel guilty, and damn well start listening to me again.

Chapter Twenty-Three

RUTH

That's it. I've had enough of whatever's going on with David. He hasn't replied to a single text, call or email in nearly two weeks. I don't want to be needy or nagging, and I really hate confrontations, but he's my friend and this behaviour is so out of character for him that I'm worried.

I slammed the phone down for the last time and drove to his house before I could change my mind. I knocked at his door and stepped back slightly so the light didn't hit me fully. If he really was avoiding me, I didn't want to give him the chance to spot me and refuse to open the door. I don't know what I've done to upset him, but I should have been given the chance to make it right. I clasped my hands behind my back to try and stop them shaking.

When David opened the door a huge grin spread across his face, but it was quickly replaced by a look of horror. 'Ruth, what are you doing here?'

'Seems to be the only way I can get your attention.' He refused to answer the challenge, or meet my eyes. 'So you are all right then?' I crossed my arms and stared at him.

'Umm ... should I not be?'

'Well I was half-hoping you'd had some sort of accident where you'd broken every one of your fingers. Although tongue-numbing laryngitis would have done too. Either would have given you a good excuse for not returning any of my calls.'

'Oh. Sorry about that.'

'So, are you busy?'

'Not really.' He looked awkward.

'So do I get an invite in?' I wondered what was going on with him.

'I don't think it's a good idea, Ruth.' The words seemed to hurt him. 'I don't think we should see each other any more.'

'David.' I stepped forward and reached out to him, but he pulled away. 'Have I done something to upset you? Have I said something wrong?'

'No, no. It's nothing like that, nothing you've done. I just ... don't want to see you any more. I'm sorry, Ruth.'

Ouch. His words hurt as much as if he'd reached out and struck me, but I forced myself to keep my tone casual and even. Something was going on here, and I wanted to know what. I leant back against the door frame, partly to stop David from shutting the door on me, and partly to hide my shaking hands. I really, really hated confrontations. But I don't think I'd realised how important David's friendship had become until now. 'All right. I'll go and leave you in peace. But only after you've explained to me why I'm walking away. I think you owe me that much.'

'I can't.' David shook his head, unable to meet my eye.

'Why not?' I couldn't hear his reply at first, so I made him repeat it.

'I can't ... it's too embarrassing.'

'I thought we were friends, David.'

'We are.' He nodded.

'But not good friends. Not important friends who are worth fighting to keep. Because apparently you're willing to end our friendship because you're embarrassed about something. Call me stupid and self-centred, but I thought our friendship was worth more than that.' I started to lose control and my voice began to crack. 'Thanks a lot for putting me straight.' I didn't want him to see me get upset, so I turned away and headed back to my car.

'Wait. Ruth, wait.' David was standing in the middle of his driveway, barefoot. 'I'm sorry, Ruth.'

'Are you going to tell me what's going on?' I crossed my arms and waited.

He mumbled something.

'What?'

'I like you, Ruth. I can't stop thinking about you.' He couldn't meet my gaze and he turned bright red.

'Thinking about me how?' I was pretty sure I knew the answer, but I needed to hear it from him.

'In the inappropriate sense.' David forced the words out between gritted teeth.

'Oh.'

'I can't be friends with you while I think of you like that. I'm sorry.' He shook his head sadly.

'Would it help if I told you that I might have thought of you like that too?'

'Really?' David caught my gaze then looked away. 'No. No, that doesn't help at all. That's even worse. It's just not right. I'm still in love with Jenn.'

His words resonated painfully and trapped my breath in my chest, forcing my words to a whisper. 'If I'm honest, I don't think I've ever really stopped loving Chris.'

'So you understand why I can't see you any more.'

'No. Not really.'

'But—'

'David,' I interrupted. 'This isn't a conversation I really want to have on a doorstep. Can I come in?' The gap between us seemed huge as the silence stretched out.

'All right.' David slowly headed back into his house. 'Can I get you a drink?'

'Sure.' My nerves were jangling as I followed him into the kitchen, trying to work out what to say, and how best to handle the situation.

'Tea or coffee? Or something else?'

I shrugged and stuffed my hands into my pockets. It

was easier than trying to work out what to do with them. 'Whatever you're having.'

'There's a good bottle of zinfandel in the fridge.'

'OK.' I shrugged and watched as he opened the wine in silence. He poured a couple of large glasses and handed one to me. I took a small sip before setting it down on the breakfast bar. It was good, but I was driving, and I didn't think alcohol was really going to help the situation. David disagreed and downed half his glass in one go.

'Well, this is nice and awkward,' I observed.

'Yeah. It is a bit,' David agreed. 'So, how have you been?'

'All right, thanks.'

'How's work?'

'About the same as usual.'

'And Lisa?'

'She's fine. Settling into university. Not missing me anywhere near as much as I am her. David?' I waited until he looked up at me properly. 'I didn't really come round here for small talk.'

'No. I guess you didn't. Living room?'

'Sure.' I followed him through and watched as he paced and fidgeted uncomfortably, lapping the room again and again. 'David, sit down and talk to me.'

He looked around and flopped into the chair furthest away from me.

'I don't even know where to start.' He rubbed the back of his neck worriedly.

'Well, first you said you don't want to see me any more, then you said you liked me. How was it you phrased it? Oh yes, in an "inappropriate way". And when I admitted I might have thought about you that way too, you reacted in a way that some people might consider insulting.'

'Did I really react that badly?'

'It wasn't your best moment.' I sat back into the cushions.

'So how about that as a place to start? You could try explaining why the thought of us together is so utterly abhorrent to you. I mean, don't think I'm vain, but I like to think of myself as still being vaguely attractive to the opposite sex.'

'You are. That's the problem.' David shrugged helplessly.

'I'm going to need more than that, David.'

'I'm still in love with my wife. She's still around me and part of my life.'

'You feel like you're betraying her?'

He nodded silently.

'Because you're attracted to me, you don't want to see me?'

'I know it probably sounds silly to you, but I don't know what else to do.'

'Why don't you just keep seeing me anyway?' I kept my voice soft. 'Without putting too fine a point on it, Jenn's dead. Where's the harm? We're just friends. If anything else happens, and I'm not saying it will, then we can deal with it then.'

'Look Ruth, you've been a good friend and you've helped me a lot, but I can't keep betraying Jenn.'

'All right.' I wanted to argue with him, and tell him he was being an idiot, but it wasn't fair. It's not even been a year since he lost his wife. It took me a lot longer than that to come to terms with Chris's passing, and I'd had the benefit of time to prepare beforehand. This was David's grief and his life, and he had to handle that in the way that was best for him. I just wish he could find a way to do that which didn't cost me his friendship.

I stood up and brushed imaginary dust off my jeans, and dug in my bag for my keys. My fingers wrapped around them almost instantly, but I kept rummaging for long moments while I composed myself. When I looked up, I managed to give him a bright smile. It was a fake one, but I've had plenty of years to perfect it. It's the same one I used for years when people asked if I was all right, and now it's the one I use at work when people need to see a smiling confident face that tells them everything is all right, even when it isn't and never will be again.

'So, I guess we'll see each other around?' David followed me to the front door.

'Maybe.' It wasn't a big town, but I hadn't remembered ever bumping into him before we met. Our circles were different, and that was fine. My smile faltered as I opened the door and turned to face him. I let my hand fall to his on the door handle, and my fingers wrapped briefly around his.

He stood silently for a moment, watching my hand on top of his. 'I'm sorry, Ruth.'

'Yeah, me too. It's all right though. I think I understand.' I took a deep breath and forced the smile back to my lips, even though I really felt like crying. 'Take care of yourself, David.'

Chapter Twenty-Four

Winter

DAVID

I can't wait until this winter is over. I'm so tired of all the enforced jolliness. First there was Halloween, and it seemed like every kid in the neighbourhood was dressed up and knocking on my door. Jenn always used to love it, but I didn't remember to buy any sweets. I didn't put up decorations either. It just seems so stupidly pointless. Half the children don't even try any more, they just wear a plastic mask they probably bought from the pound shop, then come hammering on my door demanding some sort of prize.

I bet most of them don't even understand the point of it. It's supposed to be a celebration of the dead, a day when the veil between the two worlds lifts or becomes so thin that spirits can pass through. I know because I researched it.

I sat waiting for Jenn, hoping that somehow the old pagan magic would still work, that she'd be able to come back to me, if only for one night. But it didn't work, if anything Jenn was quieter than usual. I've barely felt her around me lately. I don't really blame her for not wanting to be anywhere near me, I can barely even look at myself right now. It must be the guilt of what I nearly did pushing her away.

But I didn't actually do anything, so I know Jenn will forgive me. It's better to feel like this and still have Jenn nearby than to have a few moments of empty pleasure with someone else and lose Jenn forever. It's just a matter of waiting for her forgiveness.

In the meantime I've got plenty of things to distract me.

Bonfire night and Diwali fell close together this year, which basically means the sky has been filled with exploding crashes and screaming rockets for days. As if I wasn't sleeping badly enough already. I'm so tired I think I need to start inventing new words for it. I was tired a few weeks ago, when I had the non-argument with Ruth. Since then, and with Jenn's disappearance, I've gone from tired through exhausted, and come out the other side. I feel like one of those mindless destructive zombie creatures that seem to be on every other channel lately. I'm just an automaton in a mask that other people seem to vaguely recognise. I don't know how they do. When I looked in the mirror yesterday, I barely recognised myself. I look haggard and drawn, and about a decade older than I did a few months ago.

I can't sleep without Jenn here. The lack of her presence around me is as choking as the thick gun powder and bonfire smoke that hangs in the air. I don't want to do anything except wait and beg for her forgiveness. Anything else seems pointless. There's no point trying to eat when everything turns to ash in your mouth, and it's useless trying to paint when all the colour has drained out of your world.

There's no point trying to talk to anyone either. What have my family done that they deserve to be dragged down into misery with me? It's a pain of my own creating, and there's no one I can ask to share it. Besides, it wouldn't relieve the burden anyway, only stretch and spread it out so it could hurt more people.

I'm being pulled back down into that pit of despair, but I don't have the energy or inclination to fight it. I'm too tired. I'm fed up of fighting and always trying to swim against the tide and never really getting anywhere. I feel old and tired and heavy. Every part of my body is weighed down under my own guilt.

It's best that I'm just left alone until Jenn's able to forgive me. Until then, there's nothing anyone can do to help me anyway.

JENN

If there was an award for doing the most stupid thing possible, but with the right intentions, David would definitely be on the shortlist for winning it.

He's cut off all contact with Ruth. Completely. I wish I had hands so I could go give him a really good shake. I love my husband dearly, but sometimes he's a complete idiot. I struggle to understand it. He's so talented when it comes to seeing the beauty and the angle that everyone else misses. How can he be so blind to this? I'm practically jumping up and down in his face and yelling in his ear, but he remains completely oblivious. The more I try to make him understand, the more he seems not to hear.

He's right that I've not been around him as much as I would like, but it's not because I'm angry or upset with him. It's because he is pushing me away. His worry and pain over something that never even happened is building a huge, impenetrable wall between us. Even my mirror trick isn't working – he's filled with so much misplaced guilt. I don't know what to do about it. He's utterly wretched and I can't reach him to help. I tried going through Lottie and Matty, but he just lied to them and pretended everything was fine.

I started leaving him things, little messages to try and break through the barrier of guilt he's built up. But he misunderstood them. He took the white feather as a reminder that I was still there. It filled me with hope at first, until he started apologising again. All I'd meant to do was let him know he wasn't as alone as he felt, and that I still loved him. But he took it to mean I was angry that he had feelings towards another woman, that I was reminding him that he still belonged to me.

I left his sketchbook and a brush on the worktop. I hoped he'd start painting again. But he didn't. He threw it, and all the nearby paints and brushes, into the bin, claiming that he was a terrible person who didn't deserve anything good or beautiful in his life. I wish I could have cried that day.

It's like he wants to hurt himself, and believes if he suffers enough, I'll forgive him. I wish I could tell him that it isn't true, and that there's nothing to forgive. I'm already with him, and I always will be. There's nothing he could do that would ever make me stop loving him.

I think there's something wrong with that tiny speck of green I found. It had been growing recently, until it was as big as the tip of my little finger. Other tiny specks appeared around it, glittering with colour and life. But they've all gone now. And the first, tiny, delicate speck seems to have shrunk again. I still don't know what they are, or what they mean, but it must be important.

I feel sad to see them go. I liked those strange little green things. They're so familiar that I feel like I should recognise them. But I'm still struggling to understand what they are. Or were.

What they mean is even harder to work out.

But it doesn't really matter. If they are important, then I'm sure I'll find out why soon enough. They would be fascinating to me, except that I have better things to concentrate on right now.

My world isn't the only one that's changing. In the living one, the shops have brought out their shimmering lights, glittering globes and shining stars to turn the town into a glistening beacon of hope, joy and Christmas cheer. I always loved this time of year. The sense of excitement that it fills you with, and the way people seem to be a little bit more cheerful and nice. I'd usually be half-done with my

Christmas shopping by now. Not because I'd plan to start early, but because I'd just see things that I'd want to buy. A top Lottie would love, the book Matty wouldn't be able to put down, and the CD that I knew David would play every time he got into the car until about February.

But there's not so much joy and happiness this year. Especially not for David. While everyone else is excited and counting down the nights until the big day, David's not looking forward to Christmas, and he isn't counting down to it either. His internal countdown is locked on a point in time a few days later, in that odd period between the end of Christmas celebrations and the start of New Year ones. He's counting down to the anniversary of my death.

While everyone else in the world is excited, David is dreading the coming weeks.

I'm hoping it won't be quite as bad as he fears, because even though I won't be doing any shopping this year, I still have a gift to give. The gift of hope. I don't think there could be anything more appropriate to give at this time of year.

David isn't listening to me. He's too busy feeling bad and worrying himself to distraction over something that hasn't even happened yet. But that's all right, because I'll just find someone who is willing to listen. I already know the perfect woman for the job. I just have to get her attention in a way that she can't possibly mistake.

RUTH

It has been a very strange few weeks. Christmas decorations seem to have sprouted up almost everywhere, and we're still weeks away from the main event.

To be honest, I'm hating it. Usually Lisa and I go shopping together, clumping around in scarves and boots until our feet hurt, but she's too busy with her new university life and friends. It's exactly how it should be, and I'm glad she's settling in so well, but it does make for quite a lonely run-up to Christmas.

But I expected all that. That's why I've been doing my shopping online this year, because it lets me avoid the crowds. It's shocking how lonely you can be in a crowd of people. But that isn't what's made the last few weeks so … peculiar. Strange things keep happening.

It started off with the feeling of being watched. For a few days, everywhere I went I felt like there were eyes on me, even when I was alone. But the really strange thing was that it didn't frighten me, even though it should have. Whatever it was didn't make me feel afraid, or threatened, but I knew I wasn't alone.

At first I thought I'd imagined it, that I was being paranoid and had just spent too much time by myself lately. At this time of year most of my friends are busy with their families, so it's harder to meet up. I started to wonder if it was something I'd created out of my own loneliness, then something happened that I can't explain away. I got an emergency call from work. One of my patients had taken a turn for the worse. I'd been dreading this call.

He's a really special case. I wouldn't usually be involved with someone suffering from chronic lung disease, but Billy is very unusual. He's only nineteen, barely past being a child, and his family have seen a lot of tragedy in the last few years, which is how I came to know them. It's also how they knew to ask for me when the specialists told them there wasn't much else they could do for Billy. He isn't terminal, or at least I'd hoped that he wasn't. He'd been on the transplant list for months, but his blood type isn't a common one. Sometimes the worst things seem to happen to the nicest people.

When I got to his house, he was in a lot of pain. Even with oxygen his lips were turning blue with hypoxia. His saturation levels were dropping even as his heart rate was climbing into ragged peaks, and his fingers were ice cold. His battered lungs just couldn't pull in enough oxygen to keep him alive any more. The best I could do for him, and his family, was keep them all as comfortable as possible.

'This … it?' Billy rasped the words out between painful breaths. 'No … lies.'

'You know I never would.' I squeezed his fingers gently around the pulse and oxygen monitors. 'I think it might be. Your oxygen levels are pretty low. If they get any lower the only thing left that might be able to help is a ventilator. Are you still sure about not wanting that?'

Billy nodded firmly, his mouth set, and my heart went out to him again. He was an incredibly smart young man, and he understood exactly what his chances of ever making it off a ventilator alive were. I had to admire his bravery.

'Shame … asked … Santa for … new … lungs.' He grinned in silent laughter. I lifted him gently forward and rearranged his pillows into a better position. It might sound silly, but even the smallest things can be a comfort at a time like this.

'Stay?' His eyes were filled with pleading as I rested him back into his pillows.

'As long as you need me to and longer,' I promised.

And I did. I stayed with Billy and his distraught parents for the whole night, watching and comforting them as best I could as his vital signs dropped lower and his breathing became more and more ragged. He drifted in and out of consciousness as the darkness faded slowly into morning. His parents sat by his side, holding his hands and talking to him even after he stopped answering. We'd talked about this often enough that words weren't needed. They both knew that their little boy was slipping away from them, and there was nothing I, or any other person in the world, could do to prevent that.

That was when it happened. The presence I'd been feeling for the last few days intensified and grew until it filled the whole room with peace and warmth so intense that it made it hard for me to breathe. Sweet, fresh fragrance filled the air. For a moment my eyes drifted shut, and I was caught in a swirl of light and warmth that I never wanted to leave.

Clanging alarms snatched me back into reality, and I whirled on the machines angrily. I'd turned those alarms off to make sure they didn't disturb Billy and his family in their final private moments. The figures that were flashing were impossible – the bloody things must be malfunctioning.

'I'm so sorry. I thought I'd shut these off.' I yanked the power cable out of the machine quickly, and its alarms faded back into silence. It wasn't as if they could tell us anything useful now anyway.

'Is all right ... am used ... to them.' Billy's eyes drifted shut as a small smile played around his lips and he exhaled slowly.

His mother looked over at me, tears in her eyes as I felt her son's wrist. 'Is he ...?'

I adjusted my fingers, not quite able to believe what I was feeling. I shook my head and grabbed my stethoscope from the end of the bed. I couldn't believe what I was hearing. I closed my eyes, listening more carefully as I moved it across his chest.

His mum's hand on my arm made me jump. 'He's asleep.' I half laughed. 'I don't understand how, but his breathing's evening out and his pulse is returning to normal.'

I clipped the pulse and oxygen monitors back on his finger, already knowing what I was going to find. After an excruciatingly long thirty seconds I flipped the screen over to his parents to show a steady seventy percent and slowly rising. Somehow Billy was improving.

I stayed with them for another hour, taking vitals and watching Billy closely. Sometimes I'd had patients who seemed to get better just before they passed, but never like this. I gave the readings to the day nurses who looked at me like I'd been drinking on duty, and left with words of thanks and miracles ringing in my ears.

When I reached my car, my hands were shaking and tears were streaming down my cheeks. I'd gone in expecting Billy wouldn't make it through the night. And I'd been right. He had been dying. I've seen enough passings to know when the body is shutting down, but something intensely beautiful and loving had saved him, at least for now. I didn't notice the little white feather tucked beneath my windscreen wiper until I got home. Even then I was too tired and shocked to think much of it. It was just a feather.

I got the call six hours later. Billy's pager had gone off. They'd finally found him a match.

The strange things have kept happening. Nothing anywhere near as dramatic as what happened with Billy, and I think I'm glad for that. Whatever it was I felt in Billy's room was too intensely beautiful. In a way, it was frightening. I'm glad I've not seen or felt that again, but the warm feeling of being watched hasn't gone away, and I get the distinct feeling that it won't, at least not for a while.

I like this feeling of being watched over. I'm getting used to this fresh, sweet smell being around me – it's comforting and yet invigorating at the same time. It seems to have a positive effect on my patients, and anything that makes their lives easier and better can't be bad.

The air seems a little warmer and brighter, and the Christmas decorations I've been avoiding now seem as magical and as exciting as when I was a little girl.

My dreams have been strange too. I didn't sleep well

today. It might be partly because I've been on nights, and the changeover back to daylight hours can be uncomfortable, but I was kept awake by the same dream that repeated over and over again. In the beginning it was lovely, and more real than any memory or dream I've ever had before. I could feel the breeze on my skin and through my hair, and the springy, cool grass between my toes.

I was walking through a beautiful wood, filled with daffodils and late winter jasmine, and birdsong echoed through the air. It was one of those gorgeous winter days where the sun shone brightly, and the sky was crisp, clear and blue.

Then everything twisted, and the birdsong became louder and more pained until it twisted into human sobs. I tried to follow them, to find the person who was in pain so I could help them, but the sobs bounced off the trees and came back to me distorted and twisted, and I couldn't work out where it was coming from. Then I woke up.

The dream pulled me back into it as soon as I closed my eyes again. And again and again. Each time I ran down what I thought was the right path and the sobbing got louder and clearer, but every time I was about to reach the source I'd wake up again. But I knew I was getting closer, so I closed my eyes and forced myself back to sleep.

Finally I found him, curled in a ball and shaking as he sobbed helplessly. Every sob seemed to wrack his entire body. I knew he'd been crying for a very long time and, that without someone intervening, he'd cry for a lot, lot longer. My hand rested on his bony shoulder, and I gasped in horror at the eyes that met mine.

They were David's, only red-rimmed, bloodshot, and filled with pain. His skin was grey and streaked with tears, but they dried up as I pulled him to his feet.

His hand fitted into mine easily, and as we walked back

together, huge, soft snowflakes that were as warm and fluffy as feathers started to fall from the clear blue sky.

Despite the broken night of sleep, I woke up feeling well-rested. I grabbed my filofax out of my bag while the kettle was still boiling. Lisa likes to tease me about it and call me old-fashioned, but I don't care. I like the feel of the paper, and the reassuring weight of it in my bag. And I can find everything I need in seconds, and never have to worry about a battery letting me down.

I flipped through pages as I waited for the tea to steep, and gasped. Stuck to the page with David's details was a single, pure white feather. It tingled between my fingers when I picked it up and studied it, wondering how on earth it had got there. As I smoothed it out, I remembered the one that had been caught on my windscreen. I wandered outside, convincing myself that it couldn't possibly be there after so long, but it was waiting patiently, a perfect match for the one from my filofax. I had to peel it off the windscreen, my mind reeling. It could be children playing a prank, but who would bother? No one else has access to my filofax.

I'm not usually the type of person who pays much attention to dreams, but then again I've never had ones so vivid. And I'd never had things from my dreams turning up in my real life. I grabbed my keys and phone, and was dialling the number before I'd finished pulling on my shoes.

'Hey, it's me. I'm coming over and I'm not taking no for an answer.' I stared at myself in the window as I snapped the phone shut. No, I'd have to change. These clothes definitely weren't going to do.

Chapter Twenty-Five

DAVID

Before I'd time to really think, or let the panic set in, Ruth knocked at my door. I wasn't sure whether or not I wanted to see her. I mean, honestly, I've missed her, but I didn't want to be around someone who made me think about betraying Jenn.

'Bloody hell, you look awful.' Ruth ran her eyes over me. 'You've not been eating properly.'

'Speak for yourself.' Shock made me blunter than usual. I'd never seen her look anything except great, but she stood in front of me in a paint-stained jumper and scruffy jeans, and her hair was scraped back to show that she wasn't wearing a scrap of make-up. 'What happened?'

'At least mine is by design.' She grinned cheerfully. 'I feel a right mess, but I've had an idea. I'll leave the skirts and boots at home. I'll wear my ugliest, oldest clothes and battered flat shoes, and I won't do my hair. I'll even forgo the make-up.' She paused and took a deep breath, and the next words came flying out quickly. 'I like you, David, and I've missed you. You make me laugh and I feel like I can really talk to you, and that you understand. I don't feel like I have to walk on eggshells with you, or pretend that I'm fine when I feel like crap. I figured you can't possibly be attracted to anyone who looks as much like a scarecrow as I do now. So maybe this way we can still be friends. What do you think?'

I tried to hide my sigh of relief. I'd been driving myself crazy over the last few weeks. I wanted to see her, and missed her company, but couldn't betray Jenn. I was so relieved she'd come up with a solution that I could have hugged her. In a strictly friends only type of way. 'I think I'd like that.'

'Good.' Ruth flashed me a smile that was distinctly un-scarecrow like, and I found myself thinking maybe her scruffy-dressing plan wasn't quite as foolproof as she'd thought, but I didn't care.

'So, how have you been?' She shot the question at me as she wandered into my house.

'All right.' I flashed her a bright smile, thrilled to have her back, but unsure of how to act. 'You?'

'About the same. Now, how have you really been?'

I rolled my eyes. 'Bloody awful. Seems Christmas is on overdrive this year, and determined to remind me of how miserable and alone I am.'

Ruth laughed, and, as cheesy as it sounds, I felt the weight lift off my shoulders a bit.

'Me too,' she admitted. 'Usually Lisa does everything with me, but she's not back from university yet. Decorating a tree by yourself is really ...'

'Depressing?' I offered the word.

'Yeah. Or it would have been if not for all the mulled wine.' She grinned. 'There was a lot of it. Still, at least your house has escaped.'

'Ha. That's what you think.' I held open the door to the living room.

'Wow. That's a lot of tinsel and glitter. I especially like the Santa cushions.'

'Yeah.' I let the door swing shut. 'Lottie did it. She knew I wouldn't put decorations up myself, so decided to surprise me the other day. I left a relatively tidy, clean house to go to work, and came back to find Rudolph had broken in and thrown up.'

'That's a bit harsh,' Ruth chided, trying not to laugh.

'I know, it's just a bit much. Lottie probably thought it would cheer me up.'

'Do you need cheering up?' Ruth's question sounded innocent enough, but I couldn't help noticing she kept her back to me.

'Yeah. I guess maybe I did.' My stomach growled and Ruth spun round and laughed at the look of surprise on my face.

'Hungry?'

'Yeah. Actually I am.' I couldn't remember the last time I'd actually felt hungry. Lately I'd just been eating because I felt like I had to, not because I wanted to. 'We could order something in.'

'At this time on a Friday it'll take ages,' Ruth argued. 'Besides, I'm not sure I fancy takeout. What have you got in your fridge?'

'Nothing worth eating. I've not been shopping.' I grimaced at the confession.

'I'm sure we can come up with something.'

'Want to bet on it?' I knew what was in the fridge, and it was precious little.

'Maybe. Depends on your terms.' Ruth's answer sent a shiver down my spine, and I made an effort not to watch her as she rummaged in my fridge. 'Well there's ham in here.'

'Only because I've run out of bread.'

'And you've got mushrooms and milk.'

'Sounds delicious.' I pulled a face.

'Well if you've got some rice, it won't be too bad.' She dropped her finds by the oven and started to dig through the cupboards until she came out with a couple of small jars of herbs, an ancient bottle of soy sauce, and a dusty looking bag of rice.

'Sorted.' She grinned triumphantly. 'It's not exactly haute cuisine, but I reckon I can conjure up a special fried rice type dish. I should have set terms and conditions on that bet.'

I dropped the dirty plates into the dishwasher and watched Ruth as she sipped her wine. She looked up and caught me staring at her.

'What?'

'You're amazing. I don't know how you do it,' I admitted honestly.

'Do what?' Ruth shook her head in confusion.

'Everything. You're so together and collected all the time. And you seem happy. I feel like I'm still struggling to get up and get through every day. How do you it?'

'Well, time does help. I know I've said it to you before, and that's a cliché, but most clichés are true.'

We fell into quiet, only this time it was comfortable, but the question I'd been pretending not to think about was still bothering me.

'What is it?' Ruth smiled at me.

'What?'

'I just get the feeling there's something you wanted to ask me. Go ahead and ask.'

'It's not important.' I shook my head to try and clear it.

'Just spit it out, David.'

'Did you mean it when you said you'd thought of me ... like that?' I blurted the words out.

'Like what? Oh, like that.' Ruth blushed slightly. 'Like I said, maybe.'

'How do you do it?' I stared at her. 'How do you even think about being with me?'

She shrugged. 'Well, we get on and have fun and laugh together. I like you, trust you, and you're attractive. Why wouldn't I think about you like that? Don't look at me like I'm some sort of sex-crazed nymphomaniac.'

'No it's not that.' I tried to reassure her. 'I mean ... what about your husband?'

She took a deep breath. 'Chris isn't here any more, but I am.'

'It's really that simple?' It felt like she was speaking another language.

'I didn't say it was simple.' Ruth laughed. 'You want brutally honest?'

I nodded. 'Don't I always?'

'Chris getting sick was the worst thing that ever happened to me. I hated watching him suffer, and I hated both of us knowing he was going to lose the fight. I hated how long it took him to die, and how much pain he was in, but at the same time I hated how fast it all happened. But I'm grateful too.'

'Really?'

Ruth licked her lips and nodded slowly. 'Sorry, I've never really tried to put this into words before. The thing his illness gave us, ironically as it took it all away in the end, was time. We had time together to take in what was happening and understand it. Even though he was the one who was dying, Chris took care of me and worried about me right up until the last. We had time together to plan.'

'Plan what?'

'Everything. We planned everything. From what to do with his car, to what colour I should paint the dining room, and how I should get the loft re-insulated before winter. We talked about Lisa and where she'd go to school, how we'd pay for her university, and how old she'd be before I allowed her to date. We planned my fortieth birthday, and his parents' golden anniversary. Right down to the gifts. I bought the cards and he wrote them, and recorded video messages so he'd still be part of the important things in our lives. He even planned his funeral with me. And his death.' Ruth's throat closed and she had to gulp back tears.

I reached out to her without thinking. 'Please don't cry. I didn't mean to upset you.'

She shrugged and rubbed at her eyes. 'You wanted brutal honesty. This is it. There will always be things about Chris that will upset me and make me cry, and there'll always be things that you'll never get over, but you have to keep on living. Maybe it was easier for me. I had Lisa. I couldn't afford to get depressed. I had to live life for her too, and show her that living isn't just about pain. She spent too much of her life knowing the worst kinds of pain. I had to show her it could be happy and joyful too. It was one of the things Chris made me promise him.'

'Did you?'

'I like to think so.' Ruth smiled, and my stomach twisted. 'Which sort of brings us back to your question. Chris even planned for this.'

'What do you mean?' I felt completely lost.

'I was thirty-eight when we found out Chris wasn't going to get better. He passed away just after I turned thirty-nine. Have you any idea how young that is? With any luck it's barely half my life. That was another of the promises he asked of me, that I wouldn't live my life alone, and that I should take every chance I had for happiness, without any guilt. Which included sex.'

It shouldn't have interested me, not with Jenn still with me, but I had to know. 'So, can I ask ... have you?'

'Had sex since? Hell yes.'

'When?' The word slipped out before I could bite my tongue.

'Why?' Ruth's eyes sparkled mischievously. 'You offering? Sorry.' She took it back almost immediately, but not before a vision of her naked skittered across my mind. 'I shouldn't make jokes like that. First time was a couple of weeks after I turned forty.' She smiled at a memory I couldn't see. 'It was my birthday that did it.'

'Some sort of midlife crisis?'

'Nope. I threw myself off a bridge for that.'

'What?' That had been the last thing I'd have guessed, and from the look on Ruth's face, she knew it.

'It was one of the things Chris planned. I got to my fortieth birthday, and a friend delivered the card and present from Chris. He'd arranged for me to go bungee jumping. He'd always wanted to do it, but I'd never really liked heights. He said that he knew I could do anything, but that I needed to know and believe it too, and that once I'd jumped off a bridge, I'd know it for sure. After that, having sex with someone else didn't seem such a huge … jump.' She grinned as she said it and without make-up, I could see that the corners of her eyes crinkled prettily, drawing attention to her sparkling eyes. My stomach clenched again.

'You know, the clothes don't work. You're still bloody gorgeous.'

'Then do something about it.' She folded her arms and challenged me.

'What do you mean?' My voice caught slightly in my throat. She leaned in closer, and I found it hard to breathe.

'I mean find a way to get over it, throw me out, or come here and do something about it.'

'I can't.' I was frozen to the spot.

'If you're attracted to me, why shouldn't you do something about it? If you're not attracted to me, what's the problem?' Her voice was soft and low, and I struggled not to watch her lips as they formed her words.

'It's Jenn.' I pushed myself away from her.

'All right.' Ruth settled back into her chair. 'Tell me.'

I took a deep breath and exhaled a couple of times before I could find the words I needed. 'Jenn is … still here. She's still with me. If I got involved with you, I'd feel like I was betraying her.'

'You really think Jenn's still here?' Ruth's tone was carefully even.

'I know it sounds a bit insane, but yes, I do. In fact I know she is. I'm not the only one.' I ran my hands through my hair and tried to find the words to explain in a way that wouldn't have her calling the local psychiatric unit. 'After she died,

Jenn came back. I could feel her around me. At first I thought I was going mad from grief and that she was just a figment of my desperate imagination, but things started to happen that we couldn't explain away. I've seen her in mirrors and glass, and felt her around. She's left gifts and messages that couldn't have been from anyone else.'

'What like?'

'Well, she used to leave my paints and brushes out to try and get me to paint, and when Matty asked her for advice about his girlfriend, she left her engagement ring in his pocket. She gave a bracelet to Lottie when she was struggling with some things.' I started to laugh. 'When she wanted us to clear out some of her stuff, she started leaving black bags everywhere. I mean everywhere, and she didn't stop until we'd done what she wanted.' I swallowed nervously. 'So, are you waiting for me to turn around so you can speed dial the men in white coats?'

'Not quite. What do you mean when you said you could "feel her" around you?'

'It's hard to explain beyond that. We just feel her as a presence around us. Like the feeling you get when you know someone's watching you, only stronger. Do you know what I mean?'

'Hmm.' Ruth nodded slowly. 'I think I do. Do you get smells too?'

'What made you ask that?'

Ruth shrugged. 'Just wondering.'

'Scent seems to be one of the things we noticed most.' David smiled. 'Whenever she's around us, we usually smell honeysuckle and apple. She always used apple shampoo and wore honeysuckle perfumes. The air changes until it feels softer and lighter, and warmer. Like somehow you're being wrapped in sunshine. Which sounds ridiculous, I know, but it's true.'

'It doesn't sound that strange.' Ruth's voice was choked,

and the colour had drained from her face. 'Has she left other things too?'

'Are you all right?'

Ruth nodded. 'Yes. Has she left other things? Or changed things? Like dreams, or bad situations?'

'Yes. All of that and more. Are you sure you're all right?'

'I think so.' She smiled shakily. 'You didn't ask me why I suddenly called you and turned up out of the blue. I thought you would.'

'I guess I was too glad to see you to care.' The casual words surprised me, ringing true even as I spoke them.

'You should have asked me. It's just ... I think I might have met your wife. Sort of.' She let out a long breath, slowly and evenly, before she spoke again. 'If you'd told me any of this last month, I'd have struggled to believe you, but recently I've been experiencing some very strange things.'

'You think Jenn's behind them?' I leaned forward in my seat, desperate to hear what she had to say.

Ruth laughed. 'Honestly, I didn't know what to think. I was starting to think maybe I had an angel watching over me. I felt this presence around me for days, it was warm and softly scented, like a late summer evening. Then I had an experience with a patient that was ... amazing. He should have died. In fact he was dying, but this ... presence intervened, and he didn't.'

'What does that have to do with you calling me?' I struggled to see the connection. But the word *presence* caught my attention. Surely Jenn hadn't ...

'Strange dreams. I dreamt of hearing someone crying like their heart was breaking, and when I found him, it was you. I took your hand and we walked back towards the sunshine in a field of feathers.' She shook her head and buried her face in her hands. 'Now I'm the one who sounds crazy. Especially because I've found two feathers that could have fallen out of the dream since. To replay the old line about things "sounding strange", they didn't feel like ordinary feathers, they felt nice, so I kept them.'

'Do you have them with you?' My heart was pounding so loudly it echoed in my ears. I was convinced it would be Jenn, because there wasn't anyone else, but I had to see the feathers to know for sure.

'Sure.' Ruth grabbed her bag and rummaged around inside.

I tightened my hands into fists with the effort it took not to snatch Ruth's bag in eagerness. After what seemed like an age, she pulled out a battered blue organiser that was struggling to stay closed against all the bits of paper that stuck out of it. She slipped the rubber band off it and flipped it open. In the middle, rested two perfect white feathers, so bright that they seemed to shimmer.

Forcing my hand not to shake, I reached out towards them. 'May I?' Ruth nodded and pushed the organiser towards me. I tried not to laugh as I picked up the feathers and felt goose pimples shoot up my arm. It definitely felt the same as the ones from Jenn. 'My family are making a collection of feathers like these. We've got dozens of them. Where did yours come from?'

'One on my windscreen the morning after I'd been with the patient I told you about, and the other in my filofax. Stuck to the page with your name on it.' She laughed. 'So I'm probably being haunted by your dead wife. At least that means my phone's probably all right.'

'What?'

Ruth shrugged. 'There's been a couple of times I've got my phone out my bag, only to find that it's unlocked and your number is on the screen. I think it might even have called you a few times. I was starting to think it was faulty and that I'd have to take it in for repairs. At least now I know it's probably not going loopy, and neither am I.'

'You're taking this all remarkably well.' I wasn't sure whether I should be worried about Ruth's reaction or not. It was a lot more down to earth than I'd even hoped for. Instead of being angry or freaked out, she seemed amused.

Ruth snorted in amusement and rested her chin on the heel of her hand. 'You forget what it is I do for a living. I spend a lot more time thinking about death and the afterlife than the average person. If I'm totally honest, I've come across more than a few odd things in my career.'

'What like?' Now that we'd started talking about this, I didn't want her to stop.

Ruth rocked back on her chair and looked away. For a moment I was worried that the question was far too personal and that I'd somehow upset her with my eagerness to hear more about Jenn. But after a moment, Ruth bit her lips together and began to speak again, her voice and eyes somewhere further away than in the room with me.

'I've seen patients, who I would have sworn couldn't move from pain and exhaustion, sit up in bed and hold out their hands and smile like they've never been happier. I've seen others open their eyes and have completely normal-sounding conversations with people I couldn't see or hear. I'm not the only one either. It's not something we really talk about, but on the very rare occasions that we do, anyone who's been doing this job for long will have their own stories. You know when someone's dying. It's something you just can't escape. You actually feel the soul leave their body. Something changes in those final moments that I can't even begin to explain.' Her voice croaked, and she hesitated, before swallowing hard and continuing. 'I don't think it's completely out of the realms of possibility to think that someone's soul could linger on. If a spirit or angel or whatever can come to welcome a dying person and soothe them, then I don't see why someone couldn't stay on after they've died. If it was what they really wanted.' She looked back at me, her eyes overly bright with emotion.

'So you really believe me? About Jenn and everything?' I was scared to hear her answer, in case she said no.

'Yeah.' Ruth nodded slowly. 'Just ...'

'Just what?' My breath was heavy in my chest.

'Just ... I'm struggling to understand why Jenn would go through all this effort to bring us back together if we can't actually be together. Wouldn't she have known you'd be attracted to me, and that it would make for some seriously awkward, friendship-wrecking situations?'

I froze, my mind reeling. What if she was right? What if Jenn had known all along that I'd be attracted to Ruth? My heart was thumping so hard I was convinced Ruth would be able to hear it.

'Well?' Ruth was watching me, waiting for an answer. Her eyes flicked to something behind me, and she jumped off her chair. 'Bloody hell!' She reached for something off the bookshelf, and I had a funny feeling I knew what it was. 'This isn't the same daffodil bulb that nearly wrote off your car, is it?' She held the brown paper globe between shaky fingers. 'Answer me this honestly, David. This has got something to do with Jenn as well, hasn't it?'

'Yes.' Denial wasn't an option. Of course it was Jenn.

'So she didn't just haunt me until I came back round here, she actually introduced us too.' Ruth laughed and tossed the bulb between her hands.

I nodded even though it wasn't really a question, and took the bulb back from her. My fingers tingled and burnt where they brushed against Ruth's, and I turned away quickly to tuck the bulb gently back where it now seemed to live.

'David?' Ruth's fingers curled around my wrist and I stared down at them numbly. I couldn't believe the heat that came from a few inches of bare skin. 'David. Answer a question for me. Just one more.'

'All right.' I turned to face her, but she was nearer than I thought, and I struggled to ignore the sheer closeness of her. Even through the baggy old clothes, I was intensely aware of the curves of her body. Desire and guilt fought for dominance. On one hand I wanted nothing more than to gather Ruth in my arms, follow my body's screaming urges and kiss her thoroughly – just to start with. But on the other hand there was my Jenn. I needed an answer, and hoped beyond reason that Ruth could give me one.

'Jenn has been around you all this time, so she's known about you being attracted to me for as long as you have. Maybe longer as you've tried to convince yourself otherwise. Given that, and the fact that I was willing to respect your wishes and never see you again, as a friend or anything else, why do you think she's gone through all this trouble to bring us back together, and to this point?' Ruth looked up at me with such warmth and openness that my stomach flipped.

'I ...' I took a deep breath, stalling for time as I considered the possibilities. 'I don't know.'

'This is your wife we're talking about. If you don't know her, who does?' Ruth's calm logic was unavoidable.

My mind reeled as my world turned upside down. For the first time in months, everything started to make sense again. If Ruth was right, then I'd misunderstood almost every one of Jenn's actions in the last few weeks. The feathers she'd left weren't angry messages, they were just reminders that I wasn't as alone as I'd felt, and when she left my sketchbook out it was just an attempt to drag me out of my misery and make me smile again.

I couldn't believe how stupid I'd been. All this time I'd been concentrating on the tiny little movements Jenn made, and ignoring the whole point of what she'd been trying to achieve. She hadn't been trying to hurt me, or punish me, she'd been trying to get me to move on.

I closed my eyes, and for a brief moment the air took on the warmth and weight that meant Jenn was nearby. I could almost hear her relieved laughter as she disappeared again, and I finally understood her point.

'David, I'm afraid I lied to you.' Ruth interrupted my thoughts and brought me back to earth. 'I've got another question. How do you feel about women who make the first move?'

Before I could even think about the question, let alone work out the answer, Ruth's hands were cupping my face. She stared at me for a second and her eyes searched mine briefly, before she pressed herself against me. Her body was warm and welcoming against mine. Her nose brushed against mine before our lips met, tentatively at first, and slightly unsure. She was waiting to see how I'd respond.

Then her hands slipped around my neck, and she drew me closer. Her touch was soothing and healing, but incredibly sexy all at the same time. Heat flooded through me from every point where we touched, bringing me back to life and pushing away every other thought except for the feel of her lips against mine.

Ruth pulled away from me reluctantly, and for a moment I felt her breath hot against my lips. She smiled up at me, mischief and desire mingling in her eyes in a way that made my stomach, and muscles a lot lower that I thought had long ago shrivelled up, clench tightly.

'Well, the roof didn't cave in on us, and I've not been pelted by leftover rice or daffodil bulbs. What do you think that means?'

I wrapped an arm around her waist, and placed my other hand at the back of her neck.

'I think it means I should do this.' I lowered my mouth back to hers in a kiss that was deep and hungry and bruising.

Chapter Twenty-Six

JENN

I'm so excited. The tiny speck of green I found isn't so tiny any more. And it isn't alone. All the others have reappeared, and dozens more of the tiny little specks have been sprouting out of the ground and stretching up in tiny green spears. The first one is nearly as tall as my thumb.

I've finally realised what they are and where I know them from. They're daffodils. Dozens and dozens of tiny daffodils, all growing out of nothing in this dead, grey world.

It was empty and lonely here, but now with this tiny carpet of green appearing, it doesn't feel like such a bad place to be. Soon they'll grow taller and burst into golden blooms.

I still don't know what they mean, but they have to be good. It's strange that they should choose to reappear now. I would think about them more, but nothing as pretty as daffodils could bring anything but happiness, and I've been distracted by other things.

I'm so pleased for David and Ruth. I know that might sound like an odd thing for a wife to say about her husband kissing another woman, but I do mean it. I've had to come to terms with the fact that things have changed.

It looks like David is finally realising and accepting it too. It's lovely to watch him at the moment. It's like he's coming back to life beneath Ruth's touch.

It is heartbreakingly sad for me, but my husband deserves better than fleeting, half-imagined touches and barely-there whispers. He deserves someone who can give him better and more. Maybe someone like Ruth.

I do quite like Ruth, and I know that Lottie does too.

She's been fantastic, my daughter. She's been encouraging her dad when I wasn't able to reach him. Although I probably wouldn't have used the term "hooking up". We called it something very different, and less vulgar, when I was younger. Back then, David and I were just "seeing each other". But whatever she calls it, I'm glad Lottie is on side.

Both of my children are adults. They're mature enough to understand the situation and not to blame David for being with a woman who isn't me. They're not going to get angry or hateful and accuse him of replacing me.

But if I had been worried about either of their reactions, it would have been Lottie's. So I'm really glad she likes Ruth, and not just because it means she won't make things difficult, but because I value her opinion too.

I have been spending more time with my children lately. As much as I like Ruth, I don't want to watch her kissing my husband. Especially like that. She's passionate and alive, and makes David feel like a teenager again.

It's also that I don't want David to sense my presence and feel bad. I won't let him feel guilty about this, so I've been giving them their space. It's not been as difficult as I thought it would be. I haven't felt the same pull to be with David as I used to.

Don't get me wrong. I still do, and always will, love my husband. But the desperation to be with him that was there in the beginning has faded. It isn't so strong and dragging, and it doesn't cause me physical pain to be away from him any more. Maybe we're both reaching the point of some kind of acceptance.

I suppose it means that he's starting to move on. Which is a good thing. It's healthy and what he needs to do. It really is the best thing for everyone involved. I know it's for the best.

Except if it is, then why do I feel so horribly restless and on edge? It's like I'm waiting for something to happen or change. But nothing ever happens here in my horrible, empty grey place. There is no change.

Except for my daffodils.

DAVID

Ruth moaned and arched her back against me, deepening the kiss. I wrapped my arms around her more tightly. Her body felt different to Jenn's. Ruth was leaner and sleeker, and her breasts and bottom were smaller. The differences were exciting, terrifying and intoxicating all at once.

She teased my lips with hers, delicate soft kisses one moment, and then deeper more intense ones the next. I bruised her lips with mine, then traced kisses down her neck.

I'm still amazed that someone like Ruth can be attracted to someone like me. She really is gorgeous, and I care about her a lot. Then again, I know she cares about me too, so maybe she sees a different version of me to the one that greets me in the mirror every morning. It's not love. Not like it was before. We both know that, but we do enjoy each other's company, and the sheer physical attraction can't be ignored.

I gently tilted her head back to look into her eyes, placed a quick kiss on her nose, then broke away and flopped back against the arm of the sofa and sighed happily. Ruth sat up and pushed the hair out of her eyes and grinned at me.

'So,' she bit her bottom lip in that incredibly sexy way of hers. 'As much as I'm enjoying messing around and feeling like a horny teenager again, I'm not one any more. In case you forgot, this is my couch in my house – there aren't any parents coming home to catch us!'

'I'm not sure where you're going with this.' Horror and desire filled me in equal measure and I sat up straighter.

'That's exactly what I'm asking. I like you David, I really do.' She fiddled with her fingers before looking up at me.

'But you're driving me mad with frustration. I know you feel the same.' She rolled her eyes. 'Hell, I can feel how much you feel the same.' She glanced at my crotch and I felt my cheeks burn even hotter. 'So if you want me to spell it out for you, why are we still down here when we could be upstairs? We've been playing this game for weeks.'

I hesitated and Ruth glared at me and thumped me gently on the leg. 'Don't you even think about telling me anything less than the truth.'

'I'm worried about ruining our friendship.' I answered her honestly. 'Right now, it's not that hard to stop and back away, and go back to just being friends, but if we ...'

'Had sex.'

It still shocked me how easily Ruth talked about sex. 'Yeah. Well, that would change everything.'

'Why does it have to?'

'It just does.' Although for the life of me, I suddenly struggled to remember why that was the case. But it was obvious. Sex had to change things, didn't it?

Ruth sighed and tucked her feet underneath her. 'Sex only changes things if you let it. We can just decide that whatever happens, we'll stay friends.'

I shook my head. 'You make it sound so easy.'

'It is that easy.' Ruth cupped my face in her hands. 'Despite the way we've been acting, we're not teenagers any more. We're both mature adults capable of making mature decisions. It is only sex.' The tip of her thumb traced its way along the edge of my lips, making me shiver. I wished I could make her react to my touch like that. 'So, what do you think?'

'I think maybe it's time that I stopped thinking.' I could hardly believe the words had come out of my mouth, but they had and for once I wasn't crippled by guilt at the thought of taking another woman into my arms.

'I couldn't agree more.' Ruth smiled in a way that made me think very, very inappropriate thoughts about her. 'So, what are you doing for the rest of today?'

'What! You mean now?' Panic bolted me upright. It was one thing to think about having sex sometime in the hazy future of maybe, but was she serious? I couldn't just drop everything and leap into her bed now. I wasn't ready. I needed time to prepare.

'Why not?' Ruth raised an eyebrow at me.

'Shouldn't I be taking you out to dinner and buying you flowers and chocolates?'

'What on earth for?' Ruth rested her arm across the back of the sofa as she laughed. 'I already like you, you already like me, and there's no question that it's in a more than just friendly way.' She leaned closer. It would be so easy to shift slightly and kiss her.

'You honestly think it can be that simple?'

'I think it's as simple or as complicated as we choose to make it. Personally, I like to keep things simple.'

'It just seems too easy.' Even as I complained, a voice in my head shouted at me. Why on earth was I arguing with this gorgeous woman who wanted me?

Ruth's eyes flashed dangerously. 'If I didn't know you better, I'd have sworn you just called me easy.'

'No, no. I didn't mean that. I'd never think that about you.' I fumbled my words, trying to apologise and take back the offence before realising that Ruth was teasing me. The panic melted under her smile, and I leaned towards her. 'I should stop talking, shouldn't I?'

Ruth nodded, her eyes not leaving mine.

'Maybe I should do this instead.' I twisted my fingers through her hair and lowered my mouth to hers, and every other thought fled my mind.

Within seconds she was in my lap, her body pressed

tightly against mine as we moved together, hands wandering over each other. Her mouth was hot on mine and our kisses and fumbles were faster and more urgent than before. I pulled away shakily and caught her face between my hands.

'Do you want to come upstairs?' Her voice was deep with lust and her eyes had darkened with excitement. 'It's up to you, David, but if it helps, I really, really want you to say yes.'

I still couldn't believe this was happening. I struggled to get my voice past the lump in my throat. 'Yes.' I cleared my throat and tried again. 'Yes.'

She stood, one hand still in mine, deliciously solid and real, and beckoned provocatively with the other, a sultry smile spreading across her lips. 'Follow me.'

Ruth pulled the covers up and I flopped back into the pillows. My ears were burning and I could feel the heat rising to my cheeks. I didn't know where to look, but I couldn't look at Ruth.

'Are you all right?' She didn't move to close the gap between us. Clearly she was as disappointed as I was.

'Yeah.' I struggled to find something to say. I had to say something. 'So that was ...'

'About what I expected.' Ruth filled in the missing words far too easily for my liking, and she was careful not to touch me. The distance hurt terribly.

'You expected me to be bad in bed?' It was getting worse and worse. I wished the ground would open up and swallow me whole. I'd never been so embarrassed.

She rolled over to face me and propped her head up on her hand. 'No. I expected us to both be nervous.' Her hand slipped beneath the sheets to find mine, and she brought it to her lips and placed a kiss on the inside of my wrist, allowing me to breathe a sigh of relief. 'You were practically shaking with nerves.'

'I guess it was pretty crap. Sorry.' I felt the heat rising in my cheeks and looked away.

'It's all right.' Ruth stroked the inside of my arm. 'If you're nice, I'll let you make it up to me later.'

'Wow.' I gawped, shocked she hadn't already made an excuse to escape and never speak to me again. Instead, she was giving me another chance. 'You really are something else.' I kissed the tips of each of her fingers, amazed at how understanding she was being, and how much that put me at ease. That was one of the lovely things about Ruth – she's so easy to be around.

'I know.' Ruth grinned cheekily. 'So, to change the subject, have you got any plans for Christmas?'

'Lottie's decided she's cooking Christmas dinner.' I tried not to grimace at the thought of a Christmas without Jenn, and the empty spot at the table, and missing gifts under the tree. 'Matty and Lucy are coming down the night before, spending Christmas Day with us, then heading off to see her parents on Boxing Day. What about you?'

'Lisa isn't getting home until the twenty-third, and she has to be back at university by the twenty-seventh. She's got a job up there and they want her at work. I guess I'm lucky to have her for as long as I will. My brother-in-law and his family will probably come over at some point while she's still here. We've stayed pretty close even after Chris passed away.'

'That's nice.' I wondered how close I'd stay with the rest of Jenn's family. As much as Sarah and I got along, and I know she'll always be there for the kids, I somehow couldn't see us spending much time together.

'Yeah. So, we're both free on the twenty-second and most of the twenty-third.'

'Sounds like it.' I twisted a lock of her hair between my fingers. 'Do you fancy dinner?' I tried to appear casual, but I'm pretty sure I didn't have Ruth fooled for a second.

'Only if you promise it's not turkey.' Ruth grinned.

'Don't you find this a little ... odd?' I was suddenly worried again.

'What?' Ruth tilted her head. 'Two friends talking about Christmas plans? Nope.'

'Naked?'

'Nope. I call that good planning.' She laughed. 'You do have a point though.' She slipped out from under the covers and pulled on her top.

'Where are you going?' I sat up, feeling cold loneliness bite where her warmth had been seconds ago.

'Getting dressed.'

'Do you have to?'

'No. I guess I don't have to.' She hesitated, then dropped the top to the floor.

'Then can we stay like this a bit longer? Please.' I caught her wrist and pulled her back into bed, where she snuggled against me. 'Hmm.' I sighed into her hair. 'Thanks.'

'For what?' Her lips tickled my chest as she murmured the question against my bare skin, and something close to joy tickled in my stomach.

'Just for ... everything.' I shrugged and tucked my hands comfortably behind my head. I couldn't remember the last time I'd been so relaxed.

Her warmth shifted next to me, coaxing me from my dreams, and I sleepily wrapped my arm around her waist. I didn't bother to open my eyes as I pulled her against me, still half asleep. I nuzzled the back of her neck, and she moaned and shifted her body closer to mine, fitting her curves around my body as I groaned and pulled her closer.

She moved against me, and with me. Her head fell back against my shoulder and a soft murmur escaped from her lips as I cupped one of her breasts in my palm and kissed the back of her neck. Her hand caught mine and drew it down across her stomach as she shifted into a better position.

I pulled her more tightly against me, whispering into her ear. 'Jenn ...'

The warmth froze and I immediately realised my mistake. Shit. Did I risk moving? Long seconds passed before she spoke.

'Damn.' Her fingers uncurled from mine and she sagged against the bed, all the delicious, exciting tension gone in a single, thoughtless word. 'Just as things were getting interesting as well.'

'Oh my God, Ruth. I'm so, so sorry. I can't believe I just did that. Shit, Ruth ...'

'You're going to want to talk about this, aren't you?' Her voice was tired as the bed sheets rustled around her.

'Don't you? Of course we should talk about it, but I didn't mean it, Ruth. It was just a slip of the tongue. Ruth, please forgive me.' Panic made my words trip over each other. 'I wouldn't blame you for running away and never seeing me again.'

'It's all right.'

'No, no it's not. I can't believe I just did that. Here I am in bed with you, and I called out my wife's name.' I couldn't forgive myself. Even if Jenn had blessed – hell, she'd kick-started whatever was happening between me and Ruth – confusing them was unforgivable.

'David, it's all right. *Ouch.*' There was a thump and she gasped in pain.

'What's the matter?'

'Just whacked my wrist on something while I was looking for the light.'

I reached up and hit the pad for the wall light. Ruth squinted and blinked as it flickered into life.

'I am so, so sorry.'

'Stop.' She held up her hand. 'Just stop and look at me.' She wrapped the sheet around her body more tightly and tucked it under her arms. 'I'm not kicking you out, or running away and I'm not especially hurt or angry.'

'You should be.' I would be if the reverse had happened.

Ruth sighed. 'Maybe, maybe not. The thing is, David, we're in a very strange position.'

'What do you mean?'

'I think it's only fair and honest to say that if either Chris or Jenn were still alive, we'd probably never have met,' Ruth explained quietly. 'And even if we had, I doubt we'd have become friends, and we certainly wouldn't be here. Neither of us is the other's first choice. That's all right, so long as we both understand and accept it. Can you do that?' Her eyes searched mine.

I sat quietly, thinking. It all made sense the way Ruth put it. She didn't want to replace Jenn, and wasn't looking for me to replace her husband. Nothing I could ever do, or be, would change the fact that she had loved her husband, and still did. Nothing would ever take away from the huge part that he had played in her life, just like nothing and no one would ever replace Jenn and everything that she was, and still is, to me. She will always be my true love, my best friend, my wife, and the mother of my children. I didn't have to stop loving her, but that didn't mean I couldn't still have laughter, friendship and even sex in my life. I laughed as the last of the guilt lifted off my shoulders.

'Yeah, I think I can.'

'Good.' Ruth pushed her hair back. 'Then I believe you have some making up to do?'

Chapter Twenty-Seven

JENN

Christmas has been and gone in a blur of tinsel, light and mistletoe-fuelled hope. Of course there's been sadness too, especially when everyone was opening their presents.

When they sat down to dinner, the space where I should have been was too obvious. Everyone fell silent, except for Lottie who shook and gulped in air as she tried to force back the tears that she knew would start everyone else crying.

They all did cry, and share more than a couple of toasts to me, but it wasn't as bad as I expected. Or as bad as it would have been a few weeks ago. The tears came with smiles and memories that made everyone laugh.

I owe Ruth a lot of thanks. She's helped my family heal in a way I could never have expected or even hoped for.

Spending Christmas with my family was the best gift I could have asked for. I let them know I was there by filling the air with warmth, the smell of cinnamon and orange, and decorating the place with tiny white feathers that looked like snowflakes.

I love this time of year so much. It's filled with so much warmth, joy, happiness, and goodwill towards others. Even if it does sound as cheesy as a bad greetings card. I've always loved all the glitter and shine, the handmade, scribbled, sticky cards from children, and the beautifully wrapped presents under the shimmering trees.

It all came to an end far too quickly. Even with the mince pies and brandy, and chocolates and mulled wine, and finally cups of tea with more mince pies, it still ended too soon.

Lucy gave up first, and it wasn't long before Matty said his goodnights and followed his soon-to-be wife up the stairs to bed. Lottie hung up the phone to Stu – he's been with his own family – and lasted another hour or so before her eyelids became too heavy and the tiredness weighing her down began to win. Which left David sitting and staring into the fireplace.

'Jenn, I know you're still here.' He spoke into his drink.

Of course I'm here. As if I'd be anywhere else on Christmas night. I let go of the cinnamon and orange I'd been wafting through the house and settled back into my usual presence.

David grinned. 'So that's another Christmas over. You've done that every year that I can remember. Flopped down on the sofa next to me and yanked off your Christmas hat and earrings. I guess switching scents isn't so different.' He sighed happily and relaxed back into the sofa. 'You know, it's not been a bad day. I thought it was going to be a lot worse, and a lot harder, than it really was. We still managed to have some laughs and fun.' He sighed quietly. 'But I miss you, Jenn. I still miss you.'

I curled up beside him and sent waves of love and warmth, and he relaxed into me.

I realised that Lucy and Matty will probably be gone before Lottie crawls out of her bed in the morning. If she even makes it up before lunch. It's difficult to think that the next time my family will be back together is for the anniversary of my death.

That's a very strange thought. A whole year since I died. It falls during that odd, often lonely time between Christmas and New Year, when people are wandering around slightly aimlessly. No one is really working, even the people who are officially at work, and there's no point to starting diets or fitness resolutions when the biggest party of the year is only a few days away. Everyone's coming down from the excitement of Christmas and thinking about the last year, while planning their resolutions for the next. It's an empty part of the year where nothing really seems to happen.

Except for the anniversary of my death.

It's a very strange thing really. Usually anniversaries are such happy and exciting things. The celebration of a wedding or a birth is such a wonderful thing. But a death? It's strange to remember the worst day of your life and the loss of someone, but equally letting the day pass unnoticed would be unthinkable. It's a little like picking at a scab. It would be best to leave it alone and let nature take its course in healing the wound, but we never do.

In the end my anniversary was actually quite lovely. There were hundreds of flowers, from my family of course, but also the children and staff at my school. They overflowed from my grave and spilled across the grass. The tree above me seemed to shimmer and flicker with light and golden ribbons from the messages that my former pupils had tied into its branches.

Lottie, Stu, Matty, Lucy and David all came to visit me early in the morning, their arms full of flowers, including specially ordered daffodils and tulips from Sarah in Germany. Matty and David fussed around my grave, picking at bits of grass that had started to grow at the base of my headstone and rubbing at patches of dirt with soft, soapy cloths.

While they did that, Stu fetched water and Lucy and Lottie cleaned out the vases before filling them with fresh water and dozens more flowers. Lottie tidied up the holly wreathes they'd brought me for Christmas, and wove tiny little narcissi among the spiky leaves. It looked so beautiful.

The most surprising visitor came later in the day, carrying a bunch of cream roses. It didn't matter that they weren't exactly my favourite flowers, or that there wasn't a tag attached, I still really appreciated the gesture.

Ruth deliberately didn't come until it was almost dark, and she knew my family would have been and gone. I suppose she hadn't wanted to risk upsetting anyone with her presence. She stood awkwardly at the foot of my grave, not saying anything for long minutes. I watched her with interest, waiting to see what she had come to do and say. Eventually, she cleared her throat and licked her lips.

'I'm sorry I didn't get the chance to know you when you were alive.' She peered up at the messages and ribbons decorating my tree. 'You were clearly very well loved.'

She fingered the petals of the roses gently before leaning them against my headstone. 'I'm sorry for what happened to you, Jenn, I really am. But thank you. For everything.' She rested her fingers against the cold marble for a few seconds, then stuffed her hands into her pockets and walked slowly away.

Chapter Twenty-Eight

Winter Becomes a New Spring

JENN

My daffodils are nearly fully grown. They'll be blooming as soon as there's some sunshine, if sunshine is even something that exists here. It is going to be lovely. I can't wait to see them.

I hope seeing some beauty here will help me feel better. Lately I've been feeling more and more uncomfortable. I don't know what it is, but I'm restless and uneasy. The feelings I had of being on edge are worse. I feel nervous and slightly sick whenever I'm back in this grey place. It seems to feel different here. Like the air is humming with anticipation of some big event. But I've no idea what.

Maybe something terrifying and wonderful. The nearest I've ever come to this feeling before was when I was pregnant with Matty. We wanted him so much, but we were both so young that it terrified me. I think I spent most of the pregnancy swinging between worrying about all the things that could go wrong, how much it would hurt, and being incredibly excited that we were about to have a baby.

A terrifying and exciting event big enough to change everything. The thought of it leaves me cold. So I try not to think about it, or focus on it too much. Instead I'm spending as much time as I can with my family.

David is spending lots of time with Ruth. I honestly don't know if their ... friendship is going to develop into anything more permanent or important. But they will always be friends, even if nothing else works out. That friendship will be worth a lot to both of them over the years.

As I'm giving my husband some space right now, I've been watching over my children more.

Lottie has settled in well to a strange sort of domesticity with Stuart and his mad dog. I didn't really expect to see my daughter living with a boyfriend so soon. I had always thought she was too independent – she'd always seemed to have a veritable allergy to the "slushy stuff" in life. She was always the first one to complain and pretend to vomit over public displays of affection.

Then again, Stuart is a very unusual, special person. He just seems to "get" her. And he loves her dearly, maybe even more than he's realised yet. My daughter adores him too. They make a good team. And he's going to change the lives of so many kids in his work, he's a natural.

Stuart supports Lottie in almost everything, and gives her the confidence to succeed in things she usually wouldn't even bother to try. She's succeeding in building a life and a career for herself.

But when she's wrong, Stuart's happy to point it out and argue with her. And he's very good at it. He's perfectly capable of holding his own and standing his ground against her, but in a way that Lottie respects and listens to.

Even I struggled against Lottie's passion and temper in the rare arguments that we did have. For some reason my default setting when arguing with my daughter was yelling. And she liked to yell back. It's strange. I could handle screaming, abusive children with the worst tempers at work, but not my own daughter. Our rows always descended into screaming matches. Thank goodness our arguments were rare occurrences. Still, I'm glad she's found someone who can survive an argument with her and come out unscathed. He sometimes even wins.

With Stuart in her corner, Lottie's career is leaping on in huge bounds. She's had more of her work published in newspapers and magazines, and she's building a fantastic reputation for someone her age. She deserves it. She's worked so hard. Things are only going to get better for her. I don't know if her work will make her rich, but it will make her happy. There's not much more I can ask for than that.

Lottie isn't the only one doing well. Matty's never been happier than he is at the moment. He and Lucy are excitedly planning their wedding, and their future together. It's going to be a wonderful day. In the end, Matty decided his future with Lucy meant more than any career, and he'd happily follow her halfway round the world to make her happy. She took the dream job and is loving it and Matty's already lining up exciting new work opportunities. They're looking for a new home nearer Lucy's office in York – but this time it will be a proper home for their future family instead of another apartment. Until then, they're only seeing each other at the weekends.

I wish I could have been there in a posh hat and dress that I probably would have spent months choosing. But none of that really matters, because they're ridiculously happy together. To the point that they nauseate Lottie. But beneath the flush of wedding excitement and the joy of getting back together when they were so close to falling apart, there's true love that should last them both a lifetime.

It won't always be easy, and there will definitely be times when they'll both wonder if they made the right choice. But so long as they remember they love each other, they'll never go far wrong.

I am so proud of both of my children. Somehow, despite the mistakes David and I made along the way, both Matty and Lottie have found happiness and are building good lives for themselves. They've grown into beautiful, successful, kind, loving people who care about others and always try to do the right thing.

The only thing that saddens me a little is that they don't really need me any more. Even if they sometimes think they do, they're both intelligent, capable adults. I don't think there's much beyond their reach once they decide they really want it.

They do still have their dad, and each other. I guess I'm just being a little selfish for still wanting to be a part of all the wonderful things they're going to do and see.

I think I finally understand. In my grey place, the daffodils have all bloomed together, bursting out into a sea of yellow and gold that waves and shimmers in a breeze I can't feel. There are thousands of them. Now that they're all exploding with colour, I can see a pattern to them that I hadn't noticed before.

The swirls and gaps cut into them are so familiar. They're the daffodils from my school. The ones that David, Lottie and Stuart, and all my friends and students, and their parents, planted for me.

I stared at them in wonder. A whole field of glowing, golden daffodils, planted just for me, with love strong enough that it reached right into this grey world of mine. Right past death and to me.

Excited yapping came from somewhere far away, and the bright red rubber ball I'd been so carefully looking after slipped out of my pocket and bounced into the daffodils. It vanished among the long green leaves, then reappeared from a different direction a few seconds later, bouncing crazily and followed by a blur of black and white fur. Daisy!

Silken ears were shoved beneath my fingers and a cold wet nose bumped against my wrist as she snuffled against me. She yipped and bounded away, darting into the daffodils.

After a few seconds she realised I wasn't following her, and raced back. She snatched her ball off the floor and danced away before I could catch her, then dropped to the floor. Her back end was tensed and her tail wagged as she waited for me to come and play. As soon as I reached for her, she shot away again, disappearing into the daffodils with a happy bark.

She was right. This time it was right. The daffodils seemed to call to me, waving and beckoning in the wind. I bent down to bury my nose in one at the edge. The instant my fingers touched the velvety petals, all the restlessness and worry that had been gnawing at me was washed away in waves of calmness and peace.

I stood to look at them, and tried to take them all in. They grew before my eyes, spreading out further than I could see, a shimmering, beckoning sea of golden scent. If I stayed here for all eternity I wouldn't be able to count them all.

I stepped into them carefully, and my world turned into golden light so bright it was like the sun reflecting off a thousand, million daffodils, spread out further than the eye could see or the imagination could ever comprehend.

The light of the daffodils was so bright and so beautiful that the colours burned into my eyes. I couldn't see anything except the bright gold petals shimmering and waving in front of me. Then I couldn't see anything.

RUTH

I wrapped my hand more tightly around David's, and tugged at his arm to pull him up the hill more quickly. 'Come on slowcoach.'

'It's bloody freezing out here.' His breath left white clouds in the air. 'Are you mad? I should be curled up in the warm, not being dragged around the frozen streets by you.' His foot skidded on a patch of ice that had been hidden by the snow and he growled as he fought to keep his balance. I struggled not to laugh. 'Why are we doing this again?'

'I told you. I want to show you something,' I explained. For the fifth time.

'Couldn't we have driven?'

I rolled my eyes at him. 'Don't be so lazy. We're nearly there anyway.'

'But there's nothing up here except the back of the school.'

'Exactly.' I smiled at his confusion.

'We're going to the school? But why? It's closed for the weekend.'

'Maybe it is if you don't know anyone with the keys. Lottie's boyfriend lent me the one to the back gate.'

'Why would he do that?' David glared at me.

'Because I asked really nicely. And because it's important.' My warm breath filled the air with clouds of white as I clambered to the top of the hill. It was harder going than I'd expected, but I wasn't going to admit that to him. I paused at the frozen fence. 'Take a look.'

David peered through the frozen railings. 'What? What am I looking at?'

'The top of the hill.' I fiddled with the stubborn padlock. 'Damn, I think this lock's frozen.'

'I wouldn't be surprised. Everything else is. I can't see the hill through all the snow.' David grumbled. 'Here, let me have a go.'

I handed the key over with a shrug. 'You don't see them, do you? You can see them from the top floors of the flats over there. I was there a couple of days ago visiting a patient. With the sun we've had, they've all come out early.'

'What are you talking about?' The lock clicked and he grinned. 'There you go. Just needed a bit of strength.'

'Oh shut up.' I scooped up a handful of snow to chuck in his face.

David shot me a dangerous grin. 'Don't start what you can't finish.'

'What makes you think I couldn't?' I raised an eyebrow. 'Actually, forget it. I didn't bring you up here for a snowball fight.' I slipped my hand around his, two mismatched gloves wrapped around each other, and dragged him through the gates and around the back of the school.

When we reached the corner of the school, I paused. This was something that belonged to David and Jenn. I didn't feel like I had a place in it.

'I'll wait here.' David turned and gave me a strange look. 'This isn't mine,' I explained.

'I don't understand.'

'You will.' I gave him a gentle shove, and leaned back against the wall, blowing into my gloves to warm my fingers.

A few seconds later I heard David swear, and grinned to myself. Ever since I'd peered out of my patient's flat window and seen the golden glow topping this hill, I knew I had to get David up here. A minute or so later he reappeared and held out his hand to me.

'Are you sure?' I asked gently. 'I don't want to intrude.'

David gave me a warm smile. 'This was your idea. You should see them. I want you to see them. It's amazing.' He shook his head, smiling. 'I still can't believe they all grew. Especially so early in the year.'

I let him take my hand and lead me back the way he'd come. He held me tightly so I wouldn't slip in the snow and ice.

As soon as I rounded the corner, I stopped and stared in wonder. Thousands of daffodils sprouted from the snow, their green proud leaves and golden petals bright and beautiful against the stark white snow and empty landscape. Despite the snow and ice, they waved to us cheerfully, defiant of the season and cold.

'It's so beautiful,' I breathed as I looked around at the thousands of golden flowers that covered the entire top of the hill. 'It looks like something out of a fairy tale. They didn't look anything like this lovely from the flats. I didn't realise there were so many.'

'And every single one of them was planted by someone who cared about Jenn.' David's voice was filled with pride.

'That really is amazing.' I squeezed his fingers tightly.

'Yeah.' David sounded far away. Even though he was staring at the daffodils, I knew he wasn't really seeing them. His eyes were focussed on something much further away, and I understood what he must be thinking.

I slid my hand out of his to let him have his privacy and space, and wandered a few steps away to brush the worst of the snow off one of the benches. I perched on it gingerly. Even through my thick coat and jeans, I could still feel the cold of the wood against the backs of my legs. I watched the daffodils dance and wave cheerfully for a few minutes before calling to David, and patting the bench next to me.

'I still miss her. I don't think I'll ever really stop.'

'I know.' I leaned up against his shoulder, offering what warmth and comfort I could. I think he appreciated the gesture, because he rested his head against mine and let out a long sigh.

'It really is beautiful here, isn't it?' David still didn't look away from the daffodils. 'Jenn would have loved this. She really would have.'

We watched the daffodils ripple and wave in the wind for long, quiet minutes. It was quiet and peaceful, and even though I'd never met Jenn in the conventional sense, I knew David was right. Anyone would love it up here.

Eventually David shifted and turned to smile at me. 'Thank you for showing me this. It means a lot.' His voice was thicker and heavier than usual, weighed down with emotion.

'I know. You're welcome.'

He looked up and smiled. 'Look at that. The sun's coming out. Maybe it'll finally warm up a bit.'

'Maybe.' I tilted my face towards the light, but it was more bright than warm. It glistened off the snow, and the tiny drops of water on the daffodils, making them shimmer as they danced in the wind. It was almost magical.

I struggled to look away from the scene even though the sunlight grew brighter and brighter. It glared off the snow, sending painful stabs behind my eyes that made them water, and filling them with multi-coloured spots, but I still couldn't look away. The glare from the sun got brighter still, digging into my vision and turning it white, and I started to panic.

I threw my hands across my eyes to protect them from the glare, then instantly felt stupid. It was nothing more than a bit of snow blindness. I rubbed my eyes until the spots started to fade, then gingerly opened them again. I blinked a few times, feeling more and more silly with every blink. When my vision cleared properly, I realised we weren't alone any more.

Though my eyes were still watery and protesting against the brightness, I could just make out the figure of a woman in the middle of the daffodils. She was bent over, cupping a delicate flower head between bare fingers as she inhaled its fragrance. Her pale, summery dress fluttered in the breeze and merged in with the snow, making her hard to see.

'Bloody hell. She must be freezing.' The medic in me took over. 'I wonder where she came from.' I was already stripping off my gloves to unbutton my coat so I could wrap it around her, and warm her up. 'Come on. I'm going to see if she's all right. She shouldn't be out in this weather dressed like that.'

David was frozen beside me, staring at the woman as she moved carefully between the flowers.

'David? Are you all right?' He ignored my concerns and stood up silently.

The woman started to walk towards us, her skirt and dark hair still moving in a breeze that I couldn't feel. She didn't look cold or ill. She looked healthier and more alive than anyone I'd ever seen. She almost seemed to glow with the light that reflected off her.

Somewhere deep inside, part of me began to panic and scream. Whatever was happening here wasn't right or normal. I knew I should be afraid, that I should run away and hide from this stranger. But I couldn't move.

Then the familiar presence that had been around me for weeks filled the air, and peace washed over me. The biting air suddenly felt warmer, and it was tinged with the scent of honeysuckle and apples.

My mind struggled to put together the scent and presence, and match it with the woman floating towards us. Then I recognised the smell and feel, and I knew who she was. It was impossible. There was no way on earth that she could be here. Except that there wasn't anyone else it could have been.

I'd believed David when he told me about her. I've long accepted there's far more to this world than any of us could see, but I never expected to come face to face with that afterlife, and have part of that other world walking towards me in the form of my lover's dead wife.

My tongue stuck to the roof of my mouth, and I had to swallow half a dozen times before I could find my voice. 'Is that ...?'

'Jenn.' David's voice was a whispered sigh of joy and hope, almost prayer-like. I felt instantly uncomfortable and out of place. I was intruding on an incredibly private moment.

I brushed the snow off my butt and rubbed my hands together, feeling awkward. 'I'm ... umm ... I'm going to go now.'

Neither of them seemed to notice me as I edged by, but I

just couldn't do it. Just as I reached the corner, I stopped and turned.

The angelic, glowing vision looked towards me, and my eyes locked with hers. Horror filled me as thoughts crashed through my mind.

This was David's wife. Or her ghost at least, or whatever she was. I'd been sleeping with her husband, and helping him move on. To move away from her. Panic bubbled in my chest and rose up in my throat. I had to apologise and make this right. I had to take it all back.

But cool stubbornness overwhelmed my panic, and I squared my shoulders. Actually, I didn't have anything to apologise for at all. David and I were adults, and whether Jenn's ghost was here or not, she was still dead. I'd done nothing wrong.

After what felt like a small eternity, the corners of her mouth started to creep up into a smile. Clearly I'd done something right. I had to unstick my tongue again, but eventually found enough voice to ask the question that had been plaguing me for weeks. 'It was you, wasn't it? Before Christmas with Billy?'

She nodded and the smile lit up her eyes.

'Thank you. From me, and him, and his whole family. You kept him with us long enough for the surgeons to carry out his transplant and save his life. Thank you.' I pulled my coat more tightly around me, and walked calmly away.

Chapter Twenty-Nine

Sometimes Endings are Beginnings

JENN AND DAVID

David stared at Jenn in disbelief, his voice frozen in his throat by the emotions that choked him. He'd dreamt about this moment every day for over a year, but now it was here, he had no idea what to say or do.

'Jenn?' The word tore from his throat, carrying a year's worth of emotion, pain and love. 'Is it …?' Hope crushed the words.

She smiled and nodded. 'It's really me. I'm really here.' Tears slid down her face.

'Oh my God, Jenn. I've missed you so much.' He rushed towards her, but she stepped away.

'I'm sorry love, but I don't think you can touch me.'

'Oh.' David stopped short. He reached for the hand that had stopped him, and tried to catch it in his, wanting to grab on to her and hold her tightly so she'd never leave again. But her fingers slipped through his, as insubstantial as smoke. His heart broke a little more as his hope crashed away.

'I've missed you too. All of you. Even when I was nearby, there was so much I wanted to say, but the gap has always been too wide.'

'Until now.'

'It's still not close enough, or for long enough.' Jenn shook her head sadly. 'I'm not here to stay, darling. I'm here to say goodbye.'

'Why? Why can't you stay?'

'Because I'm not supposed to be here. I should have left

when I died. But I couldn't.' Jenn's hair fluttered around her face. 'I couldn't leave you all. I didn't fully understand what had happened at first. When I did, I was too scared to leave. You were in so much pain, and it was my fault. I wanted to stay to make sure you would all be all right. But then you saw me.'

'Before your funeral.' The words felt wrong.

'Yes.' Jenn nodded. 'And once I knew you could see me, I realised I could do a lot more than just watch.'

'So you stayed to look after us.'

'Yes.'

'So stay for longer. Look after us more. We still need you. I love you. I still need you.'

Jenn's eyes filled with love as she looked at him. 'I love you too. I always will. But you don't need me any more. You're healing, you're moving on, and it's nearly time for me to do the same.'

'It's so unfair.'

'No, no it's not.' Jenn tried to comfort him. 'My dying was unfair, but me being here … this is a miracle. One you created for me.'

'I don't understand.' David shook his head.

'I should never have been able to come here, love. The dead and the living don't speak like this. The gap between our worlds is too wide. It's supposed to be that way. But you found a way to build a bridge so I could come back. Even if it is only for a short time.'

'A bridge?'

Jenn nodded. 'The daffodils. All the love and warmth you planted them with, gave them strength enough to grow in my world too. They guided me back here. Back to you.'

'Wow. Bloody hell.'

'Yeah.' Jenn paused and stared at the golden flowers, then shot her husband an amused glare. 'Don't you go teaching my granddaughter language like that.' Jenn's eyes sparkled with happiness and mischief.

'Granddaughter?' David's mouth hung open for a moment. 'Oh my God, Matty's going to be a dad?'

Jenn smiled and shook her head.

'Lottie? But she's so young.'

Jenn shook her head again, still smiling. 'That wasn't a "no it's not Matty", it was a "no I'm not going to tell you". Don't you tell the children either. It's a surprise.'

'Shouldn't I warn them?'

'Absolutely not!' Jenn laughed and the sound echoed through the air, and the daffodils seemed to laugh with her. 'I told you, she will be a surprise. All you need to know is that she'll be healthy, loved and very much wanted.'

'All right. I won't tell,' David agreed. 'So what happens now?'

'We sit and watch our miracle together?' Jenn settled on the bench next to him, careful to keep a finger's breadth between them.

The silence spread out until Jenn broke it thoughtfully. 'So, that was Ruth. She looks different in the flesh. Prettier.'

David jumped at the subject. 'About Ruth … I'm so sorry.'

'Don't be. I like her. She's good for you. She's funny.' Jenn turned to face him. 'And she won't let you get away with too much. She won't let you wallow in self-pity and misery. I'm sorry about how I introduced you. I really didn't think the car would pick up so much speed so quickly. I never meant to hurt you.'

'It's all right.' David laughed. 'It wasn't all that bad.'

Jenn ducked her head, and her hair fell across her face. A bark sounded through the air. David shaded his eyes as he squinted towards the source of the noise.

'Is that Daisy?'

Jenn nodded without looking up. 'Sort of. But she's

more than that. She's come back to guide me to where I'm supposed to be, and make sure I don't get lost again.'

David swallowed hard. 'Does that mean it's nearly time for you to leave me again?'

'Oh David, I'll never truly leave you.' Jenn rested her hands on the cold wood between them, wishing she could wrap her arms around him. 'You loved me too well for me to ever truly die. I'll live on in your memories and thoughts, and Matty's and Lottie's too. When you meet our grandchildren, you'll all tell them about me, and I'll live on through them as well. And I'll still be watching.'

'Oh, Jenn, what am I going to do without you?' David's eyes filled with tears.

'You're going to live, my darling. You're going to live, and you're going to be happy.'

David shook his head, unable to speak through the tears.

'Yes you will. Look at me, David.' Jenn waited until his eyes met hers again, and the life they'd had flashed between them. Days laughing and flirting at college melted into white lace and promises, then slipped into warm embraces and hot nights. Jenn screaming as she laboured with their children flashed across shared memories, along with dozens of arguments and thousands of kisses and whispers of love. Shared dinners and jokes, evenings at home, and just time spent with each other followed. Family, friends, pets. Joy, happiness, sadness and fear. It all flowed between them until the flash of pain when they were pulled apart.

David groaned and shook his head, trying to clear the last image but hold on to every other.

'David.' Jenn's voice was thick with emotion. 'Don't you understand? You have to keep living for me. Whether it's with Ruth, or someone like her, or no one at all. You have to find your happiness again. Live, and love, and enjoy your life. I'll always be in your heart, and I'll always be with you.

So long as you're really living and loving your life, I'll never be far away.'

'Will I ever see you again?' David struggled to speak through his tears.

'Of course you will darling. But hopefully not for a very long time, and after a long life. Then I'll come for you, and take you home.'

'How can you be so sure?'

Jenn laughed, and the clearing echoed with the sound again. 'Look at the daffodils, David. Our love is so strong it reached past death to bring me back to you. Love like that is too strong, too deep and too honest to fade over a few years. It was created to last an eternity. And it will.' Jenn slid from the bench and dropped to her knees in front of him. She forced her words past her tears, fierce and passionate. 'I love you, David. Yesterday, today and always and forever. I'll wait for you always. No matter where you go, what you do, or who you become, I'll always love you.'

David nodded and forced back tears. 'I love you too. Always and forever.'

'I know.' Jenn nodded. 'You'll do as I ask? You'll live, and be happy, enjoy and celebrate your life enough for the both of us?'

'I promise.'

'And if the chance for love comes again, promise me you'll take it. I don't want you spending your life alone.' Jenn's hands were almost in his.

David nodded. 'I promise. But I'll always love you. Whatever happens, I'll be always and ever yours.' He gulped in air painfully. 'I don't think I can do this. I don't think I can watch you leave me again.'

'Then don't.' Jenn smiled through her tears. 'Just close your eyes.'

'I love you, Jenn.' David closed his eyes over the tears that still spilled down his cheeks, and tried to concentrate on Jenn, pulling her presence and scent into his heart, locking her with him.

Jenn saw a flash of something small, round and red disappearing into the distance beckoning to her, followed by a joyful bark that David wouldn't hear for a lot of years to come.

The air around David turned colder and ice brushed over his lips, as soft and insubstantial as a snowflake, and gone just as quickly.

As the kiss melted on his lips and burnt itself into his memory forever, Jenn's last words whispered into his ear.

Always and ever yours.

Thank You

Dead Reader,

Thank you for taking a chance on a new writer and choosing *Beyond Grey*. I really hope you've enjoyed reading it as much as I did writing it. And while it is entirely fictional, I will admit that there may be a few unusual feathers in my life.

If you've enjoyed my writing, please remember my name – I promise there are more books on the way – and please let others know what you think by leaving a review on Goodreads, or other book review sites. You can also follow me on Twitter for news on my next book, and maybe share some of your own angel encounters – or just pop by and say hi!

Love and light,

Ella

x

About the Author

Ella is one of those people who is addicted to the written word. She's been obsessed with books since before she could walk. She decided to become a writer as soon as she realised that stringing letters together in the right order could actually be a career.

She grew up in the outskirts of London, where fairies lived at the bottom of her Grandma's garden, so it isn't surprising that she still looks for magic in every day life – and often finds it.

When she's not living in a fantasy world of her own creation, she writes bids and develops programmes for children's services, and lives in rural Warwickshire (where there are probably more fairies). She shares her house with two small parrots, one of whom likes to critique her writing from his favourite spot on her shoulder, and her husband who is ever loving and understanding and makes her gallons of tea in magical cups that can keep drinks warm for whole chapters.

She doesn't plan on stopping writing any time soon, so if you've enjoyed this book, please remember her in the future. In the meantime, please spend a couple of minutes to leave a review and tell your friends about her – it's one of the best ways for new authors to meet readers.

To find out more about Ella, follow her on social media:

Twitter: @EllaCookWrites

More Ruby Fiction

From Ella Cook

Summer's Christmas

Bringing the spirit of Christmas to a summer's day …

Summer by name and summer by nature – that's how people describe Evelyn's happy, outgoing daughter. Even if her favourite time of year is actually Christmas!

But Summer has gone through more than any eight-year-old ever should, and that's part of the reason Evelyn is leaving everything behind to return to her childhood home in the village of Broclington; just her, Summer and Summer's best friend – a Shiba Inu dog called Tilly. Unsurprisingly, Evelyn is hesitant to let anyone else in, although local vet Jake Macpearson seems intent on winning her trust.

When Evelyn receives the news that every mother dreads, it's Jake who comes to the rescue. With the help of the Broclington community, could he be the man to bring festive magic to August, and make all of Evelyn and Summer's Christmases come at once?

Visit www.rubyfiction.com for details.

More from Ruby Fiction

Why not try something else from our selection:

Evie's Little Black Book

Hannah Pearl

Is hunting down every man you've kissed the answer to finding Mr Right?

When Evie is invited to the wedding of the guy she'd fancied throughout her teens, it's the final straw. What's wrong with her and why can't *she* keep a man?

In between consoling herself with ice cream and chocolate, and sobbing her heart out to her cousin Charmaine, Evie has a brainwave – and it all centres around her 'little black book' (well, more floral patterned notebook really) – which contains the details of every man she's ever kissed or dated. Perhaps the cure for her disastrous love life has been nestled within its pages all along ...

Does Evie's little black book really hold the answers, or will learn she learn that exes are exes for a reason?